Praise for Swan Huntley's

We Could Be Beautiful

"*We Could Be Beautiful* is a sexy psychological thriller about wealth and class and the endless mysteries of romantic engagement. At the heart of Swan Huntley's sly and witty debut is the unsettling question that anyone who's ever been in love has wondered about the person they've given their heart to: *Who are you?*"
—Dennis Lehane,
author of *World Gone By*

"A novel that is deeper than its heiress-meets-man-of-her-dreams setup. The reason: Huntley's uncanny ability to detect the fault lines in Manhattan's glitterati as if flaws in a precious diamond—and make us laugh about them."
—*O, The Oprah Magazine*

"Mesmerizing. . . . As elegantly plotted as it is—and it is—Huntley's debut stands out not for its thrills but rather for her hawkish eye for social detail and razor-sharp wit. It is more than a classic psychological thriller: it is also a haunting—and weirdly moving—portrait of love and family among Manhattan's flailing upper crust. An intoxicating escape; as smart as it is fun."
—*Kirkus Reviews* (starred review)

Swan Huntley

We Could Be Beautiful

Swan Huntley earned her MFA from Columbia University.
She's received fellowships from the MacDowell Colony and
the Ragdale Foundation. She lives in California and Hawaii.

www.swanhuntley.com

)

We Could Be Beautiful

WE COULD BE BEAUTIFUL

A Novel

Swan Huntley

Anchor Books
A Division of Penguin Random House LLC
New York

FIRST ANCHOR BOOKS EDITION, JUNE 2017

Anchor Books and colophon are registered trademarks of Penguin Random House LLC.

The Library of Congress has cataloged the Doubleday edition as follows:
Huntley, Swan.
We could be beautiful : a novel / Swan Huntley.—First American edition.
Pages cm
1. Socialites—Fiction.   2. Man-woman relationships—Fiction.
3. Mothers and daughters—Fiction.   4. Alzheimer's disease—Patients—
Fiction.   I. Title.
PS3608.U5958W43 2015   813'.6—dc23   2015006065

Anchor Books Trade Paperback ISBN: 978-1-101-91218-8
eBook ISBN: 978-0-385-54060-5

Book design by Maria Carella

www.anchorbooks.com

Printed in the United States of America
10 9 8 7 6 5 4 3 2 1

For my parents, Kim and Mark

We have no instincts, only legs to run on.

—*Hannah Gamble*

THE FRAMED THING

Part One

1

I wanted a family.

I was rich, I owned a small business, I had a wardrobe I replaced all the time. I was toned enough and pretty enough. I moisturized, I worked out. I looked younger than my age. I had been to all the countries I wanted to see. I collected art and filled my West Village apartment with it. My home was bright and tastefully bare and worthy of a spread in a magazine.

I was also a really good person. I volunteered at a soup kitchen on Thanksgiving; I paid my housekeeper well and on time. I was a good sister, a good daughter. I had been a pretty good student. I'd gone to Sarah Lawrence and then NYU. I had substance. I was conscientious. I'd seen enough documentaries to make me a vegetarian. I voted. I recycled. I tipped generously. I gave money to homeless people on the street. I gave extra to gypsy mothers, their sooty babies, always sleeping, maybe drugged, hanging heavy from their necks in hammocks made from ratty T-shirts.

But despite my good deeds and my good fortune, I felt incomplete. I had always felt incomplete, even as a small child. I have a memory of myself, age four, cheek pressed against the cold black smoky design of the bathroom tiles, my hot breath fogging the smooth marble, thinking, I am dead. I am dead but I am alive. I am dead and this is a dream.

That I didn't have a family yet wasn't for a lack of trying. I felt I had always been trying. I'd been engaged twice. I'd had a million boyfriends, and even one girlfriend, but none of them had stuck. I tended to like addicts. Maybe by definition those people didn't stick around—they were always running, that was their nature. I also tended to like poor people, impoverished sculptors like Jim, who were a little too desperate for my good sheets and my big TV screens and my masseur, who came once a week.

There was something about having money that made the incompleteness sharper. If you were broke, it was an excuse for almost everything. You couldn't afford to fix the shower, so it kept leaking. You didn't have time for friends or exercise or charity. You were always working because you had to work, and work was the best excuse for your misery.

If you had money, you had no excuse. And people didn't feel sorry for you either. Instead they decided not to like you before they even knew you. They said, If you're sad, can't you buy a new house somewhere, can't you take a trip? Don't you have so many choices, so many resources? They said, We're not stupid and we know you can't buy happiness, but we also know you sort of can, too, because money means choices and choices mean you don't have the limits that we do, and that means you should shut up now and be happy. Look at everything you have—it's limitless.

And those people were right. It was limitless. I got a headache just thinking about how limitless it was. If you could afford any end table in the world, how could you be sure you were getting the right one? If you could go anywhere, where would you go? And in what order? And for how long? If you had any goals at all, why had you not attained them? If you hadn't attained them, it wasn't because you were broke, it was because you had failed.

And so it was that I felt not only incomplete but also like a failure. I went to the Gala for Contemporary Folk Art that night not because I really wanted to, or because I had planned on meeting anyone. I went because I had promised Susan I would go, and I was a good friend who kept my promises.

Wineglass between just-manicured (always manicured) fingers, I stood in the pool of people, looking up at this enormous tapestry. Buttery light, the clinking of glass, low polite voices, one person laughing too loud. Men in tuxedos pressed and crisp and smelling slightly of the dry-cleaning bags they'd been taken out of just before, and women in gowns that made them look like jellyfish, their hair coiffed into oceanic shapes. I wore white, which is funny to think about now. Of course I wore white. All I wanted was to be married, and that want was obvious, subliminal, cellular—it was in everything I did, whether I knew it or not.

The tapestry was big, as big as a swimming pool, and so intricate, all those tiny pulls of string. It was a modern triptych, three panels in brilliant colors, almost neon: a woman floating in water, a woman standing on land, a woman curled at the foot of a mountain. It was beautiful and depressing and overwhelming and all I could think was, I am forty-three years old and I am alone and where the hell is Susan?

Of course it was just when I'd decided to leave and go home and curl up in bed that I saw him. A stunning, square-jawed man with gentle eyes and elegant gray hair, full and parted to the side. He made his way closer until he was standing beside me. We watched the tapestry like it was a movie. We said nothing to each other for what felt like a long time. There was something familiar about him. Maybe he looked like an actor, or maybe he was just one of those people who looked familiar to everyone, or maybe his dry-cleaned scent reminded me of home.

"It's nice to see you," he said finally. His voice was smooth and cool, like metal, brilliantly polished. He held out his hand. On his pinkie was a ring, a turquoise stone on a tarnished silver band. That intrigued me. It seemed out of place and special. It suggested a character.

"Do I know you?"

"William Stockton."

"Catherine West."

I remember his hand felt as smooth and as cool as his voice. I remember thinking, There is something about this guy, there is some kind of electricity between us. It was big, enormous, unavoidable. From the very beginning it felt like a current pulling me blissfully toward a whirlpool. Before you drown, the spinning just feels like a dance.

2

William Stockton and I had never met, but it turned out our families had been friends. "In fact," he was saying, "I believe I remember your mother pregnant, and it must have been you she was pregnant with."

It was three days after the gala, a night that had ended in Susan never showing (the flu) and William buying the huge tapestry, and taking my phone number, and calling to ask me out for this coffee we were now having in the park, very near William's new apartment on Seventy-Eighth Street—he'd just moved back from Switzerland—and also near my childhood apartment on Eighty-Fourth, where William had apparently visited "more than once."

"If she was pregnant with me, we must have just missed each other." I twirled my long chocolate-colored hair around my fingers. The plan was to mesmerize him, and I was pretty sure it was working. More softly, I said, "Ships in the night."

"Uncanny." When William smiled, the lines around his mouth creased. Those were the only real lines on his face. His skin was strangely intact for a man of his age. It glistened, lightly bronzed, almost golden. And his hair. Despite being gray, it was silky, well conditioned. It bounced with just the right amount of bounce as we walked.

It was a warm Saturday in May, the first real warm day after what had felt like the longest winter of my life, and I was feeling alive, finally alive, and also kind of overstimulated. It was my bare exposed skin, which hadn't seen light for so long—I felt almost naked in my summery dress—and it was the buzz from the coffee, and it was this man: this handsome, extremely tall, extremely independently wealthy man who was articulate and Old World in a way that didn't seem contrived, and who knew me—not me personally, but he knew my family, and in this way we shared a history. We came from the same place. I trusted him immediately.

He had brought his dog, Herman, a long-haired dachshund with gold-brown hair that curled slightly at the ends, very cute. As we veered from the asphalt onto the curving dirt path, under the shadows of tree branches, their outstretched limbs begging for sun, children stopped to pet Herman, and William was very sweet with every one of them, lingering patiently, saying, "This is Herman, and what is your name?"

We passed a group of young boys building something with sticks, and a lesbian couple on a plaid blanket, eating scooped-out cantaloupe balls from a dewy Ziploc bag like they were really in the wilderness. A line of little preschoolers in bright white shirts moved like a twinkling diamond bracelet over the knoll. Someone far away was flying a kite shaped like a fish.

It smelled like grass and dirt, and in certain moments, when we walked closely enough together, there was the faint trace of William's clean, salt-dipped scent. I would never figure out exactly what that scent was—maybe the combination of his hair products and his detergent and the aftershave he used, and the unique way it reacted with his skin. Vaguely it reminded me of a hotel where I'd stayed on the Amalfi Coast when I was thirteen and still obsessed with pasta Bolognese.

We were talking, of course, about what he remembered. "Let's see," he said, sipping the last of his coffee and stepping in front of me ("Pardon me, Catherine") to throw it in the wiry basket, which prompted me to do the same, even though my coffee was still basically full; I'd been too overstimulated to drink it. "I remember the stone lions by the door—not replicas, because they were missing facial features—and of course the plants. There were so many plants."

"Yes—oh my God. Those plants are what everyone remembers, it's so funny." My mother loved her plants—she could almost have been called a hoarder of them. Ferns lined the walls, succulents lined the windowsills, and roses (always roses) were a mandatory centerpiece on every table. She spent a good deal of time explaining to her assistants (she called them all assistants, whether they were housekeepers or nannies or decorators) what her plant visions were, and kept a list for the florist alongside a grocery list in the kitchen drawer. Her collection of plants was the one way in which my mother diverged from her typical Upper East Side existence. It may have been the only eccentric thing about herself she let people see.

"It was nearly a forest, wasn't it?"

"It was. Especially in the fountain room. The running water made it more forestlike. Do you remember that?"

William squinted into the sun. His skin was so smooth. And his lips were just pink enough, just full enough. "Yes," he said, nodding, "yes, of course, how could I have forgotten that? It was a stone fountain, wasn't it? Like the lions, it was made of stone that had been worn away outside, by wind and rain. Do I correctly recall cherubs?"

"Yes! I thought they were so scary as a kid because they had no pupils."

"I also remember the bathroom with the yellow walls," he said. "I very distinctly recall its mustard color."

"The mustard bathroom, yes!"

"And the reclining chair your father loved."

"Yes. Oh my God, this is so crazy. You know so much about my life and I only just met you. It's crazy."

I probably said "It's crazy" twenty times. Although as we kept talking, I realized that maybe it wasn't so crazy. People in New York knew each other, and apparently not only had our mothers been involved in a lot of the same art organizations, our fathers had both been close to Pierre Mallet, the reclusive artist who lived in the Catskills with too many dogs. I remembered Pierre, of course, though not well because he rarely came to the city. What I remembered most clearly was that every time Pierre's name came up, my mother said, "He needs to quit smoking. He is going to die."

William's father, Edward Stockton, had also been an artist, William told me, "though he never achieved fame or money, which was a shame—he wanted those things very badly." He and Pierre had collaborated on many projects, including a series of orblike sculptures, one of which my parents had bought and put in the living room.

"I didn't realize that was your father's sculpture!" I remembered it exactly. It looked like a planetary system, with all white planets and one blue one, which bore a red X. I recalled many afternoons spent lazing on the couch, looking at that X and wondering what it meant.

"In part it was, yes," William said. "I believe it was Pierre who introduced our fathers initially."

"What happened to Pierre?"

"He passed away some years ago," William said. "Lung cancer."

Based on his choice of outfit for a weekend walk in the park (blue dress shirt buttoned to the neck, dark khaki pants, tight brown leather shoes), I was not surprised to find out William was a banker. He'd spent a long time at UBS and now worked at a small investment bank downtown, way downtown, south of Wall Street, at the very tip of the island. My initial response to this was: No. I had gone out of my way not to date finance guys because I didn't want to end up marrying my father, who had worked too hard and died too young, and also because I just thought finance was boring. But William didn't seem boring to me. The turquoise ring: he wasn't a typical banker. It also helped when he said, "I enjoy my job very much," and I actually believed him. The way he spoke—he was so charismatic. He could have sold water to the ocean.

"I sometimes wonder if it was your father who inspired me into this position," he said. "In my youth I was surrounded by bohemians, and your father . . . well, he was different. He made an impression. He was so very powerful—the way he dressed and the way he spoke."

I said, "Thank you. Yes, he was," and I remember I got the feeling that William could have been describing himself just then. The shine of his Italian shoes reminded me of something my father said often: "A great man's shoes should always be polished."

We walked for a long time, going through the requisite first-date stuff. School, family, hobbies. Favorite foods, vacation spots, whether or not Starbucks had good coffee. I was so rapt by everything he said and by his cool way of saying it that I looked up at one point and realized I didn't even know where we were in the park.

William did not like the coffee at Starbucks ("Too much acidity"). He had no siblings ("In fact, they hadn't planned on having me either"). During his early childhood in the city, the Stocktons had lived just near the Met, and he had gone to Dalton. ("You *would* go to Dalton," I teased, flipping my hair, to which he said, "Yes, my mother befriended the dean, and so I was allowed to attend for free.") He had studied the violin "fairly seriously" during his youth, and it was still something he liked. He was even thinking of volunteering as a tutor now, if he could find any extra time to indulge in that.

His parents had inspired his love of folk art. His mother, who had grown up in Mexico City and then Santa Fe, was drawn to it as a Catholic, and particularly loved the works of Reverend How-

ard Finster and Sister Gertrude Morgan. She made art herself—
"mostly crochet; she was very patient"—but didn't consider herself
a real artist. She was talented but lacked dedication. His father,
who William thought possessed less natural talent, was dedicated
enough for the both of them. Edward Stockton was extremely
hardworking, almost obsessed. Every day—even on Sundays,
which bothered William's mother—he awoke at four o'clock in
the morning to work. "Work was all that mattered to him, and
my mother understood there could not be two stars in one family.
My father was the star, and my mother, I suppose, was the sky. He
wouldn't have existed without her."

William went on to explain that his father's severe stutter
made him self-conscious about speaking. "But when he began to
stutter, my mother was there to finish his sentences." She carried
him through every party, every opening, every event. She had a
knack for people, and people adored her. In the art world, in the
supermarket, at church. Church was very important to her.

Yes, William was still a Catholic. "It's a part of me. I hope
you won't judge me too harshly for it," he said, and I blurted out,
"Isn't Catholicism all about judgment?" I immediately regretted
this and backtracked. "Sorry, sorry," I said, "I'm only kidding."
And he said, "It's okay, I'm used to it, really. It's not very à la
mode to be Catholic these days, I understand." In an attempt to
appear kind and interested, and also because I wanted to know
how serious he was about the whole thing, I asked him how often
he went to church. He liked to "stop in every so often," mostly to
pay his respects to his parents. Both of them were gone now: a
freak car accident on an unpaved road. It was recent—they'd died
only months before. "I regret that I didn't have the chance to say
good-bye," he said.

Now William had his own "modest collection" of folk art. I
wondered how modestly he was defining *modest*. It included sculp-

tures and tableaux in cross-stitch—he adored those, probably because they reminded him of his mother—plus all of his father's work, of course, and a few Joseph Yoakum landscapes, which were his favorites. I didn't know who that was but heard myself saying, "Oh yes, of course. I love his stuff."

When I said, "I like your ring," he explained that it was a family heirloom, dating back exactly one generation. His mother had bought it the day she arrived in the States, when she was ten. She had given it to William on his tenth birthday, and at some point in his life he would pass it on to his own child, if he was "lucky enough to have one."

He had been married before, yes. At the age of thirty-six. Gwen had died four years later. Breast cancer. He'd dated since then but hadn't found anyone he wanted to spend eternity with. I felt bad for thinking Gwen was a fake princess name, and then I felt bad for William that he had lost her. I couldn't even imagine that, I told him. He said it was horrible, but at least, unlike with his parents, he had been given the chance to say good-bye.

On a lighter note, William enjoyed skiing and running. Stracciatella gelato was his preferred treat. He could eat it all night and all day. But not literally, of course. He'd briefly lived in Italy after university at Oxford. He spoke some Italian, and also French, German, and Spanish. He'd grown up speaking Spanish with his mother, whom he'd been very close to, unlike his father, who "gave the impression that he was a man simply out of reach." His father was German (well, half German, really), though William had learned that language mostly at school. Despite their nearly identical looks ("typically Nordic—hard and pale, as though chiseled from ice"), William felt he and his father had had very little in common. He and his mother, on the other hand, had shared a "deep internal sameness." She had passed on none of her physical features ("she looked Native American—everyone thought so") except her very long limbs. When William said this, he extended the arm that wasn't holding Herman's leash. "See?"

"Wow," I said, and imagined how good it was going to feel when I had that arm wrapped around my waist.

More seriously, he said, "My mother was a wonderful person. I miss her dearly."

"I'm sure you do. I'm so sorry."

I don't know what it was that made us stop walking, or what made us look at each other then. His face was perfect, his body. The air was perfect. The electricity between us. Even Herman's bark had a musical ring to it. I remember thinking, You look like you could be the one. Even then I knew. William Stockton and Catherine West. Those two names were going to look great on an invitation. And then, without acknowledging that we had stopped or why, which made it even more perfect because it implied we understood each other without the annoyance of finding words to speak our understanding, William began to walk again, and I followed.

"And your parents? Are they still at Eighty-Fourth?"

"No. My mother moved out recently. And Dad's gone. He died of a heart attack." It had been a while—ten years—so I didn't feel completely devastated saying it anymore, but it still upset me, especially being here, so close to where we had lived. William also seemed upset to hear this news, and sighed heavily in a way that confirmed he hadn't known.

"That's terrible. I adored your father. I mean that—I truly adored him. Once he took me to an exhibit about the railroad system in America. No one would go with him—your mother certainly wasn't interested."

"I'm not surprised."

"It's odd to think of now. Where were my parents? I can't recall. But I remember that day well. Your father tipped the waitress a hundred dollars. I was very impressed."

"He did that all the time!" I wanted to tell William I was generous like that, too, but there was no humble way to say this.

We had gotten to the edge of the reservoir: joggers in their skintight Lululemons, a French couple taking pictures of each other, and the water, so still, a barely moving reflection of the sky.

"Shall we make the loop?"

"Let's make the loop," I said, as though making the loop had a much greater significance than just walking in a circle.

It had been about a year since I'd been up here, since we'd sold the apartment. My mother's Alzheimer's had progressed to the point where the task of living alone was beyond her. For a while she had caretakers, but my mother was a difficult person, and these people kept quitting. My sister thought we should put her in a home. At the time I thought it was so shitty of us, but it actually turned out to be the best thing. She had friends there, or at least other forgetful people her age who seemed friendly enough, and the interior of the place—the sofas, the walls, everything—was either cream or yellow or a combination of cream and yellow, which looked lame in the pamphlet but had a surprisingly uplifting effect in person. It was completely unlike the dark apartment on Eighty-Fourth Street, with its heavy velvet curtains and its stone animals and its long disturbing hallways filled with plants.

Even though it had been the right thing to do, I still hated it that we had sold. It felt like my father was preserved in that apartment, and without it there was no palpable evidence of him: nothing to remind me of his peppery smell, or of the particular way the air rushed in through the window of his study sometimes, blowing apart all his papers. Besides a few trips to the dentist and exactly two baby showers (bane of my existence), I had managed to avoid the Upper East Side completely since Mom had left. Which hadn't been hard. Especially since my sister, in a move that surprised everyone—everyone being me because I was the only one left, at least the only consistently coherent one—had relocated all the way across town to the Upper West Side to be near her doctor husband's practice, and now lived conveniently within blocks of our mother.

Walking with William now, I felt surprisingly at ease being here. I wasn't as pissed off or as sad as I'd expected to be. The reservoir reminded me of so many things, and I actually felt like sharing them. It was out of character for me to open up so easily. I took this as a good sign.

"We used to drink vermouth on those rocks in high school." I pointed to the gray boulders. "And, oh my God, one day, walking here with my dad—maybe I was five, six?—I threw my stuffed panda bear into the water, over this gate." I touched the metal. It was warm. Herman circled back because we had stopped. He sniffed my toes.

"Did you?" William said thoughtfully. He was a good listener. He paid attention. He understood how to draw people out of themselves. He put a hand on the metal, next to mine. "Why did you do that?"

"I don't know," I said, trying to remember, but nothing came to mind. "I became difficult around that age."

"Really?"

"My dad said I changed when my sister was born. I was jealous."

A pause. "I didn't know you had a sister."

"Caroline. She's younger, so you wouldn't have known her, I guess."

"No," he said. "Our families must have lost touch by then."

"Why, do you think? Did something happen?"

In a lower voice, he said, "I think people simply lose touch sometimes." He looked at the water. His nose in profile was long, dignified. He had the strong jaw of a warrior. I couldn't see his eyes.

Then, without words, he took my hand and led me to the street, which wasn't far. We walked over the cobblestones to the curb. We had spent almost two hours together, and I had assumed for some reason that our date would include dinner. I thought the next words out of his mouth would be, "Catherine, I would love the pleasure of having dinner with you," or at least "How do you feel about sushi?" But instead he said, "I have an appointment for a haircut," and looked at his watch—a Patek Philippe with roman numerals and a simple black band—"at four o'clock." This seemed like a too-abrupt ending (had I done something wrong?), and his hair looked great, but I said, "Okay, right, haircuts are important," and smiled (too enthusiastically; I was overcompensating), and reminded myself that two hours was a very long time and that I had to stop being unrealistic with men. It was unrealistic to think you would meet a man for coffee and then never leave his side. We weren't teenagers.

He raised his long, elegant arm for a cab. "Perfect," he said in his cool, even way. I got the impression then that William was a person who wouldn't show you what he didn't want you to see. Because it was four-fifteen and he didn't seem stressed at all that he was late. He was serene, the flat surface of unmoving water, liquid that appeared solid. I remember thinking, He must be great at his job.

Looking back, this might have been my first little warning. A haircut, now? It felt like a lie. What was he hiding? At the time this warning registered in only the vaguest way—a slight constriction in my chest, maybe, a tiny pang that disappeared, a single skipped beat I told myself didn't matter. It was just a haircut. It was nothing.

A cab stopped. He stepped forward and opened the door in one fluid movement. The way he moved had a naturally sensual quality to it. We watched Herman jump in and then jump back out. Was it odd that we said nothing about that? Was it odd that we hadn't been speaking? Then William put his fingers below my chin like my face was something delicate, and he kissed me. His lips were perfect. And his taste: of mint dipped in sea salt. He was careful, confident, familiar, strange. He was exactly what I'd been waiting for.

3

The next day Susan made a circle with her finger on the couch and said, "Is this new?"

"Do you like it?" I had bought two new couches. We sat on one and looked at the other. White, downy fabric that reminded me of clouds (who doesn't want a couch like a cloud?) paired with a low-backed, contemporary body that was long and near to the floor.

I had been redecorating. I was going through a phase of wanting everything in the house to be white. It felt cleaner to me, and softer, and, as my architect had rightly pointed out, white didn't compete with the art.

"It's good," she said, in her absolute way. Susan spoke only in absolutes. She was the most decisive person I knew. She also had good taste, so her opinion mattered to me. I was relieved she approved of the couch.

Today Susan wore a giant yellow scarf that looked more like a blanket and was feeling a lot better after her episode with the flu, though she still wanted to baby herself, which was why she was swaddled, drinking tea, and which was also why she had conveniently planned this visit to coincide with Dan the masseur's usual Sunday appointment. Dan loved me, so he usually didn't mind adding another body to the roster, especially if it was Susan.

Susan was my closest friend. We had gone to Deerfield

together and now basically led parallel lives—same gym, same hairdresser, same magazines in the bathroom. Physically we were total opposites, which was annoying only because it disproved my theory that short people and tall people didn't mix in meaningful ways, though this theory still held up with everyone in my life besides Susan. I was tall, Susan was short. I had brown hair, Susan had blond hair. Susan was fair-skinned, I was olive-skinned. Our color themes even extended to the tea we were drinking right now. Me: Earl Grey. Susan: chamomile.

"I think one of my people got me sick," she said, curling her small legs underneath her blanket/scarf.

"Who? Henry?"

"Please, don't say his name." She mock-cringed. "Oh, I need to text him. Thanks for reminding me." She rummaged around her giant salmon-pink purse until she found her phone. I was surprised it wasn't in her hand already. Susan was a little addicted to the screen.

By "her people," Susan (lovingly) meant the people who worked at her shop, Bonsai, an adorable little boutique that sold, obviously, bonsai trees. It turned out Susan had landed on a gold mine with this very niche market that combined artistry and mini-fauna, and she was killing it. Henry was her manager. He was also twenty-four and wanted to fuck her. He'd made this obvious through the many doting cards he left around the shop for her to find. With his spirited curly hair and the cutoffs he wore in summer, Henry looked like a gardener from a '90s movie. ("I half expect to find him singing into a hose every time I go in there," she said once.) But as much as she thought sleeping with Henry would be "wholly entertaining," he was too young, and he was her employee. Susan had self-respect, or at least she wanted it to appear that way. So her approach was to dismiss the cards entirely—she didn't mention them to Henry at all. Yes, of course she kept them. She kept them in a box at home, and that was no one's business.

Working was a big thing Susan and I had in common. Most of our friends didn't work, especially the ones from Deerfield. They were too busy raising kids (or paying people to do that) and taking care of the household (or telling their assistants how to do that) and going to Pilates and lunch and dotingly removing their husbands' coats at night after long moneymaking days at the office.

Susan and I, both still childless (she didn't want them) and unmarried (which bothered me more than it bothered her), owned small businesses within a few blocks of each other in the West Village, where we both also lived. Mine was a handmade stationery shop. The goal in starting it was to promote new artists and give them a way to make some extra cash while giving people cool, original, not-Hallmark cards. Susan had actually named the shop for me: Leaf. First we thought Paper, but that was taken, and Leaf—ha—went with the bonsai theme. As in bonsai trees had leaves, most of the time. (Yes, we may have come up with this idea while tipsy on pink champagne one late afternoon at Le Gigot.)

Although neither of us actually needed to work, we often did. It was nice to have something tangible and straightforward to do during the day. I hated to be such a cliché, but if I had nothing to do, I shopped. Which was bad, but better than drugs. Of course I was grateful to have the luxury to buy whatever I wanted, but I also knew I didn't fully understand gratitude for material things like other people did. By "other people" I obviously meant poorer people, which also happened to be most people. I knew I was lucky because people told me I was lucky. I knew it to the extent that I could know it. But I actually resented my good fortune sometimes—I may have had distorted, oversimplified notions that romanticized a hunter-gatherer, stranded-on-a-desert-island-in-a-good-way(?)-type life—and this, the resenting, proved that I didn't get it at all, because, as Susan pointed out, "Only trust-fund babies have the audacity to resent money." She was allowed to say this because she was a trust-fund baby, too.

I watched her beady little blue eyes scan the screen. Susan was pretty in sort of a pinched way. She had small features: a button nose and the itty-bitty mouth of a pocket-sized fairy. As a child she had been adorable. Now she was what people usually called "cute." She hated that—no one called tall people "cute." But, she argued, she did get more leg room where tall people didn't, though this would have been more advantageous if she flew coach, which would never happen.

She chuckled to herself, said, "Wow."

"What?"

"Nothing."

In a way Susan and I were still the skinny, naive girls we'd been at Deerfield. When she said "Nothing" now, I saw her saying "Nothing" at age fourteen, when she'd had a crush on Tommy Charles and didn't want to talk about it.

"Um." She looked up. She had forgotten what she was going to say. And then she remembered. "Oh, should we get sandwiches?"

"I don't know. Do you want a sandwich?"

"I wouldn't be asking you if I didn't want one."

"Okay, but let's order in."

"Oh yeah, I'm not walking anywhere."

So I called the sandwich place and ordered our sandwiches. I got a veggie hummus wrap and a Coke for Dan, like a real Coca-Cola, which no adult except Dan actually drank, and which was hilariously not in sync with his holistic approach to life at all.

I took a sip of my tea and noticed how the leaves on the tree outside my window were so much bigger and greener than they had been the week before. I thought, You can be in the same rut for so long, and then, seemingly out of nowhere, everything changes and you remember what the point is. The point, of course, is love. To love someone, to be loved by someone: that is the point.

Even in my best relationships, I wasn't sure I had ever been truly in love. This bothered me. A lot. I thought about it all the time. I was sure it was part of the incompleteness I had always felt. None of the people I'd been with seemed to be the missing piece. They were always the wrong shape, sometimes very obviously and other times in a more irritatingly mysterious way. I told myself I was not stupid to think that with William it would be different, though of course I knew I had said this many times before.

I didn't know why I was waiting to tell Susan about him. Usually it would have been the first thing out of my mouth. Maybe I didn't want to jinx it. Or I didn't want to find out that she hated him, because if she did, her opinion would be hard to cast aside. I had to tell her, though, and if I waited too much longer she'd accuse me of withholding. "Do you know William Stockton?"

Susan looked up immediately. "Stockton, Stockton," she said quickly. She was a person who talked very fast unless she was sad. When she was sad, she talked very slow. "I know Maureen Stockton, I know Callan or Cameron Stock*ard*. William. William. Will-yam. Does he do Dick or Will or anything?"

"I don't know."

"Not helpful."

I drank more tea, even though I knew it would be cold now, which it was.

"Who is he?"

I gave it to Susan in bullet points. Those resonated with her. "Met him at the gala, we had coffee yesterday, he just moved back from Europe, he knows my family, he knew them before I was born. Very good-looking, has a dog, literally just moved back."

"Huh." Susan stretched her feet out onto the glass coffee table, with one foot on either side of the lilies I had bought earlier. She curled her toes back (her toenails matched her fingernails today: eggplant), then pointed them forward. She kept doing this, back and forth, and we stared at her feet because they were something to stare at. "Is he married? Kids? Why is he back now?"

"Work."

Susan, a lover of gossip, squinted attentively as I went on to explain William's memories of Eighty-Fourth Street and of my parents, and what he looked like (very tall, maybe six-four, gray hair, sensitive eyes, strong jaw, chiseled yet childlike features; I had been thinking about words to describe him), and the kiss at the end. I skipped the part about the haircut.

"Sensitive eyes? Okay, you're fucked."

"I know. But it's good, right? Doesn't it sound good?"

"Definitely good," Susan said, "almost too good." When she looked up and saw my reaction to that—not happy—she said, "But listen, you deserve it. Oh my God, you deserve it. After the ride you've had, and Fernando—shit, girl." She pointed a finger in the air. "Good stuff is coming, don't worry."

By "the ride you've had," Susan meant: all the terrible people you've chosen, including, most recently, Fernando Delarus, who asked you to marry him and then left you for someone else—not even a young model but an old, old woman, so the only problem could have been your personality.

So yes, I was ready for the good stuff. I think, honestly, I hoped this business of getting young artists exposure and money would count as something Good I was doing, something to enhance the Good that would be returned to me by the universe. But that sounded so terrible and selfish and Bad that I wouldn't have mentioned it to anyone, not even Susan.

•

Dan arrived just after the sandwiches, wearing his usual massage outfit: coal-gray stretchy pants and a white V-neck under a colorfully striped alpaca hoodie. When he smiled, the gap between his two front teeth reminded me, as it always did, of Madonna. It was also very endearing.

"Hi," he said, and kissed me on the cheek.

"Dan-nay," Susan said.

"Susan." He went to kiss her.

"Can you fit me in or do you have a meditation retreat to go to?"

Dan paused. He did this a lot. He liked to think about things. He looked at the ceiling. He often found the answer up there. "I can fit you in."

"Good. Sit." Susan patted the couch.

Dan rubbed his hands together—he did this as a reflex; it was what he did to warm his hands before touching skin—and did as he was told.

"Okay, let's go around. Updates, Danny, updates." Dan and Susan hadn't seen each other in a few weeks—she'd been in St. Bart's avoiding the cruel end of spring. "I'm getting over the flu. Don't worry, Dan"—she touched his arm—"I'm not contagious. Other than that, I am still single. Nobody good goes to St. Bart's in May. I am considering buying a new car this summer. Not a red convertible, no. I am not having a midlife crisis, no, no. What else? My doctor told me to do yoga for my back. I hate yoga. It drives me insane, it's too slow." Dan and I laughed. "That's it. Catherine, go."

"Met someone and feeling hopeful."

"Really?" Dan said.

I shrugged. "We'll see."

"Dan?"

"I turned thirty-one this week."

"No you didn't."

"I did."

"Baby," Susan said.

"I'm so sorry I forgot," I said. "But we did get you a sandwich."

We moved to the table, the large glass dining table overlooking my tree and my street. I loved this street, and I had waited for a long time to buy the perfect home here. It was narrow and quaint and reminded me of France.

Susan said, "I'm feral for this—I haven't had real sustenance in days," and dug into her sandwich (chicken salad), and Dan thoughtfully unwrapped his. I wasn't that hungry, but I took a bite because it was there. It tasted mostly like carrots with a dash of cucumber because that's exactly what it was.

"Thanks so much for this," Dan said.

"Of course."

"You should come get a bonsai, Dan," Susan said, her mouth full, "from the store. For your birthday."

"Really?"

"Yeah." She went on to explain about the different kinds.

He nodded at the right times, said "yes" and "okay" at the right times, took small bites of his wrap and chewed with his mouth closed. He opened his Coke, took a sip, placed the butt of the can back down in the circle where it had been. I always watched Dan with a certain interest because he was so strangely at ease with himself. How could a thirty-one-year-old be this comfortable in the world? Shouldn't he be stressed, schlepping around on the subway all day with his backpack, going from one knotted back to the next, trying to make a buck?

He was also so polite. His good manners came from being raised partly in Tokyo—that's how he had explained it when Susan had asked once. He was half Japanese and exotically handsome (black hair and blue eyes), and it was odd that neither Susan nor I had romantic feelings for him. He was attractive, kind, and (I was pretty sure) straight. He just really felt to us like a younger brother; that's what we said when we talked about it. But Susan was strict about not dealing with anyone under thirty-five anyway, and I was strict about my height requirements. Dan was five-five: way too short.

Even though we all acted like friends, I sometimes worried that Dan secretly thought we were assholes. He never talked about money, but I assumed he was broke, maybe because he wore the same outfit all the time and lived in a neighborhood in Brooklyn I'd never heard of. I didn't know much about his personal life except that he had a dog and worked really long days. I tipped him a lot, of course—I tipped everyone a lot—but then that made me feel kind of pathetic: rich lady buying friendship of young masseur. It was impossible not to be a cliché of yourself. Every little choice was just another opportunity to be so obviously . . . well, you.

Susan crumpled her sandwich paper and flicked it a couple of inches away from her on the table. "I demolished that." Susan talked like a stoner sometimes because she had spent her childhood in San Francisco. Her younger sister, who still lived there, actually referred to eating as "grinding," as in "Let's go grind some food."

"This was delicious. Thanks again." Dan wrapped the half that was left and slid it into his floppy fabric backpack. He stood up, pushed his chair in. "I'll set up the room," he said, and went down the stairs.

"Can I go first? Do you mind?" Susan looked at her phone. A sly smile appeared on her face in reaction to whatever she was reading.

"No, that's fine."

"Thanks." She threw her yellow blanket/scarf/pashmina thing over the side of the couch, placed her phone on top of that, and walked her little fairy feet down the stairs.

I cleaned off the table and put my uneaten wrap in the fridge. I knew I wouldn't eat it later but felt too guilty throwing it away. This was a habit left from Jim, who had called me wasteful once.

I could hear Susan laughing. I opened a book about apartheid. It was one of those books everyone said you *had* to read. From at least three people I'd heard "It takes some time to get into, but you *have* to read this book." I read the opening paragraph and closed the book. (I had done this at least twelve times.)

I looked around the room. It looked good. My gorgeous white house, my art: red Mark Rothko on one wall; lithographs of an obscure French printmaker on the other; Asian vases, huge ones, in the corner. A modern chandelier that looked like it was made from white rose petals floated above the table. Of course I couldn't stop myself. I was always looking past what was good to what was wrong, and right now what was wrong was that the vases needed to be dusted. I knew Lucia was scared to touch them, but we had already gone over how to dust them lightly. I would bring it up again. A voice in my head said, You have become your mother. Another voice said, No, you're fine, and you pay the cleaning lady to clean things, so she should clean them.

Earlier that morning, before I had gone out to buy the lilies, William had written me an e-mail, which I reread now.

> *Catherine,*
>   *It was lovely to see you. I will be in touch very soon.*
> *Yours,*
> *WM.*

Even though I knew what it said, I reread my response: *Look forward to hearing from you. C.*

Was my response too cold? Fernando used to call me cold. He'd even called me a bad hugger once. My mother was cold. But no, it was fine. He would be in touch very soon.

I Googled him again. The thumbnail next to his bio showed William in a red tie, smiling with those brilliant-white teeth.

"William Stockton, MK Capital. Head of Corporate Client Solutions. Mr. Stockton served as head of European investment banking at UBS, and prior to that was head of European rates trading. Mr. Stockton holds an MBA from Oxford University."

He was smart. He was fashionable. He was practical. He was

classy. And as the time between yesterday and today widened toward dusk, he became smarter and more fashionable and more practical, and classier, and taller, and a more caring dog owner. His gait, which I now found a word for, was stately.

I sat back on the couch, folded the computer. Kids on the street played with a ball—someone shrieking, "Arthur!"—and birds made noise, swarming the tree, and the traffic on Seventh Avenue whirred like a distant stream, or like the hum of a small and comforting appliance. The noises of the city reminded me of its constant movement, and this soothed me. Because I hated silence. Silence made me anxious.

Sundays also made me anxious. I hated Sundays more than anything. Every week it was like time stopped to show me how lonely I was. People meandered in lazy, loping patterns, rudely forgetting how sidewalk traffic works. They had no direction, no goals. It was brunch time and family time and time to enjoy yourself, and it felt like an immense amount of pressure to be happy.

I wasn't unhappy, though, I reminded myself of that. Look at this house. How could you be unhappy here?

I got up to look out the window—yes, there were the kids with the ball; one of them was the famous actor's son—and I reminded myself that my home and the light in my home were beautiful and welcoming and that I was open to new, great people in my life. It would happen. And maybe—I thought and then unthought; I would not get ahead of myself—great things were already happening.

I moved back to the dining table and began to fill an online cart with Frette pillowcases. I had been meaning to get some more for the guest room. These were sand-colored and Egyptian cotton, a thousand thread count. I clicked to see a closer view. Buying fabrics online was hard. It was better to touch them. But returning things was so easy nowadays. You just put them back in the bag.

I often thought that a person could spend her entire life buying things and making returns. I was glad I was not that person.

•

Susan emerged looking jet-lagged and dumbly contented. "I'm leaving. And I'm taking the rest of the day off."

"Sure you are," I said. Susan was terrible at relaxing. She wouldn't take the day off unless she was bleeding from the head. This was another thing we might have had in common.

"Seriously." She poured herself a glass of water. "That man has the magic touch."

"I know." I had been hovering the cursor over the Add to Cart button, and then I pressed it. I turned around to find Susan gulping the last of the water in the glass. Her yellow hair was sticking straight up from the middle of her head. She looked like a parakeet.

"Aaaaah." She set the glass in the sink and made her way over to her phone (quick look at the screen) and her yellow thing, which she put around her shoulders. She bent slowly to pick up her bag off the floor and started down the stairs. I followed her down and smoothed her parakeet hair on the way. "Your hair looks crazy. I'm helping you."

Dan stood in the doorway on the second floor. "Dan, aaaaaaah," Susan said. I could see he had already changed the sheet in the room. He was so good. "You're a miracle." She patted him on the chest. As I watched her kiss his cheek, I thought Susan was a little touchy-feely with Dan today, but then she kissed me and I remembered that no, Susan was like that with everyone.

"Call you later." She hugged her yellow thing tighter around her little body as she made her way down the last flight of stairs and out the red door. That was the one thing that wasn't white—the red front door.

Dan, mocking the experience of a more formal—or a Japanese?—massage, gave me a short nod with prayer hands and motioned for me to enter. He could be pretty dorky.

He waited by the door as I changed behind the shinju panels. It felt nice to be in this room. The windows were tinted to make the light feel bluer, and I'd chosen a nice thick carpet. The towel folded on the black lacquer chair was warm from the sunlight through the window. I didn't really need to use it because I knew Dan wouldn't look, but I threw it around myself anyway. I walked the few steps to the table, let the towel drop, and lay facedown and looked at the carpet, which, yes, had been a great choice.

"Okay," I said, "ready."

I heard his footsteps. Then I saw his feet, clean and manicured, with a normal alignment of nice-looking toes and a tattoo of a scorpion on his ankle. He smoothed the blanket over my back. It felt wonderful to be touched so sweetly. Dan did have the magic touch. He just got it. He knew how much pressure to apply and when. He knew what I wanted. From the first time he massaged me, which had been about a year before, around when we had sold Eighty-Fourth, I knew I needed him on the payroll. I wasn't in love with the masseur I had before Dan anyway. Donald, a rough Swede, was all business and no warmth. While I had been dating Fernando, I used Dan's touch as a point of comparison. During the week I would tell myself that Fernando was fine, and then every Sunday Dan would remind me that no, Fernando was seriously lacking in the touch department.

Sometimes we liked to talk. With me on the table like that and Dan at work, he had more nerve to say the things he might not have said if we were sitting face-to-face, and so did I. Today he said, "So, tell me more about this guy." He ran his hands up and down my legs, warming them.

"I mean, it's just out of nowhere. He seems very together."

"That's a good thing."

Dan had this nonjudgmental nature that made me want to tell him things. I told him about Herman and how William had been so good with those kids at the park.

"I can see why you feel hopeful," he said.

And then we said nothing for a while, and I drifted off. That was the other thing I liked about Dan: he knew when to talk, and he also knew when to stop talking.

At some point I may have noticed that I was imagining Dan's hands were William's hands and that Dan's breath was William's breath. With Fernando, I hadn't done that. With Fernando, all I could think was that I wished he would touch me like this. Fernando hadn't been love. He was a stand-in, he was filler. And he wasn't even great filler. After we broke up, I was finally able to admit that he smelled like salami most of the time. When Fernando wasn't around, I didn't pine for him; I didn't even think of him much. He was like a figurine I moved around to the places in my life where I needed a plus-one: Fernando in a tux at the ball, Fernando in Sperry loafers on the boat, Fernando, the figurine-man who posed in pictures beside me.

4

I woke up Monday morning with the feeling I always had on Monday mornings: relief. Sunday was over. We could get back to our real lives now.

My tree outside the bedroom window looked like a painting of itself, flat and grainy purple in the early light. It was drizzling. Often in this hazy state, still half asleep, I would see my life as though it belonged to someone else. What did this room say about the person who lived in it? The pretty chaise longue under the window, cast in lavender light; the threaded floral embroidery on the duvet, white on white; the Roy Lichtenstein, the Shepard Fairey, the Renoir. These were interesting, tasteful choices. The person who lived here was tasteful and interesting.

I checked my phone. An e-mail from William. I felt myself smile.

Would you like to have dinner tonight at Joseph Leonard? 8 p.m.? Yrs, Wm.

Would I wait to respond? Yes. But wait. No. No, because I would not play games. No. I would just be myself. Just be yourself, I told myself.

I wrote back: *That sounds perfect. C.*

The new skylights meant I didn't need to turn the lights on. This fact gave me a small pleasure every time I remembered it. I got in the shower. When the water had woken me up more fully, I remembered how my night had ended, postmassage: nachos

ordered in, a bottle of dry white wine, *Us* magazine with my reading glasses, another hate letter to Fernando written on a greasy
nacho napkin with a very expensive fountain pen.

So I wasn't perfect. So I had my vices. A fleeting thought:
What would William think of a woman who wrote hate letters on
greasy nacho napkins? And: Did he have vices? Looking at him,
none were apparent. But I'd been with enough people to know that
everyone had at least one hidden weirdness. Fernando trimmed
his nose hairs obsessively. He also ate salami in the middle of the
night—only salami, not other meats. Jim couldn't get in bed without washing his feet, which he preferred to do in the sink instead of
in the shower for some reason. Shelly, my one girlfriend, ate half a
pack of honey rice cakes every single night in bed while scrolling
on her iPad, making extreme and lofty plans for the future and trying to get me excited about them. Hey Cat, do you want to go to
India? Hey Cat, we should definitely go to the Amazon. Hey Cat,
I might become a psychologist. She always said "Hey Cat" like she
was calling me from another room, when I was right there, right
next to her in bed, wanting to strangle her for making me sleep
with all her sticky rice-cake crumbs.

Shelly flipped houses for a living. She would have appreciated
this shower. It was gorgeous. Small rectangular gray tiles, all the
way up to the ceiling. It had been a painstaking process to line them
up so perfectly. Jeff, my handyman (who'd grown up in Alaska; he
could do anything with those hands), had recently installed three
glass shelves in the corner for my shower products. You were supposed to use the microdermabrasion scrub only once every three
days, but I loved how soft and new it made my skin feel. I used it
almost every day. Another vice. As I rubbed gently in an upward
circular motion for two to three minutes, I imagined that this would
be the thing I'd reveal to William if he asked me about vices.

The running list of plans in my head today included calling
Jeff about getting automatic blinds. I always had a running list of

plans in my head. I woke up with a checklist and spent the day trying to check as many boxes as possible. Sometimes, usually when I
was overtired, I would think, Am I living a check-box life? But no,
I was just organized. I was just productive.

I would call Jeff. I would stop by the shop. I would go uptown
for lunch with Mom. I would invite Caroline because I had to—
she would be upset if I didn't. I would work out. Would I buy a
new outfit for dinner with William? Maybe I would. I felt myself
smiling again. I touched my cheek. Smooth. Microdermabrasion
was a miracle.

I turned off the water, stepped into the steam. For this bathroom I'd chosen plush white towels, a plush white rug, and long-
necked, elegantly curved faucets on his-and-hers sinks. On the
walls were a tiny Matisse drawing—dancers on grass—and a big
blue painting of the ocean that Susan had assured me was too
expensive to be cheesy. I reminded myself that it did not look like
Florida at all. (It looked exactly like Florida.)

My ass looked good in the mirror. For forty-three, my ass
looked really good. Face, too, looked good. Yes, I'd gotten a little
Botox to fill the creases, but it wasn't obvious. The trick with Botox
was to leave the forehead alone.

My incredibly long hair—almost down to my hips now—was
kind of my trademark thing, and had been forever. I'd begun to
consider cutting it, but I wasn't ready. I didn't know whether that
was because it was so much a part of me (and a part people liked—
lots of hair compliments) or because I refused to age, and cutting
your hair short, unless you had a genre (punky, sporty), just meant
that you were old.

•

It was still drizzling, but not enough to need an umbrella.
Jeans, white shirt, Burberry rain jacket, boots. My usual nonfat

latte and a banana from the coffee shop on the corner. The air felt nice and cool as I walked and I didn't even mind getting a little wet. The shop was only three blocks away.

When I turned the corner and saw our sign—*leaf*—just like that, all lowercase, so simple, I felt content. I owned this. This was mine. I hadn't planned on buying, initially. I was going to lease, like everybody else, but the landlord wouldn't let me gut the place, and it needed to be gutted badly. So I bought it. Or my mother did, really. She gave me $2 million to buy it.

I opened the door to find Vera in her usual spot on the backless chair at the computer. She peered around the big screen and jerked her head back when she saw it was me. "Oh, Catherine, it's you," she said. She pulled her crumpled green shirt off her stomach. It had tiny dandelions on it. On her wrist was a matching scrunchie (as in: the same exact print) and the calorie-counting bracelet she never took off. (Once Susan had summed up Vera's look like this: Anne of Green Gables meets REI.) A Starbucks Venti with dried brown drip marks and her cell phone sat on the desk. She always had her phone there in case her kids called, or so she said. She had four of them under the age of eighteen. She didn't stand to greet me, but she did straighten her back. "How are you?"

"I'm great." The first thing I wanted to do was complain about the nachos, but Vera was actually fat. She wouldn't understand. She also had other "real problems," like kids and a lazy husband and bad roofing on her house. And it would have been unprofessional. I was, after all, the boss. Mostly, though, it would have tampered with the image Vera had of me, which was of someone who was very lucky and very together and very happy, or at least as someone who wore quality clothing and who appeared to be moderately contented a good amount of the time. "How are we doing today?"

"Okay." Vera sounded unsure. She was constantly worried that the shop would close and she would be out of a job. Even with the commute from Jersey, it was a good job. I paid her a lot, probably too much.

I didn't want her to worry, and I also didn't want to get into it, so I said, "Good, I'm glad," instead of asking about specific numbers. The accounting stuff didn't interest me anyway. I hated math—it just didn't resonate. I unzipped my jacket and hung it on the back of the door.

"Wet out there." Vera tucked her short hair behind her ear. Her chunky highlights gave the impression that several skunks were parked on top of her head. This was a common New Jersey mistake. "Not good for business."

That was probably true. It was eleven in the morning and we had no customers. But the shop did look great. Blond wooden floors, just cleaned, and it smelled nice. That was important to me. I insisted that Vera have at least three Jo Malone candles burning at all times. Yes, even in the morning. And I was happy to see them there, two on the center table with the journals and scrapbooks and one by the computer, although maybe it was a little too close to the computer. "I'm just going to move this over a tiny bit," I said. "I think it's better by the business cards, don't you?"

I wasn't a micromanager. It was my shop. Vera nodded. She was good at being pleasant. Yes, she may have tensed up a little when I was around. She tucked her hair and pulled her shirt off her stomach incessantly. But that wasn't my problem. If it had been Vera's shop, we would have done what Vera wanted.

Overall, she did do a wonderful job, and I wanted her to know that. It also made her easier to work with when she felt good. I walked around the center table—I couldn't help but tweak those candles, too; the labels should face out—and said, "These walls look great, Vera," which was true. They did.

"Thanks." A sincere pleasantness rose in her voice, and I knew she was smiling, though I didn't turn back to look.

Latte in one hand, I straightened the cards out with the other, just to make them a little more perfect. They were arranged not by occasion but by artist. All the cards were blank inside, so they could be used for anything. Or at least that was the idea. The artists who'd been selling here longer knew it was smart to have at least one or two event-themed cards, like this one by P. J. Klein (he was brilliant) with a drawing of a little girl sitting on top of a five-tiered birthday cake, a star-topped wand in her hand. Cards that subtly said "Birthday" or "Christmas" tended to sell faster. My interpretation of this was that most people were uncreative morons who needed to be told what to do.

"Has Dorothy sent anything new?"

Dorothy was a seventy-four-year-old out of Alabama who'd e-mailed me pictures of her work. Her son (who did "big business in the Big Apple") had wandered into the shop and decided his mother's stuff belonged here, and he was right. It was my ideal scenario: someone I had discovered myself whose work was legitimately good. Dorothy's photographs were simple and hopeful and sad and not decidedly southern (a good thing): an aerial view of a child's chipped wooden train set, the condiments on the counter of a dusky diner, an old woman's papery hands folded in a lap.

"She did send something," Vera said slowly. I could hear her clicking through the in-box. Vera had jurisdiction over all the e-mail, both to the shop's general address and to my personal address at the shop, but she knew I liked to e-mail the artists myself. That was my passion. The sales stuff—I didn't feel passionate about that at all. "Here it is. I'll flag it for you."

"Thanks."

In the back room, I ate my banana and read Dorothy's e-mail. There was one new image—of a lone swing at a playground on a fall day; I loved it—accompanied by Dorothy's description. I didn't know why she insisted on explaining the images. I thought it killed the magic, and I had already politely told her it really wasn't necessary. But she had apparently chosen to ignore that. This one said:

On this swing, I was molested over sixty-five years ago. The man was never taken to trial, but he died young. That was the Lord taking him to trial.

Holy fuck.

Dear Dorothy, I wrote quickly, *while we love your work, we are only interested in the content of the work itself. No text is needed. Please stop sending. Best, C.*

I deleted the e-mail and decided to tell no one about what it said, though my guess was that Vera had already seen it.

I scrolled through the other e-mails Vera had flagged for me—nothing too exciting, no new potential artists—and made a few calls: to P.J. about a check we had for him; to Bird, a female artist in Queens, asking if she would be open to doing a mural for my friend's rec room; and to the florist. I made sure the back room looked organized and emerged to find a few people milling around, taking cards off the shelves and opening them despite the cute sign I had asked Vera to make that said *All These Cards Are Blank* ☺. It was amazing how many people still felt the need to check for themselves.

I smiled at the fashionable man in dark denim with the open card in his hand, and when I got to Vera, I said, "Feel free to talk to them about the artists."

She flinched, tucked her hair in a disjointed, robotic way. "Oh yeah, I was about to."

"I ordered flowers. They should be here within the hour."

"Okay." She nodded, doing her best impersonation of a perky employee. "Will you be back later this afternoon?"

I knew I wouldn't be back but I said, "Maybe." I wanted to keep Vera on her toes. I wanted her thinking there could always be a chance I would appear. We had cameras in the shop I could watch from my iPhone, and every once in a while I would remind Vera that I was watching the live footage on the days I didn't come in. I'd say things like, "You wore nice pants yesterday." Most of the time it wasn't true. Watching the footage was incredibly boring.

"Call me if you need anything, okay?"

Vera made her way off the chair with great resistance. "You got it."

A part of me—this was so fucked up—wanted to stand there until she had actually started talking to the man in dark denim, but I was running late. I took my jacket off the door and stepped out into the puddles. The pregnant sky suggested thunder. At any moment we might hear the roar and start running. For now, there was no rain.

•

Mom's designated lunch hours were eleven to one. Her days were structured, predictable, designed to give her a feeling of security. Breakfast, Bingo, lunch, a nap, TV or reading, dinner, shower, bed.

Even though I wasn't in the mood to see her, I texted Caroline from the cab, which had the gray leather interior of a dry, dead elephant and smelled like cigarettes and hot sauce. The name of the cabbie was Dev. He looked pixelated and constipated in his little laminated picture. I liked to make note of cabdrivers' names in case I got kidnapped. I had done this instinctively ever since seeing *The Bone Collector*.

We inched up the West Side Highway slower than I could have walked. I didn't mean to sound rude when I told this to Dev, but it came out sounding rude. Dev grunted.

Caroline, somewhat surprisingly (I hoped it might be too last-minute for her to come) and also not surprisingly at all (she never said no), wrote: "Yes! Italian place!" Which was great—she'd walk Mom there, I could be a few minutes late—and it was also so typically Caroline. She loved to involve herself in anything that involved me. She'd been like that since we were kids, always trying to make my friends into her friends, adopting my interests as her own. I wanted to take horseback riding lessons, Caroline wanted to take horseback riding lessons. I wanted blond hair, Caroline wanted blond hair. That had happened when we were teenagers. Our family Christmas card that year was ridiculous: two platinum-blond children between our dark-haired parents. It looked like they had adopted us from Sweden. Now that we were adults, I knew I was supposed to be flattered by the way Caroline looked up to me, but most of the time it was suffocating.

I also had a lot of opinions about Caroline's life. One would assume that a normal mother of three wouldn't have the flexibility to just run out for lunch with half an hour's notice, but Caroline's mothering techniques were turning out to be exactly like our own mother's: fully dependent on nannies. Caroline actually had three nannies, one per child. Betty and Caleb, the two-year-old twins, often ran to the nannies when they were upset, which didn't seem to bother Caroline at all ("Good for them," she said once). And Spencer, the poor five-year-old, who was such a lovely boy—delicate and feathery, he reminded me of the character in *Le Petit Prince*—was going through a phase where he seemed genuinely confused about who to show his little Play-Doh sculptures to. I knew Caroline's lack of involvement bothered her pediatrician husband, Bob, because she had let that slip once in a vulnerable moment. Her main point of defense when the nanny thing came up was that she had had those children with her own body! She could just as easily have hired a surrogate. If Bob couldn't wake up and smell what year it was, and see how much she had sacrificed (hello, stretch marks!), then that was his problem.

I arrived just in time to find them at the door of Da Castelli. Caroline held Mom's elbow in a way that suggested this was a very stressful thing to do. I told myself to be perky—if Vera could be perky, I could be perky—and said, with way too much enthusiasm, as though I had just popped out of a cardboard birthday cake in a stupid hat, "Hey guys!"

"Hey!" Caroline dropped the elbow and threw her arms around me. It was her signature hug-you-to-death hug, designed to squeeze the love out of you by force. I held my breath, braced myself. I knew it would hurt and it did. Our bones pressed together.

She'd obviously just gone to the gym and hadn't showered yet. Her dark brown hair (long, same as mine) was matted to her forehead, and she looked even thinner than usual, in spandex pants that were scary roomy around her pencil-straight calves.

"Hi." I held her barely. I didn't want to break her. "Hi Mom," I said with my birthday messenger fervor, this time as though it were a child's birthday I was arriving for. I had promised myself when Mom started to lose it that I would never be one of those ladies who addressed children and animals and old people in miniature, cooing voices, and here I was, doing it. I guess my hope was that if I sounded excited, Mom would take it as a cue to be excited herself. It had never worked, and it didn't work now either.

"Hello, Catherine," she said, her eyes wide and bewildered.

I gently touched her shoulder—red rain jacket, slick from the drizzle—and kissed her very rouged cheek. Her makeup looked good, if a little heavy, but at least she looked like herself today. Some days the women who worked at the home made her up so severely. She would emerge with thick foundation and blue eye shadow and crusty eyelashes, looking like a pimping madam in a Broadway show. But even on those days she always smelled like herself: Lancôme products and rose oil. Despite my mother seeming less and less like my mother all the time, and more like a stranger lost in the street, these smells always brought me back. Lancôme and rose oil. This was my mother.

My mother and I looked a lot alike: hazel eyes, almond-shaped; eyebrows that cut straight across, barely any arch. This gave us a serene and pensive expression, which was funny for being so wrong. We were anxious people, prone to constant shifting and stirring and paranoia. My nose was larger—it was my father's nose—and hers was small and upturned. She'd had it done to look exactly like Caroline's (whose nose was nearly perfect), and we had all been very impressed with the surgeon's work. The three of us were obviously related—same coloring, same hair—but up close, other than her nose, Caroline's features were just slightly off, just slightly askew. Her eyebrows grew in wildly different directions— one looked like a fucked-up tadpole—and her eyes were a few important millimeters too far apart, and her smile on one side was unable to achieve the height that it did on the other.

Da Castelli was dark wood, cherry-red booths, white linen tablecloths, mirrors everywhere. It smelled like garlic bread. The bald maître d', whose name we should have known by now but didn't, took a stack of menus from his podium. "Ciao, ragazze West, follow me."

Caroline held Mom's hand, leading her toward the table, and I walked close behind, ready if she fell. We were such idiots at this, such novices. Even the small task of lunch was almost too much, and we watched Mom with wired eyes, full of fear that something bad would happen and it would be our fault. I hoped the people at the restaurant—the older couple by the window, eating pizza, the guy in a Yankees hat at the bar—interpreted this not as fear but as extreme loving cautiousness.

One of the reasons I wanted to have a child was that I knew it would change me into a person who was capable of really caring for another person. My plan, if it happened—an "if" that felt less promising every day—was to hire no nannies at all. To which Susan had said, "You're not serious. You don't even know how to iron a shirt." But I was serious. And (this had come to me later, and I planned on telling Susan the next time it came up) raising a child had nothing to do with ironing a shirt. I planned to hire someone to iron the shirts while I breast-fed, swaddled, got no sleep, sacrificed my life to another human being, etc.

"Your usual table." The maître d' knew how important it was to keep things familiar for Mom. He pulled out a chair.

"Caroline, Caroline, Caroline, Caroline," our mother was saying.

"What?"

She pointed to the ground. Caroline's foot was on her coat.

"Shit, sorry," she said, and lifted it off. We all looked at the wet tread mark left by her Reebok.

"Don't curse," Mom said, and decided to ignore the chair and sit in the booth instead. She scooted herself down it in a series of incremental thrusts until her placemat was square in front of her.

Caroline sat next to me instead of Mom. Of course she had to be as close to me as possible.

The good thing about Da Castelli was that Mom liked it now. A year ago she hated it for not being Silvano's on the Upper East Side, and would order only the veal with rosemary, because that's what she was so used to saying: "Veal with rosemary, thank you." The very nice chef here had replicated it for her for months, until one day Mom, for no apparent reason, decided she would have salmon pasta, light on the cream sauce, and a glass of your driest prosecco, thank you.

Now we all ordered the same thing every time. I would have the salad with goat cheese, and Caroline would have three bites of her penne, extra-extra pesto. (Caroline had the palate of a child.) It was an act of solidarity that had evolved by accident.

We took the menus from the maître d'. Only Mom opened hers. She looked at it confidently, even though I knew the cursive was too small for her to read because it was too small for anyone to read.

"You look good, Mom." I felt a little bad that I always said this, whether it was true or not, but at least today it was.

"Who did your hair, Mom?" Caroline smiled at the waiter who filled her water glass. She was right. Mom's hair—a high bun today—was overteased and oversaturated in hair spray. It looked like a bird had misplaced its nest on top of her head.

"The girl," Mom said.

"Which one?"

"Don't do that," I said.

"Do what?"

"Don't quiz her."

Caroline buzzed with her usual high voltage. "I thought we were supposed to ask questions about what's going on in the present."

"Yeah, but don't push her." I managed to say this more calmly than I felt it.

We looked at our mother, who had taken her coat partway off (we should have taken it off for her before she sat down) so that one arm was in and the other was out. With her free hand, she was buttering a slice of warm bread.

"Mom, let me take your coat," I said.

Mouth full, she shooed me away, but I stood up anyway and freed the other arm before she yelled, "Stop!"

"Okay, okay," I whispered, to illustrate that she had been too loud. The now empty arm of her rain jacket stuck out awkwardly beside her like it still contained something living inside it.

"Mom, you seriously want to sit on your coat during this whole lunch?" Caroline scratched her neck. It was probably itchy with the dried sweat from her workout.

"Yes," our mother said, "I would like to sit right here where I am."

Caroline rolled her eyes and smiled at me. I smiled back. Our shared stress over Mom was the closest thing to a connection we had, and it reminded me that, okay, fine, I was glad she was here. Doing this alone would have been a nightmare.

When the waiter came to take our orders and Mom said hers right, we exchanged another look. "Go Mom," Caroline said.

"How's Bob?" I asked her.

"Good. Busy. How's the shop?"

"Good."

Caroline hummed along to a song in her head (there was always a song in her head) until her eyes landed on my nails. They were a deep red right now. "Do you get gel or regular?"

I wanted to say, You have ADD. But what I said instead was, "Regular. The gel ruins your nails."

"Seriously?" Caroline frowned, looking at her own nails, which were fire-engine red and had obviously just been done, probably with gel. "Mom, let's see your nails."

"Absolutely not." Mom curled her fingers into her palms and hid them under the table.

"Mom."

"Catherine, I'm not interested in you right now."

"Mom, it's me, Caroline. Ca-ro-line." To me Caroline said, "I hate that."

"Mom, why did you give us such similar names?"

"They are not similar," Mom said.

"It's not that," Caroline said. "She calls me Catherine because she loves you more."

I made a look like "No," but everyone knew that was true. For some reason Mom had never really liked Caroline. I knew this not just because I could feel it (everyone could), but also because of the things Mom would whisper to me as a child. "You are the strong one," she would say, gin-lime breath and her hand firm on the back of my neck.

The bread in Mom's hand had lipstick all over it, and there

was lipstick on her teeth. She was still beautiful, or at least she was obviously someone who had been beautiful once, and she carried herself like that—like a person who understood the value of outward appearances in the world. Despite being old and confused now, she still possessed a grace. I knew I had inherited some but not all of this grace. I moved well, but not as well as my mother in her prime. Caroline had actually inherited more of Mom's great body, but she moved like a wrestler: hunched shoulders and a waddling hustle.

Her phone rang—some ridiculous rap song that was cool right now—and she answered. After a second she said, "Well, can you go to the store?" and then, more sternly, "Leave Caleb with Amelia and go to Fairway."

Our mother looked out the window. I would have liked to say that before this, I might have known what she was thinking, but my mother had always been a difficult person to know. She was cold and detached and thought emotions were a handicap. She had said "I love you" only two times that I could remember, both in dire circumstances: when I broke my leg horseback riding and on the turbulent flight to Paris when she was sure we were about to die. She had probably never said it to Caroline. My father had been the warm one. He hugged us; he told us he loved us often. In college a psychic had told me that our mother was the moon and our father was the sun. Caroline, sensing our mother's distance from her at an early age, had clung to our father like a monkey to a tree. Literally. I remember him trying to leave for work, dressed in his suit, smelling of coffee, and Caroline wrapping her arms around his neck and refusing to let go.

Caroline hung up. "Oh my God. These people can't do anything without me. It's like a full-time job telling them what to do."

"Why? What happened?"

"Apparently my son is out of fish sticks and the nanny can't figure out to go to the store."

"I love how your nanny doesn't even have a name."

"Tonia. You don't know her because she's new." Caroline dipped a piece of bread in olive oil and set it on her plate.

"Fine," I said.

"Can you please be nice to me?"

Mom, in her stern voice, said, "They must know you're the one in charge, Catherine."

Caroline sighed. "Thanks, Mom."

I felt bad for Caroline. She seemed like she was coming a little unglued lately. I put my hand on her shoulder. I was aware that I did this not very gently but more like a basketball coach. For a second I thought she might cry. Of the three of us, she was the only one who might actually do that in public.

"Thanks, sis," she said, her face full of rejection. Caroline so badly wanted to be best-friend sisters. She had always been searching for a deeper connection that I just never felt we had. Sometimes I thought she was living in a fantasy world, a world where life could be like the movies. Caroline loved movies. She had seen everything. It often felt like her actions were taken from a scene in a movie she'd just watched. When she said "Thanks, sis" now, for example, I wondered in what film some bleary-eyed actress had said "Thanks, sis." Her efforts came off as staged because they were staged, but her desperation was so authentic that it was hard not to feel very sorry for her all the time, and it was exhausting.

When I said "I love you," it might have been more for me than for her. I was making a serious effort to become softer. I was practicing. It made me so uncomfortable to utter these words that I actually felt dizzy for a second, and distractedly reached for my water glass to avoid eye contact.

Caroline looked surprised (this was only the third time I had said "I love you" to her; yes, I was counting), and then she looked exhilarated. This felt like too much responsibility. In the mirror behind Mom, I could see that my cheeks had turned pink. Mom looked disgusted.

"I love you, too," Caroline gushed. Of course the actress among us could say those words the most easily. But I sometimes wondered if it was Caroline's imitations of a cinematic existence that had gotten her so far in her real life. Because after all, she was the married one. She was the one with babies.

Our plates arrived at the table, followed by a moment of worrying about an unexpected reaction from Mom. Sometimes she suddenly hated the thing she usually liked. But today she picked up the fork and twirled her pasta with the rhythm of her old self.

"She's in a good mood," Caroline whispered.

"I know."

"What are you two saying?"

"We're saying this is good food, Mom."

Mom looked suspicious, and then her face melted into calm. Her emotions changed so quickly. It was hard to keep up, and there was no real point in trying.

Alzheimer's, we had learned, was a progressive disease. The longer it went on, the more Mom's memories would go further and further into the past, replacing the memories of the things that had just happened. "So that by the end," one doctor explained, "she will have settled on the earliest memories, things from childhood that make her happiest to talk about." Mom had never liked to talk about the past, especially her early past. She'd grown up without money and she was ashamed of it. She had a stock answer for people who asked her questions about her childhood: "I have lived nine lives—how can I remember them all?"

For now, what Mom liked talking about was our father. How they'd met in Greece ("Ios, fabulous place") and moved to the Upper East Side ("I thought we had become stiff, but your father assured me it was the only place we belonged"), and their marriage

("Thank God I was pretty, or he wouldn't have stayed"). Sometimes she called out for him—"Bruuuuuce!"—but most of the time she remembered he was dead.

Mom's other favorite subject was how her caretakers were thieves. Evelyn had stolen her comb, "the fat one" wouldn't give her "the good shampoo," they were all trying to pinch her purse, even though she no longer carried one.

I took a few halfhearted bites and moved the food around my plate. Of course I was thinking about William. I didn't want to ask in front of Caroline, but I also didn't know when Mom would be feeling this good again. I started slowly.

"Mom, I met someone you used to know."

"Yes?" Her eyes focused on me. Sauce dribbled down her chin. I was happy she noticed and wiped it with her napkin.

"Do you remember the Stocktons?"

"Edward and Donna," she said automatically.

"Who's that?" Caroline asked.

"Donna and I served on the New York City Children's Art Fund. It was very successful. We raised a lot of money." It was obvious she'd said this many times before. She sipped her prosecco. She was almost fooling me into thinking she was back to her normal self. "Edward and your father were great drinking buddies," she said. "Scotch."

"When did you meet?"

"Long ago. Your father and I were still"—Mom paused, looking for specifics, and, when she found none, chose something general (Alzheimer's pointed out how crafty the sufferer could be)—"at the beginning."

"Do you remember their son, William?"

My mother's eyes went fiery, then blank. She stopped chewing. She spit the food from her mouth into her napkin and pushed her plate away.

"Mom?"

She wouldn't look at me.

"Mom."

She took her prosecco glass by the stem and lifted it, looking out the window at the rain because it was raining now, hard. The sound of the water beating on the pavement drowned out all other sounds in that moment.

It was important to be clear. "Mom, do you remember William Stockton?"

"Who *is* that?" Caroline asked again.

My mother's nostrils flared involuntarily.

Caroline said, "Well, whoever it is, Mom's not a fan."

"Mom, please."

"Drop it," Mom said.

"Whoa," Caroline said.

"I won't drop it," I said.

"Oh my God, are you serious? She's having a good day, Catherine!"

"Mom," I said.

"Catherine!" Caroline yelled.

"Mom!" I yelled.

But my mother was done. She was putting her coat on. She was putting it on backwards, but she was still putting it on. "I am ready to leave," she said.

Caroline was signaling to the waiter for the check.

"Fine, I give up, I give up." I dropped my napkin on top of my uneaten salad, maybe a little too dramatically. To Caroline I said, "I can't take this sometimes."

"I know, I know." She rubbed my back with the eagerness of a clawing animal.

"Stop." I moved her hand off me. Where was my phone? No matter what time it was, I would say I was running late. I had to go. This was too much. When I found my phone, I saw that I actually was running late. "I have to go. Caroline, do you—"

"Go."

"Thanks." I kissed her sticky face and stood up to kiss my mother, who still wouldn't look at me. When I said, "Mom," she held her palm up and turned her face farther away. What else was there to do? I said good-bye and walked out of the restaurant (what was that couple by the window thinking now?) and got into a cab heading back downtown. My driver's name was Sadat.

•

Of course Mom's reaction bothered me, but I couldn't trust it either. Even pre-Alzheimer's, she'd had a tendency to hate people for no apparent reason, or for reasons that were insignificant and unfair. Growing up, I loathed the moment my mother would meet a new friend. She was extremely judgmental, and if the person fell short of her impossible standards, it was bad. Sophia, for example, my roommate at Sarah Lawrence, was pretty and smart and the kind of person who was hard to dislike. But she chewed gum. Constantly. There was always a piece of gum in that girl's mouth. The day she came over for the first (and last) time, Sophia was midsentence about her love of soccer when my mother said, "I'm sorry, I can't hear what you're saying over the smacking of that gum in your mouth," and left the room. After that, whenever I mentioned Sophia, Mom gave me the silent treatment. Sophia the gum chewer was dead to her.

So. If she didn't like William (if she even knew who he was; maybe she was confused about that), it was probably for a very stupid reason.

I got worked up and pissed off in the cab, thinking about my mother and cataloguing all the things in my life she had ruined. She had barely raised us herself, and then she had sent us to boarding school. She had alienated us. No, I wasn't a victim. I was simply taking note of the facts.

We were stuck in traffic again. I called Jeff and left a terse message about the blinds. I called Vera to ask her where she had put the flowers. "At the front, Catherine." She sounded defiant. "Good," I said, and hung up.

I inhaled deeply, told myself to relax. I noticed I wasn't breathing, which was something I'd been noticing a lot lately.

When I finally got to Equinox, I waved at the desk person, who tried to stop me. "Excuse me, ma'am, can you scan please?"

I kept walking as I said, "I'm in a hurry. Can I do it later?" I had no intention of doing it later. That girl should have known who I was by now.

In the locker room I wondered yet again why these women sauntered around so sexually. Were we in a porno? Did the tween-looking model with the belly-button ring really need to sashay to her locker like that? It wasn't jealousy. Even when I had had that body, I had walked like a normal person.

Sex with William was going to be great. I may have had a history of being nonsexual (this had been a big problem between me and horny Fernando), but I was so attracted to William. I wasn't worried at all.

I changed into my workout gear—all black Lululemon, purple Nikes—and met Chris by the treadmill. Chris was a gorgeous gay black man with crystal studs and the most defined quads I had ever seen. He liked to put his hands on his hips to air out his biceps, which looked like perfect dunes on a postcard horizon. I loved Chris—he never failed to put me in a better mood. When he saw me coming, he said, "Hey baby!" and gave me a kiss. "Get on up here!"

"I'm so sorry I'm late."

"No problem," he said.

"Ugh, I'm never on time, I just have so much to do." I put my hair in a ponytail with a sigh and stepped onto the treadmill. Maybe I was being a brat, but I was stressed. I was allowed to be stressed. My life was stressful. Even though I was richer and luckier than most people, that didn't mean I couldn't be stressed. It was all relative. Wasn't it? If I were making minimum wage and living in a bad apartment, I'd be stressed about that. Was that stress equal to the stress I felt today about my family? I asked myself this type of question a lot, and I always answered in the same way: probably. It was probably relative, which meant there was nothing to feel guilty about.

Chris put me at level three and the track started moving. "We'll start you slow today, baby, don't worry."

"I am just so stressed out!" Complaining made me feel better. And then I smiled. It wasn't like I didn't have a sense of humor.

"Yeah? What's wrong?"

I didn't feel like talking about my mother. "My legs are killing me."

"Woman, smile," he said, which made me smile. "Happy face!"

Chris was big on happy face. If you made a face like you were in pain, then you *were* in pain, and it made your workout a lot harder. I thought that was the stupidest thing I had ever heard, but it also worked.

It felt good to walk it off. Working out made me happier; it always did. I didn't have a therapist because the gym was my therapist. That's what I said to people all the time.

I looked at Chris. I should ask him a question. So I asked the question I always asked. "How are auditions going?" Of course Chris was an actor. Every personal trainer I'd ever met was an actor.

"Good," he said. "I'm working it."

I was breathing harder now. "Remind me to give you my friend's number."

"Yeah," Chris said, "for sure. I'll give you my card."

"Okay." I wiped my face with the towel. "Didn't you already give it to me? I must have lost it. Sorry."

"No worries, baby, no worries. All right." He reached over. "Moving you up to six now. Keep it going, you're doing great."

I had been meaning to hook Chris up with my friend who was a casting director. It was the least I could do to help someone who was really struggling. Chris had moved to New York from Ohio or somewhere, not knowing anyone. I couldn't even imagine how hard that must be. And he lived in Queens, which was so depressing. I had barely been to Queens, but I knew there were a total of four trees in the whole borough.

After the treadmill, we did burpees and weights. My anger was making this a great workout. Chris and I talked about food. That was sort of our bonding thing. We had decided the carrot cake at Whole Foods was the best on earth. We couldn't believe Jamba Juice ("the McDonald's of smoothie places") was still in business. Organic Avenue was obviously the best juice place. We voted Juice Generation "most innovative." Today Chris was praising the nuances of their Coco Açai smoothie. "It is an ugly color, but, girl, it tastes like heaven."

We did our final stretches on the mat by the window. The air outside was gray, foggy, one big puff of smoke. As I reached for my toes, Chris pushed my back. We had our routine down; I knew what to expect. This was the part where I felt relaxed and accomplished. I had worked hard. I was a hard worker. Good things would come to me because of this hard work.

5

He sat there with such confidence, his arm hanging easily over the chair, telling me the funniest things I had ever heard. His shorter hair was an improvement—he looked even better. He wore a navy-blue suit that angled his body in all the right ways. I wore the cream dress with the super-deep V-neck I'd picked up at Alice + Olivia after my workout. It appeared to be stitched from large silken petals that flowed around me when I walked. The lingering eyes of other people told me we looked good. We looked like we belonged together.

William wasn't funny funny, but he was so charming. It was his vague Europeanness and his overly articulate way of speaking—the way he never said "Yeah" but always "Yes," and how he constantly said my name. Catherine. Yes, Catherine. That's incredible, Catherine. I had the lamest smile plastered on my face. My cheeks were sore already.

We ordered martinis and looked at the menu, sort of. He looked at the menu while I looked at him. "What strikes you, Catherine?" he asked.

I scanned quickly. In yet another opportunity to be my clichéd self, I was exactly that. "The salad looks good."

When the waiter reappeared, William said, with such assurance, and also like it was 1952, "The kale salad for the lady, please, and I will have the Hudson Valley duck confit."

We smiled dumbly at each other across the table.

"So tell me about what you do all day," I said.

"Specifically, you want to know? Are you interested in banking?"

"No." I flipped my hair. "Not at all."

He smiled and studied me for a long moment. He looked at my hands on the table. I thought he might touch them. I wove my fingers together, keeping his interest there.

"Tell me more about you, Catherine. Tell me more about your shop."

I took a sip, preparing. "It's right near here. It's called Leaf."

"Yes, right. What a clever name. And you sell greeting cards?"

"Original prints. We have some great artists."

"Anyone I would know?"

I thought of P.J., and Bird, and Dorothy—ugh, that e-mail. "Probably not."

"Do you make any art yourself?"

"No, it's so sad—my sister's the creative one, not me." I briefly recalled my favorite painting of Caroline's, a realistic oil of a man getting out of a bathtub, and the way his hand reached for the towel, which was just out of reach. It was a shame she'd stopped painting. She'd done half an MFA at Yale and then dropped out when she got pregnant. "I'm not creative at all."

"How interesting, about your sister. I suppose sisters aren't always alike." He sipped his martini. "Do you look alike? You and your sister?"

"Sort of," I said.

"I'd like to see a photo sometime. That would be interesting. It's always interesting to see people's siblings."

Was that true? I guess it could be interesting, but it wasn't *that* interesting. "Sure, I'll show you sometime," I said. Was it a little odd that William wanted to see a picture of my sister? But no, I told myself, it was sweet. If he cared to know about the people in my life, that was because he cared about me.

"Splendid," he said. "And I am envious of Caroline's creativity. I'm not creative either. When I was younger, I made cutouts. Simple designs mostly. But I inherited none of my parents' skills. I've often thought that might be a reason I value art so highly. I respect it because I am incapable of creating it myself. But you, you seem like a creative person. Were you artistic as a child?"

"Not really." I smiled slyly, aware of how he watched my mouth.

"Violin was my art, I suppose. I began playing when I was very young. And in fact, on this subject, I got a call back today from Dalton."

"You did?"

"About tutoring the fourth graders who need extra help."

I made a face like I'd just seen the cutest puppy in the world. "That is so sweet. Oh my God, so sweet."

He said nothing to this because he was modest, and smiled as though slightly embarrassed by how cool I thought he was. He had the jawline of a superhero, the strapping shoulders of an athlete. The soft glow from the candle cast him in a warm and easy light. He was too big for the furniture at Joseph Leonard, but he still somehow managed to look comfortable, sitting there with his manly biceps slung over that chair. He could break that chair into sticks if he wanted to. And yet despite his mighty build, there was something delicate about William, something soft and small. He was almost like a teenager in a growth spurt—he carried himself as though he didn't fully understand his own heft. I wondered what this boyishness meant, if anything, and what it had to do with the Dalton boys. Maybe he wanted to be near them because he still felt he could be one of them.

The restaurant was cozy and bustling, filled with good-looking people and a few tourists in windbreakers. The drums of an African song beat alongside throaty French lyrics. Silverware clinked. I felt good in my dress. I moved my hair from one side to the other.

"How's Herman?"

"He's doing very well, thank you. I think he had a good time with us at the park."

"There are other nice places to take him to up there," I said, "but I guess you would already know that."

"Yes," he said, "there are so many parks."

We paused there, looking at each other dumbly again, and then picked it back up with a conversation about how New York City had more green space than people generally realized and how lucky this made us and how we should take better advantage.

When the waiter returned with our meals, William ate his and I picked at mine like a dainty lady. That's how I would bring it up—carefully, like a dainty lady. I tossed the rest of the martini back in one cool sweep (I was glad I pulled that off without spilling) and said, "I saw my mother today."

"Yes?" He wiped the corners of his mouth with the napkin, his expression attentive, as always.

"Caroline and I had lunch with her. You'll have to come see her at some point, and meet Caroline."

"Right, of course," he said. "And how is your mother? Elizabeth, is it?"

"Good memory." I speared a piece of kale. Too big for my mouth. I removed it from the fork, tried a smaller piece. "She was okay today. You know, it's very hard. We never know what version we're going to get."

"Right, yes." He began to twirl his hair.

"Anyway, I asked her about you."

"Oh? Did she remember me?"

"She did." I didn't want to hurt his feelings, but I did want him to know what the situation was. If they were going to meet again, he should know. "I'm not sure she liked you very much." I laughed to ease the blow.

"No?"

"Which is odd—you're so likable." I stopped there, smiled at him. "But, well, you know her. You knew her, I mean. She's . . . how should I say this? Hard to please."

William looked concerned. He continued to twirl.

"Oh God, don't take any of this personally. She's just, well, yeah, like I said, very hard to please. And she could have confused you with someone else. It's . . . Ugh." I threw my hands up, a little more dramatically than I meant to. Blame the martini. "It's so hard to know, you know?"

He removed his hand from his head as though he suddenly realized where it had been and took a bite. He looked stressed. He probably wasn't used to being disliked. "What did she say? Did she say anything about me at all?"

"No, she didn't."

"I see."

"Why? What would she have said?"

"Oh, nothing, no, I haven't the faintest idea."

"You didn't steal anything from her, did you?"

"Heavens, no."

"Don't worry, I'm kidding. She thinks everyone steals from her."

"Oh, I see. All right."

"You didn't tell her her plants were ugly or something?"

"No."

"Were you a gum chewer?"

He considered that and answered sincerely. "I chew gum, but not regularly."

"Okay."

"Your mother did know me when I was very young. And, well, let's just say I was something of an obtrusive child. Overly curious. I asked too many questions."

"Oh." I laughed. "Mom hated that."

"Yes. Yes, she did," William said. "So perhaps it was that."

"Did something happen?"

"Well, yes, something did. I'm a bit embarrassed. But it was so long ago."

"What happened?"

"One day in the fountain room—I remember the sound of that water so clearly—we were hanging around, the adults having tea and me walking around with a yo-yo I had gotten that day. I was twelve or thirteen, I believe. It was right before we moved to Switzerland. Your mother said, 'Be careful with that, please,' and my mother of course agreed, and I thought I was being careful, but then, well, I must have been trying to do a special trick, and I lost control of the yo-yo, and suddenly there was a crash and broken glass at my feet. Your mother leapt off her seat and screamed, 'That was very expensive, William! That was a very, very, very expensive vase!' I think she even went on—yes, she did—long enough for my mother to intervene and say that we were so very sorry, we would replace it. But it was irreplaceable, unfortunately. It was something very special I had broken, and your mother, rightly, was inconsolably upset."

"Oh no," I said. I could see the whole thing happening. My mother turned into a very scary person when she was angry. "You poor thing."

"So that must have been it." William draped his arm over the empty chair next to him again. He seemed relieved to have gotten this off his chest.

"You must have been traumatized. I'm so sorry. God, my mother. She traumatized us all."

"Well, I'm okay now."

"Yes," I said, studying him, "you seem pretty okay to me."

The waiter cleared our plates. Of course I said, "I always have room for dessert," because that's what you were supposed to say when you were fun and dating and wearing a pretty dress. And of course by *room* I meant I would have one dainty lady bite.

We ordered the chocolate mousse. When it appeared and he spoon-fed me that bite and I said, "I feel like I have known you much longer than I have," I forgave myself for being so cliché. If happiness really was a Kodak moment inside a Hallmark card inside a Diamonds Are Forever commercial, then that was fine with me.

We walked arm in arm back to my place. The air was thick with dew. It made everything look like a dream. The Open sign on the bodega blinked red in peaceful throbs like a beating heart. Our footsteps barely made a sound. Under the dimly glowing streetlamp in front of my house, he kissed me. Those lips.

"Do you like the red door?" I asked, gazing up at him, his strong jaw.

I distinctly remember the words he used to answer. He said, "I do."

"Do you want to come in?"

"Yes."

He closed the door behind him, said the requisite thing. "What a stunning home you have."

He was gentle; he moved my hair away from my face gently. His sensitive eyes. The shapes the shadows made on his cheeks: hollow, eager. With just one finger, his pinkie, he pulled the strap of my dress off my shoulder and kissed the spot where it had been. He was good at this, better than I had imagined he would be. I wondered if he'd been with a lot of women.

I unbuttoned his shirt. I knew I was supposed to do that. Sex made me nervous. I disconnected. I would float up out of myself and watch the woman, me, unbutton the man's shirt, watch her take it off, maybe too quickly, and kiss the center of his chest, and undo his belt and rip it away, maybe too quickly again. It helped that I was tipsy. It also helped that William was so sure of himself. He compensated for my uncertainty.

He took my dress off so I was standing there in heels and a nude thong, and carried me up the stairs, our breath heavy, and his hands, my God, his hands, they were huge. How big William was, how tall. He made me feel safe and small in a way I had never felt. He saw the bed through the open door and moved toward it. We didn't turn on any lights.

He was so strong. Black boxer briefs and legs like a centaur's. He fucked me like an animal, like he had to fuck me, it was instinct, it was the only thing. It was good, but it was painful. He was big, very big. He was huge. I didn't want to fake it. I didn't want to fake anything with William. I wanted this to be different. I wanted to be honest. I tried to settle into the pain, I tried to get past it. But it was too much. I faked it because I needed it to be over. Yes, he was bigger than the men I'd been with, but the truth was that it had nothing to do with him. I had never not faked it, with anyone, ever.

Afterwards, he kissed me. He trailed his fingertips down my cheek. He traced my ear. "Was that okay for you?"

Maybe he knew I had faked it. But I couldn't admit to that—it would hurt his feelings, and it would make me a liar. "It was," I said, which was also a lie, but a smaller one. And I was about to say something about how huge he was, maybe as an excuse, in case he knew I had faked it, but then he kissed me again. Later, when we knew each other better—we could be more honest then.

He held me, his breath on my neck, me stroking the length of his back. The sheets were damp, but just barely. This was different from Fernando. Fernando was a sweater; he drenched the sheets in sweat. While he lived here, I'd had Lucia wash the bedding three times a week.

"May I stay?"

I kissed his forehead. "Of course you may stay."

When I woke up later that night, I found him sleeping in the most perfect position. You could have taken a picture and called it *Sleep*. He was on his back, hands clasped over his chest, head on the pillow. His body was even, balanced, not tangled up like most people's. He looked like a pharaoh, serene and elegant and almost too angelic to be real. His chiseled face, the weight of his arms, the weight of him on the bed, and yet the lightness of him, like he could have been floating, like he could have been hovering just above the sheets.

6

He moved in two weeks later. We wanted to wake up together in the morning and sleep in the same bed at night and watch bad TV together and drink good coffee together and talk about art and walk the dog and make love. This is what we said when we talked about it, looking at each other dumbly—we looked at each other dumbly a lot in the beginning—at a Vietnamese fusion restaurant where all the dishes came with a decorative spattering of bright multicolored sauces. We said we were infatuated. We said we were blessed. We said we were insane.

Of course I knew everyone thought we were moving too fast, and my response to that was, I am too old to care. That was a lie. Of course I cared. I probably cared too much. But the hourglass was running out of sand. It sounds so cheesy, but I had a constant image of that, literally: the hourglass I pictured was the blue plastic one that came with the Boggle game Caroline and I had played with as kids at the beach house.

The move was easy. He'd only been subletting on the Upper East Side and had barely lived there long enough to unpack his things. And he didn't have many things. He'd sold a lot of them before leaving Switzerland. He wasn't a packrat. What he did have, besides Herman, who he assured me was potty-trained, was art, good art, and I loved it. Well, most of it.

There was this one crocheted piece that said the Lord's Prayer, the entire thing: "Our father, who art in heaven," etc. I didn't like the content of it or the look. Red stitching on white gauzy fabric, it appeared to have been made by either a child or a mentally ill person with fat fingers. The words sloped in the center like a hammock and got very small at the end so they would all fit. The artist was an actual artist, William said, a protégé of Sister Gertrude Morgan named Zoe, and Zoe had given this piece to William years ago, while William was at university. He held the piece up with his long arm. "Isn't it wonderful?"

"It's interesting," I said.

"Where shall we hang it?"

"Well . . ." I looked around the room. Herman was sniffing the boxes lining the wall, and then he was following one of the movers, who said, "Hey, little guy."

"I'm not sure it belongs in this room," William said. "How about the massage parlor?"

"I love how you call it a parlor."

"Well?"

He looked so adorable there in those cargo pants, waiting for me to answer. "Okay, sure," I said, and laughed at how easily I'd given up.

"Why are you laughing, Catherine?"

"Oh God, I don't know."

He gave me a look. He seemed upset.

"What? What's wrong, babe?"

"Well," he began, his eyes on the mover, a round man with a back brace that appeared to be on too tight, who was placing another box in the pile along the wall. He waited for the man to descend the stairs before saying, "I suppose I could say that I personally feel that using the Lord's name in vain is a bit dicey. But"—he put his hand on my shoulder—"that should in no way inform what you choose to do. It's just a personal preference of mine."

"Okay, that's good to know." He was being clear. Clarity was important. Communication was important in relationships. "Would you rather I say *gosh* instead?"

He shrugged, and dusted the frame with his elegant thumb.

I shrugged, too. "That's fine with me." And it was fine—*God* or *gosh*, who cared? If this was something that meant a lot to William, then it meant a lot to me, too. But I wasn't going to be a doormat either. "What about *fuck*? Can I say *fuck*?" I laughed.

William eyed the skinny mover (nappy mullet, no back brace) who had entered the room with another box. He seemed slightly disturbed that this man had just heard his woman drop the *F* bomb, and I found his old-fashionedness kind of endearing. "You can say whatever you like, my darling."

"Good." I craned my neck for a kiss and he kissed me.

We hung the tapestry in the dining room, above the glass table. It took up almost the entire wall. I wondered what it meant—woman in water, woman on land, woman curled at the foot of a mountain. From any point in the room, the woman's eyes seemed to be fixed on the viewer. "It's like she's watching us," I said to William.

"Yes," he said, considering. "I wonder if that's what Rick intended. I'll have to ask him."

"Rick?"

"Rick Blass. Brilliant man. He studied under my father. He owed my father a lot, hence the gift."

"He gave that to you?"

"He did."

"Why was it at the gala, then? Why didn't he just give it straight to you?"

"This way he gets a little press, my darling."

"Sneaky," I said.

"Smart," he corrected. "It's a smart business move. Everyone wins."

I tugged at his belt loop. "Is that smart business? When everyone wins?"

"Absolutely," he said. "When everyone wins, or when everyone *thinks* they have won. There is no difference."

•

William had more folk art than I did, but overall we shared an aesthetic, artistically and otherwise. He said his house in Switzerland had been a lot like this house—clean and minimalist, with the art at the forefront. He loved Calder, and hung two of his mobiles side by side above the entryway. Together they complemented each other, became one grander thing.

I kept bringing up the color of the door. Was he sure he liked the red? Yes, he said, he thought it was lovely, and why did I keep asking? I didn't know, I told him, although I did know and was too embarrassed to say it. I'd read somewhere that a red door would invite love and power into a home. I'd had it painted the week Fernando left. I was feeling raw and unstable; it wasn't a choice I would have made under better circumstances. Now it felt sad to me, and desperate—a bright, bold symbol of my wanting, exposed. I didn't want to want anything so desperately, and I definitely didn't want other people to know about it. I wanted to be calm and neutral and stable; the white walls were calm and neutral and stable. White said nothing about a person. It gave away nothing. Of course I was being paranoid. No one looked at a red door and thought anything besides "That door is red." No one would have guessed, based on the color of a door, how hard I was trying to be the opposite of my mother—warm, loving, open—or how badly I wanted to feel differently about my life.

The only furniture William brought was a huge desk, made from one piece of oak, irregular at the edges, and an ergonomically correct forest-green chair, which we put near the windows in the den downstairs. This would now be William's office. The den was the only room in the house that wasn't all white. The walls were the color of deep soil. The designer and I had chosen espresso leather couches and a richly patterned carpet to offset the whiteness of the rest of the house. The big-screen TV and these dark choices were "meant to invoke a movie theater experience," the designer had said.

Now, instead of calling the designer, I deferred to William. He knew the brand of the remote-control blinds Jeff should buy. He introduced me to European furniture companies I hadn't known existed. We bought a new bed frame together; gorgeous and simple, it looked like a very upscale park bench.

It was funny: we also bought a few benches—light wood, metal legs. We dotted the hallways with them. I said, "It looks like a museum. Are we ever going to use these?" William sat down on one of them and said, "Yes." I thought that was hilarious.

And it was this moment—this simple, unassuming moment, with us in the hall, still littered with boxes, and the low light of evening glowing through the windows, and the way he looked at me, smiling just barely, the glint in his eyes—it was this moment that I became aware of my descent. I had fallen for him harder than I'd thought.

•

We settled into a routine. William went to work. I continued to work on the house. I had the rest of the art hung—William's Damien Hirst in the bedroom, yes, please. I cleaned out one of my closets for his clothes. I bought him a toothbrush holder that matched mine. I felt useful and wired and goal-oriented and I loved it. If I went to the shop less and didn't return my calls, people would just have to understand. This was a big transition.

Although William worked eighty-hour weeks (typical banker),

he never worked on the weekends, except in a rare emergency. I appreciated this. He was making time for me. It was so un-American and so unlike my father, who never stopped working.

On Saturdays we ate out and took walks along the High Line and milled around galleries. We were on an ongoing quest to find the best coffee in the city. William thought American coffee tasted like wet socks. So we went to all the artisan cafés—in the Village, in Chelsea, in SoHo. So far, he thought the place right on the corner was the best, which relieved me, maybe too much. As in, Thank God I had chosen to live near the café William liked. (Thank *gosh*—that's how I said it now, always teasingly.) William was definitely a person who knew what he liked, and I knew this meant his feelings for me were real. It was as if, out of all the women, he had pointed a finger at me—I want *you*—and that in itself, the certainty of that desire, was intoxicating.

On Sundays he tutored the Dalton boys. Yes, he wanted to teach them how to be better violin players, but he also wanted to prime himself for parenthood. That's exactly what he said. "I want to prime myself for parenthood. I want to practice."

There were two Dalton boys, Max and Stan, both nine years old. Stan (I felt bad for Stan) was chubby and awkward, a redhead with the serious face of a French aristocrat and intense dark eyes. I was glad when William told me he was much better than Max at playing the violin. At least he had that. Max was tall, oddly tall for his age, with long curly black hair that swirled in ringlets by his ears and a few well-placed freckles on his nose. He was adorable in his hoodie and jeans. He could have been a model for Gap Kids. The funniest thing about him was the way he walked, with his feet trailing on the ground behind him, like he was ice skating all the time.

They had their sessions at the house. We made the study on the second floor into a music room. We bought two tall chairs and a music stand. Each boy had an hour with William. Stan came first. He lived nearby and walked over by himself. He carried his violin with great pride; I loved that, it was so cute. Max was second. His mother dropped him off, sometimes a little early. I didn't mind. It was fun to chat with him in the kitchen while we waited for Stan to be done.

I found such unexpected comfort in listening to the boys play the same beginning of a song over and over and over. I bought them sodas (which I bought especially for them; I was so nurturing). I could tell the boys liked that, especially Max. He was such a sugar freak.

During Max's session, Dan would arrive for our usual appointment. He massaged me and then William. During William's massage I would shower and dress for dinner, and then we would go out and talk about the day and the boys and our plans for the upcoming week. Sundays now had a rhythm and a purpose, and I actually found myself looking forward to them.

•

As time went on, I fell deeper and deeper. My love for William consumed me. It consumed me entirely, and I wanted it to. Because it made me feel different than I had felt before. It made me feel like I was changing. It made me feel free.

I loved the way he made espresso with such care. I was much lazier. His espresso tasted a lot better than my espresso. He took time to press the grounds in. He was patient enough to wait for it to cool when it was done. Me, I just added cold water.

I loved his hand on the small of my back as we walked down the street. I loved his hand on the back of my head when he hugged me. His hands were so big. I felt so enveloped. When he hugged me like that, it was like I existed in the smallest, safest, warmest room. He was my armor.

I loved the way he moved through the world. He was like a dancer almost. So fluid, flowing, like he was under water, like he was swimming, like he was floating, like he was made of feathers.

I also loved his smell. I loved it because it was inhuman. He never smelled like sweat, he never smelled like a body. His scent was clean and new and streaked with salt. It was a deserted beach filled with fine white sand that stretched to horizons. It suggested we could be better. We could cover the swampy human parts of us, and we could be better. We could be new again, and we could be beautiful.

7

One morning after an early workout with Chris, I stood in the kitchen drinking a green juice and going through the mail. Lucia wiped down the counters with the Soft Scrub William had suggested "in lieu of 409." She rubbed in her usual quick circles, bent over her working hand. Her messy ponytail bounced with the rhythm of each new circle. I thought, Lucia does not make cleaning look easy. She makes it look like hard labor. She was sweaty, as usual. The pits of her oversized gray T-shirt were soaked. Lucia actually had a great body, probably from the constant workout of cleaning so hard. Her face was nice to look at, too: light green eyes, caramel skin. All the people who worked for me were good-looking. Sometimes I wondered if this was intentional. (Should I hire an ugly person?) But it wasn't intentional. Of course it wasn't. I was just lucky.

I had inherited Lucia from Mom when we sold Eighty-Fourth. She'd managed not to get fired for ten years, which was a miracle. Only one other assistant had made it that far. I'd been more than happy to get rid of Griselda, who constantly gave me the evil eye and who had gained so much weight because of her thyroid condition that she couldn't even finish the whole house every day anymore. She actually asked me if she could bring a friend in to help. So I could pay double for the same amount of work? Definitely not. When I fired Griselda, she actually cried, which upset me more than I wanted it to. I told her it was probably for the best; maybe she could get a desk job at an office or something, a job where she could sit all day. I remember the scary rumble deep in her throat when she sighed. I thought she might go postal and shoot me. I even pressed the 9 on my phone, ready to add the two 1's if she sighed like that again. "I cannot work in the office, I have no papers!" I told her I was happy to write her a reference whenever she needed one and shooed her out the door. I gave her $100 on the way out and hoped the image of her limping away down the street would be blotted out and forgotten as soon as possible.

Lucia and I were friendly. I had known her for so long. She knew all my little tics, she knew how I liked things. She was one of the few people who actually *knew* me knew me. And I didn't feel the need to impress her. I felt relaxed. I actually loved having her around. She was like a built-in friend. Sometimes (and I wouldn't have admitted this to anyone) I wondered if my truest friends were the people who worked for me. I just spent so much time with them. The people I would have listed as friends were more like acquaintances. Everyone was just so busy. People had jobs and lives and children, and it was hard even to get together for dinner. Susan was the one exception.

"Lucia, what do you think of William?"

"William?" She stopped rubbing. "William es muy hombre."

"What?" I said. "English, por favor."

"William is a real man." She flexed her arm. "Fuerte. But this dog, I don't know." We looked at Herman, whose head was poking out of his padded dog igloo in the corner. "I hope no peepee."

"He better not peepee."

Herman's presence in the apartment was definitely not ideal. He hadn't done anything stupid yet, but I knew if he peed anywhere, or ate anything that wasn't food, I was going to lose it. Honestly, when I looked at him, I thought, Wow, my fear of dying alone has made me more open and malleable than I ever expected to be. Herman was cute, but I was not an animal person. I agreed with my mother on this front: animals belong outside. And yet here I was, compromising. Compromising with my partner. That felt good. It felt like progress. I had even hired a dog walker to take Herman out three times a day. Her name was Trish and yes, Trish was very good-looking. Her light skin and her dyed red hair reminded me of Tori Amos. She was a grad student at NYU, working on her thesis, and this job was her way of "getting off her ass." I liked her thrift-store look; she actually managed to pull it off. Her winged black glasses would have looked ridiculous on other people, but on Trish they looked great.

Lucia had moved on to the living room, where she was fiercely wiping down the coffee table. The water in the flower vase was low. She brought it to the sink to refill. The vases should be full at all times.

"William is better than Fernando, right?"

"Sí, Fernando was no very smart."

"You never told me you thought that, Lucia!"

"His pants, no no no. No for a man, those pants."

"I know, the leather pants were bad—you're right."

"Very bad, very, very bad." Lucia set the vase back down on the table.

I took the last sip of my green juice. I always drank my green juice standing up in the kitchen while I checked the mail and talked to Lucia. Today it was bills, bills, bills, coupons, catalogs from Saks and Barneys, and a letter from the place that managed the trust fund Dad had left us, which I didn't open; I never opened those. All I knew was that around $80,000 got direct-deposited to me every month. And actually, these people should stop sending me mail and get online. They were wasting paper. Maybe I would call and let them know. As if I had time for that. I threw all the mail into the recycling and sighed loudly enough for Lucia to say, "What wrong, Miss Catherine?"

"Nothing."

"Maybe you eat. You very skinny today." Lucia sucked in her cheeks like a fish; this was her "skinny" impression.

"It's the stress diet." I frowned, touched my stomach. Of course I was happy she'd called me skinny, even if she hadn't meant it as a compliment.

"Ah, stress."

We frowned.

"Lucia, do you like this?" I pointed at the tapestry.

She scrunched her face. "No." Lucia's opinion of art was the best—totally uninformed, unadulterated by hype and fame.

"Why not?"

Lucia pulled her lips back like a snarling dog, cocked her head. "This lady"—she motioned with the dirty rag in her hand—"she crazy."

I sighed again. "Everybody's crazy, Lucia."

"No me."

"Well, okay, not you."

"No. Me." She shook the rag back and forth to accentuate her point.

"I'm taking a shower."

"Oka-ay, Miss Catherine."

•

On Sunday I looked through the hole in the table at Dan's scorpion tattoo—we could hear Max fumbling over a familiar-sounding song—and asked him, "So, what do you think of William?"

Dan adjusted the towel over me. "He seems great."

"You would say that about anyone though."

Dan laughed.

"You're too nice. What do you really think?"

"I really think he's great. I mean, his shoulders are tense. It's a good thing I'm working on him."

"Mmm-hmm."

"This new piece on the wall is interesting. Is it a sewing?"

"Crochet," I said.

"It seems"—he paused but kept rubbing—"like it was made with a certain amount of desperation."

"Do you like it?"

"I guess I appreciate it for what it is."

I thought that was a great answer. Noncommittal without being rude. Appreciate it for what it is. I would use that later.

•

In the evening, before dinner, we stopped by the shop. I wanted William to see what I had built. I was nervous. I opened the door for him.

"Ladies first," he said.

"Of course, right." I walked in.

Maya, who worked weekends, was talking to a customer. Great. She was so much more sociable than Vera. I thought it was because she was younger. She also played better music. I didn't even know what the music was, but it was very hip. There were five customers, normal for a weekend. The space was so small, it couldn't fit many more. She had the candles burning, labels out. The vases were fully filled. When I'd hired her, Maya had described herself as being "a touch OCD," which worked to my benefit.

"This is quite luxurious," William said. "I'm impressed."

"Really?"

He put his hand on the small of my back. "Really."

"Good. You should take a look at some of the cards. Dorothy Adkinson and Bird are my favorites."

"Okay," he said, and made his way—stately gait—to the card wall.

I thought I would go to the back, check the e-mail, but then decided not to. I stayed by the front display and watched this scene: William taking the cards off the wall, opening them, putting them back. Eventually (maybe he saw the sign) he stopped opening them. Smart man.

Maya waved when she noticed me. I waved back, gave her a thumbs-up. I was being my perfect enthusiastic boss self. Her bun, which usually looked like a doorknob, front and center on the top of her head, was cute today. She wore red lipstick and a simple black dress, sleeveless to show off the sleeves of her tattoos, which ran all the way down to her wrists and which included, among many other things (too many other things—it was overcrowded), a voluptuous mermaid with a sex kitten smile. The mermaid kind of looked like Maya, which I assumed was no accident, though I had never asked.

At the register she rang up the customer she'd been talking to—an old woman with salt-and-pepper hair who wore a long beaded sweater and was talking about Paris.

"I adore Paris," Maya said in her pat way. I knew she had never been because she had told me once she'd never left the country. She didn't even have a passport. It was a miracle she'd crawled out of Idaho at all.

"The Tuileries this time of year . . ." the woman reminisced with herself.

"I agree," Maya said.

She had sold this woman almost twenty cards. At ten bucks apiece, the total was more than the woman expected. "Golly," she said, digging into her tasseled purse.

"They're originals," Maya said. "You could send this one"—a stencil of a carousel by Marsha Pern—"to your friends in Paris. They love carousels over there."

"I suppose that's true," the woman said with new interest, and swiped her card.

Maya was a genius. The woman left looking pleased.

"Hey! I haven't seen you in so long!" Maya gave me a tight hug.

"I know, I've been busy." I sounded terser than I meant to. Boss voice. I couldn't help it. And while I was flattered by Maya's friendliness—she acted like she really liked me—I was also unnerved by it.

William made his way over. "I want you to meet someone. This is William. William, Maya."

They shook.

"Nice to meet you."

"My pleasure," he said.

We all looked around. "Well," I said.

"Is there a loo?"

"Yes, right there."

"Great. I shall return."

Once he had closed the door, Maya said, "That's your new boyfriend?"

"Yes."

"He looks like Arnold Schwarzenegger."

"Really?"

"Really."

"I'm not sure that's accurate, but okay."

"It's a compliment." She touched my shoulder. "Don't worry."

I realized then that what unnerved me about Maya wasn't just her friendliness but the feeling that she could see through me. Her ability to read people was what made her such a good salesperson. The way she touched my shoulder—it was like she knew how badly I needed that.

•

At dinner he said, "I am meeting everyone in your life. When do I meet Caroline?"

Somehow William had not met (or remet) Caroline or Mom.

Caroline and Bob were currently out of town: they'd left the kids with the nannies and taken an extended vacation to Mexico to reignite their fire. And Mom—well, I visited her on weekdays and William worked then. I kept meaning to take him during the weekend, but something always came up: the Diego Rivera exhibit, a new play, a bike ride on the Hudson because the weather was good now and it might not be later.

Really, though, it was more than just a scheduling issue. I was protecting him. I tested it every time I saw Mom. I wanted to see if I could get a new reaction, but that wasn't happening. At "William Stockton," she shut down. I thought it was so unfair, and just like Mom, to be mad all these years later over a stupid vase.

I hadn't told William anything about Mom's reaction to him after that first time. When he knew I'd been to see her, he'd ask me how it went, and I would say it went well. He never asked for specifics. But now, what else was there to do? We were just going to have to deal with it.

"Yes," I said, "you should meet Caroline. And you should probably see my mother at some point, too."

"I would love to meet Caroline, absolutely. But," he said, touching his hair, "I'm not sure seeing your mother is a good idea."

That surprised me. "What?" He had never said this before because I had never directly said, "Let's go visit my mother" before. It was just kind of distantly on the horizon.

"Do you think it's a good idea? You mentioned she is harboring negative feelings toward me."

"I know," I said. "I'm nervous, too, but she'll love you, babe. Eventually. After she forgives you for breaking the stupid vase."

"Maybe we shouldn't tell her I am the same William Stockton she used to know. Perhaps we can just say William for now. I would hate to upset her."

"William, no. It's a *vase*, and you broke it *years* ago."

He took this in, nodded. "You're right," he said, and kissed my hand.

"When she sees you, she'll see how handsome you turned out and forgive you. If she brings up the vase, you can just apologize."

"I suppose you're right," he said.

"So tell me about work."

"Work?"

"I like your assistant. Fiona? She seems nice on the phone."

"She is nice."

"You never tell me details. I want details."

"What do you mean?"

"I don't know. Maybe it's a man thing to be vague. That sounds very sexist."

"It does." He laughed. He took a sip of water. "What details might I tell you about Fiona?" He set his chin on his fist. "Well, she is from Canada, I know that."

"What does she look like?"

"I would say . . . she's a very nice person."

"Got it," I said. "Well, I'd like to meet her. And your colleagues."

"Absolutely."

"You must miss your friends in Geneva."

"I do sometimes, yes."

"Are you glad you came back?"

"I am," he said. He looked straight into my eyes. He didn't blink. "If I hadn't come back, I never would have found you."

•

Buoyed by Maya's reaction to William, and Lucia's and Dan's, I was finally ready for him to meet Susan. Susan couldn't do dinner, so we arranged to meet for drinks beforehand. William left work early to make room for this in his schedule. In his suit and tie, he looked severe. I knew that's what Susan would think.

We met at an upscale sushi place with slate walls and patches of grass in small ceramic squares on every table. We were sitting by the open window, holding hands and having a conversation about the traffic William had hit on the way up, and traffic in New York in general, when Susan appeared in a light blue jumper and over-sized buggy sunglasses, her arms full of shopping bags.

She circled through the main door. "Hello, lovebirds," she said. "William, I'm Susan." She gave a firm shake. "And hey, you." She kissed my cheek. "It's been *way* too long." She sat next to me on the banquette, said, "Sorry, sorry," to the people next to us as she arranged her bags under the table.

"What did you get?"

"Oh my God, there's this new place. I don't even know the name. Dividend? Divider? Who cares. You have *got* to go there."

"Okay," I said, "text me the address."

"I will do that right now." She grabbed her phone. A second later she said, "Done."

"Thanks."

"So, William, wow, it's great to finally meet you."

"And you," he said. "Catherine has told me only good things."

"She better tell you only good things." Susan smiled. She looked good today. Invigorated. Had she had something done?

"So you just moved back from Switzerland. It must seem dirty to you here."

"Well," William laughed, "Geneva is rather clean."

"Everywhere's clean compared to this hole." She looked at the menu. Susan and I had a long history of drinking fruity drinks at Asian places, so of course she said, "Let's order cosmos."

"Great," I said.

"I was thinking a bottle of chardonnay," William said. "It will pair nicely with the food."

"I'm not eating, so I'm having a cosmo," Susan said.

My face was hot. I definitely needed a drink. "How's Bonsai? I told you Susan owns a shop right near mine, didn't I, William?"

"You did indeed."

Susan was checking her phone again. "Look at this picture— how funny is that?"

"Ha," I said. It was a picture of a cat using a toilet. I thought, Don't show that to William.

"William, look at that." She held the phone up for him. "How funny is that?"

"Gosh," he said.

This was not going well.

"William, do you still have family in New York?"

"No, I have no family. My parents passed away recently."

"Sorry to hear that." Susan applied lip gloss and rubbed her lips together. "What about other people? Did you keep in contact with anyone here?"

"No," he said, "unfortunately not. I was quite young when I lived here. Most of the people I knew have moved away."

"Catherine and I are so lucky to still be friends. It's rare." She put her arm around me. "So you better not hurt my baby!" She made crazy eyes and laughed.

"I wouldn't dream of it," William said.

The waiter appeared. Susan ordered her cosmo. William ordered a glass of chardonnay. I said, "I will also have chardonnay, thank you."

"Shall we get a bottle, then?"

"Sure."

"A bottle of the chardonnay, please," William said to the waiter.

Susan finished her drink in ten minutes flat and said she was late for a wax, which I knew was a lie. She must have forgotten she'd told me she'd made the switch to electrolysis months before.

"So great meeting you," she said to William, all her bags in her arms again. To me she said, "Call me, bitch."

When she was out of earshot, William said, "Bitch?"

"She's from California."

"Well, she certainly is energetic."

I laughed. "That's true."

A few minutes later we were talking about Van Gogh and his ear—William thought it had been a courageous form of insanity that drove him to do it—but I was having trouble paying attention. "Is something bothering you, dear?"

"No. Well, maybe. Sorry. I guess I'm just upset you and Susan didn't hit it off."

"We had so little time together. Don't worry, Catherine. Any friend of yours is a friend of mine. I just want you to be happy."

•

The next morning, right after he left for work, I called Susan. "Well?"

"Yeah," she said. "I don't know with him yet."

"What does that mean?"

"I haven't spent enough time with him to draw any conclusions."

I didn't believe her. "Are you sure?"

"Does he kind of look like a newscaster? He looks like a newscaster whose name should be Jay or something, right?"

"Are you serious? He's gorgeous!"

"I know! He seems fine. He seems great, okay? I just want you to be happy."

"God, everyone says that. I am fucking happy!"

"Good," Susan said, "because you should be."

8

We'd been living together for about a month when I woke up one morning to find William contemplating my face in silence. It was so sweet. Elbows on the bed, chin resting on his fists. His eyes soft at the corners, his full head of gray hair adorably puffed up. His chiseled face wore a youthful expression.

"Good morning," he said. I wondered how long he'd been waiting to say that.

"Hi." My voice was sleepy. I touched his hair.

"I'd like to tell you something."

Fuck, I thought, here it comes: This isn't working, I have to move out, I can't do this, I hate your friends, your shop is stupid, I've met someone. I had never been dumped in bed before, but that didn't mean it couldn't happen now.

"I have come to a conclusion."

He touched my arm with his fingertips. If he was going to break up with me, this was a pretty twisted message to send first. He looked right into my eyes when he said it.

"I have come to the conclusion that I love you."

I may have stopped breathing. I may have wanted not to trust it, to assume he was lying. This was too good to be true. This was too good to be my life. But then I thought, Oh my God, Catherine, you deserve this, so take it.

Instead of blurting out the words and grabbing his dick—

I'd done that with so many men—I said it in parts, like all of it mattered.

"I love you, too."

We made love quietly. At least until the end, when his moan rose and rose, louder and louder, and he screamed my childhood nickname. "Kitty!"

I didn't come, but I had gotten closer. A lot closer. At some point, I knew, it would happen. If it was going to happen with anyone, it would be with William.

Afterwards I wrapped myself around him. I put my ear on his chest. I heard his heart beating. Fast, fast, and then slower. He touched my hair, stroked my back. I wanted to say it again. Maybe I wanted to make sure it was something we would keep saying to each other. I turned to rest my chin on his chest, looked up at him. "I love you," I said. My voice sounded sure and real.

•

We went to the café on the corner for brunch. Somehow they managed to have good coffee and good food, which William thought was a real anomaly. We were rosy-cheeked; we held hands. We moved together easily, like we were part of the same machine. When we were together like that, I lost concept of time. It stretched out and contracted and didn't exist.

When he would leave, even for a second, like now, to go to the bathroom (or the loo, as he called it), I missed his presence. I thought about him all the time. During my sessions with Chris, I would think, Does William know what a burpee is? And my eyebrows. Would he like the new shape the aesthetician and I had agreed on? I'd be at a store picking out dresses based on what I thought he would prefer.

When he returned from the loo, wearing the new jeans I'd

bought him—they looked so good—he gave me a peck on the lips like he had missed me, too. We sat there, so in love, drinking the good coffee, lost in each other's faces. We sat in the sun, our sunglasses on. The air was thick with the start of summer. It was a heat I normally would have called oppressive, but today it felt manageable. I even welcomed it.

"I think the house is done, don't you?"

If it had been up to me, I could have kept finding things to fix and redo forever, but William was more logical than that. He understood endpoints.

"Yes," I said, "I think it's almost done. I'm going to have Lucia reorganize some stuff in the hallway cabinets, but other than that, I think it looks good, don't you?"

"I do. Our belongings are officially integrated." He raised his eyebrows twice.

"It's true."

"I love you."

Three times in one morning. I was giddy. "I love you, too."

At the end of our meal we ordered the chocolate mousse; it had become one of Our Things. William was talking about how the island of Malta was not a place worth visiting when the waiter brought the mousse to the table and set it down incredibly carefully, as if it were a thing that could break. I actually thought this waiter had a mental problem, or was going blind.

Without asking, William spoon-fed me the first bite, and—what? What was this metal thing jabbing me in the mouth? My first thought was, Get the manager! But then, when I saw William's face, I put it together pretty quickly. The metal thing had to be a ring. He hadn't gone to the loo. He had gone to find the waiter to make this happen.

Even just feeling it with my tongue I could tell the rock was huge, and when I spit it primly into my open palm (the sunlight seemed to make a spotlight just exactly there), I saw that it was. I licked the chocolate off and William dipped it in his seltzer—huge smile, those brilliant teeth; those teeth were mine now—and when it was clean, he got on his knee and said, with so many people watching, "Catherine West, will you be my wife?"

9

The definition of insanity is doing the same thing over and over and expecting different results, but if the person you are dealing with is not medically sane, does this definition apply?

On Monday I went uptown to try again with my mother. I hoped again that today would be different. The biggest thing I had going for me was that my mother now adored Evelyn after months of hating Evelyn's guts for allegedly stealing her comb. If she stonewalled me again, I planned to tell her that she had to stop. She had to make peace with my future husband. She had to accept this. She had to accept me and my choices and my life. I got worked up in the cab with a heated inner monologue: You have to accept my choices, Mom! I am an adult! Accept my choices! Accept this! Accept me, Mom! Fuck!

My ring. It was huge. It was an ice cube. I'd moved all the other jewelry off my left hand to make room for its presence. I couldn't stop looking at it.

When Mom and I got to Da Castelli—a particularly arduous walk; she kept stopping to ask where we were—and sat down in our regular booth, I laid my palm flat on the table in front of her. "Mom, look."

She didn't look down but straight at me instead. Was there distance in her eyes? Or was this how my mother had always looked? She seemed to float in and out of herself. She was there and then not there and then maybe there again. Her hair was tied back in a severe chignon like a schoolmarm's today; her makeup was a little heavy. Were those fuchsia accents in her eye shadow? She wore a royal-blue silk blouse and a pearl necklace. She ran her fingers back and forth along the pearls.

I flapped my sad hand on the table. "My ring, Mom, look at my ring."

She looked down, and tapped the diamond once. She said nothing to me, but when the waiter appeared with her prosecco (impressive—she hadn't even ordered it yet), she said, "Thank you very much, kind sir," which was a lot more than she usually said to waiters.

"Mom, I'm getting married."

She looked at me like I was a moron. "Catherine, I am aware of that."

"You are?"

"Of course I am."

My face twisted up in the mirror behind her. "Really?"

"What do you take me for?" This was one of Mom's stock one-liners. She had said it to my father all the time: "What do you take me for, Bruce?" (My father's reply: "Certainly not an idiot, Elizabeth!")

"Okay," I said. It was hard not to keep looking at myself in the mirror. Not because I was obsessed with my reflection, not because I was a narcissist, but just because it was there. "Do you know who I'm marrying?"

"Fernando Delarus."

"No, Mom," I said, "no."

"Who then?"

I braced myself. "William Stockton."

"Who?" She looked confused, like she had never heard the name. I thought this was good. I thought I might be getting a new reaction.

"William Stockton."

Then her face changed. She was still looking at me, but her gaze had turned inward. Her eyes went blank; she was no longer there.

"Mom," I said, "I'm so sorry William broke your vase." I tried to sound like I really was sorry. Intonation was important. "I'm sure he didn't mean to do it. I'm sure he'd be happy to buy you a new one now."

"It's *voz*, Catherine, not *vayce*."

"You're right, Mom." I looked distressed in the mirror. "I'm sorry William broke your voz."

"I don't understand anything you are saying to me, Catherine."

"William broke your voz and he is very sorry."

"William Stockton?" She said this as though she had just thought of the name herself, as though I hadn't just said it.

"William. Stockton. Yes."

For a second this seemed to register, and I thought I could feel my mother, the old version of my mother, sitting there with me at the table. She took a long inhale through her nose. One nostril turned into a slit and the other one didn't. This was a side effect left from the nose job. "He . . ."

"What? What?" I looked distressed in the mirror. "What?"

"He's not good enough for you," she said finally.

"Why? Because he doesn't come from money?"

"Catherine," she said.

"Why? Tell me why."

She closed her eyes—her lids were like tissue paper now, her eyelashes like black lace ripped apart—and when she opened them again, I could see even before she spoke that she was gone again. She was no longer my mother. She was just another parent who had been taken away from me, and I felt very sorry for myself.

"Where is my veal with rosemary?" she said.

I didn't have the energy to explain that this wasn't Silvano's or that the dish she would be having was salmon pasta, or that it was very good here. I didn't tell her that she lived in a home now that was all fucking yellow, or that she had Alzheimer's, and that it was so hard to deal with, so incredibly hard, and that sometimes I didn't know if her life was worth living.

In the mirror I looked so honest that I almost believed it myself. "Don't worry, Mom," I said. "Your veal is coming."

10

It was a small engagement party. *An Intimate Gathering of Friends and Family,* the invitation said. I wore pink chiffon. William wore a blue blazer. Dierdre who was married to Russell who worked with William said, "You two look like you belong on the top of a wedding cake!" She was drunk, but she was right.

It was a pretty afternoon, sun-dappled and not too hot. Crisp champagne and well-dressed people, smiling and laughing, and my heels were even comfortable. At least they were a little more comfortable than usual. I checked the doorway for my mother—no, still not here.

The jazz band wore cream suits with bright green handkerchiefs and played just loud enough, and all the caterers with their little trays looked like models. I had chosen the very best canapés: smoked salmon with dill crème fraîche on sesame lavash, tequila prawns with bacon, cucumber with whipped feta and sun-dried tomatoes, roasted cinnamon pear bruschetta, olive crostini. These were presented on glimmering silver trays with green napkins that matched the handkerchiefs on the band.

Jeff had done a spectacular job of improving the roof garden with not much notice. He had modeled it after the plants on the High Line that William and I liked so much—long grasses and purple wisteria in ten-foot-long gray wooden beds. Bouquets of baby's breath lined the entire perimeter of the roof in ascending tiers. Jeff had installed a surrounding staircase just for that. It gave the impression that we were on a cloud, a dreamy little slice of heaven, albeit a rectangular one.

A dozen people from William's work were there. He was so likable. In just a few months he'd gotten this many people to come to his engagement party. Besides Russell and Dierdre, there was a blond guy named Kurt from Arizona, who looked more like an actor than a banker, and Stellan, a short Swedish man with too-wide lapels and a buzz cut, and Fiona, William's assistant, who was pleasant and frumpy (I was glad about that) and who spoke in an even more overly articulate way than William did, with the separated syllables of a GPS machine.

Stan and Max had come with their mothers, Beatrice and I had forgotten the name of Max's mom. Both women were stylish and trim. Beatrice was Australian, and oddly pale for being Australian, and wore a large straw hat with a purple bow on it. Max's mom was slight—her big blue Birkin miniaturized her even further—and when she lifted her sunglasses at one point to remove something from the corner of her eye, I noticed the worry lines on her face. They seemed natural and permanent. It was hard to imagine that face asleep.

The two of them were blending in nicely. Beatrice got into an animated conversation with William's boss, Michael, and Max's mom nodded politely as my architect, Carl, who was such a Chatty Cathy (he never shut up), explained something with his hands. I did wonder where their husbands were, and felt a small sense of pride about William being a sturdy male figure in their lives.

Max and Stan were hanging out in the far corner drinking orange juice and taunting Herman with branches of baby's breath they'd pulled from the pots. They wore dress shirts and blazers: Max in navy and Stan in red, which had definitely been a poor choice on his mother's part. Redheads can't wear red. It never works.

Maya's short yellow dress was working. She gave me a heart-felt hug and said, "Hey William," as though they were already friends, which was so sweet. For maybe the first time ever, her hair was not in its doorknob bun. It hung down to her ass instead.

"Your hair is longer than mine!" I said.

"I haven't cut it for five years."

I had a feeling she meant that literally. "Wow."

Besides having a fabulous time—this was a day to enjoy, Catherine, a day to enjoy—I was anxious. The host is always anxious. I checked the doorway again. Still not here. And there was a dead leaf on the ground. And one of the model-caterers seemed to be perspiring too heavily. I knew all those guys did coke and thought, No one better OD at my party.

"Are you having a nice time?" I asked Maya, who sipped her champagne with her pinkie extended straight out.

She swallowed and said, "Oh my God, are you kidding? This is fly." She touched my arm. "So fly."

"Good," I said, trying to give the impression that it barely mattered to me what she thought.

In the doorway, not my mother but Vera with one of her sons.

"Hey you guys!" Maya wrapped her arms around them both.

"Hi Vera." I hugged her lightly, a boss hug. "And hello," I said to the boy, who must have been about fourteen.

Vera nudged him. "Introduce yourself."

The poor thing was covered in volcanic acne, and when he opened his mouth to say, "I'm Dorian," the sun glinted off the metal braces in his mouth.

"So good to meet you finally," I said, sensing right as I said it that the *finally* had been too much.

"Yeah," he said, the end upturned like a question. I wondered what terrible things his mother said about me at home, and hoped she was a good enough mother to tell only her husband these things and keep the kids out of it. Not that I cared.

"You look great," I told Vera. At least she was looking more serene than usual. Her outfit was a floral polyester nightmare from T.J. Maxx, but she did look relaxed.

"Hey," Maya said to Dorian, who was on his phone now, "don't drink too much, okay?" She winked.

He smiled without teeth—the braces smile.

"No drinking," Vera said, too seriously. That woman could not take a joke.

"Mom, I won't," Dorian whined.

"Let's go get you a nonalcoholic beverage from the bar," I said, and motioned for him to follow.

"Lucia!" Maya said. She had spotted Lucia and Jeff standing over the flowerbeds. They tended to stick together at these things.

"Hola, ciao."

They started speaking in Spanish.

"Hey, no working," I said to Jeff, who was still wearing his gross work pants. "You're here to have fun!"

A fleeting thought: Yeah, Catherine, take your own advice.

"What do you want? A Coke?" I asked Dorian. We were standing in front of the bartender now, who waited with his hands behind his back. This one looked less sweaty. Good.

"Ummm, yeah," Dorian said.

"Be polite," Vera said.

"Coke?" the bartender asked.

"Yes, please."

"Vera, what would you like?"

"White wine if you have it."

"Of course. We have chardonnay, pinot grigio . . ."

A hand on my shoulder and I turned around to find Dan, who looked great, and also like someone else. I'd never seen him in a suit before.

"I almost didn't recognize you."

WE COULD BE BEAUTIFUL

He smiled in his easy way. I was glad he was there; maybe his calm would rub off on me.

"You look great," he said.

"Really? I shouldn't put my hair up?"

I moved it to the other side. I was beginning to feel too hot. Also, did Maya's hair look better than mine? When I looked again—she was still talking to Lucia—I thought, No, mine looks better. Her ends were weirdly tapered.

"Can I get you a drink? Champagne?"

"I'll have a Coke," Dan said.

"Of course."

He ordered it from the bartender, then said to Dorian, "What's that, buddy?"

"Coke."

"Cheers."

Dorian still looked like he was hating life, but maybe a little bit less.

"Catherine!" Susan yelled. There she was in a gorgeous periwinkle dress, her makeup perfectly fresh and her arm around a man. It took me a second to realize the man was Henry, Susan's too-young-to-date manager, who was apparently now her date. He had grown a short beard and looked older.

When I hugged her, I whispered, "What the hell?" into her ear, and she whispered back, through a plastered smile, "Tell me about it."

Since the sushi restaurant, Susan hadn't been calling with her usual frequency. This was because of Henry, I now saw. This meant that we were fine. We were just focusing on our love lives right now.

"Dan!" She kissed his cheek.

"Henry, it's so nice to see you," I said.

Caroline greeted me by punching my arm and saying, too

loudly, "I can't believe you got engaged while I was gone!" People turned to look because she was so loud, and then she took my hand and said, "Oh my God, this rock!" I loved her so much in that moment.

Bob was there, too, with Spencer and his large Jamaican nanny. It was afternoon; the twins were napping. Caroline and Bob looked tan and jovial. She wore a super-tight black dress (it looked good; she looked more like a socialite than a hooker today), and Bob was plump in his khaki slacks and his white button-up, which he'd unbuttoned too much—his curly gray chest hairs were offensive. Bob hated dressing up. It wasn't his thing. He was from Maine.

"Where is the man in question?" Bob took two glasses of champagne off a passing tray and handed one to Caroline. "Take us to him," he bellowed, ridiculous, like a cartoon king.

"Come, come," I said, and led them to William, who was talking to Michael now. It seemed serious. Michael stood with his chest puffed out—he had a wide torso and disproportionately small legs—and was wagging his finger at William. William was captivated, or pretending to be, saying, "Yes, absolutely, yes."

"No work talk." I took William's arm. "Hi, babe."

He kissed me. "Hi."

"Lovely party," Michael said. His reflective glasses were expensive and gaudy, and his bronzed skin shone like a penny.

"Thanks all to my future wife." William kissed me again.

"I want you to meet Caroline and Bob."

Caroline dove in for a squeeze-the-life-out-of-you hug. "Soooooo good to meet you."

William respectfully patted her back. His face looked shocked, scared. My sister was scaring him. "You, too, Caroline," he said.

She pulled back and held his arms. "Yay!" she squealed, like a kindergartner.

"Yay indeed," William said, studying her face. I assumed he

was comparing her face to mine. I wondered what he saw. He still looked shocked. I remember thinking he must have expected Caroline to look different somehow, or be different somehow; that explained his surprise.

"And Bob," I said.

"Hello there," Bob said in his ridiculous regal voice. He shook William's hand with one firm jolt.

"He's hot," Caroline whispered to me.

Spencer pulled at my dress. "Aunt Catherine, I want to blow bubbles!"

"I don't know if I have any bubbles, Spencer." I looked around for Jeff.

"You want bubbles, sweetie?" Caroline touched his fine blond hair and Spencer smacked her hand away. "Where's Tonia?"

Spencer pointed at her, his arm snapping straight. Tonia, the large Jamaican nanny, was at the buffet, making herself a plate of food.

"Go ask Tonia to buy you bubbles." Caroline patted his back twice. "Go, go."

Spencer took off running.

Bob was telling William about the epic boating conditions in Playa del Carmen. "I prefer sailboats as well," William was saying.

"Mom's here!" Caroline announced.

My body flushed and tingled with a wave of anxiety. "Great," I said in my best hostess voice, nearly out of breath because I wasn't breathing again.

Caroline waved like a lunatic. "Mom! Over here!"

William looked at me, unsure. I gave him a look that said, It's okay, don't worry, we will get through this together.

"Mom! Over here!" To me she said, "Oh good, she's with the one I like."

Caroline meant Evelyn, whose name she should have known by now.

Evelyn led Mom by the arm to an empty gray wooden bench that matched the flowerbeds. Mom wore a red dress, high at the neck, with flowing see-through sleeves and gold flats. It was a miracle Evelyn had convinced her to wear flats. She looked at her feet as she walked, holding on to Evelyn, who shaded Mom's face with the large white hat she held up like a parasol. Mom looked old, hobbling along, her footsteps small and timid as though the earth would open up and swallow her if she stepped too far. I reminded myself that now she was the child and I was the parent, and nothing she said could be taken to heart.

"I'll go talk to her." Caroline pressed her birdlike body into mine and squeezed, and then she teetered away in her strappy silver heels toward Mom.

The band finished their song. In the pause before they started again, a woman in the street yelled, "Cunt fucker!" and I thought, Why me? It's always something with me.

"Catherine, I love this guy." Bob's bald head looked like a turkey basting in the sun.

"So do I," I said. William put his arm around me. We kissed. Bob said, "Oh, you two," and someone else (was it drunk Dierdre?) yelled, "Get a room!"

"Should we go say hello to my mother?"

"Wonderful," William said in a cheery way, though it was clear he didn't think it was so wonderful. He squinted, dutiful, looking around the crowd until his eyes settled on my mother's red shape. "I'll go," he said. "Excuse me."

Bob started saying something else about boats—"It's like a catamaran, but bigger"—but I wasn't paying attention. I was watching William make his way through the crowd.

"Sorry, Bob, I'll be right back." I touched his arm so he would stop talking and left him. "One second, one second," I said to all the people who wanted to start a conversation on the way.

Evelyn stood behind my mother like a secret service agent:

serious rectangular sunglasses and her hands behind her back. She wore an unflattering, tight blue dress that accentuated the pearlike curve of her childbearing hips.

"Mrs. West?" William was saying. "Mrs. West?"

My mother looked straight ahead into nothing, saying nothing. Caroline, who had been nibbling on a cracker, now plopped herself down on the bench and put her arm around Mom.

"Get off me," Mom said, recoiling.

"God, sor-ry."

"I know you?" Evelyn said. It was unclear who she was talking to at first, or why she was talking at all. "I know you, mister?" She was looking at William.

William put his hand on his chest. "Me?"

"Yes, you."

"I'm sure you have me confused with someone else," William said.

"Huh," Evelyn said. She obviously thought she was right, and she was obviously wrong.

"Mom?" I didn't want to squat in my dress, but I did anyway. Because I was a good daughter. And it was just a dress. I put my hands on her knees, looked up into her face. Her eyes seemed to focus and then detach. Her lipstick had smeared onto her chin. I did the kind thing and pretended not to notice.

"Mrs. West doesn't like crowds," Evelyn barked, and scanned the perimeter.

"Want a drink, Mom? I'll go get you one," Caroline said, and sprang up, and I took her place there on the bench. William, who was standing squarely in front of my mother, put his hands in his pockets. Then Evelyn, out of nowhere, having apparently decided the sun was suddenly too much, decisively stuck my mother's white hat on her head.

"No! Don't touch me!" Mom took the hat off and held it up, expecting it to be taken from her. Evelyn waited. Mom waved the hat in jerking motions, threatening to throw, but before she could, Evelyn swiped the hat and put it firmly on her head again. "You will wear this hat, Mrs. West."

Mom conceded with a frown.

"Here, Mom, I got you champagne." Caroline held out the glass.

Mom seemed pleased with this. She took it gently by the stem and sipped.

"Mom," I said, "do you remember William?"

Mom took another sip.

"Mom?"

"Where's the girl?" Mom said, panic rising in her voice.

"Right here, Mrs. West. I'm right here behind you."

"I need my purse."

"No purse, Mrs. West."

"I need my purse." Mom turned to face Evelyn but couldn't see her because the brim of her hat was in the way.

Evelyn pulled the brim back and said into my mother's face, "No purse, Mrs. West. Drink your champagne."

William kneeled now. "I apologize for breaking your vase, Mrs. West. I'm so very sorry. Will you forgive me?"

My mother looked at his face, her eyes wandering over every part of it. It took a choked gulp of air to make me realize I had stopped breathing again.

"Who do you say you are?"

"I am William." He smiled. Beads of sweat gathered at his hairline because it was so hot.

"I know you," my mother said slowly.

"Yes," he said.

"Your parents."

"Edward and Donna."

"Stockton," she whispered. Her hand began to tremble; the champagne swished up the sides of the glass, almost and then not quite spilling. She became aware of the problem and used her other hand to steady the glass. I remember thinking, I should have taken the glass out of her hand. Why hadn't I thought of that faster?

"Mrs. West, I am sorry I broke your vase." William's face took on a strained apologetic look and froze there. The poor guy. He looked so innocent.

"You," she said, and we all waited. "You, you, you. You . . . are, you are, you must, you . . . you must leave."

"What the hell?" Caroline mouthed.

Evelyn rubbed my mother's shoulders with force, and my mother seemed fine with that, her head bobbing like a ragdoll's. "Be nice to the man," Evelyn said. "He's apologizing to you, Mrs. West."

Mom turned away. Of course she did. That was so like her. William looked very disappointed. I felt so bad for him. He didn't deserve this. I stood and softly, sadly wrapped my arms around his waist in a way that said, At least we have each other.

When the band paused between songs this time, the woman in the street yelled, "Rats, rats, rats, rats!"

"And now," the bandleader said into the microphone, "I think it's time for a little toast. William, my man, where are you?" The bandleader shaded his eyes with his hand. The chatter on the roof receded and receded until all eyes were on us.

William said, "Come," and took my hand and led me toward the band. I was aware of everyone watching and smiled. We stood in front of the stage. Someone handed us fresh glasses of champagne.

William took the microphone. "First, thank you all for com- ing." His voice was strong, firm, even. I thought I would faint. I couldn't see my mother's face. I could only see her hat. When I looked at the crowd, that white splotch was all I saw.

"We are gathered here today," he said, and everyone laughed.

"Catherine and I met only recently, but we have fallen very much in love." He looked at me then, squinting. "Sometimes the heart sees what is invisible to the eye. Though Catherine is not difficult to look at"—more requisite laughter—"it is my heart that knows she is the one for me." So poetic, especially when he repeated, "It is my heart that knows, darling."

We kissed. I was so happy. I was also so self-conscious. My expression was caught between delight and disbelief. It was hard to know how to look, and hard to sustain these emotions in front of all these people for so long.

"And so a toast."

"Toast!" someone yelled, raising a glass to catch the light.

"A toast to my fiancée, Catherine."

We clinked, sipped, kissed again. I had no idea what was happening; my hands were just doing things.

"And now," the bandleader said, "a special presentation by the talented Max and Stan."

Max and Stan had somehow appeared onstage behind us with their violins. They stood on either side of a music stand. Max looked bored. Stan looked determined, and also sweaty as hell, poor kid.

They played "When You Say Nothing at All" by Alison Krauss. My first thought was, How cliché. My second thought was, Or maybe it's perfect. "This is our song," William whispered in my ear as we swayed together, watching the boys. It sounded like a pulsing heart. The pulsing started soft, and then rose and rose until I felt out of control and my body was moving without me. William guided me, our bodies pressed close. His salty breath, its touch of mint. With his face hot on my face, he whispered, like it was the only word he knew, "Catherine."

•

People danced. Dusk fell. The sky turned a brilliant tangerine-pink and then settled into a blue glow that was almost too stunning to be real. Susan and Henry did silly moves like the fish and bait, Maya moved like an interpretive dancer—I imagined her inner dialogue was something like, "I am a tree, I am a burning bush, I am a whale"—and Dan slow-danced with Vera, who was obviously very happy about that. Spencer, Max, and Stan played leapfrog. Tonia enjoyed a big slice of cake. Caroline took off her heels, and Bob danced in spurts, stopping to make conversation; he must have talked to every single person at the party.

My mother, the white splotch, stayed on the bench. People went to talk to her there—Susan, then Caroline for a while. Eventually Evelyn came to tell me they had to leave in order to make it back in time for Mom's shower.

"Yes, that's a great idea," I said. "Good-bye. I'll see you later."

This was not good enough for Evelyn. She put her hands on her hips and looked at me like I was an asshole. "You going to say good-bye to your mother now, aren't you?"

No, bitch, I wasn't going to. After a pause—breathe, Catherine, breathe—the right words came out of my mouth. "Of course I was going to say good-bye. How can you ask me that?"

"Well then."

"Well then, go get her," I heard myself say.

Evelyn rolled her eyes and trudged off.

Meanwhile other people started to leave. I stood in the doorway, saying, Thank you for coming, thank you so much for coming, thank you for the card, thank you for the flowers. I was on autopilot, my attention concentrated on the approaching white splotch.

My mother looked cold, stiff. She had been sitting for too long. I was very proud of myself for making this correlation.

"Thanks for coming, Mom." I kissed her cheek. And then, just to piss her off, I said, "I love you."

Without hesitation she said, "Good-bye, Catherine," and then—what?—she bowed at me, one hand on her back, the other on her chest, like a ballerina, a male ballerina, at the end of a show.

My mother was losing her mind. Nothing she did or said could be taken seriously.

"Let's go," Evelyn said, looking behind her at the procession. "People are waiting here, Mrs. West. Let's go down these stairs now."

•

Caroline and Bob stuck around for a while. We drank wine in the living room and picked at the leftover canapés. Spencer was downstairs watching a movie with Max and Stan, whose mothers had left to have dinner together and would be back soon to pick them up.

William and I sat on one couch, Caroline and Bob sat on the other. I took my heels off, finally conceding to the fact that they had been very uncomfortable, and leaned into William. "The music was wonderful," he said, and kissed my forehead. "I forgot how much I love to dance." I felt his rib cage expand and contract as he breathed. I felt his warmth. I might have been proud of how comfortable we appeared in this loving posture in front of Caroline and Bob.

As I smiled at them, I thought they looked like such a funny couple. She was a bird and he was a ferret. He leaned forward, elbows on his knees, talking to William. He looked like a coach strategizing a play. And Caroline sat back, her lanky bird body, all angles, with one lazy foot that was basically in Bob's armpit.

"So, Caroline, Catherine tells me you're a painter," William said. I remember thinking it was so sweet that he had remembered that. He was making a real effort to get to know my sister.

"I was," Caroline said, a little sadly. "I haven't painted for a while."

"She's great!" Bob said, squeezing Caroline's knee. "So William, where did you sail in Europe?"

"Well," William began, and the conversation turned back to boats. Bob and William got excited talking about a specific yacht on the Mediterranean—it was the oldest one, or the one with the most gold on it—and then there was a pause, and the movement of the caterers in the kitchen, putting things away, and Caroline said, "I can't believe you're engaged."

"I know—isn't it crazy?"

"That ring is crazy," Caroline said. She looked at her ring, jokingly hit Bob. "It's way bigger than mine."

"Hey now," Bob said.

"I think I'll go check on the boys," William said. "Who knows what they're up to down there."

"Good idea." As he hoisted himself up to go do this kind thing no one had asked him to do, I knew that William was going to make a wonderful father.

•

A few minutes later we were talking about Evelyn—"I think she's kind of mean to Mom," Caroline said—when Stan's mother called. She was on her way. "I'll go down to let him know," I said.

"Yep," Bob said, scarfing a shrimp.

Tonia, whom I'd completely forgotten about, was sitting on the staircase, playing a game on her phone. "What's up?" she said. I hoped they were paying her a lot. Unless you were still in high school, taking care of other people's children was the most depressing job in the world.

The door to the den was a swinging door with a circular window at the top. It reminded me of a window on a ship. When I looked in, it was very dark. I could see Stan and Spencer lying on the carpet in front of the TV, their little heads propped on their fists, their faces illuminated in flashes by the changing light of the screen. William and Max were on the couch. I could see their faces light up, too, only less brightly because they were farther away.

When I pushed the door open, William said, "Hi, honey."

"Hi," I said, walking closer. "You look comfortable. Are you hiding in here?"

"I'm sorry. I suppose I might be hiding, yes. There's been so much social interaction today, sweetheart. I feel overwhelmed."

"Tell me about it. But now it's just Bob and Caroline. They don't count. We don't need to impress them." As I said this, I wondered if it was true.

"I know, my darling, but I do feel the need to impress them. Your sister is a big part of—"

"Shhh," Stan said.

"I think this is the good part," William whispered.

The music in the movie sounded like an epic conclusion. Long-haired people with too-big ears in New Zealand, or somewhere very green, drew swords and slowly brought them together until the points touched. Then a gold zap, and the screen was bleached in light.

11

Planning the wedding took over my life. I barely worked, I couldn't sleep, I kept canceling lunch with Mom. My hair was falling out, and it was clogging the shower. Lucia showed me a clump of it one day. A dark gnarl in her bare palm, it looked like a wet nest. "This is no good," she said. I tried to meditate twice, but I couldn't stop checking my phone. So I gave up. Meditating just made me more anxious. I finally had Bob write me a Xanax prescription.

I don't know why I thought I could do it myself. Pride, probably. And a need for change. I'd hired wedding planners with my first two fiancés, and I hadn't liked either of those people. They were glorified salesmen, always trying to add on features you did not need. The problem was that once you had become aware of these features, you couldn't possibly live without them.

In the beginning we said, Let's have something small. Small, easy, local—maybe the Hamptons in September. This, I knew from experience, was how all weddings started. First you wanted just your closest friends and family, windswept and barefoot on a beach. Then you opened a bridal magazine and it was over.

This time I swore I would not get carried away. I had gotten very carried away planning the wedding with Fernando—Isle of Capri, a dress with a ten-foot-long train, hundreds of our closest friends and family and every person we had ever passed on the street—and then, well, Fernando had married his grandmother. Or somebody's grandmother.

It might have been their announcement in the *Times* that set me off. (Of course I would make this connection only later.) The grandmother, Anabel, heiress to a nail-polish fortune, had actually managed to look a few years younger than she was, thanks to makeup, Photoshop, and the grainy low-resolution black-and-white newspaper-grade picture. Fernando looked like an imp. And excruciatingly content. I couldn't believe they had gotten married in the Hamptons. "No," I said out loud. So the Hamptons were out. I started thinking that their announcement was puny anyway. Simple, small, Hamptons—how boring, how cliché. It was that same afternoon that I mistakenly purchased the current issue of *Brides* at a newsstand, along with a pack of Mentos to angrily chew on while I whipped through the pages.

Talk about the tyranny of choice. There were so many choices. Hawaii, Aspen, the Keys? A ranch in Wyoming was an untapped resource for pastoral ceremonies? What about Mexico? Or fucking Alaska? Sleeveless, backless, endless. Everything was endless. An endless veil of lace, an endlessly flowing fondue fountain, a heart-shaped monogrammed key chain for the gift bag that would be endlessly meaningful to guests as they left the greatest celebration of their lives.

And then there was the food, and the silverware, and the color palette. The accommodations, the reception, the flowers. The extras—oh my God, the extras. Did we want a poet to write poems about hearts and roses on her antique typewriter, under the shade of a fake baobab tree, like Jackie from Chicago in *Brides*? Horses—did we want those? How about a bunch of cheese and a cheese expert? Oh, and music, there was that. And the bridal shower. And the bachelorette party. And the Mentos were gone and I needed a lobotomy. Since I couldn't get a lobotomy—did people have those anymore?—I made an appointment for a facial instead.

•

When William got home, I said, "I think we're going to end up getting married at a horse ranch in the Gulf of Mexico with edible confetti at the end."

I expected him to laugh, but he barely smiled. He sat next to me on the couch, tired. A long day at work. Herman jumped onto him, licked his face. That dog licked everything; there was something wrong with it.

"Are you okay, babe?" I put my hand on his forearm.

"Yes, I'm okay, honey. Thank you for asking." He took off his tie, rolled it up, put it in his pocket.

"Is there a lot going on at work?"

"There is."

I waited for more. I wanted details. But I sensed now was not the time to ask for them. William had a tendency to pull away when he was stressed. He just got overtired—he worked so hard—and it made him quiet. Maybe that was okay. Some couples didn't talk that much. It implied there was an unspoken understanding, a certain level of comfort. My image of this included a serene-looking couple in their nineties, reading the newspaper on a park bench, looking out at the pigeons every once in a while, and not speaking for hours. I was learning to accept the quiet, distant version of William, but it still made me nervous. What was he thinking?

"I've been thinking," he said, scratching his temple. "I would like to get married in a church." He turned to face me, and smiled. That made me happy. The thought that I had the power to make someone smile like that. It reassured me. This man loved me very much. "I should have mentioned it before, perhaps, but I didn't want to scare you. Now that we are into the logistics, though, I have to tell you that I've been thinking about it, and getting married in a church is very important to me. My mother wanted me to be married at St. Patrick's Cathedral, where I was baptized, and, well, I think it would be nice to do that, if it's possible. What do you think?"

"I think . . . Well, I'm relieved you're talking. I hate it when you're quiet, honey. And yeah, the church thing. I mean, if it's important to you, then it's important to me."

"Really?"

"Of course."

He touched my face, and brought my head to his chest. The smallest, safest, warmest room.

"Does it matter that I'm not Catholic?"

"It shouldn't be an issue."

"Good, because I don't think they'd let me be Catholic. I've done bad things."

"Have you? Like what?"

"I stole a shirt in high school. And I cheated on all my tests in high school. And college. And I've driven while under the influence way too many times in the Hamptons."

"None of that is so bad," he said, stroking my hair. I could feel his heart beating under my ear. His heart, his body, the needs of our bodies. That's when I realized maybe he just needed to eat. Maybe he was just hungry.

"Are you hungry, babe? I have dinner ready for you." It was on the table. I had even put a cover on top so it wouldn't get cold.

"Did you make it?"

"I made a phone call when I ordered it."

He laughed. "Catherine." He squeezed me. "We're going to have to get you to start cooking. It's so nice to cook. I love cooking."

"I love ordering. I got you Chinese! You can't be mad."

"I would never be mad at you." He looked at the table. "Looks delightful. Where's your plate?"

"I already ate."

I sat with him while he ate the spring rolls and then the beef and broccoli he liked so much. "This is delicious," he said, and leaned down to feed Herman a piece of beef, which was gross. I told myself not to be judgmental.

"You look so adorable when you eat," I said, flipping my hair.

"You look so adorable always."

"Mmm." I reached my legs out and touched his knees with my toes under the table. We could see them through the glass.

He put his napkin down, took my feet, held them. His arms were so long. And we just looked at each other for a while like that, just enjoying our dining room, and us in it, under the steady glow of the neon tapestry.

•

Herman followed us to the bedroom. William took off his shirt, took off my shirt. Herman sat in the corner and began to pant. I had gotten used to him watching us. It probably wouldn't have been the same without him there.

He went down on me that night, and I shuddered in a way I had never shuddered. In that moment I knew he was definitely, definitely the one.

Afterwards, I expected us to make love in the traditional way, the way we always did. But instead he lifted himself off me, stood up on the bed, and pulled my arms up until I was standing there with him. "Catherine," he said, moving my hair off my shoulder and kissing my neck, and then biting my neck and squeezing my sides. He was in his animal mood, he couldn't get enough of me—I loved it. "Can we try something new?" He turned my body away from him so he was behind me and lowered us to the bed.

At first I liked it better. It seemed to hurt less. And I was feeling very open to the pleasures of sex at this moment. It still wasn't painless—not even close—but it was better. And then he said, "Sit up for a second?" So I did. And when he pulled me back down, he entered my ass. I thought it was an accident. "Oh my God," I said. But he was already thrusting, he couldn't help it, the animal had taken over. "Is this okay?" His voice was so sweet—he was so sweet, I loved him—but his body was merciless, it didn't stop. He clenched my sides, rocking me with him. His ring had turned around on his finger and it pressed into me hard, the metal pressed right into my ribs. "I don't know if I can do this—it hurts," I said, and he said, "You can, you can," his breath heavy. I clenched my teeth. I was waiting to rip open, I was waiting for the sound of ripping open. Herman had curled into himself. He was whimpering. I was whimpering. "Is it okay? Are you okay, my darling?" William asked, thrusting over and over and over and over and over. "I—" I said, but I could barely speak, it was too much. He came like crazy. This was clearly the best sex he'd had with me. And that was good, I wanted to make him feel good. But I also felt terrible. What had just happened?

He put his arms around me. "Are you okay, are you okay?" he kept saying. He held me in a tight lock. I felt small and breakable—my bones were the wishbones on a chicken. I was paralyzed by the welling of tears. My throat tightened. I didn't move. I was exhausted. I stared at the turquoise ring on his finger. I wondered if he and Gwen had had sex like this. I wondered how she had reacted. "Please, please, tell me you're okay, please talk to me." I was faced away from him. That's how my body had landed. He got up and knelt by the bed in front of me, so his face was very close to my face. He touched my hair. Looking at him, I didn't want to cry anymore. His face was flushed and concerned. I loved how concerned he was about me. I remember one sweat droplet rolled down his forehead in that moment. He was sweatier than usual that night.

"I'm just surprised," I said. "I didn't know we were doing anal." I forced a laugh, which sent a pang down my spine.

"I'm sorry, babe, I should have been clearer with you. I'm so sorry. I just—I got caught up in the moment." He looked ashamed, and then he looked at the floor.

"It's okay, honey."

"I worry you don't trust me now."

"No, William," I said. "Come here, come lie next to me." And when he did, I looked into his glassy eyes and said, "I trust you, don't worry. Of course I trust you."

•

When I called St. Patrick's, the woman who answered the phone told me they would have no weddings for the next two and a half years. They were closed for construction. I was secretly pleased about this. I wanted to be open-minded for him, but I was very judgmental of Catholics, and of all religions, and had been since my Sarah Lawrence days. I hadn't been brought up with religion and I didn't understand it. I thought God was an imaginary friend to people who couldn't admit they were talking to themselves.

"If you'd like to start the process, you would begin by presenting the baptismal certificates of both parties," the woman said.

"My husband was baptized there, actually."

"How wonderful, dear. Is he still a parishioner?"

The word *parishioner* stuck out. She used it so conversationally.

"Yes," I lied, "he just hasn't been in a while."

"Well, you should both come out and see us soon." She pronounced *out* like a Canadian. I pictured her as a squat little Canadian who wore a cross the size of a banana around her neck at all times, even when she went swimming.

"And if the bride wasn't baptized, what can we do about that?"

"It would be a mixed marriage, in that case."

"Mixed?" Were we talking about race relations? I ripped off a piece of my stationery. My initials were embossed at the top: C.L.W. I uncapped a pen. I doodled a cross. Jean Paul Gaultier came to mind.

"Yes, mixed, dear. Where do you attend services?"

"I don't go to church. I'm not Catholic. My fiancé is Catholic."

"I see. Ideally, the priest of one's regular congregation marries the couple."

"So we have to go to church?"

"It is recommended, yes."

I imagined going to church. For two and a half years. "I worry it's too long to wait."

"I know it may seem like a long time, but given that you will be married for eternity, it's not so long."

I wrote the word *eternity* on my pad. And then I thought of something good to say. "Well, my mother is old, and she really wants to see us get married before she dies."

"I understand, dear. That makes absolute sense to me."

"Thanks for your time."

"Good luck, dear. May the Lord be with you."

•

That night William got home late after a client dinner. He kissed my forehead. "I'm going to go for a run."

He had started going for long runs on the Hudson at night. It kind of bothered me, which I knew was unfair. He worked so hard, and he still wanted to exercise. I should be happy about that.

"Okay, babe, have fun."

He left and returned an hour later with a healthy flush on his face. I was in bed, surrounded by a semicircle of bridal magazines. In an effort to feel less crazy and more in control, I had decided color coding with Post-its would be a good idea. Pink for yes, green for no, yellow for maybe. Then I had decided blue could mean maybe/yes and purple could mean maybe/no, which felt good for about five minutes, and then I felt insane. I chucked everything onto the floor while he showered, and waited until he was relaxed and in bed to tell him about the two-and-a-half-year wait.

"You think it's too long," he said. He took a sip of water from the glass on the nightstand. Herman curled up in his crotch.

"I think it's a long time, don't you?"

"My mother wanted me to get married there very much." He looked at the sky through the skylight. What did he see up there? Did he see what I saw? Stars? Or were those God's freckles to him?

"Well, there's another St. Patrick's in the city. Did you know that? It's not the cathedral, it's the 'old cathedral.' I found it today in my Google searches. It's in Nolita, and the pictures look really nice." What appealed to me most about this other St. Patrick's was that you only had to book three months out. And the neighborhood—I liked the neighborhood. "Do you think your mom would notice the difference?"

He considered this. It was a good sign. I stroked his cheek while he was considering. "Let me think about it," he said.

He kissed my forehead, turned off the light. In the dark I said, "The church woman asked me if we were parishioners on the phone."

He forced a laugh. "You say 'church woman' like it's a bad thing to be, Catherine."

"Sorry, I know. I'm trying to be open-minded."

"What did you say?"

"I lied."

"You lied to a nun?"

"Oh God, was she a nun? I mean gosh, babe—sorry."

William put his arm around me. "Would you like to go to church with me sometime?"

"I wouldn't go without you, that's for sure."

"Let's go then. To the old cathedral. Let's see how we feel there. Would you like that?"

"If you want me to go, I'll go."

He cradled my skull in his big, warm hands. This was what it felt like to be safe. "Will you do anything I ask you to do?" He laughed.

I pressed my nose against the smooth skin of his neck. I inhaled the scent of him like it was a drug. I always went stupid around him, and in bed it was worse. "Probably," I said.

12

Church was what it looked like in the movies: glossy brown pews and a red carpet that rolled down the center aisle to the stage, where the priest in small glasses and gray hair looked just like the pope. He wore a long green robe embellished with gold. A few other men onstage also wore green robes, and sat in chairs. This was confusing. Who were they? One, a young Latino man, appeared to be sleeping. Another twisted the tapered end of his long Merlin beard with great concentration. A man in a Pat Robertson outfit (cobalt-blue blazer and corn-yellow tie) stepped up to the microphone. His black hair was slicked back like a mobster's. I didn't trust anything he was about to say.

We were lit from above like in a bad dressing room. But the stained glass was exquisite—it couldn't have been better. And the intricate detail behind the stage—twelve alcoves holding twelve apostles, marvelously carved—reminded me of Rome. Five biblical palm fronds stuck out of a pot in front of the altar. Did that mean something? Off to the side were buckets of flowers arranged in an irregular pattern, as if different people had dropped them off at different times. Their colors and forms didn't match at all: red roses, sunflowers, something pink, something orange. Between the apostles hung a realistic portrait of Jesus, frozen in the stance of the most flamboyant shot-putter I had ever seen, about to throw the ball that did not exist in his empty hand. At least here, though, he was joyful and alive. In the nearby sculpture of him, he was very dramatically dead: his arms outstretched and nailed to the cross, his head hanging limply, the flaps in his stone loincloth suggesting a strong wind. As if the slow, torturous death in the story weren't enough, the weather had also been shitty that day?

William had said, "Perhaps the black dress with the longer sleeves," and so I had worn that. It was hard to know if I was overdressed or underdressed. The woman in front of me wore flip-flops and cutoffs. Another woman wore a full face of makeup and a tailored green dress. Her boyfriend wore a tight checkered shirt tucked deeply into tight black jeans. He looked constricted. He reminded me of the *American Psycho* guy. William wore a suit and tie. He was definitely overdressed.

It smelled like a musty wooden cupboard filled with old-lady perfume. Which might have been coming off the old lady next to me, who was clad in a Chanel tweed jacket and skirt despite the weather. "Hello," she said. "I'm Marge. How are you today?"

"Fine."

"Are you new?"

"Yes."

"I can tell."

"Hello. I'm William." He reached across me to shake her hand.

"Marge," she said, her breath hot on my face. It smelled like mushroom soup from a can.

"Have you been to church before?"

"No."

"I can tell. I'll walk you through it, don't worry," Marge said, adopting me. She appeared to be alone, no husband, not even a Golden Girl friend. I thought that was very sad. Being old and alone was just the saddest thing in the world. I may have felt superior with William by my side, and also safe, and I hoped that later, in the winter of our lives, William and I would either die at the exact same time or I would be the one to go first.

"In the name of the Father and of the Son and of the Holy Spirit, amen." We stood. The organ started. It sounded like haunted-house music. The priest opened a huge Babar-sized book and began to sing-read the words. It was odd. He did not commit to song or to regular speech—he was sing-speaking. When he was done, a woman in mean glasses, who looked like the type of person who would work at the DMV, spoke to us in a thick, smoky Bronx accent. I had no idea what she was talking about. Then one of the green robes took the spiral staircase up to the turret and spoke to us from there, reading again from the Babar book. There were so many characters onstage, so much to watch. Church was like going to the theater. Except for the participation element, which I thought was a lot to ask.

We stood up, we sat, we stood up, we sat. The pews were so uncomfortable. A young man in a striped T-shirt a few rows ahead obviously felt the same way: he kept rubbing his shoulders. Sometimes we knelt. People clasped their hands in prayer. I made mine into fists, which felt like a generous compromise.

We sang from a book. The words were separated into syllables for us. Marge had an operatic voice. William's was a monotone. I didn't sing, but I politely looked on since Marge was eagerly holding the book out for me.

Catholics had a lot of information memorized. There was some chant that included the line "We have sinned, we have sinned," which was accompanied by softly beating one's chest? And then raising one's arms in a Pilates-like repetition?

"Christ has risen," the priest said.

"He has truly risen," everyone said.

"Christ has risen."

"He has truly risen."

William said these words like he'd been born saying them. At church he went into a trance. He sat straight up like a soldier, total attention on the stage. I kept waiting for him to break character—to look over at me and smile, to roll his eyes at this talk of Christ truly being risen—but he did not.

Pat Robertson announced that the baskets would go around. He asked that we be generous. In return we would receive the gifts of bread and wine. The collectors wore plain clothes. The baskets were attached to long sticks. William put a twenty in, which I assumed was for both of us. Marge put in a folded check. As the haunted-house music played, the collectors ceremoniously dumped their baskets into a larger wooden basket at the front of the stage, which was supposed to be reminiscent of something handmade on the Nile, maybe, and which looked like a hamper from Pier 1 Imports.

Then it was time to say "Peace be with you" to our neighbors, which was my favorite part for two reasons. One, it allowed me to see that these robotic chest-beaters were actual people, and two, William actually made eye contact with me then.

"The chaaaaa-lice," the priest sang-spoke, and people formed a line to eat the body and blood of Christ. "You stay here during this part," Marge said, and scooted past my legs.

That chalice looked exactly like the one from *Indiana Jones*. The priest was holding it up with such intensity, his eyes squeezed shut in either rapture or fear, it was hard to know. A tiny part of me might have been jealous—these people actually believed in something beyond their boring human selves—but most of me was judgmental. The theatrics of church were just absurd.

I watched people chew their wafers as they walked back to their seats. Some looked indifferent, others looked forlorn. I assumed the forlorn ones had committed bad sins recently, and they were mentally repenting as they ate the body of Christ.

When it was over, we stood in another line to say good-bye to the priest, who was shaking hands by the door. Marge said, "You did great, honey."

"Thanks." I laughed.

"Do you pray at home?"

"No."

"Well," she said, leaning in confidentially, "you should start. It'll make you feel better." To William she said, "Did you grow up in the church, William?"

"Yes, as a matter of fact I did," William said.

"I can tell."

When it was her turn, the priest said, "Marge, is that you?"

Marge whipped around, took his hand. "Oh, Father, that was a magical service. Thank you."

"Thank *you*," he said. "How are you doing? How's your knee?"

"Much better." Marge extended her leg, rotated it. We all looked at the knee, which looked . . . like a knee.

"Good, good," he said.

"Peace be with you," she said.

"And also with you."

Marge continued out the door. William and I took her place in front of the priest. "Hello. I'm William, and this is Catherine."

"Hello there." The priest shook our hands. He was a gangly man with ropy neck skin and a large head that seemed dismembered from his body in that robe. His twinkling eyes and that encouraging smile—this person looked too happy to me. Which meant he was delusional. "I'm Father Ness."

"A pleasure."

"Come back now."

"Absolutely," William said.

We made our way down the crowded steps. The parishioners congregated in insular little circles. Marge put her arm around a frail man in a wheelchair. Oh good, she had a friend. "See you next week! Oh, and Catherine, there's a ladies' bowling league we have here. You should join us!"

The woman in Chanel went bowling? "Yeah, okay, bye," I muttered, and continued to walk away from her.

On the street William put his hand on the small of my back, looked up at the clay-brown cathedral, and said, "I feel a strong connection to God in this space."

"Are you saying you want to get married here?"

"I think it would be nice. I think my mother would approve."

"Good," I said, and craned for a kiss.

•

Dan arrived with a gorgeous black orchid. The center was purple with two yellow dots. "I didn't bring a gift to the engagement party."

"Oh, Dan, thank you." I took the plant and hugged him. "These are so rare. Where did you find it?"

"Brooklyn."

"I should go to Brooklyn."

"It's a nice place."

I tried to think of something clever to say to that. Nothing came to mind quickly enough. "Come in," I said.

"You look very nice today."

"Yeah, we went to church." I rolled my eyes. I waited for him to say "Why?" But of course he didn't say that. He just nodded. I put the orchid on the table in the entryway, and we went upstairs.

"So," he said, "how's your week been?"

"I'm fine, but I'm stressed about the wedding."

He nodded, taking this in. "Why don't we sit for a few minutes today?"

I laughed. "Sit as in meditate?"

"Yeah," he said.

"I'm not very good at meditating."

"Have you tried?"

"Sort of."

We sat on pillows in the massage room, facing each other, legs crossed. Dan faced the crochet and I faced the other wall, which had an intricate wood carving on it—William's—of lovers and their picnic at the foot of a sprawling tree.

"Cover one nostril, breathe in." I watched him do it. "Cover the other nostril, breathe out."

I couldn't seem to stop sighing. "This is hard."

"It gets easier."

I watched him, little Buddha, continuing to breathe. Maybe being half Japanese made him calmer. Maybe being calm was a cultural thing—it was ingrained in you or it wasn't. Which meant that if it wasn't ingrained in me, it wasn't my fault.

After the longest ten minutes of my life, we actually Om'd together. I felt ridiculous doing that and wondered if William had heard us over the sound of Stan playing.

"How do you feel?"

"Better." I sighed heavily, and we laughed at how I had sighed.

"Good." He helped me up off the floor. "Breathing usually helps."

Behind the panels, I stripped. I got under the sheet, said, "Ready."

I watched his bare feet through the hole in the massage table, saw his toes tighten when he pressed into my back.

"You're very tight here today." He tapped a spot on my shoulder.

"I am?"

"You are."

"I blame the wedding."

He laughed.

I don't know why I chose that moment to ask him. Maybe I wanted him to say, Yes, I am seeing someone and we have semi-nonconsensual anal sex all the time and it's completely normal and don't even worry about it. And maybe it was the norm for him, at least the anal part, because maybe he dated men. I still wasn't sure.

"Are you seeing anyone, Dan?"

"You know, I was, but we broke up recently."

"Oh, sorry. Are you sad?"

"I am heartbroken." Dan said this so easily. It was the type of thing I would never say out loud. I was glad we weren't looking at each other.

My response was more like a noise than a word. "Aaaawwwwoooh."

"Thanks. It's okay. I know I'll feel better once more time passes."

We didn't talk any more after that. I started wondering about Dan's life. After Japan, he had grown up in Santa Monica or Santa Barbara, one of the Santas. Where had he gone to college? And who had broken his heart? That's what I really wanted to know.

At some point I actually fell asleep on the table. That had never happened before. I must have really needed the rest. A whispering "Catherine, Catherine" woke me up.

"I need to change," I heard myself say, my voice cold and abrupt.

"Sure," Dan said. "I'll leave the room."

I put on a robe and felt fuzzy walking to the door. When I opened it, Dan was standing there, hands clasped behind his back, talking to William. I didn't know why the sight of them together seemed so wrong.

"How was it? You look relaxed." An arm around me, a kiss on the forehead. My embarrassment at Dan watching, but Dan was watching the floor.

"I am. But planning a wedding is stressful." I made a sad face like a child.

"We'll figure it out," William said.

"I know," I whined.

He kissed me once more and walked into the blue light of the room.

•

At dinner he said, "I understand your apprehension, but I really feel we should hire a wedding planner." The restaurant was packed. We were on the sidewalk, too close to another couple. They were younger than we were, and both had very oily faces. "You might find it will make things easier."

"Did Gwen hire a wedding planner?"

William, for a flash, looked uncomfortable, but then he was quickly composed again. "No, she didn't."

"Did you and Gwen get married in a church?"

"We did, yes." He was looking around for the waiter, then looking at his empty glass.

"Where did you meet Gwen?"

A chuckle from William, who was now holding his empty glass up so the waiter could see it. "At an art show, in fact, in Lausanne."

"Is that where you go to pick up the ladies? L'art shows?"

"I suppose so," he said, twirling his hair. "You know, Catherine, I don't like to talk about the past." He took my hand. He slid the ring halfway up my finger and then slid it back down. He adjusted the rock so it was facing straight up. He looked at me. He said, "Everything I care about is right here at this table." He smiled. His teeth were so white. They were blinding.

13

Marty Williams was a short, flashy Colombian with carnie hands and thoughtfully contoured eyebrows, and he knew everything. He was also straightforward as hell. He reminded me of Susan in a way. He called the church thing "severe." "But," he said, "it's so passé it's almost chic again."

His pin-striped suit and his gelled-back hair made him look like a crook. The only thing that didn't go was the hot pink handkerchief in his breast pocket. He was like a cartoon, squat to the ground and quick in his movements. He'd been recommended to me by a friend from Deerfield who'd had the most fabulous wedding I'd ever been to, so I knew he had to be good.

"So what's the deal? It's booked? What's the date?"

"William's secretary is sending the baptismal certificate."

"They're called administrative assistants now, Cat—no one says 'secretary' anymore. Which church? I'll call them."

"St. Patrick's, the small one."

"The *small* one?"

"In Nolita."

"Okay. Don't call it 'the small one' ever again. And don't even say St. Patrick's. That will confuse people. Say 'a quaint church in Nolita.' Got it?"

"Got it."

He Googled the number on his phone, put the phone to his ear.

"Yes, hello, I'm calling on behalf of Catherine West. Have you received William Stockton's baptismal certificate?" Marty cracked his knuckles, walked in circles around the living room. "Uh-huh . . . uh-huh . . . uh-huh." Stupid Herman ran right into Marty's leg, and Marty mimed a scream. "Good. When is your next available date?" Herman followed Marty in circles now around the couch. "October seventeenth at ten a.m.? Uh-huh. It's a Saturday, okay. One moment—hold please." He pressed Mute with one deft chubby finger. "Cat? That work for you?"

"Ten? Isn't that a little early?"

"Do you have anything later in the day?" Marty said into the phone. "You don't. And the next available date would be what? Okay, December?"

"No," I said, "that's too long."

"We'll take October."

Ten o'clock in the morning was the most unromantic time for a wedding, but it would have to do. October seventeenth, though—that sounded good. I could go with that.

"Uh-huh . . . uh-huh . . . uh-huh. A meeting with the priest, great. September?"

"Sure," I whispered. Why was I whispering?

"That works, praise the Lord. Thank you. Bye-bye now." He did a curtsy for me. "You have a wedding date, my friend."

"At ten a.m.? Is that the worst?"

"No, it's normal for churches. Get over that right now."

•

We made a list of all the things I wanted. I wanted lots of flowers, good music, and the best champagne. Marty said, "Your desires are vague, Cat. You sort of know what you want, but not exactly. But that's fine. That's where I come in."

And he was right. When I didn't know what I needed, Marty knew what I needed. He also took it well when I disagreed with him, and usually I didn't even have to verbalize—he took cues from my facial expressions very well. When he asked, "Do you like geraniums?" he took one look at my face and said, "Understood."

Marty said the reception should be near the church, at the gallery space of a friend of a friend in SoHo. It would be "très," he promised. Everything was très with Marty Williams.

"Do you think the church thing is très?"

"No, the church thing is chic."

"What's the difference?"

"It's subtle."

After our debriefing we walked around the neighborhood to get a feel for what my style was, even though Marty said he already had me pinned from seeing the inside of my house. "You are L.A. simple meets Upper East Side traditional meets obsession with white. Are you a virgin?"

"Are you serious?"

"Had to ask."

Marty walked surprisingly fast for a person with such short legs. "Chop-chop," he kept saying. He stopped in front of a furniture store. In the window: two unimpressively basic chairs with vomit-green cushions. "You like these?"

"No."

"Good, they're ugly."

He said whatever he wanted all the time, and walked around touching things as if anything could be bought. At Jonathan Adler, Marty went right ahead and stuck his hand into a display case to feel the heaviness of some napkin holders that looked very très. The salesperson was standing right there, trying to speak, and

Marty said, "No, no, we got it, honey, thank you." He half closed his eyes, really feeling the weight of these napkin holders, shaking them in his hands like little maracas. "Nope," he said, "not for us."

At Magnolia Bakery he said, "What would you order here?"

"A cupcake?"

"Traditional."

We went to Starbucks. I ordered a latte. "Wrong about that," Marty said. "I was sure you were an Americano girl. But no, you like milk. Wholesome."

"Okay."

"You like this song?"

It was Sarah McLachlan. I felt like I was supposed to say no, and then I felt like I was supposed to say yes. It was so hard to know what the right answer was sometimes. I knew that if I said yes, I would have to say it with confidence. "Yes, I do, actually."

"You have a soft side. That's good." Marty threw back his double espresso and slammed the paper cup on the bar. "I'll walk you home now."

"Great."

"Catherine West and William Stockton. It sounds like a British fairy tale."

"Thanks."

"Where'd you meet?"

"At a museum."

"Good. Oh, yes, that's perfect for the announcement."

Our announcement was going to squash Fernando's announcement, not that I cared.

"Is this your first wedding?"

"It is."

"What? You're a tall drink of water, girl—what the hell have you been doing?"

"Dating the wrong people."

"Honey," he said, "tell me about it. Everyone's got a weird mole and a yoga tote full of bullshit." He checked his phone. "When am I meeting William?"

"Soon."

"Better be."

When we got to my door, he said, "This is going to be a good one, I can feel it." He kissed me on both cheeks. "I'll be in touch."

•

With Xanax and Marty in my life, I was back to my fully functional self. Susan and I decided it had been a mutual falling off the face of the earth—we were both sorry—and agreed to meet for lunch at the Thai place. The music there reminded me of a spa: water droplets and a light techno beat. It smelled like limes. Susan was already at a table drinking a cosmo, eyes on her phone.

"Hi." I hugged her. "You look rejuvenated."

"You look skinny," she said.

"Good skinny or scary skinny?"

She eyed my shoulders. I was wearing a new tank from Miu Miu.

"You want me to answer that?"

"No. But if I start to look like my sister, let me know."

"Okay. You're not there yet, but you might be on your way."

"Rejuvenated," I said again. "What did you have done?"

She touched her cheek as if it weren't actually hers but some foreign surface. "Oh, just a little chemical peel. I can't stop touching it."

"I want one. It looks great."

"Dr. Butterworth. I'll text you her info right now." She did. My phone beeped.

The waitress appeared. "Hello," Susan said. "We would like a cosmo for this one. I'll have another. And we'll take two cucumber salads." She looked at me. "Okay?"

"Perfect," I said. It was always a relief to go to a restaurant with Susan because she made all the necessary decisions for me. I didn't even have to think about what I wanted.

"So tell me. What the hell is going on?"

"You go first."

"Fine." She took a too-big sip, shook her head out from the shock of it. "I am still seeing Henry. Who is still twenty-four years old. I have nightmares his mother is going to come to the shop and shoot my head off. With a gun. You know he's from Arkansas. They love guns down there. He told me he grew up killing deer. Isn't that just vile? But I like him. He knows where the clit is, thank God. And he is a sweetheart. I just don't know if I have time to be in love right now."

"That's ridiculous."

Susan sighed. "You wouldn't get it. You're a love junkie."

"Why do you always call me that?"

"Because you're addicted."

"I'm not addicted." I uncrossed and recrossed my legs under the table. They did feel skinny today.

Susan carefully brushed her yellow bangs out of her eyes and turned her hands in circles, either to stretch her wrists or to find her thoughts or both. Then she held up one finger. Her eyes were a little crazy.

"You and I"—she pointed to me and then to herself, clarifying—"have different definitions of love."

"I'm going to need you to expand on that."

"Okay, let me ask you this." She tapped my diamond. "How many times have you been in love?"

I didn't know if I was finding this conversation fun or stressful. On the one hand, I'd been in love many times. On the other hand, was it real? Maybe I'd never been in love at all. I went with the less complicated answer, the one Susan would expect. "I don't know—five times, ten times?"

"See? That's what I mean. I've been in love twice. Two times, that's it. Just two." She held up two fingers and then got distracted by something moving out the window. It was a bus. "You're just—you *want* to be in love more than I do."

Susan was in therapist mode. Which had the potential to be very amusing, because she'd be even more brutally honest than usual, but it backfired when she hurt your feelings.

"Susan, everybody wants to be in love. Come on."

"Yeah, but you—you want, like, the little man with the little picket fence." She said this in a wee little voice.

"I do not want a picket fence. And William isn't my little man, he's my fiancé."

"No, William is a big man." She said this in a big ogre voice.

"What do you think about him? Tell me the truth."

Her eyes came unfocused, her bottom lip jutted out, she rocked her head back and forth. "He's cool. Cool, cool, cool." She touched her face again; she couldn't stop. "I mean, no, he's kind of cold. Isn't he? Like a German colonel."

"Well, he is German."

"Well, so am I."

"Okay."

"He's hard to read."

"He can be at first. It's called being mysterious. It's a good thing."

Susan made a face that said no.

"He grew up in Switzerland. People aren't as expressive there."

"I have many Swiss friends I would call expressive. Also, wasn't he born here? Why does he have an accent?"

"He barely has an accent."

"Listen, I'm happy for you, okay? I'm very, very happy for you." She held my hand. "I am just saying, as your friend, okay?

As your fah-riend." She paused until she had my eyes. "I think he's a little Talented Mr. Ripley, and I don't want you to get hurt again, that's all I'm saying."

"You don't even know him. You've met him twice."

"I have a sixth sense."

"Well, it's off."

The waitress, sensing tension, placed our drinks timidly on the table.

"Fine," Susan said, hands up in surrender. "Agree to disagree."

"Fine."

"Are you upset?"

I didn't answer.

"I'm sorry, baby. I'd be a shitty friend if I didn't tell you how I felt, okay? But I'm done now. I'm done. I've said my piece. So tell me about the wedding. Let's talk tablecloths."

"Susan." I was desperate. "I need you to like him."

Susan nodded once. "Done—I like him. If anyone asks, I like him."

She kissed my ass for the rest of lunch, asking all about Marty Williams and the color palette and what kind of food we were going to have. I ended up telling her about my mother and the vase, to which she simply said, "Interesting."

"You know I have Dan coming over once a week now. Isn't that hilarious?"

I set the fork on the plate. "Are you going to sleep with him?"

"Whoa."

I laughed, and then I kept laughing. And then I was laughing uncontrollably.

"What is going on with you? And no, I have Henry." She pronounced it *Henri* like he was French. "I have it all!" Susan fluttered her hands open. They looked like sea anemones on speed. Then she turned dramatically to face me, like a singer preparing to belt out a number. "That's our job in the one percent. To look like we have it all." She touched her raw cheek again. "My face feels like the ass of a babe." She grabbed her glass. "Cheers," she said. "To having it all!"

●

When William got home, I gave him notes about my day while he changed out of his suit. Lunch with Susan, workout with Chris. Marty Williams was great. October seventeenth was going to be the happy day.

"October seventeenth—I like it," he said from inside the closet.

"You do?"

"It's perfect."

He reappeared in a tank top and those faded Adidas shorts he liked so much and sat on the bed to put on his sneakers. I was in bed, adding maybe/yes Post-its to *Brides*.

"I can't wait to be married to you."

I could feel my heart beating in my chest. I didn't know what to say. I said, "Ha." I just couldn't believe it. This was what I had always wanted, and here it was, happening.

"I'm going to go for a quick run."

"Okay."

He put his ear buds in, stood up. From the doorway he blew a kiss.

"I love you," I called after him, but he must not have heard me. The music was already playing.

14

At the end of every day, Vera or Maya sent me an e-mail about the shop. These e-mails contained information about foot traffic, the day's clientele (anyone important/famous? any homeless interlopers?), what items had sold, what needed to be restocked, and our total sales.

Vera, next to the total sales number, often inserted an opinion about how little money we were making and how this worried her greatly. "This worries me greatly!" My honest reaction was, Poor Vera, who lives in New Jersey and cares so much about her little peon job.

Today she had written: *Catherine, unfortunately we made $135 today. This is not due to my lack of performance as your manager. There is only so much I can do. Our account balance is $1,233.67. This worries me greatly.*

I wrote back: *Will transfer funds ASAP.*

I'd been bailing the shop out for a few months with my personal funds. I hadn't told anyone. Nothing had ever been this bad though. One hundred thirty-five dollars—even I knew that was a bad number.

Giving up the shop was simply not an option. I loved telling people I was a small-business owner. It made me relatable. It gave me substance. Without it, what was I doing with my life?

The trust my father had left dispersed money to the three of us every month. Caroline and I got $80,000 a month, our mother got more. One stipulation of the trust was that Caroline and I could buy real estate under $8 million. (We both got as close to that number as we could. My house cost $7.85, Caroline's $7.82.) I also had some money saved, so there was no reason to pay close attention to these monthly deposits. Even without savings, I doubt I would have paid attention. I had never worried about money. My entire life, I had never worried about money. I had always had enough.

So when I went to the bank to make the transfer to the shop's account (I liked to do this in person sometimes; I think it made me feel legit, not that the people who worked at the bank cared), I was surprised at the low balance. I assumed it was a clerical error. I assumed a few zeros had been lost in cyberspace. I would speak to someone and it would be resolved.

A hair-sprayed woman who looked like a flight attendant told me in her flight-attendant voice that no transfers had been made in the past three months. When I asked why, she said she had no way of knowing that information, ma'am.

I called the accountant, Ted, who'd been a family friend for years, and explained that a clerical error had occurred and he needed to fix it right now. I hadn't spoken to Ted in a long time but had fond memories of him. He had come to our Christmas party every year and brought Caroline and me Peeps. Which, now that I thought about it, was unseasonably odd.

"What's the problem? The trust contains $500 million. Which is enough for everyone forever!" I was sure about this number because my mother had said it so many times.

"Five hundred?" Ted sounded unsure.

"Is that wrong?"

"That is indeed wrong. Your father may have had that much at one time in stocks, but when the market fell, those funds were dissolved. The full amount at the time of your father's death was closer to $100 million."

"What about the money from Eighty-Fourth?" We had sold for $20.5.

"The house was left to your mother. What's left remains in her name. But there isn't much left. She donated nearly all of it to charity."

"She donated $20 million to charity?" I laughed. "That's insane, Ted. That has to be wrong."

"Unfortunately, it is not wrong."

"I'm coming to your office."

"Okay, let's set you up with an appointment. When would you like to come?"

"I'm coming right now."

•

I had never been to Ted's office. It was a big gold building on Fifty-Fourth Street, not far from the bank. I showed my ID, was given a badge. I took the wrong elevator up and had to come back down and go to the other elevator bank. "This," I planned to say when I saw Ted, "has been an unnecessarily degrading experience." When I found the office, finally, I was a total bitch to the headband-wearing receptionist, and I had every right to be. "Ted Adams," I said. I didn't take my sunglasses off.

"If you'll just have a seat, I'll call him."

Why was everyone speaking like a flight attendant today? "Tell him to hurry up."

I refused to sit down. I paced the waiting room. The plants were fake. How tacky. In a large conference room, with a view designed to impress (I was not impressed), two suits appeared to be having an unserious conversation. They were laughing. It was unprofessional.

"I'll take you back now," Headband said. I followed her through the cubicle maze, where people's cat pictures were sadly tacked onto the sad blue fabric walls of their cubes, to the back, where the real offices were. Ted's door was open.

"It's nice to see you." He stood behind his desk. "It's been years." He walked around, hugged me.

"Yeah." I patted his back. He smelled strongly of Old Spice.

"Please, sit."

I did, in a gaudy leather chair with too-high armrests. I looked out the window. Flying pigeons, and I swore one of them was shitting.

Ted looked like he'd just stepped off the golf course: baby blue polo, white pants (really?), the unnaturally orange skin pigmentation of an Oompa Loompa. As if I had given him a compliment on his tan, he said, "Just got back from Florida this morning."

I sighed as loudly as possible.

"Do you want some water?"

"Yes. No. I— Yes. Ted, I am distressed."

"I can see that."

He filled a glass of water at his tacky personal sink, touched my back in a fatherly way when he gave it to me. I recoiled. I was not a child anymore. I was a small-business owner with a serious problem.

"How much money is left, Ted?"

"It's gone," he said, taking his seat across from me.

"It's gone? Gone?" This wasn't registering. "Gone? What does that mean?"

"It means you will no longer receive monthly payments, Catherine."

"No," I said. "No no no no no." I was going to tear my hair out. I was going to die. "There must be some way around this. Tell me there is. Please. Tell me there's a loophole."

"There is something additional you should know. In your father's trust, it was stipulated that you and Caroline would receive additional funds if you had children. And you must be married to receive those funds. I believe he added that later. Your father rewrote his will more often than anyone I've ever known—it was hard to keep track. He loved the idea of a large family. Well, you know that. He thought this would give you and Caroline an incentive to have kids. Ten million dollars per child is the number he chose. A separate account holds that money. I believe it accommodates up to eight children. If that number isn't reached, the remainder will be given to the Met."

"What? I've never heard that." As the words came out of my mouth, I realized I was wrong. I had heard this before. Ten years before, when Dad had died, Caroline, Mom, Ted, and I had sat at the dining table (I remember the roses had been red that day) going over these logistics. I had barely paid attention. Of course, I'd been distraught. My father had been everything to me, and he had died so suddenly.

"But how can it be gone? My mother said the trust contained $500 million!" I was repeating myself. This still wasn't registering. I was going to pass out. I was going to die. "I'm positive about that."

"And you never asked your mother to see any printed record of this? The statements I sent you would have negated that figure."

"No, Ted." I said his name like it was something ugly. "Why would I? Why would I check? I believed my own mother. Wouldn't you?"

Ted pressed his lips together. His wispy white hair looked like sprinkler mist above his head.

"Does Caroline know about this?"

"Yes," he said.

"Yes?"

"Correct me if I'm wrong, but Caroline has three children?"

"And?"

"Right."

I managed to set my jittering glass of water on Ted's idiotic desk without spilling it everywhere. "This is not real. This can't be real."

"I'm sorry. I thought you were aware."

"How could you not inform me that my monthly payments wouldn't be coming?"

"I did inform you," he said certainly. "I have sent you a letter every month for the past year."

"I didn't get any fucking letters, Ted." I saw myself in the kitchen all those mornings, throwing the letters away.

"Catherine, please."

"Please? How could you not have called me? Don't you think this warranted a phone call? Or an e-mail? No one reads their fucking mail anymore, Ted. It's a waste of paper!"

Ted waited. He seemed unfazed. He had probably been in this situation more than once.

"How much money does Mom have now?"

"I am not at liberty to say."

"But it's enough to pay for her to live in that home?"

"Your mother's facility is paid for by the money she has saved in her account, yes. She has enough saved to cover her living expenses until the age of one hundred and ten."

"What?"

"She wanted to be safe."

"A hundred and ten?"

"It's a creative number. It should not be taken literally. That number just means she has padding, so to speak."

I covered my face with my hands. "I'm going to pass out."

"After your father died, your mother wrote a living will. In this will she stipulated that in the case of dementia or any other degenerative condition that left her unable to think coherently, the art collection—everything you and Caroline did not want—should be donated to museums and charities, along with most of the proceeds from the sale of the apartment on Eighty-Fourth Street. She wrote an extensive list of charitable organizations, in fact. I can pull it up now if you'd like."

"So she gave all that money away, knowing we would run out?"

"I can show you the will. And the list of charitable donations. It will just take a second." He turned the computer on. The computer hadn't even been on.

"I think you need to get off the golf course and be better at your job, Ted. And turn your fucking computer on!" I stood up. I may have made wild gestures with my hands.

The door opened. A suit stood there, his eyes wide, like sunny-side-up eggs. "Everything okay in here?"

"Fine, Bernie, thanks."

"See how Bernie is dressed? This is how you should be dressed for work, Ted."

Bernie gave Ted a look: She's crazy.

"E-mail me the documents. You'll hear from my lawyer."

It was like a bad movie. I tore through the cubicles. I jammed my finger into the elevator button too many times, as if that would make it come faster. And I was so skinny then—the gaunt-actress version of myself. I had gotten a blowout that morning by a stylist whose vision of "feathery, feathery!" had left me looking like a Farrah Fawcett drag queen. I was a woman playing the role of a small-business owner on a tirade, and I was playing it badly. I'd even worn a pantsuit. With pinstripes. Who was I trying to be that day? I think I was trying to be myself, but in all the trying, I had missed her completely.

15

I invited Caroline out for dinner that night without telling her why. Of course she came. "The nannies are here tonight," she said, as if they weren't there every other night. We went to a French bistro we used to like as children, which had since become a hokey chain that gratinéed everything in oozy, oily cheese. The smell was killing me. Even the cone-shaped sconces on the walls appeared to be made of cheese. People crammed in, filled the booths, made too much noise. Of couse Edith Piaf was playing. How cheesy.

We ordered food to appear civilized. We chose the macaroni because that's what we had chosen as children. We didn't eat it because we were wasteful, and we drank instead because we were in pain. Yes, I was feeling dramatic. My life as I knew it was ending.

I was still in the pantsuit. I had walked to the restaurant from Fifty-Fourth Street, earbuds in, head down. I listened to Metallica the whole way. I stopped only once, to buy a water bottle at a bodega. I drank the whole thing on a busy corner and threw the bottle into a trash can with force.

Caroline was her chirpy birdy self, quacking away about how it was so wonderful that she could practice Spanish with the cleaning lady. I thought, When I'm poor, I won't have a cleaning lady.

Caroline always gave me compliments. I waited for her to comment on my blowout. Instead, when she finally shut up about the romantic cadence of the Spanish language (what movie was that from?), she said, "You look like hell."

"*You* look like hell."

"What? I meant it like how are you feeling?" She gulped her red wine. Her knobby elbows on the table looked like gnarls on a twig. "Don't be mean to me."

"Oh God." This had been one of Caroline's favorite refrains since childhood: Don't be mean to me, Catherine, be nice to me, Catherine, love me, Catherine, be my best friend, Catherine, I'll do anything. "Let me tell you why I'm being mean to you. I just found out—" and I told her the whole story, including the part about Ted's funky tan. "And who knows, maybe Ted stole the money from us."

"Ted did not steal the money from us."

"Oh my God," I said, "what if that's what happened? That kind of thing happens all the time."

"No, that didn't happen." She traced an eyebrow—her good eyebrow, not the fucked-up tadpole. "How could you not have known about this?"

"How could I not have known? How could you not have told me?"

"I didn't tell you because I thought you knew."

"And you're not freaked out that we're out of money?"

"Catherine," she said, "we planned for this. I thought we were all planning for this. Why do you think Bob and I went to Playa del Carmen instead of Cabo?"

"I didn't even think about that, Caroline. Why would I stop and think, Oh, Caroline and Bob are going to Playa del Carmen because we are about to lose our monthly deposits and Mom gave everything to charity? Why would I *ever* think that?"

Caroline's mouth looked dry, wrinkled. It looked like an ass-hole. Maybe she was smoking again. "Catherine, we never talk about money. That's how we were raised. I don't talk about money with anyone except for Bob."

"That's so codependent."

"Please be nice to me."

"Oh my God, you're like a three-year-old." Caroline made the face of the girl in the movie who's about to cry, so I said, "Sorry, but it's true."

"It seems like William has money, doesn't he? I kind of thought that was one of the reasons you picked him."

"That is disgusting, Caroline."

"Sorry, I just— I didn't mean—"

"Is this why you've been popping out babies? To get more money than me?"

She actually looked pissed off in a real way then, not in a movie way, which rarely happened with her. "I love my children, Catherine."

"Fine, sorry."

"I love them," she said again.

"But it's $10 million per child. And if you knew that, you had to be thinking about that. I mean really, come on."

"Well . . ." Caroline readjusted herself in the booth. "Yeah, I guess I was thinking about it, to be honest. It's a lot of money. Why would I *not* be thinking about it?"

"So you had more kids to get more money."

Caroline looked at me, looked at the table, looked at her split ends. She twirled them around her fingers. "It's not that simple," she said.

"Isn't it?"

"No."

"And why didn't you tell me to have Fernando's baby? That was only last year! I wouldn't be broke now if you had told me to have it!"

"You're not broke. Stop."

"But I'm going to be."

"Would you really have had that baby?"

"Fuck! Probably."

"And you're accusing *me* of having babies for money?"

"Yes, because you actually had them. I didn't."

"Well, it wouldn't have mattered anyway, because you wouldn't have been married! And Catherine, this is not why we had kids! Have you met my husband? He's obsessed with kids. He's a pediatrician! Jesus!"

"Yeah, with a pediatrician's salary. Did he know about this special trust when you guys decided to get pregnant?"

"Of course he knew."

"Well how convenient for Bob. Now he can retire early."

"That's a mean thing to say."

"Maybe it hurts because it's true."

Caroline twirled her split ends but didn't look at them. She was looking at me. "I feel like you're blaming me because you don't . . ."

"What?"

"Never mind."

"Tell me. Don't do that. Tell me."

"Because you don't want to blame yourself."

"I'm blaming you because I don't want to blame myself?" This struck me as being more insightful than I thought Caroline had the capacity to be. And it bothered me because it was probably true. But then she ruined her moment of wisdom by saying, "I am your blame receptacle."

"My what?"

"Blame receptacle."

"Is that a real term or did you just make it up?"

"I heard it on TV."

"Of course you did."

Caroline rubbed her temples with her knuckles. "Catherine," she said, "you are stressing me out."

"I'm stressing you out? I'm— What if I have to sell the shop?"

"No, you won't. You'll be fine."

"No, Caroline, I won't be fine. Things are not fine!"

An old man in a light blue beanie looked over. I wanted to flick him off. If I were young and rich and flicked off an old man, I'd be a brat. If I were old and poor and flicked off an old man, there was no excuse.

"Why did Mom donate the money from the house to charity? Why everything?"

"I have no idea. Bob and I were very surprised. But the money's rightfully hers. The house was left to her. We got our own houses. We hoped we would get some of that money, too, obviously, but we haven't been counting on it. We actually didn't find out about the living will until the house had sold. And by then she was already so out of it. I thought about talking to her, but there would be no point."

"Have you asked her why?"

"No."

"Really?"

"I don't want to upset her. You know how she is."

"Oh my God."

"You ask her if you want. She's more likely to tell you anyway."

"Why did she lie and say we had more money in the trust than we did?"

Her look said, Are you serious? "You know how Mom is always throwing numbers around. I never believed it was as much as she said."

"You didn't?"

"Catherine, remember when Mom told us our horseback riding lessons cost $1,000 an hour?"

I somehow still thought this was true.

"And didn't she tell you Sarah Lawrence cost something like three hundred grand a year?"

"Yes."

"Well. And also, that was always money that was *coming*. From stocks. If you look at the statements, the balance is right there."

"Oh my God. What the hell am I going to do?"

"If we can help you, we will, okay?"

If you were rich and your sister annoyed you, you could avoid her. If you were poor and your sister annoyed you, you might have to sleep on her couch anyway.

"I know. Thanks. I'm— Yeah, thanks, really."

"I mean this in the nicest way, but maybe you should eat something. I'll eat something, too. Not this macaroni though." She piled her uneaten plate on top of mine. It looked like yellow maggots. "How about a salad?"

"Fine."

She flagged down the waiter. "Hi. Can we have two green salads?" She looked at her empty glass. "And some more wine."

"No macaroni?" The waiter looked disappointed. He was probably poor. He probably commuted here from an armpit in Queens. That macaroni would probably feed his whole family for days.

•

I came home drunk and delirious. I walked up the stairs, muttering, "Sell the stairs, sell everything." I yelled for William too loudly and too many times. William William William! He wasn't there. He was still at work. Herman skittered toward me, his nails

tapping on the wood. "Fucking dog," I slurred. I got to the bedroom, popped a Xanax, fell asleep.

•

In the morning William sat on the bedside, freshly showered,
newly dressed. A hand on my hip. Concerned gaze. Fuck. I was
still in the pantsuit, minus the jacket, which was on the floor. I
reeked of cheese. My tangled hair on the white pillow like nasty
dead vines, the unopened Pellegrino on the nightstand—oh yeah.
My legs like metal pipes, the mucus-caked corners of my eyes,
my head echoing, pounding like an empty room with rocks being
hurled at the walls.

"You weren't here last night," I said. My voice sounded like a
bulldozer.

"I was at the office."

I smoothed out the fabric on his pant leg, rolled onto my back,
put a helpless hand on my forehead. "I must look terrible." It
occurred to me then that with someone else I would have said, "I
must look like shit," but with William I said, "I must look terrible."
I had a habit of adopting my lovers' language and mannerisms. I
assumed all people did this.

"You look lovely." He smiled. "And not a day over thirty."

"You always say the right thing." I sat up and gently rubbed
underneath my eyes because I imagined there was makeup there.

"What are your plans for the day?"

I sighed. Would I tell him? I wanted to, but I was ashamed.
"I'm, uh . . ." I fumbled. I unscrewed the warm Pellegrino, took a
sip. It tasted like cheese.

He looked earnest when he said, "You know, Catherine, I love
you very much."

"I love you, too," I said.

"The door was unlocked last night when I came home."

"No." I put a hand over my mouth.

"Is everything okay?"

"Yeah." I sighed. "Yes."

"Are you certain?"

I couldn't seem to breathe in deeply enough. "No, actually, things are not okay. My mother—my mother ruins everything."

"She's ill. I know it must be very hard."

"No, it's not that. It's money. I— There's no more money. There is no more money."

He looked around the room as if to say, But yes, there is money here.

"She drained the proceeds from the house. Before she lost her mind, apparently, she made stipulations to donate almost everything. And the trust is gone. It's gone. The art is gone, the money is gone. Caroline knew the whole time. I am such an idiot, I am such an idiot. And the shop isn't doing well—it's not doing well at all and I might have to sell it. And the wedding, and I am stupid, I am so stupid, and what are we going to do?"

He listened. He held me. He put a hand on Herman, who was freaking out next to us on the bed. "There must be more. Your family has so much. She couldn't have possibly donated everything."

"I think she did."

He inhaled sharply. I remember he briefly touched his heart, maybe to see how fast it was beating. "It must be wrong."

"That's what I thought."

"Do you own this house?"

"Yeah."

He looked relieved. "That's something."

"And there's a loophole. Ten million dollars for every kid Caroline and I have. Oh, and we have to be married—that's part of it. Which is so outdated."

"Ten?" William was stunned. "My goodness."

"I know," I said. "It's a lot."

His shock made me proud. I was proud I came from so much, proud I could bring this to the table, proud I could provide for us. This lasted for about one second and was followed by an immense sense of dread, because I knew, deeply—deep in my body, deep in my heart—that I would never get pregnant again. I was forty-three years old. I'd had too many abortions. Nature had given me what I wanted and I had said, "Not right now, please come again later." And nature didn't work like that. You couldn't make appointments with nature. When I pictured my insides, they were ravaged and dry. My period barely came anymore. I may have looked good, but I knew I wasn't exactly healthy.

William twirled his hair, smiled. "That certainly gives us an incentive to follow in Caroline's footsteps."

"Because it's something we want anyway," I clarified.

"Of course it is," he said. "Of course. Catherine, there is nothing I want more than to have children with you." He trailed his fingertips over my wrist. "You don't think it's too late, do you?" he asked, and then he seemed to be holding his breath.

I didn't want to tell him that it was probably too late. What if he left me? What would I have then? I would have nothing. "I hope not," I said.

"Me too," he said.

"William?" I pressed my legs into him. "Can I ask you something?"

"Anything, my darling."

My face got hot. I almost said, "Never mind, I'll ask you later." But I was desperate. I had to know. I remember looking at his hands. I remember he was fidgeting. He was straightening his tie, he was twirling his hair again. I remember my eyes losing focus in the detail of his charcoal suit. I remember his cuff links were simple silver squares that day. It took me a long time to say it. "Are you going to love me no matter what?"

"Catherine," he said, as though surprised I had asked. "Of

course I will love you." And then he leaned down so his face was touching my face and said exactly what I wanted to hear. "It's only money," he whispered. His minty aftershave, his smooth cheek. "It is only money."

"What about the wedding?"

"Don't worry about the wedding. I'll take care of it. I will take care of everything."

"You will?"

"I will."

"Promise?"

"I'll get us a joint credit card."

And then I just blurted it out. "How much do you make a year?"

"Only three hundred thousand." He scrunched his face. "Not nearly enough."

He was right. That was not nearly enough. But it might be all we would have later. If, years from now, we sold the house, spent the money, ran out of everything, this would be all we would have: his measly three hundred grand a year.

"Will you stay home with me today?"

"I wish I could, but I really should be at work."

"Please."

"Maybe you can go to the shop this morning. It might make you feel better."

"I don't think I can."

"You can. You will go in, you will find all the records pertaining to the finances of the shop, and you will bring them home and I will take a look at them." He didn't say this sternly, but like it was the only obvious thing to do.

"Okay."

"Good. And then tonight you and I can spend a romantic evening together. If we want a child, we should start trying now, don't you agree?"

I punched the air with my fist like a tired cheerleader. "No more condoms," I cheered. "Hoorah."

"Hoorah." He kissed my forehead. "We have a plan. We have a perfect plan."

As I watched him walk out of our bedroom in that expensive suit, I felt almost spiritual. Maybe I had prayed for disaster. People had cancer and car accidents and awoke clear-eyed, happy. Those people understood how lucky they were. They were awake. They were together. Disaster had brought them together. Maybe this was why I had always dated poor, chaotic men. I had thought their deprivation would rub off on me and save me from my silly life. But it was never equal. They were deprived, they siphoned off me. I had this power I didn't understand. It always became me saving them. But William was different. William was strong. William, I knew, would save me from my silly life.

THAT HUNG UPSIDE DOWN

Part Two

16

We were early. We stood, browsing the wall of pamphlets, waiting for Evelyn. Caroline braided her arm into mine and I let her.

The Avalon smelled like wet moss and dryer sheets. Yellow-and-white-striped chairs, thick with padding and upholstered in sateen, dotted the waiting room. Yellow diamonds made patterns on the grass-green carpet, and large photographs of smiling old people (youthful-old, not sad-old) in sunny, manicured parks hung on lemon-yellow walls. The fan of magazines on the white table— *Redbook, AARP*—looked like it had never been touched, and the potted plants with their domed hedge tops stood with a whimsical pride like lollipops in a wonderland.

The plan was to stay here for lunch instead of going to the Italian place. Mom might be less disoriented if we stuck to her regular routine. I hadn't seen her since the engagement party. Caroline had. Once a week and sometimes more. I would have felt guilty, but I reminded myself of how horrible she had been at the party and how stressed I had been about the wedding. It wasn't personal. I'd barely seen anyone. So, okay, I felt a little guilty. And nervous. I checked my purse again. Yes, there it was: a copy of the living will. Ted had e-mailed it to me and I planned to show it to Mom if it came to that.

"Ladies." Evelyn looked tired. Evelyn always looked tired. She strained her neck back to see us under the heavy hoods of her eyelids. The bright colors of her scrubs suggested we should be on an island: magenta pants and a manic floral top. Her shoes used to be white but had now taken on the coloring of an old, scratched-up dolphin. She had tied her long braids up in a purple scrunchie, but she had missed a lot of them. The loose ones dripped all over her shirt like a mess of electrical cords.

She motioned for us to follow with a sluggish hand, the nails of which were expertly painted in a zebra pattern, which was too perfect—those had to be stickers. "Come with me."

We followed her down the yellow hall, past the few offices and into the residential area. The bronze placards on the doors said *Community Room, TV Room, Bingo Room.*

"Oh, how was bingo?" Caroline asked.

"No bingo today," Evelyn said.

"Did they play a different game?"

"No games." Evelyn did not explain further.

Caroline accepted this with a nod. "How's Mom feeling?"

"Mrs. West has turned on me again." Her voice became animated. "Thinks I stole her earrings this time."

"Oh no," Caroline said.

"Which earrings?" I said.

At this Evelyn turned. "You, too? You accusing me now, Catherine?"

"No, I'm not. I was just wondering which ones."

Evelyn didn't answer. When we got to the placard that said *Dining Room,* she said, "Ask her yourself. She's right there," and pointed to our mother, who sat alone at one of the round tables. It was a large room with a white tile floor and columns that attached to a very high ceiling. The other tables were sprinkled with residents and caretakers in paler scrubs than Evelyn's. One wall was all glass. The light poured in on that side.

Our mother sat on the shaded side. She looked small in her

black blouse. Too small. Disappearing-small. Her posture was excellent, as it had always been: straight spine, hands clasped elegantly on the table. She gazed ahead at a light yellow pillar.

"I'm taking my break," Evelyn said. "You text if you need me. I can come back."

I realized then that Evelyn was one of those people who worked too hard so she could complain about how she worked too hard.

"Thanks," we said.

"Ease into it, okay?" Caroline pulled her spaghetti strap up onto her shoulder. She was wearing a microscopic black skirt. It was inappropriate, especially for a nursing home. People were looking. An old woman gawked. Her mouth hung open. There was food in it. My heels made a conspicuous tapping noise on the tiles. I tried to walk with more weight on the balls of my feet, which was uncomfortable and didn't help.

When we got to the table, my mother did not look up. She was busy winning a staring contest with this pillar. I looked at the pillar to make sure there was nothing going on with it, and no, there was not. It was just a pillar.

"Hey Mom," Caroline said.

She looked up then, her muddy green eyes. They used to be a much brighter green. Emerald, almost. It upset me to think that the people who met her now wouldn't know this.

"Mom," I said. "Hi, how are you?"

Caroline bent to kiss her on the cheek. I did the same. My mother took my wrist. This was new. She had never been one to initiate physical contact unless a social situation called for it. Her skin was old-person soft. "You look wonderful, Catherine."

It was not surprising that my mother would say this now, on a day when each of my ribs was clearly delineated through my thin white T-shirt like a xylophone waiting to be played. Mom had always liked us thin. ("Fat people are weak people.") She let go of my wrist. I sat on one side of her and Caroline sat on the other, looking sad that Mom hadn't told her how great she looked, too.

She brushed a speck of nothing off her collar. "What are we doing *here*?" she asked, as if *here* were definitely the wrong place to be.

"We're having lunch, Mom," Caroline said too loud.

"Don't yell, she's not deaf."

"I'm not. That's my normal voice."

I rolled my eyes and regretted it. I could not fight with Caroline today.

"It's very loud, I agree," Mom said.

"Sorry. God." Caroline pulled her skirt down so she would have something to sit on.

I was relieved Mom didn't ask me where I had been for the past few weeks. It appeared she hadn't noticed. That was the thing about Alzheimer's. It was easy to take advantage. It asked you to do the right thing, whether the sufferer noticed or not, and it also asked you to let it go when your good efforts went unnoticed.

"It's really good to see you, Mom," I said.

She unfolded the white cloth napkin that had been standing in a triangle on her plate and put it on her lap. "Yes," she said.

An Indian man dressed in black filled our water glasses and gave us salads from a wheeling cart. Mom happily speared a cherry tomato and chewed vigorously, her mouth politely closed.

"Your ring," Mom said to Caroline.

"She keeps doing this," Caroline said to me, and I wondered if Mom's interest in rings had started when I'd shown her mine at Da Castelli.

"She? Do not refer to me as 'she.' I'm right here."

"Sorry, Mom."

"What about Caroline's ring, Mom?"

Caroline laid her hand flat on the table so we could see her diamond. A circular cut, a gold band. Mom laid her hand on the table. She still wore the ring our father had given her. It had been considered huge at the time, and was now considered average. Her gold band was shaped like a staircase that ascended on both sides to meet the diamond in the center, which was also circular. I put my hand down. My block of ice, and the band, also made of diamonds, sparkled ridiculously.

"Yours is the biggest," Mom said.

"It's huge," Caroline said.

"How is Fernando?"

Caroline and I exchanged a look.

"You really liked that guy, Mom," Caroline said.

"I adore the Italians."

"Well, Fernando and I aren't speaking. He married someone else."

"Here," Caroline said, "I'll show you." She took her phone out of her tiny purse. The size of that purse matched her skirt perfectly.

"Married who?"

"Anabel," I said, annoyed she had a name.

"Look." Caroline showed Mom the picture of Fernando and Grandma Anabel from the wedding announcement.

Mom squinted.

"Put on your glasses," I said.

She held out a hand, expecting them to be passed to her.

"They're on your neck, Mom."

Her fingers followed the black beads down the chain until she found them. She put them on and looked at the photo again, holding the phone closer, then farther away, widening and squinching her eyes.

"Who is this?"

"Fernando," I said.

"Yes," she said. "And the woman?"

"His wife."

Mom had never been a person to admit she didn't know things. She was very smart, and able to piece information together without letting on that she was clueless. She had always been this way. Now was no different, except that she wasn't fooling anyone. When she said, "His wife, how wonderful," she had a look of uncertainty on her face that hadn't existed pre-Alzheimer's. It was this same look that passed across her face when she asked a question she had just asked. I suspected she vaguely sensed the repetition, but of course she wouldn't have admitted to that, and maybe she didn't quite know either. The kind thing to do was to fill in the blanks and then to fill in the blanks again when she forgot again.

"Fernando and I broke up. He married this woman instead." I tapped the picture.

"I am aware of that, Catherine," she said.

"Now Catherine is—" Caroline began.

I shook my head in a very exaggerated way: Let's not talk about William.

"What?" Mom said.

"Very happy," Caroline said.

"Well," Mom said, "I'm glad you kept the ring."

"Do you like *my* ring, Mom?" Caroline couldn't help herself.

"Yes," Mom said, "it is quaint."

"Quaint," Caroline repeated, and frowned at her diamond.

"So you didn't play bingo today, Mom?"

"I abhor bingo."

"Why?" Caroline asked.

"A trashy game. The girl insists I play, but I won't."

I looked at Mom's earrings then. She was wearing her pearls today.

"Evelyn said you think she stole your earrings," I said.

"She did," Mom said simply. She seemed unemotional about this. She was just stating the facts. She wiped her mouth and set her fork and knife to three o'clock to signal that she was done, and only a second later the Indian man was there, removing our plates.

"Do you remember which ones?" I said.

"Of course," Mom said.

"Which ones?" Caroline said. "Maybe they're in storage."

"Don't be redundant, Caroline. The girl is stealing from me. That is the point."

Caroline said, "You thought a lot of your assistants stole from you, Mom, but they were never caught."

"That's the problem," Mom said. "They were never caught."

"Do you want to see pictures of the kids?" Caroline said.

"Yes," Mom said, though it was unclear if she knew who the kids were.

Caroline handed Mom her phone again. "Here," she said. "This is Spencer at Lucy's annual costume party. He was a robot."

"Adorable," Mom said.

"Here are the twins. They were flowers." A photo of the twins being held by two nannies, who were dressed as Thing One and Thing Two.

"Oh my God, you make your nannies dress up?"

"They wanted to," she said. "And here are the twins at the park." Caroline was in this picture, standing between the two swings that contained the twins. "Do you recognize them, Mom?" The twins were only two, and Mom hadn't spent a lot of time with them before she was diagnosed.

"The twins," Mom said.

Good answer.

"Here's another one of Spencer. Remember this?" It was Spencer in his little suit at the engagement party.

"Spencer, what a doll," Mom said.

"Do you remember this day?" Caroline said.

Mom evaded the question. "Adorable," she said again.

The main course arrived—mushroom fettuccine with frisée and walnuts on top. I took a bite. It was heavy and delicious. Mom ate all of hers—good, I didn't want her to disappear—and Caroline pushed her plate away. She wasn't in a pasta mood.

We talked about Dad—"He must stop buying golf equipment, he has far too much of it," Mom said, as if he could have been out golfing right this minute—and then we ordered espressos and Mom told us about how Dad had assured her the Upper East Side was the only place where they belonged. "He wouldn't have stayed with me if I hadn't looked the way I did."

Despite Mom's shunning of her past, we still liked to ask about it. Was it just curiosity or were we trying to make sense of our own lives? I think we both sensed the opening Alzheimer's provided us. Maybe this version of our mother would tell us more about herself.

"Was it hard to grow up as an only child, Mom?" Caroline asked.

"No," Mom said, "it was not."

"Did you have a lot of friends?"

"Of course I had friends. Everyone has friends."

"Why do you hate New Jersey so much?"

"New Jersey was a fine place to grow up."

"You never miss it?"

"I simply wasn't meant to stay in the country."

Our mother had been raised on a farm. This was what had initially inspired me to take up horseback riding. I knew it was something she had done as a kid because she had a picture of herself on a horse. It was one of maybe three pictures she had from her childhood. Her horseback riding was the one thing she did mention to people—it was pedigree enough—though when she did, she made it sound as though the farm where she took lessons had belonged to someone else.

"I do love horses," Mom said. "I was quite an equestrian at one time."

When Evelyn returned, looking slightly more awake, Caroline told her, "We'll take Mom to her room today." This was obviously a new routine that had been formed in my absence.

Evelyn touched our mother's shoulder. "How was your lunch, Mrs. West?"

"Don't touch me."

Evelyn did not move her hand. "Okay, Mrs. West. I'll see you after quiet time then."

•

Mom's suite—bronze placard 314—was not a bad place to live. We had chosen the most expensive option. It included a living room, a bedroom, a kitchenette, and a large bathroom with a tub. Its shallow design and gold safety handlebar were designed to make drowning impossible.

Like the rest of the Avalon, Suite 314 had the anonymous quality of a country club, but with Mom's art and smell. The rose oil was almost too much. "Wow," I said, "it's pungent in here."

"Mom spilled her oil on the carpet last week," Caroline said.

"I did not," Mom said.

I was jealous they had been spending so much time together without me. I hadn't even been to Suite 314 since Mom moved in, when the room had looked exactly like the pamphlet.

A photo of Mom and Dad on their wedding day at the Ritz and a photo of Caroline and me as kids, standing by the stone lions at our front door, were propped on the entranceway table, along with a few animal figurines. Mom had replaced the shoddy landscape art that had come with the room (I remembered the thick, Vegas-style textured gold frames) with her own stuff. A large Tina Barney of two overprivileged lanky teenagers eating Hostess cupcakes hung on the living room wall. An Egon Schiele hung above her bed. It was interesting that these were the things Mom had picked from the huge collection. The Tina Barney didn't surprise me—she was one of Mom's favorites. But the Egon Schiele did. A gaunt man peered creepily (lasciviously?) over his shoulder at the viewer. This seemed like a very wrong choice for bedtime.

"What kind of tea do you want, Mom?"

"I need to use the bathroom."

"Okay." Caroline opened the cupboard. "Let's have peppermint. Do you want some, Catherine?"

"Sure."

"I would like peppermint," Mom said, and closed the bathroom door too hard behind her.

I sat on the pale yellow leather couch and watched Caroline in the kitchenette. She found the right cups and opened and closed the cupboards like someone was timing her. If she had been a child today, she would have been diagnosed as hyperactive. But she was also impressing me with her usefulness. Besides her skimpy outfit, she actually seemed more like a mother to me in that moment than she ever had before.

I took the will out of my purse and unfolded it. Our mother was taking a long time in the bathroom. The water boiled. Caroline brought the tea to the coffee table on a tray, which was unnecessary; the kitchenette was right there.

"Oh," she said when she saw the paper in my lap. "Are you just going to hand it to her?"

Why was I so nervous? Maybe because Mom was in a good mood and I was about to ruin that. "What do you think?"

"It's going to be awkward no matter what."

A thud in the bathroom. Caroline went to the door. "Mom, are you okay in there?"

"Leave me alone."

A minute later our mother appeared with newly applied lipstick all over her lips, and above and under her lips, and on her chin. She sat in the leather chair that matched the couch, crossed her legs. She wouldn't touch her tea yet; it was still steaming. ("Never trust a steaming beverage.")

"Mom, go like this." Caroline rubbed her chin.

Mom looked at Caroline, considering her request. "No," she said.

Caroline shrugged. She was picking her battles, and this wasn't one of them. "Fine."

I folded the paper. Maybe I didn't need to show it to her. Caroline looked at me as if to say, Go ahead.

"Mom, I have a question about the will you wrote."

"Yes?"

"Why did you give everything from Eighty-Fourth Street to charity?"

Her answer was stock. "Those are charities I care about deeply. You know I am a philanthropist. It was what I was meant to do in my life."

"But you knew the trust would run out of money."

"Your father's trust?"

"Of course our father's trust."

"Yes." She readjusted herself in the chair. "I hate this chair—it has zero support."

"You knew Caroline and I would run out of money."

"Yes."

I looked at Caroline, who looked at her tea. She wasn't going to help me at all. "Well, why did you do that?"

"Why did I do what?"

"Why are you letting Caroline and me run out of money?"

"I gave it to charity."

"Instead of your own children?"

"Yes."

"Why? Mom, we're your *kids*."

"There are lots of kids."

"Yeah, but—"

"This conversation is over." Mom pressed the armrests away, twisting her torso back and forth. "Get me a new chair."

Caroline sprang up and grabbed a wooden chair from the small table in the kitchenette. "Here Mom, take my hand."

"No." With some effort, Mom got herself out of the leather chair and into the wooden one. She smoothed her blouse. "Your father would never have stayed with me if I hadn't looked the way I did." She laughed to herself, enough to let us see her teeth, which was rare for Mom. She had imperfect teeth and she had perfected the art of hiding them.

I put the will back in my bag. "I'm going to the bathroom."

"Don't touch my makeup," Mom said. This was another familiar refrain.

"Don't worry, she won't," Caroline said.

On the granite countertop in the bathroom, I found Mom's lipstick. Or the remains of it. The lipstick itself was outside the closed plastic holder, lying in its sticky residue. Lancôme, of course. She must have decapitated it without noticing. I cleaned it up with a Kleenex and threw it in the trash. I would mention it to Evelyn.

Above the toilet was a shelf with a stack of magazines. *W* was at the top. Next to the stack I noticed a scrap of paper that had been rolled into a ball, and a pen. I don't know what possessed me to uncrumple the paper. Maybe it was the pen. In her long cursive letters (which always reminded me of the lists in the drawer on Eighty-Fourth), Mom had written: "Guilt is cancer."

I thought that was interesting, and very strange, and put the paper in my pocket. On the way back to Caroline and Mom, I opened the drawers of Mom's nightstands, looking for more balled-up papers. I found none. There were earplugs, a Danielle Steel novel, hand cream, a day planner with not one thing recorded.

"I'm very tired," Mom said.

"We'll let you take a nap then."

"Send the girl."

"Yes." Caroline texted Evelyn.

Mom stared out the window. She had her hands around her tea, which was no longer steaming.

"What are you thinking about, Mom?"

Mom looked at me. Her muddy green eyes. "We're here," she said. This was the other thing about Alzheimer's. No one could say you weren't living in the present moment all the time.

"We're here? That's what you were thinking?" Caroline said.

"Yes." Mom brought the tea to her lips. "We are here."

17

My lawyer said everything checked out. William agreed. I still wanted to sue Ted (I was so angry), but there was no basis for a lawsuit. I should have been opening my mail. I should have known. Especially if Caroline knew, I should have known. There was no excuse. How could I not have known? A quiet, gnawing voice in my head wondered what else I wasn't knowing on purpose. Of course nothing came to mind. Another voice said, Stop it, you're overreacting, this unfortunate scenario indicates nothing about a great fondness for denial—it's just unfortunate.

The situation seemed too far-fetched to happen to anyone in real life, and I couldn't stop feeling like I was a character in a made-for-TV movie, or a bad headline on a gossip site: "Catherine West Loses Everything!" I didn't know what I had done to deserve this. I was a good person. I was a good daughter. Why was our mother making us suffer?

I kept her strange scrawl in my wallet, hoping that at some point I would understand it. That hadn't happened yet. I had no idea what it meant, except that Mom was a person I didn't truly know. I had always felt that way. It was something I'd thought about a lot when I was stoned at college. I even talked about it then. But as the years passed, I had stopped talking about it. It seemed dramatic. I was an adult now. But it was amazing how much this scrap of paper seemed to weigh in my purse. I thought about it all the time.

•

William looked over the financials for the shop. He said it wasn't good. I could keep us afloat for one more month, but if things didn't turn around, I would have to start thinking about selling. He reminded me that it wasn't a failure. The market was simply not in an opportune place right now. He also said this might be something to pray about at church. I glossed over that with a noncommittal "Yeah" and asked him what the chances were that we would survive. He said, "The chances are fairly low, Catherine." The look in his eye told me they were lower than "fairly." He stood there, sweaty from his run, drinking water over the sink. "It might be a good idea to let your employees know."

I thought about what Vera's face was going to look like and decided to write an e-mail. An e-mail made sense anyway. I was not avoiding anything. An e-mail also meant that I could tell Vera and Maya at the same time. That was the respectable and fair thing to do.

But I didn't write the e-mail.

Instead I told Vera the money for the month had been deposited. And I wrote: *PLEASE SELL A LOT THIS WEEK! You need to talk to everyone who comes in. EVERYONE.*

I didn't write to Maya, because Maya was great at selling. Maybe if I had two Mayas and no Vera, this wouldn't be happening. Or if our location were two stores down, a little closer to the corner, this wouldn't be happening. Or if the cards weren't blank. I lay awake at night scrolling through the list of reasons for my failure. I couldn't stop. And it was impossible not to compare myself to Susan, who was flourishing on a block that got far less foot traffic than ours. I didn't tell Susan what was happening. I didn't tell anyone. Only William knew.

•

The next time we went to church, William reminded me about the praying. "It couldn't hurt." Just before we walked in—the organ had started its Halloween tune—he said, "I feel closest to you here."

I thought it was a waste of time, but since I had nothing else to do while I waited for church to end, I prayed. I sat in the pew and looked at William's strong legs in those slacks and I thought, God, please keep me and William healthy and don't let us get divorced and please let me keep the shop and I really, really, really want a baby. I'll do anything. I'll be so good. I'll be perfect.

This started me on a long list of all the other things I wanted. The service went on, and I kept adding things to the list. God, please don't make me go gray too early, please let Caroline be less irritating, please make my knees hurt less after I work out, please think of something more permanent than Botox soon, please kill Herman. Okay, fine, no, I take that one back. Please let Herman run away to a meadow somewhere and never come back.

When the priest said something about stealing, I added, And please don't let anyone steal from me.

When he said something about children, I added, And I really, really, really want a baby. Even if it's only just one. And please don't let it get any tattoos. But even if that happens, I'll accept it. Please just let me be a mother. Please.

Then the priest said, "I would like to share a story with you. It's about my friend Catherine. One day Catherine called me. Catherine was a very successful lawyer at the top of her field. She had one child, a son. She told me she had recently been diagnosed with stage four uterine cancer. I told her, 'Catherine, we are going to pray for you.' Later she called me again. She said, 'I feel that God is calling me. I don't know if it's just because I'm sick that I feel he is calling me, but I want to get closer.' Catherine had not been to church in a while. She had become disconnected from her faith. I said, 'Catherine, do you remember what your baptism meant? It meant you became an apostle. It meant God would never leave you. And then later, when you came into communion with God, do you know what that meant? That meant you received the body of Christ. That was the second milestone. Last, you received your confirmation. When the bishop placed his hands on your head, you were given the Holy Spirit.' God's gift to us is the Holy Spirit. All we need to do is take it. I said, 'Catherine, God will take you into his loving arms when you are ready.' Catherine got sicker every day, but she seemed more at peace every day, and less afraid of death. Like Catherine, we all have the Holy Spirit within us. It was given to us by Jesus. When we are in doubt, we ask the Holy Spirit to shine his light on us."

Of course it bothered me that the uterine cancer victim's name was Catherine. And what had happened to her? Had she died or been miraculously saved by the Holy Spirit?

Please, God, don't let me get uterine cancer.

On the way out (after a brief conversation with Father Ness; he was ecstatic that we would be married there and looked forward to learning more about us at our meeting), a homeless woman asked us for change by the gate. I decided this woman had been placed there by God, or the Holy Spirit, or the Lord (why did he have so many names?) just for me, maybe as an opportunity to avoid uterine cancer. I took a fifty out of my wallet and gave it to her slowly enough for us all to see the number on the bill.

"God bless you, baby," she said.

Yes, of course I noticed she had used the word *baby*.

Maybe William heard it too because he raised his eyebrows twice and said, "Shall we go home, darling?"

"Sure," I said, and we went home and made love for the sixth time that week. It had begun to feel like a job. Afterwards, I held my knees to my chest so the sperm would have a greater chance of survival. I felt like I was going through the motions, like I was performing. Like the actress I had seen do this in a movie once— that was where I'd learned about it. I didn't know if it actually helped, and even if it did, we were probably beyond help. Maybe I did it for William. To show him I was trying. To pretend we had a chance. The truth was that I wanted to believe my own lie. I wanted to pretend we had a chance, too.

•

I didn't have time to go to the shop. When I wasn't busy having sex or recovering from sex—yes, it was still painful, and I'd started icing my lower back regularly—I was busy pouring every ounce of myself into the wedding. At one point Marty said, "You need to back off. You are micromanaging and I cannot take it. I will fire you." I said, "Okay, sorry," and then continued to text him at four o'clock in the morning about scalloped versus nonscalloped cutlery and where exactly the flowers would go inside the church. He worked for me. It wasn't the other way around.

We chose, unsurprisingly, simple white invitations embossed with an elegant floral trim. The Save the Date was printed on the same white stationery and included a picture of William and me from the engagement party.

We chose David Burke for the rehearsal dinner and Marty's friend's SoHo space for the reception. Both were dangerously close to Canal Street, which meant close to Chinatown, which was not ideal, but David Burke was quality and it was also big enough, and when I saw Marty's friend's gallery space, I fell in love. Huge windows, expensive flooring, good acoustics. I commissioned Bird to paint a 360-degree mural of flowers, fields of them, human-sized in the foreground and tiny in the background, to give the impression we were standing, very small, on the ground among them. I had stolen this idea from one of my magazines and passed it off as my own. ("It just came to me, I'm not sure from where.") The tables would be round—better for conversation—with white tablecloths and white orchid centerpieces.

The wedding lunch—lunch, not dinner, since the ceremony was at ten a.m.—would be catered by Blue Hill. For starters, guests could choose a salad of baby field greens with goat cheese crostini or a cauliflower soup with truffle oil and crunchy glazed pears. The main course would include the following options: filet mignonette wrapped in bacon with balsamic-drizzled white asparagus, free-range rosemary lemon chicken with duchess potatoes, and a deconstructed ratatouille. Marty thought there should be a fish. I wanted only three options. William would want the filet, the free-range chicken from Blue Hill was supposed to be the best on earth, according to everyone on earth, and we had to have a vegetarian for the vegetarians. After a very long conversation, Marty won. We added an Atlantic salmon option.

Marty insisted we go to cake tastings. I thought they were unnecessary—I only cared about what the cake looked like—but welcomed the filling of time slots in my schedule. I wasn't avoiding the shop. No, I wasn't avoiding it at all. I was planning my wedding.

We went to five bakeries. Marty tasted cakes. I drank champagne. ("Have to fit into that dress!") We decided on a five-tiered white number with light green flowers—the green was a major departure from what Marty called my "repressed virginal weddingscape"—from a new place that had been started by an important French dessert chef whose name was full of vowels and impossible to pronounce.

Dress: that was easy. Monique Lhuillier. Chantilly lace V-neck, low open back, white silk with reembroidered lace appliqué detail.

I had chosen different renditions of this dress for my other two nonweddings, and this one was even more exactly the dream.

Our guest count was 182, which was extremely reasonable. It helped that William was inviting only people from the office plus Max and Stan and their parents and a few administrators from Dalton. I had learned not to push about people from Geneva. William clearly didn't like to linger in the past, and I would continue to respect this. He was forward-thinking, he was about momentum. He was not into ruminating. Also, it was a long way to travel. William assured me that one day he would take me to Geneva and introduce me to everyone he knew, including the baker Gerard, who baked the most wondrous bread I would ever eat.

The seating arrangements weren't hard because I'd done them before for most of the same people. William's people—they would stick together. The only problem was Mom. I didn't know if I should put her at our table. She would be upset the whole time. But it would look bad if I banished her to another table. I couldn't do that. The tables were large. They sat twelve. As long as she was as far away from William as possible, it would be bearable. I would make our centerpiece bigger, fuller. Not an orchid but a meaty bouquet. That would create a barrier.

William didn't want groomsmen, so I wouldn't have bridesmaids. This upset me at first, but Marty assured me it was for the best. ("Bridesmaids equal drama.")

There were still tons of small details to figure out—a text to Marty, 5:32 a.m.: "We need something more unique than chocolate in the gift bag"—but we were okay. We had time.

The people we met with—wine people, flower people—were unapologetically judgmental when I told them we were getting married in a Catholic church. One gangly sommelier had the audacity to say, "I wouldn't have thought you were Catholic." This may have been because I got a little drunk with Marty and started talking about my ex-girlfriend and the queer spectrum. Marty's jittery leg—it never stopped jittering—vibrated under the table. I told the sommelier I was offended (jokingly, even though I was serious), and when he walked away, I told Marty we would not be using him, to which he said, "Fine, he looks like a grasshopper anyway."

•

On a gloomy Thursday, after a hard workout with Chris, I finally went to the shop. I wanted to meet with Marty instead, but he wouldn't have it. "I asked for this day off a month ago, Catherine. *Do not* text me today."

My feet felt like bricks as I walked through the door. I was ready to say, "You need to go talk to that customer, Vera," but she was already doing that. She even looked engaged, nodding her head and smiling and then reaching up to grab a card and show it to the twenty-something girl in Louboutin heels.

"Hi," she said as I walked by her into the office. I responded with a tight smile. She should be talking to the customer.

I had 1,084 e-mails. Fuck. Why hadn't Vera been dealing with these?

Everybody wanted something. The *Village Voice* wanted us to advertise with them. The people who cleaned the floor wanted more money for cleaning the floor with new, eco-friendly cleaning products. The artists wanted to know how their cards were selling.

I watched Vera through the office window. Poor Vera, who shopped at T.J. Maxx and lived in New Jersey, looked uncomfortable in those shit-brown slacks. After she rang Louboutins up, I called her name.

She stood in the doorway. I did not turn around. I looked at the computer. "It's nice you came in," she said. This felt backhanded.

"Of course I came in. It's my shop."

"Yes," she said carefully. "It's just been a little while."

"Why haven't you answered these e-mails? There are over a thousand."

"I thought you told me you wanted to answer them yourself."

"How can I answer a thousand e-mails when I'm not here, Vera?"

I knew what she was thinking: Can't you open a computer anywhere, you tyrant?

"After what happened with the toilet paper, you clearly stated that you did not want me making any major decisions."

"Well, you did order eighty rolls of toilet paper at the same time. Where did you think we were going to put all that? Out for people to see?"

"I thought we would put them in here. I bought in bulk because it saved us money. It saved us twenty dollars."

I heard myself laugh. "Twenty dollars?"

"Yes," she said. "We are in dire straits financially."

The money would run out very soon. I couldn't bring myself to tell her this. I convinced myself that protecting her was the kind thing to do. Right now, at this very moment, I was preventing Vera from having a heart attack.

"So do you want me to answer the e-mails now?"

"Yes, and you can answer the ones from the artists, too."

"Really?"

I always dealt with the artists directly. So of course Vera was surprised. "Really."

"Okay."

"But sign my name."

I turned to look at her then. I thought her face would be full of judgment, but it wasn't. She didn't even flinch. That disturbed me. She wasn't surprised. She expected me to be terrible. I turned to face the screen. "That will be all," I heard myself say.

18

Leaf was just as appealing as Bonsai from the outside. A kitsch wooden sign hung above the door. Susan had made it herself. Somehow her chicken scratch had translated into homemade charm. Lucky. She was luckier than I was. Maybe I should have hired a reiki master to come balance the energy in my space before it opened. Maybe I should have made my sign myself, even if only as a gesture. (A sign company had made our sign.)

I had to remind myself that the problem was not how we were running our shops, it was what we were selling. People wanted tiny plants. People did not want blank $10 cards. How was I supposed to control what people wanted? I couldn't control that. People were morons.

It was very big of me to be here today, considering what was about to happen. I also might have been interested in checking out the space with new eyes: how could it be split between us?

Bonsai was dark. It felt like being in a womb. The sound of running water from the fountain plants in the back was soothing. And it smelled delicious, like vanilla and orange and pine needles.

"Hey girl." Susan hugged me. Her face still looked amazing. Had she gotten another peel? She wore jeans and a white shirt and salmon-pink loafers. "Why are you here? You never come here. I always go to you."

"What's the fragrance in here?"

"Glade."

"No."

"It's incense." Susan pointed to the back, where some incense was burning.

"So hippie of you."

"Henry found it."

"Did I hear my name?" Henry popped up so I could see him over the plants.

"Hey, Henry, nice to see you. Thanks for coming to the party."

"Thanks for inviting me." Those cutoffs. He really did look like a gardener from a '90s movie.

"All right," Susan said to him. "We're going shopping. Don't burn the place down." She grabbed his head with passionate force and pressed into his lips and I couldn't help but think maybe that's what Leaf had been missing: love.

•

We went to Barneys. I bought a $3,000 bag. A gold Alexander McQueen. I had to have it. Susan got a snakeskin Fendi for $5,500. I hated that I even noticed these numbers. Was this going to be my life now? Was I going to start budgeting? Cutting coupons? Strangely, I thought, If things get really bad, I can sell my hair. For someone's cancer wig. I had heard of people doing that.

We took a cab to our favorite nail salon in the Village. We soaked our feet in the warm water, complimented each other's purchases.

"The snakeskin is nice," I said.

"Yours is perfect for summer," she said.

We told the technicians we wanted our nails round, not square. We chose colors to match our new bags. "Matchy-matchy today," Susan said.

I told Susan about how my mother was ruining my life and about the baby clause, but I couldn't bring myself to tell her about the shop. I felt physically incapable of saying the words. I was so ashamed.

"Do you think you can get pregnant again? The clock is ticking pretty loud."

"I know."

"Remember that abortion in your twenties? What was his name?"

I could never remember if it was Jim Stanwick or Jim Stanhope. "Jim."

"Right. Your eyelashes looked so good after that."

"I remember. You told me."

But I didn't remember much more than that. Both my abortions were blurry when I thought of them now. With Fernando, I'd had it done at eight weeks. That was terrible, because I found out he was leaving me at six and then had to wait. I was so angry at the time. I hated him so much. There was no way I was going to keep it. That thought didn't even cross my mind. If I felt symptoms then, I drank them away. I'd done the same thing in my twenties. I barely remembered that pregnancy, even though it had lasted sixteen or seventeen weeks. I do remember the abortion was painful. I took painkillers and watched *Who's the Boss?* reruns for a week straight. The only good part about it was that I didn't apply mascara that whole week, and my lashes looked very plentiful and healthy by the end. I probably wouldn't have noticed this unless Susan had told me. She stood at the end of the couch and said, "I should take a week off mascara! Your eyelashes look so plentiful and healthy!"

"What are you going to do if you can't have a baby?"

"I don't know."

"It's a lot of money."

"I know."

"And, holy shit, your mother," Susan said. "Money to charity is one thing, but when you don't have enough for yourself?"

"Thank you. Exactly."

"And she did this right after your dad died? What does that mean?"

"I have no idea."

"There's missing information here. And she said nothing when you asked her?"

"Nothing. She's too out of it now, she won't tell me."

"She wouldn't have told you before either. That woman is a steel fortress."

This was not the first time Susan had called my mother a steel fortress. "I know."

"You want me to go and talk to her?"

"No."

"Why not? It couldn't hurt."

"Did I tell you about this piece of paper I found in her bathroom? Look, I'll show it to you."

I grabbed my wallet from my purse, handed Susan the scrawl.

Susan read it like she was in grade school, learning to read. "Guilt. Is. Cancer. Your mother wrote this?"

"It's her handwriting."

"There's a skeleton in the closet here."

"You think?"

"Obviously. Have you looked through her stuff? Where's her stuff? Where's all the stuff from the house?"

"In storage."

"That's where I would go if I were you."

I imagined us breaking into the storage unit with flashlights, a pair of caricature Nancy Drews. We would hold the flashlights like dirty foreign objects, trying not to break a nail. "That seems crazy."

"It's not crazy. And don't you want to know what art is left? You might need to sell some of it, if things get bad. Those could be some pricey pieces."

I watched the technicians silently painting our toes. They were so patient.

"Maybe that's not such a bad idea."

"Let's go tomorrow. I think I'm free in the afternoon." Susan looked at the calendar on her phone. "Yes, free. Let's do it."

"I need to figure out how to get in."

"Do it," Susan said, punching my name into her phone. Then she was squinting at the wall with her therapist eyes. "You know, it's true." She nodded. "Guilt is cancer."

●

Caroline would have one of the nannies drop off the key to the storage unit in the morning. Spencer had art class in the Village. They would stop by on the way.

"Thanks, Caroline."

"What are you looking for?"

"Old photos."

"We already went through that stuff, I thought."

"I want to go through it again."

"Catherine." Her voice sounded heavy.

"What?"

"Can I tell you something?"

"Sure."

I heard movement. I heard a door close. She whispered, "I think Bob's cheating on me."

"Really?"

"I think he's punishing me for not wanting another child."

"Oh."

"As if three isn't enough."

"Do you know who it is?"

"No. But it's probably someone I know. It's usually someone you know, isn't it?"

"Not necessarily. Why do you think he's cheating on you?"

"I don't have any proof. It's just a feeling. Do you think I should bring it up?"

"I don't know."

Caroline sighed. She sounded desperate. And I was pretty sure she was hiding in her closet.

I had to say something comforting, so I said, "Why don't you wait and see how you feel in a few weeks?"

"You're right." She sounded very happy to receive this action item. "Okay, I'll wait. Thanks, sis, you're the best."

19

We showed our IDs to the drowsy security guard and took the elevator up to the fifteenth floor. Susan had worn jeans and a tactile vest for the occasion. I had worn $300 athletic pants.

As we made our way down the windowless hall, I said, "Caroline thinks Bob's cheating on her."

"Gross," Susan said. "Does she know who it is?"

"No."

"It's probably one of his nurses."

"What?"

"Or the secretary."

"They're called administrative assistants now. I told her not to say anything yet."

"She should find someone for herself."

"Is that what you would do?"

"Probably."

We kept walking. "It's spooky in here," Susan said. "And it smells rank."

"I think it's this one." I put the key in the lock. The door opened to a large, dark room. I flicked the light.

"Thank God it's organized."

It was very organized. The movers had done a good job. Caroline must have tipped them well. She had dealt with the move because I'd been too busy planning my future with Fernando.

"Wow, she got rid of a lot. Did she auction it? There's barely anything here."

"Yeah, and gave the proceeds to fucking charity."

"Fucking charity," Susan said, stepping past me into the room.

I didn't recognize much because it was all wrapped in light blue mover's blankets, except for the baby grand piano—the shape of that made it obvious. Other than mummified furniture, there was mummified art: tableau after tableau, stacked vertically like records in a record store. In the back were a bunch of clear Rubbermaid bins stacked tall in two columns. Each was diligently labeled. "Elizabeth's Bells"—that contained Mom's eccentric aunt's collection of, obviously, bells, all of which were wrapped in beige packing paper that made them look like just trash. "Elizabeth's Flowers"—that box contained stacks of pictures Mom had taken of flowers. Someone had inserted wax paper between each one to keep them from sticking together.

"'Bruce Legal'—that looks good," Susan said. It was at the very bottom of the stack. "Let's take everything into the hall."

"Great idea."

We stood there, hands on our hips, looking at the towers of boxes and not moving.

"Yeah," Susan said, "you have to get the ones on top. You're the tall one. God, it smells like a thrift store in here."

We moved all the Rubbermaids into the hallway. It turned out there were more behind the ones we had initially seen. We moved those, too. We were sweaty by the end. Susan got us waters from the vending machine, and we started opening the boxes.

"Bruce Legal" contained nothing of interest. It was filled with old contracts from his job. "Someone should scan this stuff," I said.

"If it's worth scanning. Look at this." She didn't hold it up, and I was too far away to see it anyway. "It's your birth certificate. You weighed nine pounds and two ounces."

"Is Caroline's there?"

"No."

"She must have taken it."

I moved on to one of the "Miscellaneous" boxes. Seven of the fifteen boxes were labeled "Miscellaneous."

I found Caroline's first tooth in a vial, old report cards, notes from Grandma Jane, tons of Christmas cards. At first I lingered. I wanted to take a lot of this stuff home with me. I started making a pile. An hour later I said, "We might have to come back another day to finish."

"No way," Susan said. "I'm not coming back here."

Next I opened "<u>Miscellaneous</u>." I had a feeling the underline meant something. Mom liked uniformity. There must be a reason one was underlined and the rest were not.

Inside was a black lockbox. Cards and letters had been placed around the box so that from the outside it looked like a paper mess. Of course there was no key.

"Have you seen keys in any of your boxes?"

"No," Susan said. "What is that?"

"I don't know."

I handed her the box. She shook it. Sounded like more papers. She grabbed her keys out of her bag. She inserted a small one, probably her mail key. The box opened.

On the top was a note:

Dear Viewer,
   Kindly do not read the contents of this box unless I am dead.
ELIZABETH R. WEST

"This is going to be good."

Under the note was a journal. Susan opened it and read aloud. "'February 16, 1980. The Harrisons for dinner tonight. We will have lamb. Carmen and I practiced. Better be good. Mrs. Harrison is a food snob.'"

"Did she really write that?"

"'February 28, 1980. Steiners for dinner. Ribs and corn bread. Mrs. Steiner is a fat pig from Texas. Carmen is stealing, I know it. Eyes on her. Bruce distant. Seven-year itch? He's stressed with merger. May need better in-house gardener. Troy makes me uneasy. Caroline more outgoing than Catherine ever was. Catherine shy, self-conscious, sweet. Caroline needs too much attention. I hope I can start loving her more.'"

"Let me see that."

Susan handed me the journal. It felt heavier than I'd imagined. "I hope I can start loving her more." That was clearly written.

"That's really sad," Susan said.

In March 1978, Mom had written, "Catherine prettier than Caroline."

"That is brutal," Susan said.

I flipped to the end. We were here to find out about money. I'd read the other stuff later, maybe without Susan around.

"'December 8, 2005. Miss Bruce. More than I expected. Even miss his sleep talking. He would not like this, but it's for the best. Decided to leave this house to charity, not to C + C. Money has made this family and money has ruined it. Bruce spoiled those children. This will give them a taste of real life. Call it kindness. Cowardly, as it will only happen when I'm likely dead. But might not affect them at all, if they are smart. Caroline will be smart, Catherine no. Other motive is possible building named in my honor. Not a gym, I hope.'"

Susan looked even more shocked now. "What. The. Hell."

"'A taste of real life'? What does that mean?"

"It means she grew up poor."

"So she'd rather give money to a gym than to us?"

"No, she said 'not a gym.'"

"But she'd rather give money to *not* us. And Caroline will be smart and I won't be?"

"Well, she was right about that. No offense."

"Oh my God."

I lay back on the cement floor.

"Don't get comfortable here. We need to leave."

"I can't believe her."

"I can't believe your mom kept a journal. Like, the woman had *feelings*."

"Barely."

"Okay, get up, please. We need to get out of here. I'm dying." Susan started moving the boxes back in. Eventually I got up. I put the black box in my Barneys bag with a few of Mom's flower pictures and the rest of the pile I had made.

•

William got home that night to find me in my bathrobe drinking white wine and reading the journal. "What's that?" he asked.

I still don't know what made me say, "Nothing." It wasn't like me to keep things from him. But I was embarrassed. I was embarrassed and horrified that my mother hadn't embraced William with open arms, and I saw how much that upset him, and I didn't like seeing him upset. I was protecting him. He didn't need more details about my dysfunctional family. And the fact that William didn't like to talk about his past—that made me feel justified in not telling him I had gone to the storage unit to dig up the past. He probably wouldn't want to know anyway.

I also don't know why I pretended to cook a dinner I had actually ordered. Maybe embarrassment again. I was embarrassed I didn't cook. Gwen had probably cooked, so I should cook. I should be better. I should be perfect. If I wasn't going to be super-rich anymore and if I couldn't give him a baby, I had to be good in all other ways.

I was sneaky about the dinner lie. I buried the wrappings at the bottom of the trash can. In an effort to make my lie more believable, I even set the greasy chicken on a pan for fifteen minutes and then left the pan conspicuously in the sink to soak.

"What did you use? Tarragon?"

"Mmm-hmm," I said.

"It's very good."

"Are you okay?" he asked me.

I was not okay, and I didn't look okay either: my hair was tangled, half wet. I hadn't applied body lotion after my shower, a step I only ever skipped when I was feeling really stressed, and I was wearing the huge pair of sweatpants I never wore around William because they were so unsexy.

"I'm a little stressed."

"About the shop?"

"Yes."

"Have you told your employees?"

I looked at him. He looked so earnest and good, eating chicken after a long day at work. I felt myself nodding.

"Great," he said. "How is our wedding coming along?"

"It's going really well."

"I'm glad. I can't wait to marry you." He ate a dollop of mashed potatoes off his fork. "Oh, I may need to go to Europe in a few weeks. I found out today."

"Really? For what?"

"We want to build connections in Switzerland, and it makes the most sense for me to go. I have connections there." William fed Herman a little piece of chicken. "Are you sure nothing else is bothering you, Catherine?"

"I'm just stressed."

"I'm sorry you're stressed, honey. But you know, we must push on." And I remember exactly what he said next. He was neatly carving the white breast of his chicken when he said it, and I remember there was a bloody patch that didn't seem to bother him at all. "We mustn't be victims."

I sighed. "You're right."

•

I initiated sex that night. On all fours, I said, "Like this?" I just wanted to feel close to him. I also thought doggie style would make him come more, and that would increase our chances of getting pregnant.

"Are you sure it's okay?"

"Yes."

Marty had made a lube suggestion. It didn't help. It was as painful as it always was.

"Kitty!" William moaned.

And then his phone rang—"I'm so sorry, honey, I have to take this"—and he left the room. I stayed in the bed. I didn't move. I told myself to breathe through the pain. He came back looking handsome and naked with a smile on his face. "Shall we go again? The traditional way?" He swung a leg over me, hovered over my body, kissed my face.

His messy pouf of gray hair. Those sweet, steely eyes. "Yes," I said.

Afterwards, he collapsed onto the bed, his wet mouth on my ear. "Did you have a nice day? I didn't ask you before."

"It was okay. I went to the shop," I lied. And I told myself to remember what I'd just said, because that was the problem with lying. You couldn't be a good liar unless you had a good memory. "How was your day?"

"Very good, thanks."

William draped his strong arm over my stomach. I listened to

Herman's dog snore and thought of all the things I wasn't telling him. It felt wrong. But I was sick of complaining about my mother. I didn't want to burden him with that, I didn't think it was fair. I wanted to figure out what was going on first. For now, he didn't need to know. An invisible space seemed to bloat with the weight of our silence. Or maybe that was just my imagination. I pulled his arm tighter around me. I told myself that maybe this was part of what it meant to really love someone. You protected the person you loved from the ugly stuff, and you made a bright, beautiful home together that was full of air and light.

20

The next morning I took the black box to the study. I asked Lucia to bring me coffee there. She did, along with some yogurt she'd put in a dish with bananas and blueberries. The high chairs and the music stand stood alone in the center of the room.

"You eat, Miss Catherine," she said.

"Gracias."

I sipped the coffee. Lucia was still standing there.

"Yes, Lucia?"

"Is from your mom?" She pointed to the journal.

"Have you seen this before?"

"Yes. From Mrs. West."

"Yes," I said, "from her."

Of course the housekeeper knew more about my own mother than I did. I put my head down and started reading. I didn't feel like talking anymore. Lucia closed the door quietly behind her.

FEBRUARY 4, 1971

Mother gave me this journal to get thoughts down. Not sure I want that, but might be nice to keep records. Met a man recently. Bruce West. Anita introduced us. He's NYC born and bred. Handsome. Banker. Too thin for a man, but forgivably so. Might be my ticket. As the song goes, we gotta get out of this place! Loathe

*living w/Rita. Stupid girl. Want job helping people but there is no
money in social work. Need $$$$$$$.*

AUGUST 16, 1971

*Marrying Bruce! He's perfect. Rich AND kind. He proposed
at Harvard Club over shrimp cocktail. Ring perfect. Everything
perfect.*

MARCH 12, 1972

*Married. Can't believe I haven't written for so long! Wedding
was gorgeous, though lobster not fresh. I feel different married. Feel
more solidly in my place. Moving to huge place on Upper East.
Stale neighborhood, but Bruce says it's the only place we belong.*

MAY 3, 1972

*Apartment is palatial. Need more furniture. Eye on chaise
longue seen in Christie's catalog. Must hire more help. Bruce wants
baby. It's what I signed up for. Part of the deal. I do want a child,
I suppose. Not having one would be wrong.*

DECEMBER 1, 1972

*Stocktons for dinner. Adore Donna. Very classy and amicable
woman. We will have caviar and champagne to celebrate Edward's
show in Switzerland. They plan to move there. Will miss them.
Although son William broke Venetian vase! Twelve-year-old boys
should be quarantined. Do I even like children? Spending lots of
time w/Hilary Eagelton. She says I should focus solely on art
foundations, not medical. Good idea!*

MARCH 16, 1973

*Catherine Lily West born four days ago. Looks like me with
Bruce's ears. Huge baby. Painful labor. Arrived home to find
bouquet from Mom and Dad. They'll visit soon. Stomach looks like*

deflated balloon. Dieting now. Everyone says Catherine is the most adorable baby. People say this about all babies. But think it's true. I can tell she'll be pretty. (I hope so.)

MARCH 23, 1973

Catherine cries all night. Normal, says doc. Breastfeeding painful, want to stop soon. Bruce helpful. Loves her so much. Loves kids so much. He should have been a schoolteacher. Asked Anita for mother's helper reference. Catherine is smart. Big eyes, very observant. I see myself in her. Scary.

MAY 30, 1973

Bell-bottoms are not for short people. Stick to what works, Elizabeth. Don't try to be anyone else. Style is knowing who you are.

DECEMBER 12, 1973

Pregnant again. Bruce made bad deal, lost money. It's OK. His parents left us lots. Bought Kandinsky to celebrate pregnancy since no champagne allowed while pregnant. Bruce elated. He wants six children. No. Pregnancy is hell.

JANUARY 31, 1974

Lost baby. Normal, says doc. Dinner with Lorimers tonight. Carmen will prepare flank steak. Frank loves that.

JUNE 5, 1974

Catherine happy with Stella. Hope she will stay. Last two quit on me. Too young. Breast Cancer benefit tonight to commemorate Bruce's mother's battle. Bruce will make speech. Want to get on Breast Cancer board. Bruce says no problem. Bought lavender dress. Hermès. Also, Condé Nast may photograph plants. Everyone loves plants. Bought more recently. Best idea I ever had.

JUNE 19, 1974

Condé Nast says not now, maybe later. They suggested trying smaller publications. Bruce knows someone at the Times.

AUGUST 1, 1974

Times came to photograph today! Photographer called me a visionary. During interview with reporter, I said, "There is something very soothing about bringing nature into your home, where the wild can be tamed and appreciated." They photographed me near the fountain. Wonder if it will be color or black-and-white. Hope I look good in picture. Made sure to jut neck forward to avoid double chin.

AUGUST 23, 1974

I am so sick of pot roast, I could die. Might become a vegetarian like Gloria Steinem.

SEPTEMBER 20, 1974

Article printed in Times! They called it "The Forest in the House." Photographs marvelous. Article painted complimentary picture of me as dazzling socialite and innovative art/plant collector. Must admit I love the attention. Will frame and put up. In the kitchen, it will not be tacky.

JANUARY 14, 1975

You can never have enough sunglasses. I bought three more pairs today. In total, I have sixty-six pairs.

APRIL 1, 1975

April Fool's, what a stupid holiday. Stella quit. Hired Mae. May be too young but speaks English. Catherine talking more now. Bruce has gained. Needs to diet. Wants another baby. All

*he talks about. "Large families are happier," he says. Please. Feel
indifferent. I know I have to give him two minimum. One not
acceptable. Dyed hair auburn color. Subtle difference. I prefer it.*

OCTOBER 30, 1975

*Halloween is truly the world's worst holiday. Bruce and I will
go to Hilary's again this year. Cleopatra and Sphinx. Catherine
will be a ladybug. Mae will take her to the parade. Must get nails
done. Gold for Cleopatra. Still no pregnancy. We will try again
tomorrow night, I'm sure. Bruce loves Halloween.*

OCTOBER 31, 1975

*Bruce late! Don't want another baby. Why does he work so
much? He doesn't have to. Feel he is avoiding me! Feel distant from
him lately. Is he angry? Why? Feel sad. Called Hilary, told her
staff we would be late. Blamed it on Catherine. She stubbed her
toe, I said. What a stupid lie! Life is so hard!*

JANUARY 4, 1976

Winter makes me blue. Added more plants. Projects projects.

JANUARY 17, 1976

*Bruce to Spain. Still no pregnancy. Found three gray hairs
growing near my temple. Inconsolably depressed about this. I am
obsessed with youth. I want to be young forever.*

MARCH 2, 1976

*Browns for dinner. Esmeralda will make halibut. Catherine
drew picture of family. "Mommy" has Mae's short hair. Threw
it out. Took Catherine to park. Motherhood duties overrated. Will
enjoy her more as an adult, though worry she is spoiled beyond
repair.*

MARCH 7, 1976

Maureen and Tyler Smith for dinner. Esmeralda will make chicken parmesan and stuffed peppers. On board of five foundations now. Feel like I might be helping. Hilary is on ten boards.

MARCH 8, 1977

Spoke today at women's luncheon. Hate public speaking. Will not do again.

MARCH 19, 1977

Stocktons visiting. They'll stay with us. Pierre will come for dinner. Esmeralda will make steak and potatoes. I feel fat.

STILL MARCH 19, 1977

Stocktons happy in Switzerland. Maybe we should move there? Are Edward and Donna happier than we are? Grass always greener.

MARCH 21, 1977

Fired Mae. Will not tell Bruce. They are set to go back as it is. Will cut off contact. Will make sure of it. This is the right thing to do.

APRIL 1, 1977

Stupid April Fool's. Catherine asked me today why people take buses if they can take cars instead. I told her not everyone is lucky enough to have a car. Also said I used to take the bus. She was visibly confused. Note: do not tell anyone about your poverty, Elizabeth, not even your own children. Will send her into Mexico as a volunteer when she's a teenager.

APRIL 14, 1977

Still not pregnant. Bruce thinks something is wrong. Doc says I'm healthy—no reproductive issues. We'll check Bruce's sperm. Now I WANT another. So Bruce will shut up.

APRIL 29, 1977

I feel guilty. Guilt is cancer.

MAY 4, 1977

PREGNANT!!!!!!!!!! No exercise. No drinking. Have been vigilant. Bruce happy. Very happy! If girl, he wants to name her Caroline. If boy, Travis. Better be girl.

JUNE 14, 1977

Bruce's sperm results came back today. His comment: "Well, it all worked out, didn't it."

JULY 9, 1977

This pregnancy easier. Catherine doing well. Speaks a little Spanish with Gloria. Bruce doing well. Feel close to him again. He's getting more handsome. Unfair how that happens for men as they age. Still, there is nothing like youth. My hair looks great— pregnancy makes it silkier. Trying to focus on the positive. Bought four pairs of shoes today.

AUGUST 23, 1977

Feel depressed. Pregnancy makes me emotional. Bruce says therapist. No therapist. Can't tell Hilary. Feel alone.

AUGUST 30, 1977

A new project! Art foundation for kids with disabilities needs my help. Put me on board and asked me to help interview potential leaders for new programs. Working gives me a sense of purpose. This cannot be ignored, Elizabeth.

SEPTEMBER 15, 1977

Project going well. Pregnancy fine. Bruce fine, though still fat. Sometimes I think he is angry with me? He assures me he is not. He already rewrote will to include unborn baby. Why is he obsessed with dying? Staff is good group right now. Why is there a coffee stain on the bureau? Who put coffee there? Was it me?

FEBRUARY 2, 1978

Caroline Iris West born. Looks a lot like me, I think. Very small. More energetic than Catherine. I am done having children.

•

On the next page was a letter, which my mother had diligently taped in.

My Dear Darling Baby Kitty,

This is your nanny, Mae. I worked with you when you were three and four years old. Being a nanny is strange business. I know so much about you, but you might not remember me at all. In twenty years I might see you at a restaurant and know so many personal details about you, like the birthmark on your hip and the long black hairs on your ass (sorry to embarrass you and I hope those went away!), but to you I will be just another stranger.

In case we never talk again, there are some things I want to tell you. The first is that I am in love with you. I want to kidnap you and bring you home with me. When I told you this last week, you said, "With Duck?" Duck is your favorite stuffed animal. I'm sure you still have him.

You love art. You draw sunflowers like Van Gogh and you like to write the letter C over and over. Pink is your favorite color.

You are a watcher. You watch people intently. Other children fascinate you. At the playground you pick someone (it's usually a boy) and imitate everything he does. It is the funniest thing I have ever seen.

You are an organizer. You have organized your books by color. I think it's a great idea. Before dinner you make sure your fork, napkin, and plate are in the right places before you eat.

I believe we are born as the people we will be forever. We might grow, but at our core we do not change. You are a beautiful child. You are so beautiful. You are also kind. If you ever read this letter, I know you will still be beautiful and kind.

I will never forgive myself for not being there when you needed me. We cannot trust anyone to care for us fully. People are inherently selfish. That's what I have learned. If you don't know what I mean, that's okay. Maybe it's for the best. I still want you to know I am sorry for what happened. I will be thinking about you all the time.

I love you very, very, very much,
MAE

21

I arrived during naptime and waited in the living room for her to wake up. It still smelled too strongly of rose oil. As I sat there listening to my mother's soft rumbling snore, I texted Marty about Bird's mural. She needed to have access to the space whenever she wanted. She liked to work in the middle of the night. She needed keys. "On it," Marty wrote.

My mother awoke murmuring to herself (I couldn't make out the words) and went immediately to the bathroom. Was she writing more notes on little pieces of paper in there? When she emerged, she greeted me like it was the most natural thing in the world for me to be sitting in her living room. She sat in the pale yellow leather chair and crossed her legs.

"Hello, Catherine." She covered her mouth when she yawned, and clasped her hands in her lap. She wore black silk pajama pants and a matching top, her initials embroidered on the breast pocket. My mother had always believed that sleeping in silk did wonders for the skin. She also believed that by monogramming all her clothes, she would be able to catch her thieves easier later on.

"Hi Mom. How are you?"

"I am rested," she said, pulling her shoulders back.

"Did I ever have a nanny named Mae?"

"Mae Simon," she said automatically.

"Mae Simon," I repeated.

"Yes."

"How long was she my nanny?"

Mom scanned the space above my head. "A while."

"Why did you fire her?"

"She was a thief."

"How old was she?"

"Who?"

"Mae Simon. How old was Mae Simon?"

More scanning of the space above my head. "Young."

"Where did Mae go to school?"

"How am I to know?"

"What did Mae look like?"

"Mae . . . was a shrimp." Her eyes sparkled. She was happy with herself for recalling this fact.

"Why did you stop talking to Edward and Donna Stockton?"

"Edward and Donna . . ."

"And their son, William."

A pause. Mom scratched her elbow, looked away.

"Mom, William Stockton. Do you remember him?"

"No."

"He broke your vase. Do you remember that?"

She shimmied herself to sit higher up in the chair. "No."

"Did you keep a journal, Mom?"

"My mother gave me a journal once."

"Did you write in it?"

"Of course. It would have been rude not to."

"Were you ever depressed?"

"Depressed? Catherine, please, I would never be depressed."

"Did you want to have more children?"

"No," she said, defiant, as though I were asking her to get pregnant again right now.

"Why did you have nannies raise us if you were home most of the time?"

"If one can afford help, one should hire help."

"Did you love Dad?"

"Yes."

"Did you love us?"

"Yes."

"Is there anything you want to tell me?"

"It's too hot in this room."

"What does 'Guilt is cancer' mean?"

"I haven't the faintest idea."

I took out my wallet, passed her the scrap. "Did you write this?"

"No."

"It's your handwriting."

She squinted at it. "I can't see without my glasses."

I handed her the pair that was on the table. "Put these on."

"No."

"Please?"

"I have a headache. Get the girl."

"Mom."

"Get the girl!"

I texted Evelyn. We waited in silence. Evelyn appeared a minute later.

"Mrs. West? You in here, Mrs. West?" Evelyn walked into the living room.

"You stole my earrings," Mom said.

"I wear no earrings, Mrs. West. Look." She tugged her earlobes. "You see for yourself. No earrings."

"Guilt is cancer," Mom said.

"Excuse me?" Evelyn put a hand on her hip with attitude. "It's time to take your pills, lady darling."

"Get my husband."

"Pill time." Evelyn took the MTWTFSS container off the counter.

"Bruuuuuuce!"

"Take these." Evelyn handed Mom two pills.

"I won't."

Evelyn sighed and plopped herself down on the coffee table. "We will just sit here until you do."

I was already looking up the name. There was only one Mae Simon on Facebook. Brooklyn, New York. The photo was a clear head shot of an older woman with short, badly bleached hair. "Is this her?"

"Who?"

"Put your glasses on, Mom."

Evelyn, without a word, put them on Mom's face.

"Is this Mae Simon?"

"Oh." Mom touched the face on the screen. "Mae."

•

Dear Mae,

My name is Catherine West. I think you may have been my nanny. I am very interested in meeting you. Please reply ASAP.
CW

22

On a bright August morning when the air was heavy with heat and exhaust, I officially sold the shop. It was the first time in my life I had wanted something tangible I could not have. We'd managed to survive three years and two months. Everyone kept reminding me of that. William, my rock of logic, put it in non-emotional terms: "To lose any more money on this venture would not be optimal."

We sold almost everything and gave the rest away. It was hard to watch people who had only discovered the shop during its Swan Song Sale (Maya came up with that—I refused to call it a Blowout Sale) say, "Why are you folding? I love this place so much!" But those people were mostly tourists from Ohio or wherever, and they were buying product at 10 percent of its usual price.

Maya was "honestly jazzed to collect unemployment," which at least made Vera laugh. "Vera," she said, "you can eat popcorn all day in your bathrobe and still make money. It's going to be great!"

"It's tragic," Vera said.

Caroline said we should throw a dinner party in the space on its last night. She would be in charge of putting everything together. I didn't love the idea, but nobody ever said no to a party held in their honor.

•

There was such a spirit of togetherness those last few weeks. We were on a ship that was going down, and we banded together with the common goal of just getting through it. I probably learned more about Vera and Maya then than I had in the last three years. Vera had been a kindergarten teacher? Maya preferred to date trans guys?

If this spirit of togetherness had existed the whole time, would we have survived? Of course I wondered that. But William kept assuring me that it was just a numbers game. People didn't want expensive cards in today's economic climate. End of story.

Susan and Henry dropped by with three dozen bonsai trees to give away to customers. "People aren't going to want these," I said. But Susan was right: people wanted anything that was free. Tourists found extra pockets in their backpacks. One guy put his in a baggie and hung it off his belt loop.

The artists who were actually making a little money were upset, but most of them weren't. Artists were used to curve balls. It was part of the gig. Bird dropped by to take some of her cards. She would sell them herself at an upcoming show. She said I was paying her so much for the mural that she couldn't be mad. She assured me she had gotten keys and was working hard and yes, it would be done on time and not to worry.

After that, I decided to send each of the artists a stack of their cards in thanks. That was the right thing to do. And it made me feel better. Swept up by the intense wave of my own do-goodery, I somehow decided that going to the post office myself, instead of asking someone else to do it, was a great idea. I hadn't been to the post office in years, and I immediately remembered why. It was overcrowded, and everyone there was in a bad mood. A woman wheeled over my foot with her grocery-cart thing and didn't even look back when I yelped. I stood there in line and checked my phone. Still no response from Mae Simon. Forty-five excruciating minutes later, when the package was finally out of my hands, I promised myself I would not return to a post office for a very long time.

•

The evening before he left for Europe, William and I took a stroll around the neighborhood with Herman. A girl in pigtails sat on the curb reading a comic book, a *Lemonade* sign resting against her knees. A woman with a shaved head and exceptionally strong shoulders pulled her spotted pit bull back when it leaped at Herman. "No, Tiffany," she scolded. The dog ignored this and leaped again, barking madly. "Sorry," she said to us.

Herman, from behind William's calves, squealed like a wimp. "Hermaaaan," William cooed.

"It's okay," I said to the strong woman, who was still there, her eyes like a kid's, waiting for affirmation.

Somewhere on Charles Street, where a man in a wool holiday sweater (why?) was kneeling on the ground, tying his shoe, William said, "You seem in good spirits."

"I know—it's surprising. I expected to be devastated right now, but I feel okay."

"You're thinking about the future."

"I am."

"About becoming my wife?"

"Yes."

"What do you think that will entail?" We stopped. Herman was peeing. "How do you think your life will be different when you are Mrs. William Stockton?"

"I will be officially yours then, and that makes me very happy."

"I feel the same." He took my hand and we continued walking like that, hand in hand around the city. I remember thinking, Catherine, this is what you have always wanted, and now you have it. Pay attention. Be happy. But as usual, I was worried. There was always so much to be worried about.

"I hope Mom will like you better by the wedding. She seems to be really holding on to this whole thing with the vase."

"Do you talk about me when you go there?"

"Of course."

"Has she said anything?" His eyes were on Herman.

"No, she just seems mad."

"About the vase."

"I guess so."

We walked through the arch at Washington Square Park and then around the fountain. It had been turned off for the day, but there was still water inside, and a curvy blond woman was standing there in a seashell-print bikini top and bright green basketball shorts, inspecting her belly button.

"Our mothers got along, right?"

"Yes, famously. They loved each other."

"Did you ever come back to visit us after you moved to Switzerland?"

"Not that I can recall. My father often returned for business, but I was in school."

"In boarding school."

"Yes. Catherine?"

"Yes?"

"May I ask you why you have these questions now? We've already talked about our mothers. Has something sparked your interest? Something in particular?"

"No." I coughed, which I had a tendency to do when I was lying. "I'm just curious."

"Are you sure?"

"Yes."

"All right. Well, I am of course happy to answer any questions you may have. Regarding anything. I am an open book."

"I know, I know, honey." I wrapped my arm around him. We watched the voluptuous bather make her way up the steps, her basketball shorts stuck wet around her thighs. "I want to ask you something. Not for any reason. I've just been wondering. Have you ever cheated on any of your lovers in the past?"

"No," he said. "Monogamy is important to me. I value commitment. I would never step out on you. Have you ever cheated on your lovers?"

"No. Well, okay, maybe once, but it was in high school. It doesn't count."

"Sounds harmless," William said.

"It was." I remembered the hot summer night that happened, and Ben's braces scratchy on my tongue. The weather that night had been a lot like this: balmy and still, a cloudless sky.

"I'm very sorry I'll miss the dinner at the shop. It sounds like it will be quite lovely."

"I hope it's not too stressful."

"You look wonderful this evening," he said. "Have I told you that already?"

"I think so." I laughed. I wasn't wearing anything special, just jeans and a blouse and black flats. "William?"

"Darling?"

"Do you believe in fate?"

He put his hand on the small of my back. "I believe God has a plan for us all."

"So that means you don't believe in coincidence?"

"I suppose not. Coincidence is merely a form of superstition."

I imagined a black cat walking under a ladder because that's what I always imagined when anyone said the word *superstition*. It was very limited of me, I know.

"Did you look for me when you came back to New York?"

"Look for you? Catherine." He laughed. "I didn't even know you existed."

"But you knew my mother was pregnant, right?"

"I did, you're right. I suppose I could have looked for you. But I would have had no way of knowing your name."

"You could have Googled it." I laughed.

"That's true." He put his hand on his head then, twirled his hair. "But West is a very common name."

"But you could have Googled Bruce and Elizabeth West."

"I suppose I could have. But I wasn't bright enough to do that."

"I guess it was fate then."

"I guess it was."

On the way home we passed a young man on the street with a change bucket and a cardboard sign that said *I'm an artist*. That made us laugh. I gave the guy a hundred bucks. William said, "So much?" I said, "Yes, your parents were artists! You know how hard it is!" And then we laughed again. I remember thinking, The couple that laughs together stays together. I was always doing that. The couple that strolls together stays together. The couple that goes to restaurants together stays together. The couple that hangs art together stays together. If there was anything to hold on to, I was holding on to it very tightly.

•

In the morning I was the best fiancée in the world. I handed him an espresso and straightened his tie when he walked into the kitchen. Lucia said, "Good morning, Mr. Stockton. I dry-clean everything."

"Thank you, Lucia. And please, call me William," he said for the eight hundredth time.

"William," Lucia said, though she pronounced it more like

"Willem." Sometimes I got the feeling there was a flirtation between them, more on Lucia's side than William's. Lucia showed an adoring deference to men in general, though. It had something to do with being raised in the extreme patriarchy of Mexico, where anyone with a penis was just one rung below God.

"It's going to be a great trip," I told him.

"Yes," he said. He slid one long arm into his jacket, and Lucia darted over to help him with the other. "Thank you, Lucia."

The gorgeous Trish emerged at the top of the stairs, ready to take Herman for his morning walk. How did she look so gorgeous at seven o'clock in the morning?

"Let me say good-bye to my little guy," William said. They had a long good-bye—long enough for Trish to check her watch and me to offer her an espresso, which she politely declined. Why did William let Herman lick his face like that? And why, when he kissed me a minute later, did I not object?

I did not object for the same reason I had gotten up early to make his espresso, and the same reason I had brushed my hair and applied concealer around my eyes: I needed William. I had always needed him, but now I really needed him. The money hadn't run out yet, and now I would get back what I'd put into the shop. But one day the money would run out, and all I would have would be him. I couldn't have articulated any of this at the time. What I thought at the time was, I am being a very good partner this morning. I love this man, I love this man, I love this man.

"I love you," I told him.

"I love you, too."

We all walked down the stairs together. Lucia said, "I bring your suitcase, Willem," and William said, "No, no, I'll take it, thank you." Trish and Herman walked off down the street, the driver took William's suitcase from Lucia, William and I kissed again. Then it was Lucia and me at the door, waving at the black Escalade as it disappeared around the corner.

"Very nice man," Lucia said, walking back up the stairs. She stopped to rub a spot on the banister.

"You really like him."

"He give me Christmas bonus. And we in summer!"

"He gave you money? How much?"

She widened her eyes. "Five hundred dollars."

My honest thought: That's not much; I'll have to give her more at Christmas. "Wow, that was very generous of him."

"Yes, muy generoso."

"I wonder why he didn't tell me."

"He said you no need to know."

"He said I didn't need to know?"

"Yes. He, uh, very humilde." Lucia nervously scratched her armpit. Maybe she realized then that she shouldn't have told me.

"What?"

"Humilde. With *H*."

"Humble."

"Humble," Lucia repeated. "One day I speak English perfect."

"Perfectly," I said.

"Perfect-lee."

•

His closet belonged in an advertisement for a closet: perfectly organized, all the things in it spaced perfectly apart. Suits, suits, suits. A bureau of undershirts and casual wear, all folded into orderly stacks. There was nothing tucked beneath the socks. Nothing in the pockets of the suits. Above and below, boxes of shoes. Below were the shoes he actually wore. Above were the ones he never did.

In the hall closet were his suitcases, more shoes, more suits.

On his desk, a stack of work papers. Contracts, contracts, boring, boring. Inside the desk was nothing interesting. Blank legal pads, a too-neat row of untouched pens, a stapler still in its box. The bottom drawer contained more work papers, a few gallery catalogs, a pair of Cartier sunglasses, two orange golf balls, and an X-Acto knife.

He'd added his books to the shelves: a bunch of coffee-table art books, a few boring investment books, Kahlil Gibran's *The Prophet*. I flipped to the part about the two cypress trees growing together but not in each other's shadow. Maybe I hoped to find it underlined. It was not. And actually, the book looked like it had never been opened. Maybe a gift. There was no inscription.

I sat back in William's ergonomically correct chair. It was made of a light mesh material, with a protruding headrest like a dentist's chair. The big wooden desk made me feel important. I imagined William feeling important as he sat here, in this gorgeous den, working at this desk. Did he ever turn on the TV? To watch golf, maybe, while he worked late at night?

I looked out the window. There was the trunk of my tree. There was a woman carrying a pie who said, in a deep baritone voice, "I know exactly how you feel." Was she on the phone or talking to herself? A cab drove by. I moved the mouse. The computer screen lit up. "William," it said. He'd chosen the icon of a hang glider. I couldn't get further than that. I didn't know the password. I tried his birthday. No. I tried my birthday. No. Our engagement date. Our wedding date. I tried random words. Geneva. Switzerland. Ilovebanking. No no no.

I opened the cigar box at the edge of the desk, picturing myself smelling one of the cigars and putting it back. But inside there were no cigars. There were pictures. Old pictures, in different sizes. The first one was very small, the size of my palm. Little blond William in a sailor suit. He was so cute. On the back, someone (his mother?) had written, "William, age 2."

"William, age 16," the next one said. Here William was onstage, playing the violin. He looked passionate and lanky. His shirt unbuttoned. His long hair was matted to his forehead. The photo had been taken from below the stage, by someone in the audience who was sitting very close to the front. That told me something: involved parents.

The next picture was of William and his parents on the boardwalk at Coney Island, the roller coaster in the background like a faint etching, the sky bleached. His father towered over his mother by a good two feet, looking stern. They were all overdressed. Not beach clothes but church clothes. His mother wore a blue felt hat with a feather in it and a green suit. William, who must have been around five or six (the back said nothing), stood in the center, wearing a suit just like his father's, holding his prize in a limp hand at his side: a goldfish in a plastic bag.

"William, age 14." A school picture. He wore a blazer with an emblem at the breast. The words were too small to make out. I assumed this was from boarding school. He looked like his gorgeous self, but thinner, his cheeks hollowed out. His eyes were the same: deep blue and very focused.

The back of the next photo said, "William, Michelle, Pierre, Edward, and me, Catskills." A black-and-white, no one smiling except for young William, who appeared to be seven, maybe eight years old. He knelt between Edward and Donna, hugging a dog—one of Pierre's, no doubt. And in the background, art, of course, but it was tacked to the wall, not framed. This must have been Pierre's studio. Pierre was grizzly and unshaven and smoking a cigarette. He was also notably older than Michelle, who had her arm around his waist. Michelle looked familiar to me. Her thick-framed rectangular glasses . . . Michelle, Michelle. And then I got it. Michelle Bellario, the sculptress. Famous for her sculptures of pillows. Michelle was one of those people I saw all the time at openings but didn't really know. She still wore those glasses—the exact same style. Her calling card. Smart. I did remember that Pierre had a girlfriend named Michelle, but I hadn't realized until now that it was *this* Michelle. And she'd been friendly with the Stocktons? Had she known my family, too? She must have. The art world. It was so, so small.

The last picture was of William lying next to his mother. It was more recent: 1996. He appeared to be dozing off. Her long arm was draped over his shoulder. They weren't posing; it was a candid shot. His mother wore a white tunic and sunglasses on top of her head, her hair in a loose bun. William also wore white. Their white shirts and the bright, bare glow of the sun gave the impression of Africa, or the Mediterranean. Her skin was the exact color of a Starbucks Caramel Frappuccino. She had long, sloping features, and her face was like the mold of a face set in clay and left to drip: nose stretched and thin, downturned mouth, the wide, sad eyes of a basset hound, drooping at the corners. Just as he had said, they looked nothing alike.

That was it—the box was empty. I put the photos side by side on the desk, and I began to string a story together. William had had a happy, well-groomed childhood. His dad had been a total asshole. I was sure that that fish had died three days after that photo was taken, or had lived an incredibly long time, as goldfish won at carnivals tend to do, or so people claim. He had been very good at the violin if they'd let him play a solo. This suggested greatness, which his asshole father demanded of him at every turn. He had excelled academically. He was the best in the class. He was the valedictorian, or the runner-up. He did this both to spite his father and to please him. His teenage years had not been miserable, or at least not outwardly. No acne, no braces. And he and his mother were obviously very, very close.

I hadn't known what I was looking for when I started looking through his things that morning, but when I found these pictures, I understood. I had been looking for a way in: something to make me feel like I knew William beyond the surface of what he presented. I reminded myself it wasn't William's fault that he was a private person. That was his nature. I would not try to change him. I would respect his need for privacy. Also, even if he had described these moments to me, he wouldn't have fully been able to. The deficiency of language—words could never fully capture a moment. Maybe images couldn't fully capture moments either, but they certainly helped. I now had a sense of his past. The photos filled in the blanks. They provided a picture of William's innocence. William, the innocent boy. William, the innocent teenager. William, the innocent man. I would hold on to this for a long time.

23

Sunday morning I skipped church, despite what William had said: "It would be nice for you to go and keep Marge company." I didn't like church enough to go there alone. I worked out with Chris and went to the shop instead. Maybe I should have canceled my massage—we had only a few days left at the shop, I should be there all the time—but Chris assured me I would need it after the workout we'd had, and also I was stressed. (Was I ever not stressed? Was anyone?)

At three I opened the door, expecting Dan, but there was Max, holding his violin.

"Hi, Mrs. West." He shifted the case from one hand to the other as though it weighed a thousand pounds.

I looked down the street on both sides. No sign of his mother. "Did your mom leave already?"

"Yeah, she has errands," he said, in a rote way that made it clear he said this a lot.

"Okay, well, come in. Maybe we can call her and ask her to come back. William's not here. He's out of town."

"Really?" He widened his honey-colored eyes, flushed with a new energy, so excited he wouldn't have to practice today. He even did a little jump.

My automatic response to this was not leniency. I said, "Maybe you can practice here anyway, in the study." God, I sounded like my drill-sergeant mother. When had I gotten so old? I was not old. I backtracked. "Or we can just eat cookies."

"Cookies," he said eagerly. Then, in a serious tone, "Cookies."

In the kitchen I gave him a Coke and in the pantry found a bag of cookies I'd never seen before. I grabbed a Pellegrino for myself and sat on the couch with him, thinking, If you drop a chocolate chip on my white couch, I will murder you. But he was careful, or well bred, or both. He held an upturned palm under his chin to catch the crumbs. I was impressed.

"Okay," I said, "what's your mom's number?"

He told me. I dialed. "What's your mom's name?"

"Doreen."

That was an unfortunate name. Doreen didn't pick up. I left a message. "Hello, this is Catherine West, William Stockton's fian-cée. William is out of town, so there won't be a session today. If you could come back and pick Max up, that would be great."

"She never checks her voice mail." Max chewed his cookie, looked around. He was bouncing a little on the couch. Sugar high. "I'm glad William isn't here."

"Because you don't have to practice today?"

He tapped his Tevas. They looked oddly clean. Maybe they were new. "Yeah."

"Do you like coming here and practicing with William?" God, did I sound like my mother again? What was happening to me? Also, why was I talking to Max like he was four? He was nine.

"No."

"No? Why not?"

"Ummmm . . ." He took another cookie from the bag and inspected both sides before biting. "I don't know."

"You don't know?"

"Can I have another soda?"

He'd finished that one already? "Sure." I went to the fridge, hoping two sodas and cookies weren't enough to induce heart palpitations in a young child.

"Thanks." He opened the can easily, like an adult, no fumbling.

"So why don't you like practicing with William?"

"He's weird."

Yeah, okay, I could see how a child would think William was weird. He was so tall and so strangely articulate, with his heightened dictionary way of speaking. That would be weird to a kid.

"Why is he weird?"

Max bounced on the couch. "I don't knoooooow."

"Is he weird because he's so tall?"

"No."

"Why then?"

"I told you, I don't know."

Being around Max made me uneasy. I didn't really know how to act with kids that age, because they were little versions of actual people. They knew things, but not everything. How much were you supposed to tell them? What were you supposed to say?

I thought of the picture of William playing the violin. That was a good segue.

"Have you ever played a solo?"

"No."

"Do you like the violin?"

"I hate it."

"Do you want to see a picture of William playing the violin when he was younger?"

"No."

Well, at least he was decisive.

"Can I watch TV?"

"Sure."

He took the remote from the coffee table, turned it on. He

knew how to use that remote better than I did. Was I supposed to pick a channel for him? Tell him what he could and couldn't watch? He found the Disney Channel and set the remote down. Okay, Disney seemed appropriate.

"Can I have more cookies?"

I almost said, You're going to have to watch it. Once you stop growing vertically, you will start growing horizontally if you keep eating like this. That was one of my mother's favorite lines. "Of course," I said, and got up to find more cookies. These were some artisanal chocolate-dipped wafers wrapped in a bow that I had also never seen before.

"These look weird," he said when I handed him the bag.

Good, he used the word *weird* for everything. This meant that William being weird held no weight.

"Try one," I said, impressed by the solid combination of sweetness and firmness in my voice.

I was nervous as he undid the bow and looked at one of the wafers like it was going to taste bad. But then he ate one and said, "It's good."

"You're welcome," I said.

"Thank you, Mrs. West," he said, like a machine.

"You can call me Catherine."

Eyes on the screen, mouth full of wafer, he said, again like a machine, "Thank you, Catherine."

"You're welcome."

The Disney sitcom tackled the issue of school bullying. That seemed useful. The bully pressed the nerd into a row of lockers and hissed, "I don't like *kids*," and the whimpering nerd said, "But you're a kid, too, Tony. Please don't hurt me." During the commercial break—Go-Gurt, Cinnamon Toast Crunch, Legos—I asked Max, "Are people nice to you at school?"

"I guess."

"Are you nice to the other kids?"

"Yeah."

"Do you and Stan hang out at school?"

"Only in Music."

"Why only in Music?"

"I don't know."

The answer was obvious: Stan was a nerd and Max was a cool kid. But at least he wasn't a bully like Tony, who wore a puffy duck-hunting vest and had a mullet. He'd also grown up in a trailer park. He was troubled, we should understand.

I tried Doreen one more time. No answer.

I took a picture of Max laid out on the couch (he'd taken off his shoes now and was petting Herman) and sent it to William. I wrote, "Hanging out with Max!" After I pressed Send, I worried this would be interpreted as passive-aggressive, so I added: "And having fun!"

•

Dan smelled like lavender. He wore a new necklace that appeared to be made of hemp or twine or something earthy and his usual massage uniform. I explained about Max.

"No worries," he said. "I can hang out."

I got him a Coke and we all sat on the couch. A new episode of the same Disney show had started.

"Can I have one of those cookies, man?" Dan asked Max.

"They're wafers," Max said, and tossed him the bag.

I felt awkward. What were we supposed to be doing right now? I was bad at unstructured time. I texted Marty. Facebook. Still no word from Mae.

"Where do you live?" Max asked Dan during a commercial break.

"In Brooklyn," Dan said. "Where do you live?"

"Two-twenty-nine East Seventy-Ninth Street, apartment four." His eyes went back and forth between Dan and me. "Are you guys brother and sister?"

"No man, we're friends."

As we sat there, I thought two things. One: Am I having fun right now? And two: I want to put my legs on Dan's knees. Which was strange. But it meant nothing. No. All it meant was that I missed my fiancé.

•

Doreen arrived late, disheveled and out of breath. Every time I saw this woman she appeared to have just escaped some traumatic event, which may or may not have taken place on a boat. Her wardrobe had a consistent nautical flair. Today she wore brown tasseled loafers, cream linen Ralph Lauren pants, a navy blouse, and a matching navy hat with an oversized brim. Unless she was on her way to the Hamptons right now, this outfit was out of place. She looked like a distorted, weathered version of Max: same brown eyes, but darker; same nose, but wider; same thin lips. Her face was freckled like Max's, but much more heavily, and her skin had the yamlike quality of someone who had spent a childhood in direct sunlight without protection. Maybe the hat was an attempt to reduce further damage.

She petted Max's fine black hair roughly, like he was a horse. "So sorry I'm late," she said. I placed her accent somewhere north of here, maybe Boston; it was the way she said "Saw-ry." I wondered if she'd been born into money—a shipping family, a lobster dynasty—or come into it later. Did she carry that blue Birkin with a guilt-ridden pride, knowing how much it could be replaced for?

I explained about William being gone. "We watched some TV

and had a snack," I said, hoping she wouldn't ask me exactly what
the snack was, but something about Doreen told me she wouldn't
care that much.

"Max, what do you say?"

"Thanks, Mrs. West."

"Catherine," I said, reminding him.

"Thanks, Catherine."

Max slogged down the stairs with his heavy violin. Doreen followed. Her walk was like a prance, like an Aerosoles commercial:
look at that spring! "Would you rather come with me to get my
glasses fixed or go home and watch TV?" she said, stepping onto
the sidewalk.

"I'll come with you," he said, excited he'd been given this
option. As they walked off, I thought it was sad that Max wanted
to hang out with his mom more than he wanted to watch TV. I
thought, If it were me, we'd go to the park, not to LensCrafters. I
thought, Life is so unfair. Doreen gets to be a mother and I don't?

•

Dan and I meditated again. I was better at it this time, though
I did keep opening my eyes to make sure he wasn't opening his. He
wasn't. The timer on his phone went off—the ding of a gong that
reverberated—and we Om'd. He bowed. I copied him, unsure,
feeling silly. He opened his eyes.

"See? That wasn't so bad, was it?"

"Were you always so calm, Dan?"

Dan laughed. "You think I'm calm?"

"Are you kidding? Compared to me, yes."

"That's funny. Most of the time I feel completely crazy inside."

"Really?"

"Of course."

"Do you think everyone feels like that?"

"Some more than others. But yes, overall, I'd say we're all crazier than we let on."

"Interesting."

The massage started. We kept talking. About his roommate, Florence, a mixed-media artist who was interested in photographing the insides of convenient stores, and his dog, a Lab named Gandolf. We ended up on the subject of the Counting Crows. What had happened to them? "If they're still touring, we should go see them," I said.

"Definitely," Dan said.

"I think William would love to come. I know he likes them, too." This was a complete lie. I'd never heard William listen to any music besides Berlioz. Even on his runs I think he listened to Berlioz.

"Great. We should all go."

"How are you doing with your breakup?"

"It's hard to say. We're still friends, but I'm not sure we should be seeing each other so much. At least not right now."

"Right."

"It must feel wonderful to have met someone you want to spend the rest of your life with."

"It does, yeah."

A long pause.

"What are you doing on Wednesday?"

"I'm not sure. Do you have a referral?"

"No, I'm wondering if you want to come to the shop for dinner. It's a good-bye dinner."

"I'd love to," he said, and of course I immediately assumed he was using me. He thought the party would be a good place to get more clients.

When Dan kissed me good-bye that day, like he always did, I felt guilty. I shouldn't have invited him to the party. I shouldn't have invited him in to sit with Max and me on the couch. Had we really talked about seeing the Counting Crows together? What was I thinking?

Right after I closed the door, I called William. He didn't pick up. I left a voice mail. "Hi honey, how's your trip going? I'm thinking about you. Max and I had fun together. I'm, uh, just getting dinner ready now. I miss you. I'm so happy I met the person I want to spend the rest of my life with. Okay, well, call me if you get a chance. If you're busy, that's okay, don't worry about calling. We can talk whenever you want—I'm here."

24

I spent the next three days working nonstop. My back hurt. The feeling of togetherness dissipated into a mild, chronic angst. Vera, looking haggard in a gross T-shirt that was probably her son's, was too depressed to be very productive, and Maya had school.

I brought Lucia to help me pack up the office and do errands. She was happy to be out on the town, wearing real clothes instead of her cleaning scrubs. She even liked going to the post office. There were many interesting people at the post office, she said, to which I said, "There is something wrong with you."

Dan e-mailed me about the Counting Crows. He sent a link. I didn't click on it and I didn't write back.

I kept checking Facebook. Still no word from Mae. Either she was busy, or conflicted about meeting me, or I had sent a message to some completely random person named Mae Simon.

Caroline wanted to know who else to invite to the party. I told her to call Susan. I mentioned I had invited Dan. She said that was "surprising." I was short with her. "No," I said, "it's really not that surprising."

"And William's not coming, right?"

"Right."

"Bob's not coming either. He's going to a conference," she said sadly. "You know in that movie about Enron? How the guy cheats on his wife and stops at the gas station after to spill a little gas on his clothes on purpose so he doesn't smell like perfume?"

"No."

"That's all I keep thinking about."

"Caroline, we live in New York. Bob doesn't even drive."

"We do have a car."

"Okay, but you never use it."

"That's not the point."

"Does he smell like gas?"

"No, he smells like Bob. I keep checking."

"Don't invite Mom to the dinner. I think it will be too much."

"I know. That's what Evelyn said."

"I have to get off the phone now. I need Tylenol. Lucia, can you get me Tylenol, por favor?"

Lucia gave me a thumbs-up.

"Okay, bye," Caroline said. "And don't worry about the party. It's going to be fabulous."

•

I was convinced the party would not be fabulous. It felt wrong to be standing there in a dress (Stella McCartney, black), drinking champagne and chatting when there was still so much to do. But of course that wasn't actually true. Mostly everything had been done. Besides a few candles and the mouse to the computer (I had to remember to take that stuff home), everything was packed. The movers would come in the morning. This was it. I kept looking around thinking, This is it. The space, bare as it was now, reminded me of the day I had seen it for the first time. Those were the only things you remembered about a place, really: the day you moved in and the day you moved out.

Caroline had hired a good catering company to do a buffet-style meal, which was set up on a few round tables so people could mill around them instead of having to stand in a line. Somehow they had confused Caroline's order with someone else's and brought folding canvas chairs with little drink holders on the sides instead of whatever she had chosen. They were red and blue and would have been perfect for a tailgate on the Fourth of July. They looked ridiculous. "We thought this was an outdoor event," I heard one of the caterers tell Caroline. Of course we would go out with camping chairs, I thought. It's always something with me. Everything that had happened to me in this space was just so incredibly wrong. Including the terrible saxophone Musak someone had wrongly chosen—it sounded like we had been placed on hold.

Susan put her little arm around my waist. "You're starting anew!"

"Cheers to that," Henry said. He had traded his cutoffs for slacks and still looked exactly like a gardener from a '90s movie. This meant his hair was the culprit, not his shorts.

Caroline seemed unhappy but she was holding it together. She kept checking her phone. I guessed she was waiting for a call from Bob.

William e-mailed me. I read it aloud to Henry and Susan: "'Give everyone my love. On to bigger and better things!'"

"Bigger and better!" Susan said.

Lucia was having a ball talking to Maya in Spanish, and Maya was having a ball telling everyone about her grand plans for unemployment. She planned to learn origami now while eating popcorn on her couch. "How sad," Vera mumbled, and drank more pinot grigio. When the sun went down, she said, with her head hung and her eyes glassed over, "This is the last time we'll be here when the sun sets."

"Unless it becomes a Marc Jacobs!" Susan said.

Jeff stopped by for a drink. He said the blinds for the house were coming. There had been an issue at the manufacturing plant. "Of course there's an issue!" I said. "It's always something with me!"

Trish stopped by with Herman. William had asked her to, she told me. People seemed to get a kick out of him for about one minute, and then it was time for him to leave.

Marty showed up with his boyfriend, who looked like a twelve-year-old model from Siberia. He wore a white T-shirt with a deep V-neck and a long gold necklace with a feather at the end. He stood with his bony hips jutting forward. "Hey, I'm Cass," he said, in a surprisingly deep voice that proved he was probably legal. Cass was obviously a made-up name, and I wondered if Marty had named him.

"Tomorrow we're back on the wedding full force," I said to Marty.

Marty rolled his eyes. "I'm ready for you, honey."

Cass took an olive out of his martini and held it between his fingers like he was doing a photo shoot for an olive campaign. "So," he said, "cards?"

"Yes, we sold cards here."

"That's très," he said. "I love cards. I love getting them, and I love writing them, even though I don't write them enough." Marty put his chunky little arm around Cass's tiny waist. "Except to Marty. I write Marty cards."

"I love your cards, baby. Even though they're mostly napkins."

"That's true."

They did an air kiss, and when I looked beyond them, Henry and Susan were hugging each other, swaying to the elevator music. I missed William. I felt lonely and alone. And then Dan arrived with a girl. My instinct was to hide behind someone, but none of the people at this party were tall enough to hide behind.

The girl wasn't particularly sexy. Or maybe she was. She looked like a scholar. Short hair, glasses. Anyone with short hair and glasses looked smart—unfair advantage, and it didn't necessarily mean anything. People with long hair had to work so much harder to prove their intelligence. She obviously did all her shopping at J. Crew: black stretchy jeans, a paisley button-down, black Mary Janes with girly pink stitching. She was probably from Greenwich, and she had probably gone to Harvard. Was she the ex?

They moved toward me. Dan wore a casual outfit of black jeans and a black button-down. The black on black was a poor choice—he looked like a bartender or a barista—but the J. Crew scholar obviously wouldn't have been able to tell him that.

"Hi." He kissed my cheek. He smelled like sour patchouli. "Thanks so much for having us. This is Ellen."

Her name *would* be Ellen.

"Hi, great to meet you."

"You, too. Dan has told me so much." Ellen was so confident, she didn't even need to finish her sentences.

"Are you Dan's roommate?" I knew his roommate was Florence. I hadn't forgotten that name, but I could play dumb. Women with long hair could play dumb better than women with short hair. That's what we had and I was going to use it.

"No, we're friends," Ellen said, a little too quickly, and locked her eyes on Dan. There was obviously a lot going on here. She had to be the ex.

"Well, help yourselves to drinks and food—there's so much!" I motioned to the spread.

"I'll get us drinks," Dan said, not asking Ellen what her drink was because he already knew.

"Thanks." When Dan walked away, Ellen folded her arms across her chest. She smelled like a discontinued scent from the Gap. "So what are you going to do now?"

"I'm planning my wedding. I don't know if you've ever planned a wedding, but it's a full-time job." I sipped my chardonnay, which was now warm.

"No, I'm too young for marriage. I'm only thirty."

"Yeah, I thought that at your age, too." I said this condescendingly, and gave her a look of understanding that made it even more condescending: you don't know anything about the world.

Unflappable Ellen looked at me like she felt sorry for me and said "That's interesting" in a way that showed no interest at all.

Continuing the thread of her original question—what was I going to do after this?—I said, "I am also in the middle of renovating my home, so that will take up a lot of time. And my mother has Alzheimer's."

"Sounds like you'll be busy," Ellen said. Had she not heard the part about Alzheimer's? This was when she was supposed to say, "I'm so sorry."

My heels were killing me all of a sudden. When I shifted my weight, I lost my balance, and Ellen saved me from falling by grabbing my arm. "Whoa," she said.

I stood back up, fixed my hair, and pretended the almost-fall hadn't happened. "Yes," I said, "I will be very busy."

Dan returned with drinks, and I excused myself and went to the bathroom. I wanted to text William and tell him how much I missed him, but this seemed pathetic, and then he would know I wasn't enjoying the party.

When I looked in the mirror, I expected to find a sweaty, cakey, upset-looking face. I even prepared to sigh. But I looked good. Maybe a little tired, a little thin, but overall, good. This may have been why I went to the bathroom. Mirrors reminded me that it was what was on the outside that counted. I wasn't transparent. I was real, solid, pretty. If I felt like a mess, nobody had to know that but me.

This was a good time to take pictures, I decided. Caroline had brought a camera, and she'd taken a few, but I thought Dan should be the photographer now. My sister shouldn't have to be the photographer. It should be Dan. He and Ellen were the most random people there. They didn't need to be in the photos. It made the most sense.

I took the camera off the table in the back where Caroline had left it and walked straight to Dan. "Dan? Would you mind taking a few photos of everyone? Maybe some candid shots, and then we can get everyone together for a group shot."

"That's a big camera," Ellen said.

"Do you know how to use a camera like this?"

"Sure," Dan said. He tried to make eye contact. I looked at the plate of chips and hummus in his hand. I waited for him to put it down. When he did, I put the camera strap over his head. "Please keep the strap on—this is expensive."

"Sure, no problem."

"Thanks so much."

I went to get a cold chardonnay. Ellen and Dan stood with their heads close together, pushing buttons on the camera and talking. Maybe about what an asshole I was, but I didn't care. No, I didn't care at all.

Everyone in the room looked happy except for Vera, who'd been slumped like a dead animal in that blue canvas chair for way too long, and Caroline, who was checking her phone again. I would go console my sister because despite what Ellen and Dan might be saying about me, I was a very good person.

My sister looked so thin. Her collarbones protruded like handlebars. I didn't know if I was disgusted or jealous. "Have you heard from Bob?"

She looked up from her phone. "We're having a fight over text."

"Oh, Caroline, I'm so sorry."

She flopped her arms over my shoulders. Was she going to cry? I couldn't deal with that right now. I pulled away.

"He's saying he has to stay in Chicago longer."

"For the conference?"

"Yeah."

"Well, that seems normal, right?"

"I don't know what normal is." She looked exhausted.

Dan snapped a picture of us from across the room. Good, a picture of me being a good sister. Nice job, Dan.

"William is traveling for work right now, too. It's okay."

Caroline put her hand on her cheek. "I don't like it," she whined.

"I don't like it either, but they'll be back soon." I put my hand on her bony shoulder. I was aware of Ellen watching us. "Okay?"

"Okay," Caroline said.

"Let's enjoy the rest of this party. Do you want to go sit in one of those camping chairs?"

"Oh my God, I'm so sorry about those."

"Don't worry, it's fine. I think it's kind of funny."

We sat by the wall with Vera, who was now roughly massaging her neck. I made sure Caroline sat next to Vera, not me. I felt too guilty to be near that woman.

I half participated in a conversation about MTA renovations with Vera and Caroline and kept my eyes on Dan. He was doing a great job as photographer. Ellen stood alone, eating cheese, not looking uncomfortable at all. She was so confident, she didn't even check her phone. Eventually she started speaking Spanish with Maya and Lucia. They were close enough so I could hear. She didn't know how to say *insurance* in Spanish so she said that in English. She was asking Lucia if she had health insurance. Lucia said, "Yes, yes, Miss Catherine gives it to me." Ha, bitch, take that.

"Everyone please get together for a group shot!" Dan said. He was taking his little job so seriously. It annoyed me, how good he was.

We all gathered by the front. Maya, Vera, and I stood in the center, with Caroline next to me. I tried to ignore Ellen, who stood behind Dan.

Dan said, "Okay, now let's do a silly one." Caroline immediately broke out into a crazy shape and stuck out her tongue. Vera, her face sullen, flicked the camera off. Maya pouted and looked over her glasses. I made a mean face. I meant it to be funny, but when I would look at this picture later, the funny part wasn't apparent. I just looked mean.

After that I was done taking pictures. I asked Caroline to go get the camera from Dan, which she did. I had another drink and waited for this party to be over. At ten the caterers had to go. I was glad about that. Vera said she would gladly take the leftover bottles of wine home with her. Susan said, "Call me tomorrow, bitch." Ellen, with vacant, unappreciative eyes, said, "Thank you for having me." I was not impressed. Dan said, "Yes, thanks, and I'll see you very soon." He didn't mention his unanswered e-mail about the Counting Crows.

Caroline, Lucia, and I were the last people there. I needed help getting these candles home, and I had asked them to spend the night. I didn't want to be alone. Lucia was going to come back in the morning anyway, so it was no problem. Caroline was indecisive. She wanted to spend the night, too, but she felt bad for leaving the kids, but she really wanted to stay. "If Bob gets a vacation from parenting, I should get a vacation from parenting." She texted her "team" to let them know. She had 24/7 service anyway, so it didn't really matter.

Lucia and Catherine waited on the sidewalk while I said goodbye to the shop. I walked into my office for the last time. All the hours I had poured into this. All the days spent working at this desk. What had been the point? What had I learned from this? Why was Susan a better businessperson than I was?

I closed the office door and stood in the near-dark of the space I had come to know so well. Jeff had executed the shelves for the cards flawlessly. I hoped whoever bought the shop would leave them up. I noted the small, familiar imperfection on the floor. For some reason, it had always reminded me of a seashell. I hoped the next person would leave that, too. I reminded myself of what William had said. To lose any more money on this venture would not be optimal. Over three years—that was a long time. That's what I would say when I talked about it later. Three years in this economic climate—wow.

I walked around the perimeter, trailing my fingertips on the walls. I stopped, put my cheek against the wall. I must have been deliriously tired—what was I doing? Then I kissed the wall. The imprint of my pink lipstick was so faint, I doubted that anyone would notice it later.

•

Lucia slept in the guest room and Caroline slept in my bed. I gave them each some pajamas. Lucia wanted to wear the ones she'd gotten me last Christmas. Caroline, in bed, said, "I love the skylight—I can see the moon." I felt like we were kids again. Maybe we had always been kids. We just had credit cards now, and homes, and men, and cellulite.

"If Bob is cheating on you," I said, "you should go to therapy."

"We're already in therapy."

"You never told me that."

I could see the outline of her profile. She opened her mouth. She waited for a second before she said, "I thought you would judge me."

"No," I said.

"Mom would judge me."

"That's true."

I wanted to tell her about the journal, but I couldn't do that—she'd want to read it. I couldn't let anyone read it, not yet. I had to figure out what it all meant first. Why had Mom written the Stocktons were "set to go back as it is"? And what the hell did "Guilt is cancer" mean? And did any of this mean anything? I imagined that when I found out, I would say, Oh, this was all a big misunderstanding. I was trying to connect dots that had no connection. Making something out of nothing as usual, Catherine. You are so paranoid and you have always been so paranoid and you think the world is out to get you when really the world doesn't give a shit about your silly little life.

"Bob was different when I first met him," Caroline said, her voice thinning. "I think he was nicer. His job has gone to his head."

"Really? He's a pediatrician. And he seems pretty nice to me."

"He's always nice in public."

"What's he like at home?"

"I just feel like everything I do annoys him."

"I'm sure that's not true."

"Am I supposed to change now that he's different? I don't even know how to act."

"Just be yourself."

"Are you yourself all the time?"

"Oh God, Caroline, you know I hate philosophy."

"It's not— I'm just asking a question."

"Am I myself all the time? Yeah, I am," I said without thinking, because it was the right thing to say, and I was the older sister, so I would act like the older sister.

"I don't even know who I am right now. I think I'm having a midlife crisis."

"You're only thirty-seven. It's kind of early."

"Maybe I'll die early and this is the middle of my life."

"So you'll be dead at . . . seventy-something."

"What? You're supposed to tell me I'll live forever! Or at least long enough to see my kids grow up." Caroline laughed and hit me with a pillow.

I hit her back. "How am I supposed to know how long you'll live?"

She was going to hit me back but then didn't. We were silent for a while. There was just the sound of Herman snoring in the corner. When I looked up at the skylight, the same stars were there, and the moon.

"Catherine, what am I going to do if Bob leaves me?"

"He's not going to leave you, and even if he does, you'll find a way to be okay."

I had the briefest recollection of my old psych professor in college who used to say, "The advice people give is usually the advice they need to take themselves." Then I remembered that professor had taken a semester off to take care of her own mental health (she thought it was important to be honest about this, given her field) and so everything she had ever said was easy to discount. She was crazy. But it bothered me that this line had stuck with me for so long. And I knew I should be taking my own advice. If William left me, I would probably find a way to be okay. And if I never had a baby, maybe that would somehow be okay. And if the money ran out—well, that didn't seem okay at all, and there had to be a way around it.

"You're such a good person, Catherine. I'm glad you met William. He's a good person, too."

"Yeah, he really is."

Herman stirred, let out a little bark. Maybe a bad dream.

"Even though I don't love that dog. He's kind of high-strung."

"I know, thank you. There is something wrong with that dog."

"Maybe he was beaten as a puppy."

"Don't say that, then I'll feel bad for him."

"Oh. Well, if you feel bad, go buy him a new jacket or something."

•

The next afternoon I met Susan at Bloomingdale's for frozen yogurt and shopping. She wore a hairy pink cardigan and said, "You look great," before she'd even really looked at me.

"I'm worried—"

"Order, you're up." We had reached the front of the line.

We ordered small, sugar-free, fat-free vanillas. We sat in the corner. I was cold, too cold. Why were all frozen yogurt places freezing inside? The place was packed, full of people and their Big and Little Brown Bags.

Susan set her cup down on the counter. The yellow spoon she had stabbed into her yogurt fell to the side in slow motion. She checked her phone. "Sorry," she said. "E-mails."

I stirred my yogurt. I didn't feel like eating. Food was such a waste of money most of the time.

"So how are you? I would be freaking out if I were you." She stirred in a noncommittal way. The pearly buttons on her pink cardigan shone like little moons.

"I'm worried." And I whispered the next part: "About money."

"Don't you have the money from the shop now?"

"Yes, but—"

"That's not going to last."

"Exactly. And if I can't get pregnant?"

"Shit. But William has money, doesn't he? How much is that ring worth?"

"I don't know."

"How much do you have saved?"

"I don't know. Not a lot." I was clenched, cold again. The more yogurt I ate, the colder I got. Why weren't we having hot chocolate or tea? Maybe I didn't want to be in this conversation. Maybe I didn't want to be telling Susan these things. But didn't I have to? Didn't you have to tell your best friend everything? "I have the house."

"Yeah, but Catherine, come on, that only matters if you plan on selling it."

I was positive about what would happen next: Susan would ask me how much I needed and offer me at least a million dollars, maybe two. She was richer than me anyway, very rich. Her trust was five times the size that mine had been. But she didn't offer me money. She said, "Have you thought about suing your mother?"

"What? I don't even know how that would work."

Susan stuck a pensive finger in the air. Her nails were a nude color. Not the best choice—it washed her out. "It would probably be easier since she has Alzheimer's, right? She's incapacitated."

"I think this year has been eventful enough. Also, suing my mother?"

"Sorry. I'm just looking out for you." Susan took the only bite of the frozen yogurt she would take. It was mostly melted, and dripped from her spoon. "At least when she dies you'll get something."

When I looked at Susan then, I thought, Who are you? And who does that make me? I had never questioned my friendship with Susan, ever. She was a pillar in my constantly-falling-down life. Not knowing how to address this in the moment, I did the mature thing and changed the subject.

"How's Henry?"

"He's a doll." Susan checked her phone. "An absolute doll."

"You're going to stay with him for a while?"

"We'll see," she said. "You know I would never say yes to that question. Anything could happen." She laughed. "Clearly, as your situation has taught us."

I forced a smile. "You know," I said, "I'm feeling nauseous all of a sudden. I think I should go home." I didn't bother to say this in a believable way.

"No shopping?"

"Not today. Maybe another time."

"Okay, honey. Call me. Call me if you need anything at all, okay?" If Susan believed in regrets, I might have thought she looked regretful then, ashamed that she'd suggested I sue my own mother. Or not. Her face was so frozen with Botox, it was hard to tell.

25

William came home looking dead tired and extremely tan. "Many outdoor restaurants," he explained. "And Michael insisted I go to a tanning salon with him."

"Your boss made you go to a tanning salon?"

"He didn't force me. I agreed to go."

"Oh my gosh." I thought this was hilarious. "Bankers at a tanning salon, that's great."

"It was rather comical. I'd never been to a tanning salon before. They gave us small goggles."

I wrapped myself around him. "I love how eccentric you are."

"Am I?"

"Yes."

"I've missed you, Catherine."

"I've missed you, too. Don't go to work today."

"Unfortunately, I must."

"Sit with me first. Just for five minutes."

"That would be wonderful."

We sat in bed together. With Herman, of course, who was psychotically happy about reuniting with his master. I leaned into William, put my head on his shoulder. He felt so warm and good and sturdy and he was playing with my hair and I loved it.

"What else did you do over there?"

"Nothing of interest. I saw the inside of the hotel most of the time."

I thought of the two orange golf balls in his desk and how he had never talked to me about golf. "Did you play golf?"

"No, I didn't play golf."

I squeezed into him. "I just want to hold you here all day, I'm so happy to see you."

He stroked my hair. "Yes," he said. "I'm sorry Max showed up. I was sure I told his mother I would be gone."

"It's okay. It was fun."

"How was he?"

"Who, Max? He was great. Give any kid some sugar and they'll be happy."

"Point taken. And how is Caroline?"

"She's fine."

"Bob called me. He was concerned that she spent the night here."

I hadn't mentioned this to William because I knew he was kind of particular about his space, and he might have been bothered that Caroline had slept in his spot in the bed.

"She did, yes." I raised my head off his arm so I was looking at him. "Bob called you about that? Why?"

"I think he was worried." He took a strand of my hair and ran his fingers all the way to the end.

"Caroline thinks he's cheating on her."

"Oh? I hope that's not the case. That would be devastating for Caroline." He looked genuinely upset, and I thought that was very sweet—how protective he felt of my sister.

"Did Bob mention anything about it?"

"No, he did not."

"Would you tell me if he did?"

"Yes," he said.

"Really?"

"Yes, I would tell you—of course I would. And I would tell Caroline. Absolutely." He traced his fingers down my spine. "The party was nice?"

"Yes, it was nice." I didn't feel like talking. I just wanted his body there next to mine.

He looked at his watch. "That's five minutes. I have to get dressed for work, my darling."

"No." I squeezed him. "Don't leave me."

•

After he had showered and dressed for work, he went down to his office and called my name. "Catherine, can you come down here, please?"

He had a thing about not yelling. He had actually suggested installing an intercom system to avoid yelling. So I was surprised he hadn't walked up the stairs to tell me whatever he was going to tell me.

I pushed the swinging door open. He was sitting in the green mesh chair, facing the window. He swiveled around. His hands were folded in his lap. His hair was still wet. He wore an off-white shirt, or was it white? It was hard to tell.

"What's going on?"

"Come," he said.

Why was he being so serious? Was this a role-play thing? Were we going to fuck on the desk now? But then, when I got closer, I saw the open cigar box in his lap.

"Did you open this?"

How could he possibly have known? I had put everything back exactly as I'd found it. Okay, maybe I had forgotten the order of the photographs, but who would remember that?

"Yes."

"Please don't go through my things," he said, his voice as steady and mild as always.

"Sorry, I just . . . I was in here, and I just opened it." My body was tense. I wanted him to say, Come sit on my lap, it's okay. "I'm sorry. You look so cute in those photos though. I loved looking at them."

"If you had asked to see my photographs, I would gladly have shown them to you."

"I know, I'm just . . . You weren't here."

"I need you to respect my things."

"I do respect your things."

"So this won't happen again." He closed the box, put it back exactly in the spot where it had been. It looked like he was even measuring it against one of the wooden swirls on the desk. Maybe that's how he had known: I hadn't aligned it correctly.

"No. I'm sorry."

He sat back in the chair, looked directly at me. "I accept your apology. Thank you."

"You're welcome. And you can look through all my things if you want." I forced a laugh.

"I would never do that," he said. "If I looked through your things, I wouldn't respect you."

I nodded. "I understand. I'm sorry."

"Are you sure you understand? I need this to be very clear."

"I understand."

He nodded. He was happy with my responsiveness. He opened his arms like I wanted him to. "Come here."

I went. I hugged him. I was still standing. He didn't get up from the chair. It was an awkward position. My sweat was drying on my temples now. It felt cold. He kissed my forehead. "I must get going," he said. I let go of him. He took his briefcase off the floor. I followed him to the front door. "Behave yourself today," he said to me, and winked. A young woman walked by on the street, carrying a fake Louis Vuitton and looking very insecure. She was probably new to New York. She probably wanted to be me, the long-haired woman with the hot guy who lived in the gorgeous house in the West Village.

The driver (I could never remember his name) opened the door of the black Escalade and William got in. He didn't look at me, he didn't wave. I watched them drive away and felt guilty. William was right. It was unfair of me to go through his things. William was right and I was wrong, and going forward, I would be better.

•

That afternoon I sent him tulips at work with a note: "Thank you for your forgiveness. I love you. C." I went to the expensive dog store. I bought Herman three sweaters, a dog cupcake, and a bag of bones. No, it wasn't cheap, but these were gifts. Buying cheap gifts would just be cruel. I would save money in other ways.

I went to Whole Foods and bought food that was not premade. Stuffed bell peppers had been one of our staples growing up. I would make Esmeralda's stuffed bell peppers. If Mom were lucid, I would have called and asked for the recipe. I felt sorry for myself, thinking that I couldn't ask her now. I felt sorry for myself thinking about how cold it was in the produce section. With heavy fingers, I typed "stuffed peppers" into Google on my phone.

I bought brown rice and mushrooms and garlic and onions and a bunch of spices. When I got home, it turned out I already owned all these spices. I would have Lucia take the doubles home. I didn't want William to see I'd made a mistake.

I texted William: "Did you get the flowers? ☺"

He wrote: "Yes, thank you."

Fine, I thought, don't give me a smiley face, I don't deserve one.

I wrote: "I'm making dinner! ☺ What time will you be home?"
He wrote: "7."

I put on a cute apron with cherries on it and I slaved. This assuaged my guilt. The more my makeup melted off my face, the better I felt.

"Stuffed bell peppers are easy and fun to make," the recipe said.

"Or not," I said. I could never understand why people liked to cook. It was so much work for the twelve minutes it took to eat the thing you had made. I preheated the oven, I cooked the rice, I sliced the tops off the peppers and removed the seeds, I sliced the onion. When my eyes watered, I thought I deserved that. I put on my sunglasses to reduce the tears. It helped, sort of. Lucia laughed when she saw me. "Miss Catherine!"

I kept chopping. I was trying to get it done quickly. I could barely see. "Lucia, take these spices home."

She picked up the red pepper flakes, shook them. "Okay." She stood there, watching me.

"Yes, Lucia?"

"I stay and help?"

She had already changed into her street clothes: a jean jacket and jeans. Was she on her way to a square dance? Her shift was over. But that wasn't why I said no. I wanted to keep slaving. I deserved this punishment. "No, go home and rest."

"Okay." She took a wooden spoon from the drawer and stirred the onions for me. "You stir," she said.

"Yeah, okay, thanks. Bye."

"Bye-bye." When Herman jumped up her leg, she said, "No! Bad! Bad!" Herman actually stopped, and retreated to his igloo.

I forgot about the rice and it burned and I had to cook more rice. I managed not to burn the onions. I managed to stuff the peppers and put them in the oven. I set the table. The good china. And candles. I thought about the better china I had registered for.

That would be nice. We could get rid of this old stuff. Lucia could have it.

Caroline texted: "What are you doing?"

I wrote: "Cooking."

She wrote: "Why?"

I decided to write to Mae Simon again, even if it was the wrong Mae Simon. "Hi, it's Catherine West. If that name rings a bell, please respond ASAP. I will pay you to respond at this point."

At 6:59, when the table was all set and the peppers had been plated, William wrote: "Sorry, client dinner. Don't wait up." I might have been glad. I had done all this work, and he hadn't showed up. I was the good one now, he was the bad one.

I put the peppers in the fridge with attitude, and I left our place settings and the unlit candle on the table so he could see what a thoughtful homemaker I was.

The woman in the tapestry watched me. Her worn and hollow gaze, she was always watching. I hated her. Especially in the last panel, curled at the foot of that mountain like a weak little bitch, I hated her.

I wrote back to William: "No problem, honey!"

Then I went for a run. I took William's route up the Hudson. These were the things William saw. The lights on the water, and New Jersey, so close. It was windy, the water was choppy. My hair flipped around violently. I pumped angry music. I felt strong and alive. I ran for half an hour straight before turning back, and I ran the whole way back. It felt good to know that I was capable of running for this long. If I could run for this long, I could endure anything. I wondered how long William could go without stopping.

•

The next morning I awoke to him watching me. "Hello, my darling," he said. "You look like an angel."

I smiled, touched his leg.

"It's Saturday."

"I know."

"Thank you for the lovely dinner. I saw it in the fridge. And for the flowers, and I also saw the things you bought for Herman. You are going to make a wonderful wife."

"You're welcome."

"I'd like to spend the day with you," he said, "unless you have other plans."

"No," I said, "the weekends are for you."

"For us."

He seemed to be waiting for me to say it, too. If he wanted me to follow him, I would.

"For us," I said.

After we made love, William pressed my knees into my chest for me. I smiled convincingly and tried to breathe.

•

We went to a new gallery on the Lower East Side. The outside looked like a warehouse and the inside was renovated. Well, partly renovated. This meant it was in the perfect stage of gentrification—on its way up but not yet overly popularized, and still a decent distance from the nearest Whole Foods. The walls were freshly painted, and the cement floor was covered in a mess of drippy accidents, which was either authentic or staged to look artsy—it was hard to tell.

William thought it was important to expand our collection with more Asian pieces. The artist whose work he had brought me here to see punched holes in canvases and sold them. The small canvases had one hole. The larger canvases had more. They all looked the same, except for the slightly different ways in which the canvas material had happened to rip.

Connie, the gallerist, who wore jeans rolled up to her calves and four-inch stilettos, assured us these were very important pieces. They intoned movement. She used the word *violence*. She used the word *post-postmodernism*. This artist was blowing up in Japan and the American market was only just catching wind. It was the perfect time to buy.

"Yes," William said, "he's getting quite big. He's a lovely man, he deserves it."

"You know Chino?" Connie said, obviously impressed.

"I do. He owes me a piece, in fact. He sent me here today to pick one out."

Connie took a long look at William. And then she said, "Cool."

"I like this one," William said about a larger piece with three holes.

"This one is very diverse," Connie said.

It took me a second to realize they were waiting for my take. "Diverse," I repeated.

"Do you like it?"

"I appreciate it for what it is," I said. It was definitely something people would talk about when they came over. A great conversation piece. "Can you frame it?"

"Of course, and you'd want to, to protect the canvas."

"Right."

"Connie, may Catherine and I have a moment?"

"Of course."

Connie teetered back to her little black desk in the corner.

I looked at the canvas. William set his chin on the top of my head. "What do you think, Catherine?"

"I'm not sure. What do you think?"

"I like it. But if it's not your cup of tea, we can hold off."

Was it my cup of tea? It could be, I guess. I knew Susan would like it. Caroline probably would, too. And Dan— But who cared about what Dan thought and why was his existence even crossing my mind?

"I think it will spark conversation," I said, and gave myself two points for using the word *spark*.

"I agree."

We stood side by side, looking at the piece. We were close but not touching. I felt the electric field between us. I wondered what color it was, if it had a color, and came up with green. The electric field between us was like a bunch of green fireflies, lighting up at random. My eyes had focused on the shape of one of the holes. I wanted to say it looked like a star, or an octagon, but it didn't. Its shape wasn't obviously anything I could name.

"Should we take it then?"

Obviously he wanted it, and he was getting it for free, so there was no reason to disagree. "Sure," I said, "let's take it."

"Wonderful." He seemed suddenly more awake. His eyes flickered and then settled back on the punctured canvas. He put his arms around me. Acquiring art always turned William on. It probably made him feel powerful.

"Connie, we'll take this one," he said, barely raising his voice. The echo carried easily through the expensive garage.

"Good choice." Connie teetered back toward us. "I'll just have to check with Chino. I believe he's in Ireland at the—"

"You can deliver it next week," William said.

"Right. I—"

"Thank you, Connie. Have a lovely day." William took my hand and led me out of the cool, shadowy space and into the sun.

•

We went to lunch to celebrate. A hole-in-the-wall Italian place. William ordered us a bottle of prosecco. I thought of my mother.

"Cheers to our new piece," he said.

"Cheers." We clinked. The couple that acquires art together stays together.

Still high from the acquisition, he ordered oysters and said, "I'd like to take you skiing in the Alps someday. There is a small town on the Swiss side, Crans. You will love it. Maybe Caroline and Bob can join us."

"That would be great." I didn't like to ski—I didn't like any sport where the getting ready took thirty times longer than the sport itself—but skiing in the Alps was different. It was the Alps. I also didn't like oysters, but I didn't tell him that. Gwen had probably loved oysters. Later I would tell him. I would tell him once we were married. Once we were married, he couldn't leave me so easily. Once we were married, I could be more honest.

"Does Caroline like to ski?" he asked.

I wanted to say, Why do you care if Caroline likes to ski or not? But then his phone beeped, and he said, "It's Michael. He'd like to go tanning here in the city."

"Maybe Michael has a crush on you," I said.

He didn't answer. He was typing.

"Are you going to go?"

A pause. We sipped. He chewed a morsel of bread.

"He is the boss."

"Well, the color looks great on you."

"Thanks." He smiled.

"It makes your smile so white."

He smiled more, still looking at his phone. "It says on my calendar we meet with the priest tomorrow—is that right?"

"Yes. What kind of stuff is he going to ask us?"

"Have you not done your Catholic research, darling? I'm surprised. You're so good at research." He winked. This was obviously a reference to my snooping.

When I said, "Please be nice to me," I reminded myself of Caroline.

"I will be," he said, and touched my hand. "So, tomorrow." He sat up straighter. As usual, the restaurant furniture made him look huge. "The priest—Father Ness, right?"

"Right."

"He'll ask us what readings we might want, and about our relationship. What our plans are in terms of the future. Finances. He'll ask us if we plan to have children." He smiled. "Have you been feeling any symptoms?"

"Of pregnancy?" I reached for my prosecco. "No signs yet. I'll let you know, don't worry."

"Good." He squeezed my hands. "And finances. I don't think those are a problem for us. And, well, especially if we have a baby, they won't be a problem."

Convincing smile.

"Although it might be beneficial to talk about that in more detail—the everyday purchases. I noticed, for instance, that you spent over $200 on things for Herman."

"How do you know that?"

He ripped off a new morsel of bread. "I saw the receipt."

"Is that a problem?"

"No, I'm not saying it's a problem." He put his hand on my hand again, moved my ring from side to side.

"I still have my own money, William. And I'm happy to keep using that for as long as you want me to." I said this very sincerely because I didn't mean it at all.

"Oh, Catherine, no. I can see you're upset that I've brought this up. I am merely saying that when one is no longer receiving deposits from one's trust, one might like to be careful."

"I think I am being careful. I cooked a budget dinner last night. That whole dinner barely cost anything to make." That wasn't completely true. I had somehow spent $140 on my ingredients.

"Yes," he said, "and the bell peppers looked lovely. I will eat one later."

"They were lovely." I pouted.

The waiter set down the silver tray of oysters, their greasy bodies like oil spills. Those shells probably weren't even real. They were probably from the 99 Cents store. And the big cubes of ice—how tacky, they couldn't even get the small ice. William took an oyster, diligently squeezed lemon and then Tabasco on top, and tipped it back into his mouth. I could see the knob of his Adam's apple working as he swallowed.

"Please, have one," he said, and put an ugly oyster on my plate.

I added lemon slowly, then added more lemon. He was watching. I waited for the right moment. I wasn't sure if I would really do it or not, and then I did it. When he looked down, for just a split second, to adjust his napkin, I dropped the oyster on the ground. "Oops," I said, and in the commotion—the waiter coming to clean it up, William saying, "Oh, what a pity"—I topped off my prosecco and quietly drained the glass.

26

We attended mass before our meeting with Father Ness. The theme of the day was grace. How does God's grace save the believer? I tried, but I just couldn't connect the dots. Save the believer from what?

William was his usual serious church self, sitting upright like a soldier. He held the book for us when it was time to sing. I sort of hummed along. William preferred me in a dress. I wore the blue one he had called "breathtaking" once. He wore his usual suit and a hand-painted tie with imperfectly spaced dots on it.

As I watched him take communion, I thought, as usual, that he was the most handsome man in the line. I didn't see Marge anywhere. I hoped she hadn't died. She was my favorite thing about church.

•

The small courtyard behind the church offices was scattered with leaves. Our white wrought-iron chairs were chipped and uncomfortable. Just as Father Ness appeared in the doorway, William leaned over and said, "Don't mention that we live together. It's against protocol."

Father Ness had taken his robe off and now wore black pants and a black short-sleeved button-down with a white band at the neck that looked like a dog collar. His skin was sagging, and the whites of his eyes were a yolky yellow, and his cheeks were hollowed out to almost nothing, but his friendly face was working hard against all this decay. He reminded me of an overanimated preschool teacher. This was clearly a man who was determined to be optimistic despite it all.

"Hello, folks." He sat down, opened a ratty binder. "How are we doing today?"

"Very well, Father, and yourself?"

"Always feel better after a service." He clapped twice. "So." He flipped the pages in the binder. "I assume you want a marriage service?"

"Yes," William said.

"What does that mean?" I asked.

"It's shorter than the nuptial mass, darling," William said.

"Great," I said.

"Any preference on readings? We'll pick one from the Old Testament, one from the New, and one from the Gospels, in case you didn't know, Catherine."

"No, I didn't."

"What would you suggest, Father?"

"Genesis two-eighteen from the Old Testament, Letter to the Hebrews from the New Testament, and from the Gospels, I like to recommend Mark ten-six."

"I see," William said, considering this. "Those sound perfectly fine to me."

Father Ness wrote that down with his golf pencil. Without looking up, he said, "Catherine, does this sound good to you?"

"Whatever William wants," I said.

"Very accommodating," he said slowly, concentrating. "All righty." He turned to a new page in his binder, with a badly pixelated heart icon at the top and a list of questions. "Now for the fun stuff. How did you meet?"

"At an art exhibition," William said.

"Here in New York?"

"Yes."

"How long have you been together?"

"Since May."

"Love at first sight then."

William put his hand on my knee. "Yes."

"And where do you live?"

"I live on the Upper East Side and Catherine lives in the West Village." I was impressed by the ease with which William delivered this lie. I'd never heard him lie before. He was confident. I would have believed him if I didn't know the truth.

"Catherine, what do you love about William?"

"Oh, wow, putting me on the spot here. Okay. Well, I love William's kindness, and how hardworking he is." William smiled. "His smile."

"Good. William, what do you love about Catherine?"

"Her good nature, her home-cooked meals, and"—he looked at me—"how I feel safe in your arms."

"Great." Father Ness wrote that down. "Now let's talk about family planning. Here are some pamphlets." He flipped back and forth through the binder, finding none. "Where could they be? Oh, here we are," he said, producing a wilted pamphlet. "I only have one. You can share. Sharing! An important tool for marriage!" He handed it over. It was called "Together for Life." On the cover, a catalog man and woman stood together, with hokey rays of light expanding brilliantly between them. "Now, if you open it up, we'll start at the third section. Find it? Okay. These are the points we're going to hit." He peered over and read them upside-down, though it seemed like he had them memorized. "Develop effective communication skills. Practice Natural Family Planning. Pray together. Enjoy romantic time together. Managing your finances. Okay, number one. How is your communication?"

William and I looked at each other. "I would say we are good communicators," William said.

"You express love for each other frequently?"

"Absolutely."

"Catherine, you agree?"

"Yes."

"How do you communicate when there is an argument?"

"We don't argue," I said.

"Well, darling, sometimes we do. I do have one example. May I share it?"

"Please," Father Ness said.

"Catherine?"

"Please," I said.

"Recently Catherine went through my personal items. This upset me. I brought it up and asked her not to do it again. I think we resolved that well."

"Do you agree, Catherine?"

I was in shock—was he really telling the priest about this?— but managed to say, "I agree."

"Good. I know how you feel, William. I don't like it when my roommate cleans out my backpack."

I thought, Roommate? Backpack? Are you a freshman in college?

"Catherine, were you cleaning?"

"No."

William laughed. "Catherine isn't very fond of cleaning."

"So you clean then, William?"

"We have housekeepers," I said.

"Ah, how nice for you." Father Ness looked us over then, looked at our clothes. It seemed it had taken him until this moment to realize we might be rich. "William, I understand your distress. But when a couple is married, everything is shared. That is some- times hard, but it's how it goes. One must not have secrets."

"There are no secrets," William said.

"Catherine, would you agree?"

"Yes."

William squeezed my hand.

"Let's talk about the family. Do you plan on having children together?"

I looked at the dead leaves on the ground.

"As soon as possible," William said.

"Do you know how many?"

"One, at least," William said. "Or two if we're lucky."

"Great." Father Ness wrote a two. "Children are a real gift."

We smiled politely.

"Okay, on to the next. This can be uncomfortable, but we need to touch on sex. Until you are ready to have children, the rhythm method is the way to avoid pregnancy, as you must already know."

"Yes," William said.

"And as far as the sex itself, only moral sex acts are acceptable."

William didn't even flinch. "Of course."

"Enjoying romantic time and praying together. Tell me about that."

"Catherine and I are very romantic," William said. "We go out quite often."

"Where do you go?"

"Dinner," William said, looking at me. "Galleries."

"We walk the dog," I added.

"Good. And praying together?"

"Well, we could be doing a little more of that," William chuckled. "Right, Catherine?"

"Right," I said.

"You can start by saying grace before dinner," Father Ness said. "Even in restaurants, people do it. My roommate and I do it all the time."

"Uh-huh," I said. I wondered if they shared a backpack when they went out for dinner, too.

"Absolutely," William said.

"Finances. Tell me about that."

"I think we're okay." William squeezed my knee. "Right, Catherine?"

"Definitely," I said.

"Well," Father Ness said, "if you should ever find yourselves at a point where budgeting is necessary, I'm a fan of Microsoft Excel. I'm sure you know it."

"Yes," William said.

"A spreadsheet can be very helpful in getting down to the nitty-gritty."

When the leaves on the ground began to swirl madly and the first raindrop hit my face, I said, in a tone that suggested emergency, "It's raining." When Father Ness said, "I think that's about all we need to cover anyway," I thanked God for making it rain. It came down so fast, we all got wet. We stood in the doorway, watching the water pound down in sheets. "I need to laminate these pages," Father Ness said, brushing the droplets off his crappy binder with a sweep of his weathered, energetic hand.

•

In the cab William put his arm around me. I was wet and shivering. I probably wasn't even that cold, but shivering was something to do, and it was something that said, I am not happy.

"I think that went well, don't you?"

"I guess so." I put my arm around his chest. "But it was a little uncomfortable, honey."

"Because I was honest? About you looking through my things?"

"Why did you tell him that?"

"They always want to hear a little bit of dirt. This way, Father Ness knows we're working through our issues. If there were no issues, there would be nothing to work through."

"Okay, but why do you care what he thinks?"

"He's our priest, darling. It's important to be honest."

"We weren't completely honest though."

"We were honest about the things that matter."

"You're such a good liar," I said. "Oh my gosh, I even believed you."

"Well." He kissed my forehead. "I promise never to lie to you."

I remember we were driving by the Jamaican juice place on Houston Street, and I remember the island-blue color of its awning through the rain, and I remember a dad standing outside with a child on his shoulders. Though this could have been wrong. There could have been no dad. We could have been on a different street. I could have made it all up, I could have been seeing things. I could have been seeing only what I wanted to see and not the rest. "I know you'll never lie to me," I told him. "I know that."

•

As usual, Doreen was early with Max. He wore a black hoodie with bright white strings and an expression of defeat. "I'm in a rush," Doreen said, tapping her long umbrella on the ground. Her tangerine Ralph Lauren polo shirt was wet in splotches. The street was slick and black. For now it had stopped raining. "I hope you don't mind."

"No problem. We'll see you later."

"Thanks, Catherine."

"Mom, I want to go with you." Max groaned.

"Honey, you can't come with me. It's violin time. You need to practice. You want to get better, don't you? I'll be back in an hour." She looked at her watch. "Hour and a half. Okay?"

Max rolled his shoulders spasmodically. "I don't want to practice the violin today."

"Honey, I've got to go. Violin is important for college—trust me." Doreen blew a kiss and jogged away in her pin-striped skirt. The umbrella in her hand looked like a spear.

"Mom!" Max shouted. She turned and waved and then kept jogging.

I knelt to meet him at eye level, which was really, really nice of me. I was so nice. His eyes were the glowing color of a beehive. His long curly black hair hung over his face. "How are you, Max?"

"I don't know." He let the violin drop from his hand. It landed on the doormat with a thud. "Sorry," he mumbled.

"It's okay." I picked up the case. It was heavier than I thought. "I'll carry this up for you. Do you want some cookies?"

"Yes please, or wafers," he said, and followed me up the stairs, past the room where Stan was playing a song expertly, or at least that's how it sounded to my novice ear. I wondered if this bothered Max—the fact that Stan was better at the violin. Maybe that's why he was so upset. He sat on the couch, and seemed a little happier when Herman jumped on him. I brought him a Coke and some Oreos.

"Thank you, Catherine," he said.

I sat next to him with my Pellegrino. We listened to Stan play. "Do you know what song that is?"

"Yeah."

"What is it?"

"Allegretto, by Suzuki."

"Oh, do you like that one?"

No response. He twisted the Oreo until it came apart and licked the white innards.

"Have you been watching that show on the Disney Channel?" Wow, I sounded so lame.

"I don't know." He licked. "Sometimes."

"You like Oreos?"

"Sometimes."

"Are you okay? Is something bothering you?"

He tapped his black Converses together. "Yeah."

"What is it?"

When he looked up and I saw his eyes, I thought he might cry. "I don't know."

The violin lay heavy on the floor. "I know, the violin isn't your favorite thing."

"Can we practice in the living room with you today?"

"I have my massage."

"Oh." He slumped deeper into the couch and put a hand on Herman, who had curled up next to him.

"Don't worry, it's only an hour. And you can have another Coke afterwards, okay?"

"Yeah."

I wanted to hug him, but this seemed inappropriate, so I got him more Oreos instead. Then Stan stopped playing and we heard the door open.

"Want me to walk you down?"

"Yes please," he said. I picked up the violin case, and Max put his small hand in mine, which surprised me and sent an embarrassed rush of blood to my face. It also made me very happy. I was mother material.

When Stan saw Max, he said, "Hi Max!" He looked so excited.

"Hi Stan." Max barely looked up.

"Hello, Max," William said.

"Max, today I played our new song all the way through!"

"You certainly did." William clapped Stan on the back. "Great job today, Stan."

"Thanks William!"

"So," I said to Stan, "you're walking home by yourself?"

"Yes, Mrs. West. I walk everywhere by myself," he said proudly, his chest out.

William raised his eyebrows twice. "Be careful."

"I will. Don't worry, I never talk to strangers, and I always stay on my route."

"Good," I said.

Stan threw his case over his shoulder. "I'm going to go now. Bye Max. See you in Music!"

Max pulled at the white strings of his hoodie. "Bye."

"Ready, young man?" William put a hand on Max's shoulder and Max flinched. Then he walked into the room, his head hung, and joylessly took his violin out of its case.

"Bad mood today," I whispered to William.

"Maybe girl troubles," he whispered back. "Enjoy your massage, darling."

●

Without my asking, Dan told me that since the party, he and Ellen had decided to stop seeing each other, officially. "It's very hard to be friends with someone you've been romantically involved with and just stay friends, you know?"

I watched his toes curl as he pressed his fists into my back. "Yeah," I said.

"Did it bother you that I brought her to the party?"

"No," I said. "Why would it bother me?"

"I'm not sure. I'm not even sure why I'm asking." Did Dan sound nervous? He changed the subject. "I meant to bring you a peach from the farmers' market, but I left it in Brooklyn."

I thought of Mae Simon, who still hadn't written me back, and said, "I need to go to Brooklyn." Maybe I'd run into her there. She probably went to farmers' markets. She probably sat in cafés with her laptop, drinking the same drip coffee for hours, which is what I imagined everyone in Brooklyn did all the time.

"Please let me know when you do. I'll show you around," Dan said. "You and William."

"Great."

I drifted off. And then I was brought back to full consciousness when I heard yelling. It sounded like William was yelling at Max in the next room. It was muffled at first, and then I heard a distinct "This is unacceptable!" Dan stopped working, unsure of what to do. "Do you want me to go check?" he said.

"No, I'll go."

Dan faced the wall. I grabbed my robe and went to the music room, opened the door. Max was crying hard, his face pink and wet, and William was standing in front of him, hands on his waist. "Hi," he said to me. And then to Max, "Stop crying now, please." He put his hands on Max's shoulders and Max flinched. "Max, please stop."

"What's going on?" I said, moving closer.

"Nothing. Max is just feeling a bit lazy today. Aren't you, Max?"

Max buried his face in his hands.

"It's nothing to worry about. You're fine, aren't you, Max?"

Max said nothing.

"I'm only being hard on you because I want you to do well, Max," William said. "Because I care."

"That's right, honey. William cares about you a lot," I said.

"You don't even like kids," Max said. "That's what you said."

"When?" William said. "When did I say that?"

"Last time." Max wiped his face with his sleeve.

"That is a lie, Max. Little boys shouldn't lie."

"I'm not," Max said, looking at me. He was looking for help. But I honestly didn't know if I believed him or not. Max was a troubled kid—that was obvious. From what I had gathered about his mother, who was clearly unhinged, Max stood no chance. I also hadn't forgotten about the Disney show, how Tony the bully had said exactly what Max was claiming William had said, down to the words *I don't like kids.* This seemed like a too-big coincidence.

And though he shouldn't have yelled, I understood why William was frustrated. William loved the violin, and he wanted Max to love it, too, but Max hated the violin. This was a frustrating place to be.

I had to make a choice, and I chose William. I put my arm around his solid body and said, "You must be confused, Max. William loves kids."

27

"We're a month out, Cat, and I have bad news." Marty pulled his pink handkerchief out of his pocket and wiped his forehead. "Also, my God, can you please get an elevator? I despise these stairs."

"It is Marty," Lucia announced, too late. She was taking an English class now (Maya's suggestion), where she was learning the importance of enunciating (though she could not enunciate the word *enunciating* correctly) and taking every opportunity to practice.

Marty gave her a look. "Yes, it's Marty."

"Thanks, Lucia," I said.

"You are welcome." She swatted her rag at a fly on the counter and killed it. Then she picked up its dead body with her fingers and flicked it into the sink.

"My God," Marty said.

"No good," Lucia said, and walked away.

"That's right, Cat. No good. Problems. We have problems."

"What? Tell me. You're scaring me." I put my hands on my stomach. I felt nauseous. I was sure he was about to tell me the reception space had flooded. Maybe I'd been going to church too much; the idea of a great flood had been implanted in my mind.

"The photographer canceled."

"Can't we get another one?"

"I have two backups. Take me to your computer."

I pointed to it on the dining room table. The Neiman Marcus Web site was on the screen. I'd found a strapless teal Chloé dress I was very excited about.

"Good. And I need some water. It is too hot here. No one should be in this city today. What a nightmare. I'm dripping, look at me!"

It was true, Marty was dripping. "Sparkling or regular?"

"Sparkling, thank you," he said, and sat with a high-pitched sigh. "This is a hideous dress."

"Really?"

"Cat. You, in teal? Come on."

I grabbed a Pellegrino and two glasses and filled them at the table. Marty downed all of his and covered his mouth with his handkerchief when he burped. "Sorry, that was disgusting."

Yes, it was. And I looked good in teal.

"Okay. So here"—he turned the screen my way—"is the work of a very nice person, but her work might be too cheesy for you. And here"—he opened a second page, typed in a name—"is the work of a woman who is a total bitch, but her work is very avant-garde artsy-fartsy, which might be more you."

Their names matched their personalities. The first one's name was Trudy Beetle. And yes, her work was cheesy. The second one was Miranda Ply. She had lots of black-and-white and interesting angles. Her work seemed to capture the mood of each couple more accurately. It was almost unsettling. As I clicked through, I thought a few of the couples even looked melancholy. Happy, maybe, but also melancholy. In one picture the bride was crying, and I honestly couldn't tell whether those were tears of joy or tears of regret.

"Let's do the first one."

"Really? I'm surprised. But okay, I can see it. I already know Miss Trudy is available on the date because I called her this morning. That's how good I am."

"Perfect."

"I'll call to confirm." He dialed, held the phone a good inch from his sweaty face, leaned back in the chair. "Sure, I love holding. Who doesn't love to be on hold?" After Marty rolled his eyes, they settled on the tapestry and moved from one panel to the next— one, two, three, one, two, three—like he was reading. "Why'd she give up?" he said.

"What do you mean?" I turned to look at the woman in the last panel, her body curled at the foot of the mountain.

"Girlfriend gave up and went to sleep."

"Maybe she was tired." I didn't know why I was coming to her defense. It was true she had given up.

Trudy Beetle, or her assistant, took Marty off hold. "I need to book October seventeenth," he said. "Stockton."

Five seconds later he hung up. "Done. Crisis averted."

"Good."

"Now, other logistics." Marty took a folder out of his Marc Jacobs murse on which he had written *Stockton* in his very precise penmanship. I thought it was kind of interesting that Marty was a person who could call himself a perfectionist and still be overweight. Maybe everyone thought they were a perfectionist. He opened the folder, scanned the list inside. "Brunch. Where is brunch?"

"I don't know."

"How about Lupa?"

"Last time I went there, they were out of seltzer."

"But it's très. I'll make sure they have your seltzer, don't worry."

"Fine, let's do it."

"Done." He fingered his way down the list. "I got the plates you wanted. I texted you that."

"Good."

"We still need to figure out hair and makeup. I'll make appointments."

"Okay."

"What's the deal with the bachelorette party?"

"I don't know. Caroline's working on it."

"Good. I want to be invited."

"I'll let her know." I laughed.

"I'm serious."

"I know."

"Party favors. What are we giving people? You said no chocolate. What are you thinking? Tell me what you're thinking."

"I was thinking olive oil?"

"No. We aren't in Tuscany, Cat."

"Fine. What do you think?"

"Something artsy. Little sculptures of you and William. If they could also be salt and pepper shakers, that would make them useful. I'll look into it."

"Great."

"What's the deal with the honeymoon? Has William booked that?"

The honeymoon was the one part of the wedding William insisted he do himself. "I have no idea. It's a surprise."

"Any clues yet?"

"I have no idea. I'm hoping it's a beach."

"Tulum is very hot right now." As he continued down the list, he hummed a tune that went *ta-da, ta-da, ta-da.* "Done with this, got that. Okay, this is it for now." He put the paper back in the folder and the folder back in his murse and sat back in the chair with his hands clasped behind his head and said, "Aaah, thank God for air conditioning. I'm never leaving."

"We met with the priest."

"Tell me." He wiped something out of one eye. His lashes looked great. It occurred to me then that he probably got them dyed.

"It was interesting."

"How was the Catholic stuff?"

"Yeah. I mean, I guess it's kind of nice to have these traditions."

"You are a bad liar, Cat."

"I'm serious," I said, in an overly serious way. "But wait—you think I'm a bad liar?"

"Yes, you should never lie again. You're terrible at it."

28

Catherine!!
Thank you so much for writing!! Sorry it took me so long to respond. I never check Facebook!! I'm so happy to hear from you. ☺ I can't believe you're writing me and I would love to meet!! Are you free to come over on the 7th? We can make peanut butter bunnies!!
X X X
Mae

Dear Mae,
I would love to come over. Give me an address and a time please. I look forward to discussing things with you.
CW

Groovy. How about 3 p.m.? My address is 79 S. Portland in Fort Greene. Ring the lower doorbell because the upper one doesn't work anymore. Can't wait!! ☺
X X X
Mae

That works.
CW

29

I asked Evelyn to bring Mom to the dining room early so I could ask her about Mae Simon again. She was well coiffed and even gave me a smile, or the beginning of one, when she saw me. Evelyn was having the worst day of her life, as usual. They walked toward me, arm in arm, Mom taking careful steps and Evelyn a languid blob of frenzied tropical patterns.

"Hello, Catherine," Evelyn said.

"Hello, Catherine," Mom repeated.

Evelyn helped Mom into the chair.

"What are we doing *here*?"

"Lunch," Evelyn said. She pushed Mom closer to the table.

"I'm not hungry."

"Then don't eat," Evelyn said. To me she said, "Text me if you need me," and shuffled away.

"How are you today, Mom?"

"Hot."

"Really? I think it's kind of chilly in here."

"Don't be ridiculous."

"Mom, do you remember Mae Simon?"

"Your nanny."

"She was a student?"

"Yes."

"At NYU?"

"No."

"Where?"

Mom opened her mouth and waited a very long time and then closed her mouth.

"I'm going to go visit her."

When the words came out of my mouth, the whole thing seemed more real, and I wondered if this was a bad idea. Maybe Mae Simon was a crazy person. Who wrote letters to four-year-olds? Her use of two exclamation marks irked me. I thought people should commit to either one or three. Two was just a hyperactive version of one and a lacking version of three. I didn't want to tell anyone about my plans to see Mae Simon except for Mom, who wouldn't remember them anyway. I think that's why I went there that day—just to tell someone.

"Good," she said. "She will make you peanut butter."

"Peanut butter bunnies?"

A glint of recognition in Mom's eyes, or maybe I was imagining that. "Yes," she said.

This was consoling. If Mae had made me peanut butter bunnies, whatever those were, she must be a nice person.

Caroline appeared, ungroomed, looking like a person who might be on her way to the methadone clinic. She sank into her chair with a small "Hi." She was drowning in Bob's huge Nantucket sweatshirt. She had not showered. Her pearly white scalp was visible between oily ropes of hair.

The Indian man in black appeared with salads, and Caroline said, "Please, I don't want this. Just coffee."

"Good girl, watching your weight," Mom said.

In a flat voice—she was beyond crying at this point—Caroline said, "Bob has a mistress."

I put my fork down. Mom stabbed a crunchy piece of lettuce. "He told you that?"

She rubbed her eyes with the too-long sleeves of Bob's sweatshirt.

"Oh, Caroline, I'm so sorry."

"He has a mistress, and he wants to keep her."

"What?"

"Let him," Mom said.

"Mom," I said.

"You mustn't let him leave you, Catherine."

"He doesn't want to leave me. He wants to stay with me and keep his mistress."

"How long has it been going on?"

"They met a year ago. On a plane. She lives in Miami."

Just as I said, "Who meets someone on a plane?" I realized that Bob was exactly the type of person you would meet on a plane. He was the guy who ignored it when you put your earbuds in and asked you a question about the weather or the tray table or where you were going and why.

"I don't know." Caroline rubbed her whole face now like it itched very badly.

I would be uplifting, which was how you were supposed to be in situations like these. I made it about honesty because honesty was on my mind. "At least he was honest about it, right?"

"I don't know. I would almost rather not know. Even though I've known for a while, I just wasn't sure."

"Of course you would rather know."

"Would I though?"

"I would want to know," I said, very sure of myself, and then I wondered if that was true. Would I really want to know?

"He wants to spend one weekend a month with her. That's his proposal. What a fucking asshole."

"Don't curse, Caroline," Mom said.

"Oh my God, you called me Caroline. Thank you." She rested

her head on Mom's shoulder and was smart enough to leave it there for only a second before what we knew would happen did: Mom said, "Don't touch me."

"What do you get out of it?" I said.

"I'm now free to find someone on the side, too. That's how he phrased it. Bob is 'freeing' me." She did air quotes, but I couldn't see her fingers inside the sweatshirt. The coffee came. She looked at it like it was a brick, or part of the table, or nothing at all.

"Are you into that idea?"

"No. I mean—no. Would you be?"

"No," I said. "Sorry." Her face told me she didn't like that response, so I backpedaled. "But I haven't been married, so I'm not the right person to ask. Maybe it will end up being a good thing?"

"Yeah right."

"I'm sorry, Caroline."

Mom leaned toward me and whispered, "Catherine, you are the strong one," and ate the radish she had waiting on her fork.

"Mom, you're mean," Caroline said.

I waited for Mom's comeback—we never told our mother she was mean—but she ignored Caroline completely and vigorously chewed her radish.

I felt so sorry for Caroline that I said, "Want to get a mani-pedi after this?"

She didn't bother to look at her nails. "Not really."

•

After lunch we sat on a bench in Riverside Park. Caroline put her head in my lap and I stroked her hair because that's what I was supposed to do. I felt awkward. How long was I supposed to do this? Could I take a break? Would she be hurt if I took a break? Her hair was so oily. Did I have hand sanitizer in my purse?

I tried to keep it neutral. "How are the kids?"

"I'm a shitty mom." She curled her twig legs farther into her stomach.

"No you're not."

There was a long pause. A man, who seemed normal at first, threw half a cheeseburger down on the cobblestones very hard. It hit with a smack. I braced myself for ketchup spray. None came. A mess of crazed pigeons were on it immediately. I was hoping this event would change the subject for us, but it did not. "I'm scared of my kids," Caroline said, in the vacant, pared-down way of a person who has been completely exhausted by life. I wondered if she'd slept, but this seemed like a stupid question to ask.

"Why are you scared of them?"

"I don't know."

"Well, you love them a lot and they love you."

"And I love Bob and he loves me."

"Right."

A pause. A pause that said, Oh, but maybe that's not enough.

"Maybe you need a hobby." I was trying to be helpful, but it sounded like such a trite suggestion in this context. I continued anyway. "Why don't you start painting again? You're such a talented painter."

"Yeah?"

"Yeah. Make one of your guest rooms into a studio and just go in there and paint."

Caroline turned her face up and smiled at me. Her teeth were all perfect except for one; that one was curtain-shaped, the others were boxy. "I feel so much better when I talk to you."

My heart was pounding. My eyes blinked involuntarily, too many times. I tried very hard not to look away.

30

Susan told me to come to the shop because she had something to tell me. She waited for me outside and gave me a huge hug, which was a much grander reception than I'd expected. "Sorry for being a bitch at Bloomingdale's. I want to make it up to you. You must be so stressed. I was thinking about it last night—I couldn't sleep. Just the thought of losing all that money, oh my God. So I am going to help you."

Two million, I thought. Susan would offer me $2 million now.

She pulled me through the door. "You're going to sell your cards here."

Fuck cards, give me money! I tried to look appreciative. I didn't say anything.

"This will be your corner," she said in a hushed tone, so as not to bother the twelve—yes, I counted—customers, who appeared to be browsing with the intention to buy. "I'll ask Henry to clear it out."

"Did I hear my name?" Henry popped up into view—he was always popping up like that over the plants—with a turkey baster in his hand. He added a few droplets to the bonsai in front of him, a gnarled thing with yellow leaves.

"You're doing a great job, sweetheart," Susan said, and kissed the air.

"So put some cards here, okay? I'm worried if you don't have something to do, you'll get depressed and kill yourself," she whispered into my cheek, her scent an overpowering mix of coffee and Gucci Rush.

I coughed. "Thanks."

"Of course! I want to be a good friend!" She rubbed my arm. I smiled without teeth. And then Susan cocked her head and looked at me more closely. She was inspecting my face. "Why are you glowing? Did you call Dr. Butterworth?"

"No."

"Oh my God." She covered her mouth with her hand. Her nails were painted a teenage blue. Henry was making her young again, apparently. "Are you pregnant?"

•

I knew Susan was wrong, but I bought a pregnancy test at Duane Reade anyway. Yes, I hadn't had my period for a while, but that was normal for me. My cycle had been irregular since my twenties.

I went to a Duane Reade that was not my regular Duane Reade, because the guys at the regular one kind of knew me, and if I bought this and turned out not to be pregnant (which was what would happen), they'd feel sorry for me and I would be embarrassed.

I added some magazines and a few packs of Mentos to the pile so the pregnancy test wouldn't be alone on the counter. I thought the woman who rang me up gave me a look, though I might have imagined that. Tina Turner was playing. What's love got to do with it? What's love but a secondhand emotion?

I put the test in my purse so Lucia wouldn't see it when I got home. "Hello, how are you?" she said in her new phonetic way.

"Fine," I said, and went straight to the bathroom.

I followed the directions. I played the same Tina Turner song that had been playing in Duane Reade on my phone. I'm not sure why I did that. Maybe so I could keep the experience just to Tina Turner. If it was a no, which it would be, I would avoid listening to Tina Turner for a while.

I waited. I waited for a no, for a no, for a no. I was too old, I had fucked everything up with my abortions, there was no way.

And then, as with everything else in my life I had been so sure about, I was wrong.

In the tiny white square: POSITIVE.

•

After another trip to another Duane Reade (I had to walk a little farther, and I walked fast), I came home with five more tests and more magazines and Mentos and a strange key chain of a squealing dolphin. I'd been pretending to be interested in it so as to avoid eye contact with the clerk as she rang me up, and when she said, "You want that, too?" I said, "Sure, yeah, everyone needs a dolphin key chain, ha."

Lucia was vacuuming the bedroom when I got home. I gave her a no-talk-right-now smile and headed back to the bathroom, where I took all five tests with Tina Turner and all five said yes.

I called Dr. Rose and said, "I think I'm pregnant."

"I have a cancellation. Can you be here in half an hour?"

"I'll be there in twenty minutes."

•

Dr. Rose was a small, attractive Asian woman from Seattle who always wore spandex under her white doctor's coat. I liked her a lot. She had walked me through the Fernando abortion with no judgment. Or if she had judgment, she hid it well. She was professional. We also had a history together outside of work, which was why she fit me into her schedule so easily. She had dated Fernando's brother, Esteban, at Yale. In the past she'd said more than once, "You can call me Patricia. I know you socially." But I didn't want to call her Patricia. I wanted to think of my doctor as a doctor and not as a flawed human.

Dr. Rose had me take yet another test. (I had planned for this. I had chugged water at the sink before walking over.) I waited in the room, my eyes lost in a diagram on the wall. *Musculature of the Human Body.* I thought about texting William, but this seemed premature.

When Dr. Rose returned (there was a ruffle on the hem of her spandex crops today), she said, "The urine test came back positive. I don't have time for an ultrasound, and I'm going on vacation. Ralph and I are going to Belize. So we'll do the ultrasound when I come back, okay?"

"I'm pregnant."

"Yes. If you've been drinking, stop drinking. One cup of coffee a day, no more. Be wary of fish. I'll give you some literature."

"I'm fucking pregnant."

She put her hands on my shoulders, looked right at me. "You need to start eating, Catherine. I'm serious."

"Okay. I know. I will." I thought, For $10 million, I will eat cheeseburgers all day. Which was horrible. I told myself to delete that thought. Because I also truly wanted a child, I reminded myself of that. I had always wanted a child. The money was just a bonus, and it happened to be good timing.

"Can I call you in Belize? What if something happens?"

"You can call the office. Dr. Maslow is great. And listen, don't worry too much."

"I'll try."

"Just eat. Three meals a day at least, okay?" She wrapped her slender arms around me, which was both nice and, I thought, slightly inappropriate. "I'm so happy for you."

•

After it was confirmed, I walked through Midtown aimlessly in a tan Donna Karan dress, wondering about which day exactly the lucky sperm had made it. My breasts, which Dr. Rose had said would grow a lot in the next few weeks, suddenly did seem larger to me. And I had been hungrier. Was that true? Yes, I thought it was.

I was about to call William, and then I decided not to. I wanted to tell him in person. I would tell him in person when he got home from work.

I got myself a vanilla milkshake from Shake Shack and called Susan, who said she knew it, she was always right. And she was so, so, so happy for me. She also told me about something called pregnancy mask, which was a skin pigmentation that could happen during pregnancy. How had I never heard of that? Your face broke out in brown splotches. She'd seen it happen to a friend. But only one friend, only one out of a million, so I would probably be fine.

Caroline was ecstatic, of course. She also said pregnancy mask was incredibly rare, and since it hadn't happened to her and we were from the same gene pool, it probably wouldn't happen to me either. She was feeling better. Bob was in Miami, and she was painting today. "An angry painting. No one will want it," she said, "but I don't want to talk about that. I want to talk about you. I'm so happy for you, sis."

I called my mother next, whose reaction was, "Good." She sounded out of it, and distant, and disengaged. I imagined her sitting there in all the yellow, looking into space. "Are you happy for me?" I said. "Yes," she said, flat. I asked her if she knew who she was talking to, and she did. "Catherine," she said. I might have been hurt that she seemed to care so little, and sad that no matter how old I got, it seemed I would never stop needing my mother's approval. I would never be adult enough to grow out of that need. She was so withholding. She left so much unsaid. There were so many things I wanted her to say, so much more to want. I told myself what every pregnant woman tells herself: With my baby, it will be different.

•

I made dinner that night. I had a clever idea: eggs. The main course was an afterthought; I threw a salad together. I added black beans for protein. The important part was the eggs, which I hard-boiled. I presented them on little egg holders.

When William got home, I poured him a glass of wine.

"You're not having any?"

"Nope," I said.

"This is an interesting dinner." He cracked the eggshell with his spoon, peeled the shell with ease. He dropped the egg on top of his salad and sliced it up into neat, uniform slices.

I accepted that this clue might have been too obscure and said, "I have something to tell you. I made eggs for a reason."

William looked at his plate. "What reason is that?"

"I'm pregnant."

He swallowed quickly. I thought he might choke. "Truly?"

"Can you believe it?"

"Are you certain?"

"Yes."

He got up and walked around the table, Herman skittering in tow, and wrapped his arms tight around me. "I can't believe it. This is wonderful," he said. "Oh, Catherine, this is wonderful. I'm so relieved." He put his big hands on my stomach. "This is going to make everything right."

31

South Portland Street was the West Village on steroids: the trees were bigger, the buildings were higher. Moms and dads pushed strollers toward the park at the end of the block. Number 79 was a tall brownstone like the others, with tattered Chinese take-out menus and bits of newspaper littering the front. The doorbell set off a familiar tune inside. It sounded like the background music from Pac-Man. Someone shouted "Door!" and then there was the sound of tramping down stairs.

I might have been holding my breath as the huge door opened with a creak. "Kitty Cat!" said a dismembered voice, and then she was there: Mae Simon, my overweight hippie ex-nanny. Her round body and her twinkling fingers—she reminded me of a fairy godmother. Glasses with Glinda-pink lenses, a dress with Andy Warhol's face on it, which was so short I wondered if it was actually supposed to be a long shirt, and dirty bare feet. Her toenails were painted a shimmering purple. She threw her arms around me before I could say anything. "I'm so glad you're here! Oh my God! Your hair! It's so long!" She smelled like garden mulch, especially near her neck. In the mornings Mae Simon probably dabbed her neck with garden mulch oil.

"Let me look at your face," she said, and squeezed both my arms as she looked me over. "Yep, wow, it's definitely you." She had gray-blue eyes and gray-yellow hair, colors wrapped in a smooth fog that dulled them. Her skin was luminous like pearls, and dewy. "This is unreal. Just a second ago I was thinking, It's not going to be her, it's going to be someone else. But no, it's you. Do you remember me?"

There was something familiar about her presence, maybe, but she didn't look familiar. "I'm not sure."

"It's fine if you don't. You had so many people in that house all the time, it would be a trip if you remembered me."

"Yeah." I pulled my sweater tighter around me—something to do with my hands.

"Come in, come in." She backed away and held the door open. "Careful of the bike," she said about the bike that was hanging above the doorway. "Let's go down to the kitchen first. I'm making bunnies! And then we can talk upstairs."

"Great," I said, stepping into the big old house, which smelled deeply of yellow curry. A bookshelf was stuffed full of shoes—girly flip-flops and big construction boots—and then there were hats, too, and belts, crammed in and spilling out onto the rugs. Rugs of all different sizes and colors covered the wooden floors. Some were actual rugs. Some were just oversized pieces of felt.

Through an open door—the doors must have been ten feet tall—a huge mirror reflected a chandelier that had been strangled in a flurry of Tibetan prayer flags. The ceiling was covered with them; they'd been strung from different points along the wall to meet at the chandelier in the center. In a gallery with a price tag, this might have been called artistic genius, but here, in the dense curry air, it seemed more like the work of a stoner on an ill-advised mission.

"This house was built in 1892," Mae said. "Everything's original."

"Is it yours?"

"I wish." Mae laughed. "This is Philip's house. He's at work right now."

It was cooler in the kitchen, and dark. Pots and pans hung from a makeshift beam that was tied to the ceiling with thick, dirty ropes. At a large wooden table, two long-haired young men looked up from their tiny game of travel chess. The pieces were as small as fingernails.

"Catherine, this is Carlo." She pointed to the small one, whose spotty facial hair looked like continents on a map. "And this is Logan."

"What's up?" Logan had a full beard and a full head of hair tucked beneath his beanie. There was a tennis ball–sized hole at the elbow of his flea-market sweater.

"Nice to meet you," I said.

Above them was a large piece of loosely hung cloth that said, in bubbly letters, *Free Education for Everyone!*

"Come here, Kitty," Mae said, waving me over to the kitchen island. "Do you remember these?"

On a chipped dandelion-print plate were two pieces of toast cut into bunny shapes. Mae had spread them with peanut butter and covered them in banana slices.

"Oh my gosh, I kind of do remember these." I was pretty sure I was telling the truth, but the feeling of remembering them was so vague, I couldn't be sure.

"Groovy," Mae said. "Take one."

I did and bit into it. Exactly what I thought: peanut butter and banana. But it did taste better because of the care Mae had taken in preparing it.

"Mmm," I said. Some peanut butter got onto my chin. Mae held out a smelly rag. I hesitated.

"It's clean, don't worry," she said.

I wiped my chin quickly because she was waiting.

"Did you make us bunnies?" Carlo said.

"Yes!" Mae said. "There are more in the fridge."

"That is so thoughtful of you, Mae. You're the best." He looked at me. "Mae is the best."

"You guys!" Mae said, pulling out a chair at the table. "Come," she said, "sit."

I sat. Logan retrieved the other plate of bunnies from the fridge.

"So what do you do?" Carlo asked. A banana slice fell off his bunny onto the table. He picked it up and wiped the peanut butter residue from the table with his finger and licked it.

"I owned a shop for a long time. We sold cards. Well, it was art in the form of greeting cards."

"Cool," Logan said.

"Catherine was a very creative child."

"I was?"

"Are you kidding? You loved to draw. And you loved glue. You were obsessed with gluing things together."

"Really?"

"Yes. I thought you might have been getting high sometimes." I laughed.

"But not really."

"How do you guys know each other?" Logan asked.

"I was Catherine's nanny when I was twenty."

"Incredible," Carlo said. "That is the most amazing thing I have ever heard. Even though working as a nanny can be very difficult. My mother used to work as a nanny. Now she cleans houses in Florida. It's very limited when you don't have papers."

"Right," I said. "How do you guys know each other?"

"We all live here," Logan said.

"It's a cooperative house," Mae said. "There are seven of us. We cook for each other and do chores. It's a community."

"It rocks." Logan was smiling. Actually, he'd been smiling the whole time. He never stopped smiling. He was probably stoned.

"Does everyone have their own room?"

"Of course," Carlo said.

"Where do you live?" Logan asked.

"The Village."

"If I were going to live in Manhattan, I would prefer to live in the Village," Carlo said, stroking the continents on his face.

"What do you guys do?"

"We're artists," Carlo said.

"And Carlo is a great writer. He just hasn't accepted it yet," Mae said.

"Mae is a great paintress," Carlo said.

"Aw, thanks, Carlo," Mae said to him. And then to me, "I'll show you some of my paintings. Let's go upstairs."

"Sure."

"Oh, and Catherine, you should come back next week. We're doing Fifteen Minutes of Doing Something Now in the living room," Carlo said.

"You can do whatever you want for fifteen minutes, or you can just watch." Logan was still smiling.

"Anything," Carlo said, a serious look on his face. "You can do anything you want."

"You can even get naked," Logan said.

"Oh, please don't scare her. Come on, Catherine, come with me."

Who were these friendly semidegenerates? And what were they talking about? Fifteen minutes of what? And it was three o'clock on a Wednesday and no one was at work? And this owner person, Philip—what was he getting in return for letting these people live in his huge, gorgeous, falling-apart house? And why was he letting it fall apart? As I followed Mae up three long flights of stairs, I made an extensive list of improvement projects for this house, starting with the stairs themselves. They made so much noise: we sounded like a wooden roller coaster going up them.

"This is my room." I followed Mae through the open door. The room was huge. It was the same size as mine. There was her bed, and couches, and an alcove where she'd laid out brightly colored afghans beside three tall white drippy candles and a well-used purple yoga mat. There was even a fireplace lined with Russian dolls, tallest to shortest, and Mae's own personal chandelier, which was missing half its bulbs. I was skeptical of the rock crystals on the mantel.

The room was painted bright green on one side and white on the other. In the yoga alcove was a big collage of the Buddha. "I made that out of cutouts from *Yoga Journal*," Mae said. I thought that was clever. It also looked pretty good.

"This is a gorgeous space," I said.

"Thanks. I love it here." Mae Simon, overweight and wearing a shirt as a dress, did not seem bothered that she was almost sixty and lived in a commune with people who were obviously much younger than she was. She seemed content, humming as she opened the shutters to let more light in. Too content, maybe. Was she stoned, too? The pink lenses of her glasses and her lack of pants were not helping my efforts to take her seriously.

"That's one of mine," she said, gesturing to a small painting between the windows. A hyperrealistic spider in an intricate web. I didn't buy this kind of stuff for myself but appreciated the painstaking work that went into it. It suggested an immense amount of patience. Or drug use.

"Wow," I said. "How long did that take you?"

"Two months."

The painting was tiny. It was the size of my hand. Mae Simon was a person who spent two months on something for which she earned no money. Besides those pink glasses and her outfit, she did have the air of someone you would trust with a child— she was matronly, warm. I could see why my mother had hired her. She also fit the bill for what my mother called an "alternative assistant," which basically meant that she was white. My mother prided herself on having white people work for her, especially the nannies. She actually once said that they were "easier to find in a playground full of Jamaicans."

Tacked on the wall near Mae's closet were a bunch of curling pictures, all of cats. "Those I saved from the street and brought to the Humane Society. They're strays." She said this with an over-compensating bashfulness, which didn't ring true. She was obviously very proud of her saved cats.

"There are so many." I quickly counted four across and ten down. "Where do you find them?"

"Everywhere. Mostly Bushwick."

This was odd. Mae Simon did a lot of jobs for which she earned no money.

"Please, sit." She motioned to the greasy corduroy couch. It was a burnt-sienna color, and the thin canals between the corduroy lines were embedded with grime. On the upside-down wooden storage crate in front of me, which Mae had painted black and was now using as a coffee table, there was a check she had written to herself for $1 million ("It's a law-of-attraction thing," she explained) and a Polaroid, which peeled off the sticky wood with a sound.

There I was in the photo, on Mae's lap, my legs dangling. I wore saddle shoes and a pink dress and an expression of surprise, my mouth open. Mae had her arms around my stomach and her head on my shoulder and she looked very loving. We were at home on Eighty-Fourth. It looked like there was a party going on. There were some figures milling in the background, and the table in the foreground was scattered with half-finished drinks.

"Aren't we adorable?" Mae sat down, way too close to me, so that our asses were pressed up against each other. She had no problem entering my personal space. Looking at this photo, though, that made sense. Mae had been very close to me for a whole year of my life. Still, it made me nervous. I scooted away.

"Oh, sorry, am I too close?" Her eyes looked worried through her pink lenses.

"It's fine." I coughed.

But she was too close. And why was she being so nice? What did she want? I didn't trust it. Had she written back finally because I'd said I would pay her to?

"You know, I'm happy to pay you for meeting with me today," I said. "I know your time must be valuable."

"What?" She looked offended. "Kitty, I am so happy you wrote me, you have no idea. I have thought about you every day since I left."

"You have?"

"Yes! You were so special to me. I was so fucking sad to lose that job."

"What happened?"

She looked at me for a long moment. "Okay." She closed her eyes and breathed like she was in a yoga class, finding her intention. Then she covered her mouth with both hands. Her hands looked young still. She wore cheap bulky silver rings on almost every finger. One was a skull. "Can I ask you first why you got in touch with me?"

"I found this letter."

Mae deep-breathed again. "That's what I thought." Another long moment. She was just looking at me. It smelled like curry in here, too, and also like the incense Mae burned, maybe to get rid of the curry smell. "Did you ask your mother about it? What did she say?"

"I didn't ask her about it. She's pretty out of it these days. She has Alzheimer's."

"Oh God." She rolled her eyes as if she knew all about what

a pain in the ass Alzheimer's was, and slapped her naked knee. "That is devastating. I'm so sorry."

"It's really hard. And my dad died—I don't know if you knew."

"Oh, Kitty." Mae put a gentle hand on my back.

"So, what did you mean in the letter about not being there for me?"

"Kitty." She inhaled again. "I have to tell you. This might be upsetting to hear."

"Okay." I still half thought she was going to tell me something totally benign, or something totally expected, like that my mother had fired her for leaving me alone for two minutes while she went to the bathroom. "Whatever it is, I want to know."

Mae took her hand off my back. Her gray-blue eyes were focused. She looked at the rock crystals on the mantel, maybe to gather their power. Then she got up, went to the crystals, and chose two, one pink and one white. "You probably think this is bogus, but do me a favor and just hold this." She pressed the pink one into my hand in a way that felt like it was supposed to really mean something.

"Okay." I readjusted the rock between my palms like it was a thing that mattered and waited for her to begin.

After another deep inhale, she did.

"This is what happened. It happened the night this photo was taken. Your mom was throwing a party for an artist. It was a big one—there were a hundred people, at least. She was raising money—you know, she was always raising money. This picture of us was taken at the very beginning of the night, after I put that dress on you. Your dad wanted a picture of you. I was going to get up, but your dad wanted me in it. Your dad was a really wonderful man. I'm so sorry he died, baby." She stopped, swallowed. "Sorry if it's weird I'm calling you baby. When I look at you, it's hard not to see this little girl."

I half smiled. I tried not to judge her. I tried to ignore her greasy couch. It was hard. I was so uncomfortable.

"Okay. Later that night your mom was understaffed, and she asked me to help. She wanted me to bus tables, basically. I said it was almost your bedtime—your bedtime was eight o'clock—and she said that was fine, she would take care of you. So I rushed around busing everybody's glasses and plates and taking them to the kitchen. I did a few laps of that and then I went to find you guys, but I couldn't find you anywhere. I thought maybe she'd taken you to bed a little early and you must be in your bedroom. So I went to your bedroom. You weren't in there. And then I heard this noise from the hall, like a shrieking sound, and I was pretty sure it was your mom shrieking. I freaked out. I thought maybe she'd fallen or something. I rushed to the guest room and opened the door and . . . your mom was in bed with a guy. And you were in the bathroom. The door was wide open.

"Your mom said, 'Get out.' She didn't yell—her voice was chilling. I didn't move. I couldn't just leave you there. I ran to you and grabbed you off the floor. You were crying. I remember looking at your mom before we left the room because I still thought maybe this was a mistake. Maybe she didn't know you were in there. But how could she not have known? You were crying, and the door was wide open, and the light in the bathroom was on. But I thought maybe she was just too drunk to notice, so when I looked at her, I thought she might be horrified that I'd found you and apologize. But she didn't look surprised at all. She just said, 'Close the door, Mae.' And the guy—he was just staring at me, kind of smiling. He was creepy.

"I took you to your bedroom and asked you what had happened. You said, 'Mom told me to wait in the bathroom while she played a game with her friend.' I remember thinking, When Mrs. West isn't drinking, she'll see how wrong this was and she'll apologize.

"I put you to bed. Your mom was waiting for me outside your door. She'd reapplied her makeup—I could tell. She handed me a check. It was for $5,000. I said I wouldn't take it. I said I loved you so much and I really wanted to stay in this job and I couldn't bear to think of leaving you. I begged her to wait until the next day to talk about this again. She kept saying, 'Take it take it take it, Mae,' and so I finally just took it out of her hands. I planned to rip it up when I left. I planned to tell your father. Once I had taken it, she said, 'Give me your key.' I pleaded again. It got nowhere. She had made up her mind. I had no choice. I gave her my key. She said, 'Don't ever come back to this house. I'll have you arrested, I swear my life on it.' I knew she meant it. Your mom—she was incredibly intimidating to work for. And I was only twenty at the time. I don't mean to be negative about her—she was definitely charming, too. But she scared the shit out of me. On my way out, I saw this Polaroid of us on the counter, so I took it.

"Downstairs I said bye to the doorman like I always did, and when I got outside, there was the guy, smoking a cigarette. I didn't realize how tall he was until I saw him standing up. Tall and blond, with crazy blue eyes. He was a really good-looking guy, but I could tell there was something wrong with him. He was missing a chip. I don't know. I'll never forget what he said to me. 'Eventful night, isn't it?' I didn't say anything. I left. And that was the last time I saw you. That night was the last time we saw each other."

Mae looked up. Her eyes were glassy. She said, "I was so sad to leave you, Kitty."

I was like ice. I was paralyzed. Maybe I was a rock, like my mother. "Did you cash the check or did you tell my father?"

Mae winced. "Please forgive me," she said. "I was going to rip it up, I was going to rip it up—that was my plan. I swear to God, Kitty, I swear."

"But."

"But I kept it for some reason. I kept it. I did call your father's office the next day, but he'd gone out of town. And later in the week I found out I was pregnant, and I used some of the money for an abortion. I was too young to have a kid."

"So you never told my father."

"No. It was the wrong thing to do. So that's why I wrote the letter. To do the right thing. So that one day I could tell you."

"Well, I hope you feel better." I set her rock crystal on the coffee table.

Mae looked confused. "Do you not believe me?"

There was the memory of myself, age four, cheek against the smoky marble tiles of the bathroom, and yes, it had been the guest bathroom Mae was talking about. But I didn't remember anything traumatic about that moment. I just remembered feeling sad. If what Mae had recounted was true, how could I possibly have forgotten it? I couldn't have.

And then I looked at the cats on the wall. Mae Simon liked to save things. Mae Simon was excited about saving things that did not belong to her. Maybe Mae Simon should have been focusing on her own life instead of nominating herself to be the Cat Savior of Bushwick. Mae Simon was addicted to other people's problems. I thought of the sign in the kitchen. *Free Education for Everyone!* Mae Simon probably called 1-800 numbers all day, hoping her complaints would get her something for free. She probably wrote notes to her neighbors about their cars being parked incorrectly. Mae Simon had an opinion about everything. And in the meantime she couldn't figure out how to put on a pair of pants.

If I saw a glint of good in Mae Simon's fogged-over eyes in that moment, I dismissed it as a play of light.

"Do you believe me, Kitty?" she asked again. "Please answer." She reached for my hands and I moved them away. The curry air began to feel even heavier. It had seeped into everything I was wearing. It had seeped into my hair and my skin and it was all over my bag.

"I don't know," I said.

The look on her face: you would have thought a volcano was erupting. You would have thought she was seeing the ocean for the first time in her life.

"Do you remember that night?"

"I don't remember anything like what you're describing."

We looked at the picture of us. She took it off the table. "The real reason I took this picture? Is because this is the guy."

She pointed to one of the figures in the background. There was the guy—most of him anyway. The top of his head was out of the frame. His face wasn't visible. He was turned away from the camera. There was only a thick head of blond hair; it looked like sheep's wool. And it looked like youthful hair. Was he young? How young? He wore a blue blazer, dark khaki pants, brown dress shoes: typical Upper East Side. It could have been anyone.

It wasn't that I thought Mae Simon was lying. I thought some version of her story must be true. It pained me to think how much, and in that moment I wouldn't let myself go there. I told myself she was exaggerating. Because my mother didn't have affairs; she was very opposed to them. She would have done anything to stay in her marriage. And even if I was wrong about that, there was one thing I knew for sure: my mother never would have left me in the bathroom like that. She never would have done that to me. That I knew. Without question. Without a doubt. I was 100 percent sure about that.

Why didn't I ask Mae who he was? This was the only question a person in my position could have possibly asked. In my recollection of this moment now, the peanut butter bunny rose up through me with a violent acid burn before, and not after, she answered the question I had not asked.

"His name was William Stockton."

IN WHAT WE CALLED HOME

Part Three

32

Denial, I have learned, is not the act of lying to yourself. Denial is not an act, it's a state. It's the state of not knowing you are a liar.

I was fixated on a certain picture of my life, and that picture was reflected on the surface of everything I saw.

We do not choose to be blind, and when we are blind, we don't know that. We see as much as we can bear to see, and we assume that's all there is.

•

What I saw was that my parents had been happy. If my mother had had a drunk kiss with some guy at a party one night, that was a forgivable mistake. I knew the guy wasn't William. It couldn't be. William was too moral, too Catholic. He was too kind. He was too polite. Also, smaller, he'd never smoked a cigarette in his life; you could tell that was true just by looking at the perfectly smooth skin on his face.

What I saw was that I loved William.

What I saw was that I needed him.

I needed his sturdy presence, I needed the way he adored me. A small, loathsome voice inside my head also knew there were logistics involved. When I had the baby, I would have what I always wanted. I would also have $10 million. There was nothing to do but wait.

•

I called Dan. We met at the park in Fort Greene and sat on a bench and he held me as I cried and cried, but I couldn't bring myself to tell him. The great thing about Dan, and the reason I had called him, was that I knew he wouldn't ask.

I told him as much as I could bear to give away at the time. An old nanny. With information that was fucking insane and very upsetting, and she might be insane, too—she saved cats and lived in a hippie commune that was maybe a cult, led by a man named Philip. And why did I come here, why did I come here, Brooklyn was horrible, I was never leaving Manhattan again. And my shop was gone and I hated church, and my mother, my fucking mother, had ruined everything.

"Also," I said, snotty and bleary-eyed, "I'm pregnant."

"You are? That's great."

"I knooooow," I cried.

We talked for a long time about my mother. This was a convenient place to put everything. I was angry, scared, hurt. I felt abandoned, alone. And I felt betrayed. I felt really fucking betrayed.

Dan listened. When I think back to this day now, I can't remember much of what he said, and I think that's because he barely said anything. He just let me talk.

I do remember that at some point, when I was all cried out, he said, "Why don't we take a walk?"

We walked to the center of the park, which was on a hill, and sat at the top of a big staircase overlooking Manhattan. We were quiet for a while. Of course I was thinking about what Mae Simon had told me and what I would do, but I thought about that less than I imagined someone in my situation would. Because I already knew what I was going to do. I wasn't going to do anything, not yet. There was not enough information. Mae Simon was not a reliable source. A misunderstanding—this had to be a series of misunderstandings.

I remember thinking, as I sat there with Dan in Brooklyn and looked at my city, that there were so many ways to live a life. I could be a masseuse, for example, or live in a commune, or buy property somewhere around this park. The life I lived seemed small, one-tracked. But when I thought about what I would change, there was nothing. I had the life that everyone wanted. My life was good. I didn't need to change my life because my life was really, really good.

I remember the orange sun on Dan's face when he said, "Dusk is my favorite time of day."

This seemed so simple. It seemed too simple. I remember how quickly my next thought flashed and burned: I was missing something. There was something I was missing. And that's when I said, "I should get back."

"Okay," Dan said. "Can I walk you to the train?"

"How about a cab."

"Sure," he said.

We walked down the stairs. He would take me to Atlantic Terminal, where there would be cabs. But then a cab drove by. Dan said, "Wow, this never happens here," and flagged it down. He opened the door. "I'll see you on Sunday." He hugged me. Meaningfully, tenderly. My response was to stand there like I was dead. I didn't hug him back. I didn't say thank you. In the cold voice my mother reserved for her assistants, I heard myself say, "See you on Sunday."

33

I moved around like I was caught in a thick and viscous gel. I was tired all the time. I wasn't sleeping. I was overwhelmed by the thought of sleep and by the thought of being awake. I hated it when William came home. I hated it when he left in the morning and I was alone with my thoughts again. I was so tired that I became a little delusional. I thought my phone was ringing when it wasn't. I thought I'd put toast in the toaster. I would run to the kitchen, expecting to find it burning, but there was nothing there. Just sparkling clean countertops and bright pink roses, huddled together in the vase, and me, alone, falling apart.

I made sure I was in bed by the time he got home at night. I didn't feel well, I needed rest. I held my breath, listened to the sound of his footsteps coming up the stairs. The doorknob would turn, the door would open soundlessly. I would keep my eyes closed. I would pretend to be asleep.

When I finally did doze off, I had dreams. Dreams I was running after my father, but no matter how fast I ran, I could never catch up. Dreams of being trapped in smoke-filled hallways. Dreams of falling, but it was never-ending—there was no ground.

When I woke up, I couldn't remember why I was in the guest room. And then I did: I had told my fiancé I needed to sleep here because our mattress was bothering my back. I had told him Dr. Rose absolutely wouldn't let me sleep on a Tempur-Pedic right now, with the pregnancy—it was out of the question. I invited him to move to the guest room with me because I knew he would say no, and he did say no. He was a bad sleeper, terrible. He needed the Tempur-Pedic; he needed rest.

•

William responded to my distance by moving closer. He saw "Dr. R" written on the kitchen calendar and insisted on going with me.

"Dr. Rose, it's so wonderful to meet you," he said in his magnetic way. I could tell by the look on her face that she was smitten with him.

"You, too," she said, her Belize-bronzed skin glowing under the fluorescent lights.

"How was your trip?"

"It was great." She opened her folder. "Okay, this is ten weeks, right?"

"Right."

"How have you been feeling?"

"Pretty bad," I said.

"Catherine's been resting a lot," William said. "On a non-Tempur-Pedic mattress, of course."

Dr. Rose, thank God, ignored this. "Rest is good," she said. "And you're eating?"

"Yes."

"Good," Dr. Rose said. "Lie back for me and lift your gown please?"

I did. I focused my eyes on a yellow stain on the ceiling. It always irked me when doctors' offices weren't as immaculate as I wanted them to be.

Dr. Rose pushed around my pelvic bone with her fingers. William towered over me. His skin. It was perfectly smooth. There was no way he had ever been a smoker. "Now I'm going to insert this." Dr. Rose held up a wand. It looked like a dildo. I thought of Shelly.

"There." Dr. Rose nodded to the screen. Black and white and yes, oh my God, the shape of a head, the shape of a tiny body, the static flicker of a heartbeat. "There's your baby."

It wasn't until this moment that my pregnancy felt completely real to me. It was hard to believe anything truly existed until you could see it for yourself. I thought, I can't leave him. He is the father of my baby. We are meant to have a life together. Why would I let some hippie in Brooklyn ruin that?

"Oh, my dear." William was amazed. "This is incredible."

I was the kind of happy that is filled with sadness. Or I was just sad. I was pregnant, finally, and I had found a partner, finally, and all my money problems were about to be solved. I shouldn't be sad. My eyes filled with tears. William and Dr. Rose looked at me, their eyes expectant. I didn't know what to say, so I repeated the last word that had been said. "Incredible."

34

But in the middle of the night I second-guessed everything.

William Stockton. Mae had clearly said that name. If it were anyone else, I would have said, This is obvious. It's him. Case closed. But because it was me, I Googled the name William Stockton instead, and felt better when the list was very long. There were many William Stocktons in the world. William Stockton was a very common name. It could have been any of them, or none of them. Not everyone was on the Internet. There was also the possibility that Mae had gotten confused. Maybe she had heard the name William Stockton around the house at some point during her year there—that made sense—and then she had transposed this name onto the guy. That was completely plausible. It could happen to anyone.

The photo. Me and Mae Simon and the guy in the background. Was it William? There was no way to know. Even if I found another picture of William wearing a blue blazer and khakis and brown dress shoes just like this, that wouldn't really matter. It was such a basic outfit.

William said he had been thirteen when he left for Switzerland. The journal confirmed this. Four years later, on March 19, 1977, the Stocktons came to visit. And two days after that, Mom fired Mae. But the Stocktons' visit may have included only Edward and Donna. Maybe William hadn't come with them. Maybe he'd been in school. But then why had Mom cut off contact? What was the reason for that? And what did "Guilt is cancer" mean?

•

When William went to work, I went back to his desk. I was careful. I didn't move the box. I lined the pictures up next to the picture Mae had given me. In none of William's pictures did his hair have the consistency of sheep's wool like the hair of the guy in the photo. Were their bodies of the same proportion? Maybe. It was hard to tell. Did William have a tendency to stand like this guy in the photo, with two feet on the ground? Yes, and so did most people.

I took photos of the photos with my phone so I could look at them later and put them back in the box in the correct order. I moved quietly so I would hear him if he came home. I opened the desk drawers. None of their contents had changed. I almost had a heart attack when Lucia came in.

"Miss Catherine, why are you here?" The sideways look she gave me implied that I was in the wrong. "Why are you no dressed today?" I was still wearing my robe, and it was ten o'clock in the morning. This was very out of character. "You sick?" She touched my forehead with the back of her hand. I let her. "No, you no sick. You pregnant. You tired. I see you very tired. You relax."

"Ugh," I said, too tired for real words.

She set her bucket of cleaning tools on the floor and began dusting the lamp.

The doorbell rang.

Lucia said, "The door rings."

It was the delivery of Chino's punctured canvas. Two men in gray clothes from the Lower East Side gallery held the box with cautious hands. "Where would you like us to hang it, Mrs. Stockton?"

I chose the wall in the entryway. William would want it some-where visible. It would be the first thing people saw when they came over. What would they see when they saw it? Something that looked expensive and important. In the context of this house, that's how it would appear. What I saw, besides an absurd piece of art, was rage—a violent outburst, silenced in a pretty frame.

35

My mother sat in her living room, draped in all the jewels she owned. When she moved, the sunlight made them blink. "The girl is stealing my jewelry," she said, "so I will wear it. That is the answer."

Evelyn rolled her eyes. "Mrs. West, I am *not* stealing your jewels." She looked at me. "Catherine, I swear to you."

"Don't worry, it's fine," I said, and Evelyn looked relieved.

My mother placed two firm hands on her necklaces. "Thief."

"I'll see you later, Mrs. West." Evelyn closed the door.

"How are you today, Mom?"

"Cold."

"Do you want a blanket?"

"No."

"I'm pregnant, you know."

"Good," she said. I waited for more, but there was nothing.

"Okay," I said, "I'm going to show you something today." My prickling armpits told me I was nervous.

I handed her the photo without introduction and passed her the reading glasses from the coffee table. She put them on carefully, adjusting each side behind each ear. She held the photo up at a distance.

"Catherine," she said sweetly. "This is Catherine."

"That's me, Mom, yeah. Do you recognize the girl with me?"

Mom looked again. "No."

"That's Mae, my nanny. Remember her?"

"Mae Simon."

"Right."

"Your nanny."

"Do you remember this night? You had a party."

"There were many parties."

I pointed to the guy. "Is this William Stockton?"

Mom's nostrils flared. She put the photo down.

"Mom, please answer me. Is this William Stockton?" I held the photo up for her, pointed to the guy.

"How should I know? There is no face."

"Did you have affairs, Mom?"

"I don't believe in affairs."

"I know you don't, but did you have them?"

"Of course not."

"Mom." My shoulders tightened. I felt nauseous. "Did you have an affair with William Stockton?"

Mom looked past me, out the window. After a very long time, she said, in a small and uncertain voice, "No."

"Are you sure?"

"Yes."

"You don't sound sure."

"Stop it right now, Catherine." It was the chilling voice Mae had described. Even now that I was an adult, that voice had the power to unnerve me.

She stroked her necklaces, looked away. Fine, we would move on.

I handed her the journal. "Here."

She ran her fingertips along the front. Simple black leather, it could have been anything. She said, "I have seen this before."

"It's yours. Open it."

"Don't tell me what to do."

"Sorry."

She showed no signs of recognition as she flipped through the pages. I watched her. It was hard to pay attention. I thought about making tea. The peppermint would soothe my stomach, but I didn't want to get up. Her jewels kept blinking. They looked very heavy around her small neck, her small wrists. I thought, Here is a woman who has so much, and who is suffering under the weight of it.

"Do you recognize that, Mom?"

"Does it belong to me?"

"Yes."

"I can't read the handwriting. It's very bad."

"That's true, your handwriting is hard to read."

She closed the journal, put it on the table. She took off her glasses. "Get me a blanket, please. I'm very cold."

I got her the blanket. I thought about leaving, but I wasn't feeling well enough to leave. "Mom, do you remember being pregnant?"

"It was awful. I got so fat."

"I'm worried about that."

"My mother ate red meat every day when she was pregnant. You should eat red meat."

I didn't bother reminding her that I didn't eat meat. "Okay."

"When they killed a steer on the farm, I was very upset. But I forgot about that when I got older."

"That sounds hard."

"I loved those animals."

"I thought you hated animals, Mom."

"I loved them. And then they were killed." She lifted one necklace from the pile on her chest and let it go.

"So you decided to buy plants instead."

"Yes. Plants can be brought back to life. A plant can be saved."

36

On Saturday morning I heard him approach. I didn't hear the door at all this time, but I felt him standing there, watching. His breath was smooth, steady. Why was he always watching me sleep? How much time had he spent doing this? When I felt myself blinking and knew my sleep didn't look believable anymore, I opened my eyes.

"Good morning, sunshine," he said. He had never called me "sunshine" before. He was trying so hard. It was almost pathetic, and I kind of loved it. I wanted him to look shitty and sad, but he looked great. He looked better than ever. All chipper on a Saturday morning, wearing a white shirt and khakis, the same outfit he had worn in the picture with his mother. "Are you feeling well enough to accompany me to brunch?"

I made my best nauseous face, touched my stomach. "I'm not sure."

"I can stay here with you all day instead if you'd like. I cook a mean chicken soup, you know. Which I can adapt to your needs, of course."

That sounded like hell. I was already antsy with the amount of time I was spending in bed.

"No, I think I can manage brunch."

I took a long time to get ready. I rationed out the hours of the day. If it was ten now and I took an hour to get ready, that would be one hour less spent with William today. When I realized I was doing this, I told myself to stop it. Every time I went back over the facts, I reminded myself that Mae Simon was not a person to trust. What she had said was most likely an embellishment, and possibly a big one, given her overly emotional response to those cats. My mother, as expected, had given me nothing. I had found nothing in the journal and nothing in William's desk. And punishing William for something I wasn't sure he was guilty of—what country did they do that in? Not ours. These were the things I told myself in the shower, where I stayed for a full thirty-three minutes, not avoiding my fiancé.

•

"You look lovely," he said when I appeared, wearing loose black jeans and a mint-green blouse. I half smiled in response. I had spent a lot of time straightening my hair and then I'd put it up in a messy bun. I wore makeup, but not as much as usual, and I moved around warily, like someone who still wasn't feeling well but who was good enough and kind enough to accompany the love of her life to a restaurant because that's what he wanted.

William folded the newspaper he'd been reading on the couch with Herman and took the last sip of his espresso. He got up and kissed me. His espresso taste made me gag. "Oh no," he said. "Are you all right?"

"Yeah, I'm just very sensitive to smells right now. The coffee. Maybe we shouldn't kiss when you've had anything pungent."

"Of course."

He touched my stomach. We looked at it. I put my hand on his hand. In that moment, with the light pouring into our clean white apartment, things made sense. For a second. The next second I was looking at him, thinking, But who are you?

And the next second: This is your fiancé, Catherine, and he's fucking beautiful and look at everything you have.

And the next: But really, who are you?

The back-and-forth was exhausting, so I concentrated on the physical pain. It was a perfect sunny day, with happy people out shopping and eating, and here I was, hobbling down the street as if I were a hundred years old, clutching my belly like I might throw up at any moment.

Our usual place had a too-long wait, so we went to the high-end diner around the corner. It was nice and cool inside, and didn't have too many smells. I wanted to order four bacon cheeseburgers and scarf them all—I was insanely hungry all of a sudden—but I ordered an egg-white frittata instead, with extra toast.

"You're eating for two now," William said. "Good girl."

The waitress with the penciled-on eyebrows scanned me for signs of pregnancy with a dulled interest and stuck her pen back in her bun.

"Is this restaurant okay?" William asked. I knew that if I weren't pregnant, he wouldn't have asked me that. I loved that he was babying me. I felt special. I also deserved it. If anything terrible had happened to me in the past, then I was a victim and the world owed me now. This was how karma worked.

"Yeah," I said, in a way that was purposely unconvincing, "it's fine."

William chose a sesame roll out of the basket. "Can I butter a piece of bread for you?"

"Yes, please. I want rye though."

"Okay." He poked through the choices. "Good, here is a piece of rye." He took time to spread the butter into every corner. "There you are, my darling."

"Thank you."

"So what are we going to do about rearranging the house for the baby? Where should the baby's room be?"

"In the study, I think."

"The music room?"

"Yeah. You guys can practice in your office, right?"

"Sure, of course. Why not?" He bit into his roll.

I put my bread down. The fennel was not agreeing with me. "I don't like the rye. Can you butter me a different one, please?"

"Of course. How about a multigrain option?"

"Sure."

"You know"—he knifed the whipped butter out of the ramekin—"on the subject of offices, I'd like to say again that I feel autonomy in one's home is paramount. I don't mean to make you feel uncomfortable, my darling, but I must ask you once more not to go through my things."

I tried to keep my face expressionless. I clutched my stomach. How had he known? I'd been so careful. "I didn't," I said, and maintained eye contact because that was what you were supposed to do when you delivered a good lie.

"Catherine," he said, sighing.

"What?"

"Lucia told me."

"Lucia told you what?"

"That you went through my desk recently, again, after I nicely asked you not to do so."

"Why would Lucia tell you that?"

"She mentioned it in passing." He tucked his napkin into his shirt. "We mustn't lie to one another, Catherine."

"Is this why you gave Lucia that bonus? To keep tabs on me?"

"I gave Lucia a bonus because she rightly deserved one. I feel we should treat our people well, don't you?"

"We do treat her well. Did you know she has health insurance?"

"No, I didn't. That is very generous."

We looked at each other for a long time. When I closed my

eyes, I could still see his face. The diner smelled like chicken-fried steak all of a sudden.

"I don't feel well." To someone else I would have said, "I don't feel good." It pissed me off that I was still speaking in a way that would impress him.

"Perhaps you'd like some seltzer." He looked around for the waitress. "I'm sorry you don't feel well," he said. "But I must know, why are you looking through my things? What is it you want to know?"

"I don't know."

"It must be something. If it is, please ask me. I'm right here."

"I guess I just feel like you're mysterious sometimes."

"Am I?" He laughed. "How?"

"I don't know. You never talk about your past."

"We've been over this, Catherine. I like to think I live in the present moment."

"But people have pasts. It's normal to talk about them. Like your friends in Geneva. You never talk about those people. And the people from your past who still live in New York. Why don't you talk about them?"

"People in New York? Everyone I knew here when I was a child is either dead or gone."

"Okay, I know, and that's very sad. But I mean just in general. You never talk about the past."

"Certainly," he said, "I simply choose not to much of the time." He leaned in. "Because I am here. With you. That is what I care about."

The more I tried to breathe deeply, the more I was aware of how shallow my breath was.

"Did you ever visit us after you moved to Switzerland?"

"I would assume so."

"You said no to that before."

"Did I?"

"Yes."

"Well, it must have been an error on my part. I apologize."

"Did you ever meet me when I was a kid?"

"If I did, I don't remember it."

"But there's a chance you did?"

"There's a chance for everything. What are you driving at?"

"I just need to know if we met before, when we were kids."

"Not that I can recall, Catherine."

"Do you remember someone who worked for us named Mae?"

"Mae." He took a bite of his roll, chewed slowly. "I don't think so. Why?"

I looked at his face, trying to find wrinkles I hadn't seen before. I had done this so many times since Mae had told me the guy had been smoking a cigarette. No, there were no wrinkles I hadn't seen. There were barely any wrinkles at all.

"Did you look me up when you got back here?"

"This again? No, Catherine," he said. "I did not look you up on the Internet."

"Really?"

"Really."

"So it was a coincidence we met."

"Catherine," he said, "it was fate. Don't you believe that?"

I didn't answer. I took my phone out of my purse, scrolled to the picture of the picture of me and Mae and the guy in the background. I told my hands to stop shaking. I pointed to the guy. "Is this you?"

I didn't take my eyes off him. He blinked a few times. Did this mean something? Did it not?

"When was this picture taken?"

"Nineteen seventy-seven."

"So I would have been sixteen or seventeen then, and this

young man appears to be around that age, possibly. It's hard to tell." He was still looking at the screen. "And these pants. I highly doubt I would have worn pants like these to a party at night. They are too light a color. I would have worn black pants." He looked at me then. His solid, cool face. His eyes, big and asking. They were asking me to believe him. "Have you asked your mother if this is me?"

"She can't remember."

"Oh," he said. He looked sorry for me. "Well, if it is me, is that a problem?"

"If it's you, then we've met before."

"A long time ago. And we don't remember it. I would hardly call that meeting."

"So you don't know whether it's you or not. That's your answer? You don't know?"

William chuckled. "Catherine, if it is me, I have no recollection of it. That's the thing about the past, you know. You don't remember everything." He carefully set the phone in front of me. I remember just then the screen went black. "And the things we do remember we cannot always trust. We cannot trust our minds. We cannot trust our memories."

•

He didn't leave my side for the rest of the day. Maybe he thought that if he was right there, opening the door for me and telling me how lovely I was and saying cutesy things about my toes as we lay on the couch watching an Almodóvar film, I would be more likely to remember how wonderful he was, or at least I would get tired of punishing him. And that's exactly what happened. The hours wore me down. As the day fell away into dusk and then into darkness, and he dotingly fed me pretzels and seltzer and even banished Herman from the room after I said his canine smell was really getting to me, I began to wonder if William was right. Did the past not matter? Was there anything beyond this moment and this room and our warm bodies inside it? And if that were true—if we had everything we needed right here—then what was I still looking for?

37

We woke up together in the guest room—William, in a move that both satisfied and annoyed me, had come to the conclusion that I was more important to him than the Tempur-Pedic—and went to church. It was a hot day, unbearably hot. You could have fried an egg on the ground. Even the people at church looked dressed for the beach. Well, either the beach or an upscale barbecue event. Marge was sadly absent.

Father Ness said, "It's almost your turn up there!" He looked especially hunched today. The weight of his backpack must have been wearing on him.

An old woman with a zebra pin on her lapel said, "Don't you two just make the cutest couple?" We smiled and held each other's clammy hands, posing for a picture no one was taking.

I sat there fanning myself with a Bible study flyer. I made my list of prayers to God like he was Santa Claus.

God, please let Mae Simon be a lunatic and a liar. Please let this child be born healthy. Please let William and me have a fantastic wedding, and please let us get the money. I just want us to be normal and okay.

William, the church soldier, sang in monotone and beat his chest at the part about sinning, and kneeled with his hands pressed together in front of his solemn, concentrated face. I wondered what he was praying for.

•

That afternoon I decided to be a caring fiancée and bring Stan and William sodas. I was trying to keep everything as normal and okay as possible. I imagined myself opening the door and cooing something like, "Just thought you boys might like a little pick-me-up." I even found straws with red stripes on them in the pantry.

I knocked on the door twice and then opened it. Stan was playing vigorously, face warped in concentration—and William was behind him at the desk, checking his phone. He was startled when he saw me; his body jolted. He stood up and went to Stan and said, "That's very good, though the C chord needs work."

Stan looked up at him. "Huh?"

The sodas were making my hands cold, so I went to put them on the desk, and I said, "Just thought you guys might like a refresher," which was the wrong word. "Refreshment," I corrected.

"Thanks, Mrs. West!" But before he got up, Stan asked William, "Can I have a soda?"

"Sure." William clapped him on the back. "Thank you, darling," he said to me. He kissed my forehead. "Though in the future, it would be better not to interrupt in the middle of a session. But we do love soda, don't we, Stan?"

"Mmm-hmm." Stan sipped from the straw.

In a too-cheery voice, I said, "Well, I'll leave you to it then!" I closed the door and stood there and listened.

I heard Stan say, "Mrs. West is really nice."

"Yes," William said.

"Is she your soul mate? Because that's who gets married. It's soul mates. I read about it in my book."

William laughed—just one little ha, just a beat—and said, "Sure, Stan, that's exactly what she is. My soul mate."

•

Max played while Dan massaged me and everything seemed normal and okay. Max seemed to be playing better than usual today. There was no yelling. I hoped William was paying attention to Max and not on his phone.

Dan and I didn't talk much because I said, "I don't feel like talking today." I didn't want to remember the reasons I had cried at the park. He said that was fine and did his job. He also said that when I got more pregnant, we could think about buying me a massage chair because eventually it would be too much to lie on my stomach. I thought it was a great idea and spent a good part of the hour imagining what kind of chair I would buy and where it would go and how it would change the feel of the room.

•

After my massage I called for him. "William?"

"Yes, darling? We're up here," he said.

I expected to find him and Max watching TV. Doreen must be running late again. But when I got to the top of the stairs, there was no Max. There was Caroline weeping and William holding her, patting her back, saying, "Ssshh."

"Caroline?"

Her face was bloated and streaked with tears and she was wearing the Nantucket sweatshirt again, or still. Maybe she'd never taken it off. She stood up and wrapped her arms around me. I held my breath and waited for her to squeeze the life out of me, but that didn't happen today. Her arms were limp.

"Bob's in Miamiiiiiiii," she wailed.

William put his hand on Caroline's back. We exchanged a look. It said, This is very sad. I hoped it also said, This will never be us; we will never do this to each other.

"Caroline, I'm so sorry." And she kept crying, so I said it again. "I'm so sorry."

Dan appeared at the top of the stairs. "Oh," he said.

"Caroline, would you like a massage? You can take my place," William said.

Caroline wiped her tear-streaked face, looked at Dan. "Hi," she said.

"Hi," Dan said, hands clasped in front of him. He looked like a waiter: attentive, ready to take the order.

"I don't want a massage right now," Caroline squeaked.

"Okay, that's fine," William said, rubbing her shoulder now. "You don't have to get one."

And then she was crying again, with her face pressed into William's arm, and he said, "Why don't we sit down? Maybe Catherine can bring us some tea. Or a coffee? Would you like that?"

Caroline, like a toddler, said, "I want juice."

"Well," I said to Dan, "I guess you're free earlier than you thought."

"That's fine," Dan said.

"Here, let me pay you." I wrote a check at the counter. I paid him for two massages and left a huge tip, even bigger than usual—my apology for throwing him into this awkward family scene.

"Thank you, Catherine," he said. Before he left, he gave me a look. It said: You are going to be okay. I don't know what my expression said back to him. Probably: I am flustered.

The closest thing I had to juice was a watermelon-flavored wine spritzer. "This is even better than juice," Caroline said, and laughed at herself.

William, who was drinking one, too—to be supportive, I thought, because wine spritzers were definitely beneath him— agreed. "It is quite good," he said, and winked at Caroline.

I sat there in my robe across from them, feeling cold. Where were my slippers? I wanted to go find them but thought I should stay and be supportive. I also stayed because I was intrigued. How

William took care of Caroline, that's how he took care of me. He was good at it. He was a good shoulder to cry on—so sturdy, so consoling. I couldn't leave him. How could I leave him? I couldn't leave him. He was such a solid guy.

When Caroline went to the bathroom—in slow motion, sadly dragging her feet—I asked, "How was Max today?"

"He couldn't make it. His mother called. He wasn't feeling well."

"But I heard playing. Who was playing?"

"I was, my darling."

I told myself not to prod, but I couldn't help it. "Would you have told me that if I hadn't asked?"

"Of course." William was defensive. "I would have told you now, if not for your sister's state of emergency. I think that should be our main focus, don't you?"

"It is my main focus," I mumbled. Hand on my stomach. "I don't feel well."

"Oh, darling," he said, "is there anything I can get you? Perhaps you can have some of your seltzer."

I picked up the seltzer off the table but didn't drink. Caroline reappeared. She'd obviously thrown some cold water on her face because her hairline was wet. She collapsed onto the couch next to William again—why hadn't she chosen to sit next to me? what about me?—and tucked her twig legs into her chest. "This is the worst thing that's ever happened to me," she said.

William put his hand on her back. "You'll get through it, Caroline."

There was something so effective about the way William called people by their names. It made them feel special. Caroline, I could tell, felt special right now.

"Caroline," I said, "you will get through it. You really will."

"Why do people do this stuff to each other?"

"Cheat?"

"Cheat, lie, steal, everything. I mean, just living is hard. Eating three meals a day, exercising, doing your hair. All that stuff takes so much energy. I don't understand how Bob has the energy to cheat on me. And he's not even calling it cheating, by the way—he's calling it 'expanding his horizons.' I feel like a doormat."

"In my view," William said, "people are sometimes consumed by impulse. When there is something one wants very badly, it may be hard to account for the pain one causes others."

Caroline whipped her head back to face William. "You're saying he wants his mistress very badly? Is that what you're saying?"

"Oh, Caroline, no, I simply—"

"You're saying he just doesn't want to be with *me* very badly."

"No, no, I am—"

"Are you defending Bob right now?"

"No, I am not defending Bob. I'm only saying that people make mistakes."

"But this isn't a mistake. It's a life choice. A 'lifestyle choice.' That's what Bob is calling it."

"I think it's terrible," I said.

"It is," William said. "It is terrible, Caroline."

Caroline was quick to forgive. She's always been like that. "Thank you," she said, her head dropping to William's arm again. "It is terrible. It's the worst thing that's ever happened to me."

The conversation ended on a light note, with Caroline staring off into space and then suddenly exclaiming to William, "Look at our hands! They're identical! William and I have identical hands!" She was all over the place today. "Catherine, come look!"

"That's okay," I said. "I believe you."

I was glad when she left. Of course we said, Call us if you need anything, anything at all. William gave her his cell number. I hoped she wouldn't call us. Bob would return in two days and everything would go back to being normal and okay.

•

In bed that night I felt like I should still be talking about it, so I said, "I feel so sorry for Caroline."

"As do I," William said. He reached for his hair, began to twirl. "But she is also so fortunate. You both are."

I knew what he meant, but I said, "What do you mean?"

"Extreme wealth," he said. "You know, when I was young, I wanted your family to adopt me. I wanted to live in your house. It was so enormous." He yawned.

When he said that, I knew the wine spritzers he'd continued to drink after Caroline had left had gone to his head because it wasn't like him to talk about the past so freely.

"I would have liked to be in your family, maybe. That bohemian artist lifestyle. It seems so real."

He laughed. "Real?"

"Yeah, salt of the earth. Or . . . you know what I mean."

"It was glamorous sometimes, but most of the time we were . . ."

"What?"

"Money was an issue. It's very difficult to make money as an artist."

"But you still went to the best schools."

"I was fortunate in that way, yes."

"It must have been hard for you, though, not having as much money as your friends." I imagined a horde of boarding school boys in Moncler jackets leaving for a weekend ski trip and poor William being forced into a lie about why he couldn't go: I have to study for this test, guys.

"It wasn't easy." William sighed. "A life without money is not an easy life."

"I know. Can you imagine being homeless? Some people

actually have no homes. And when it's cold? They have to sleep outside?"

"True," William said, "but that is also a choice."

"You think so?"

"I do. Everything is a choice. Circumstances are not created out of thin air. They are chosen."

"But what about people who have terrible things happen to them? Like tsunamis or, I don't know . . . What if you fall down the stairs and you can't work anymore and you have to declare bankruptcy?"

"Every event is a choice to give up or to persevere," William said, and I wondered if this was a line he repeated to himself a lot. "The terrible things separate the weak from the strong."

I laughed. "It sounds like you're in the army or something."

"Has anything terrible ever happened to you, Catherine?"

I thought of Mae Simon's story. Of me, young, on the bathroom floor. I still couldn't remember what I'd been doing there, and I still had no memory of my mother or of any guy. And if that guy had been William and he was right here next to me in bed now, that physical closeness would jog some sensory part of my brain, wouldn't it?

He said my name again. "Catherine?"

"A horse broke my leg once. It trampled me."

"That is traumatic."

"But it's strange. I barely remember it. I went into shock."

"That often happens during trauma," he said. He kissed my neck, and then he kept kissing my neck, and then he was moving in for more.

"Sorry. I'm not really in the mood," I said, and felt guilty. I was asexual; I was a bad partner. I made it all about me and blamed myself. Until I realized that, no, this was Mae Simon's fault; I could blame her. I hated that she'd made me feel unsure about the man I was so sure I loved.

"I understand." He patted my leg twice and moved his hand away.

Because it was dark in the room and because he was tipsy, I felt brave enough to ask. "William?"

"Darling?"

"Are we going to be okay?"

"When we have the baby, we'll inherit more money. And who knows, maybe we'll have more than one."

"I mean *us*, though. Are *we* going to be okay?"

"Oh." William fumbled. "Oh, Catherine, I'm sorry. I thought we were discussing finances."

"No, it's fine," I said. "You're right. You're being logical. We do need that money, don't we?"

"I suppose we could manage without it, but it would be more difficult."

"I don't like difficult."

"Neither do I."

And then, despite not wanting to be touched by him, I was compelled to kiss his brow. Why did I do that? Maybe to show him I understood we were bound to each other now. Maybe to show myself that I could pretend. It didn't feel like a choice. It felt like instinct.

38

Marty brought three makeup artists to the house. He explained to them in his bitchy way that I wanted heavy eyeliner, light lips, and glowing—not powdery!—skin.

As I sat in the dining room chair we had pulled up to the window for better light, feeling nauseous, Marty told me he worried that Cass would leave him for someone better-looking. My initial thought was, Yeah, probably, and you should give him a bigger allowance. What I said was, "Don't worry about it."

"You're a bad liar, Cat."

"I'm pregnant."

"Shut the fuck up."

"Oh my God," the MAC girl said. Her fingers smelled like garlic. I had discounted her already because of this. "Oh my God. I can tell, kind of, from your skin."

"So happy for you, Cat. Is William freaking out? Oh God, what about the dress? Are you going to fit into the dress?"

"Hopefully," I said, and was very surprised at how little this mattered to me.

The Estée Lauder girl smelled like cigarettes. We ended up choosing the Lancôme girl, who smelled like a fragrance that was fragrance-free, and who also kind of smelled like my mother. Plus, Marty said she had done the best job.

After they'd left, Marty said, "Cat, in less than a month you'll be hitched. Is it sinking in? Tell me all your emotions! I love this part."

He pulled up a chair next to mine. We sat facing the window. My tree was beginning to lose its leaves.

"I'm excited," I said.

"Are you? Are you nervous? What are you going to eat for breakfast on the day? Tell me everything that's going through that pretty little head of yours."

"I am a little nervous."

"Of tripping when you walk down the aisle? Oh my God, I would be."

"Yeah, I guess that, too."

"Okay. For breakfast, I recommend nothing heavy, but you don't want to be hungry either. Yogurt is good, a thick yogurt. And nothing that might give you gas. Oh my God, a horror story? I had a bride who ate a plate of spinach before the ceremony. I'm talking huge plate of spinach. No, no, no." He wagged his finger. "It was ugly."

"Thanks, I'll keep that in mind."

"Oh, and for the gift bag? I found something very clever. It's a lock-and-key box. Your face is on the lock, William's is on the key, and inside we put the gifts. Keith Haring salt and pepper shakers, also with your faces on them, and okay, I caved on the olive oil. Blue Hill's going to give us a bunch of small bottles. We'll put those in the box, add some gorgeous paper filler for padding—white, obviously—maybe in the shape of doves? What do you think?"

I thought it was tacky and too food-focused, but I wasn't in the mood to brainstorm something better. "Sounds great," I said.

"Amazing. And the scalloped silverware—I want to come back to that. I know the Upper East Sider in you wants scalloped, but I'm strongly suggesting the non. It's more modern, and I think we're going to need that after a day at church."

"That's fine, Marty," I said.

"Really? You're not even going to argue with me?"

"No, I guess not."

"Great. Also, hello, we haven't discussed the throwing of the bouquet! Is that something you want to do, or should we skip it?"

I felt nauseous again. My mother was right. Being pregnant was hard. And I had so many months to go. "I don't know, Marty. Whatever you think."

"Moi?" Marty looked puzzled. And then he was nodding. "Okay, I see, you're one of those—I get it. Some brides, when we hit the stress month, go crazy over the details, and other brides just say no, no more, you take care of it. I got you covered, girl."

"Great."

"Well." He slapped his knees. "I'm leaving. You look like you need a nap, my friend. But don't get me wrong, you look gorgeous. That makeup? To die. You're a model. No! You're a princess! Princess Catherine Stockton!"

•

I had to lie down. But then that was too much. It was too quiet. I turned the TV on. I turned it off. I went to the kitchen for seltzer. I took a sip. It wasn't good; there was something wrong with it. I threw the bottle away, opened a new one. I wandered into the study. I walked in a circle around the music stand. William's violin was propped against the bookshelf. I'd never seen it before. Cherrywood. Looked expensive. I scanned my books and felt bad, as I always did, that I hadn't read most of them. I took *The Powers That Be* off the shelf. I hadn't read my father's inscription in a long time. "For Catherine, This is the way the world works. Be POWERFUL! Love, Dad." On a different day this might have inspired me. Today I had to laugh at how unpowerful I felt.

Lucia had taken the afternoon off to do her immigration stuff, so there was no one to talk to. I could have called someone. I could have taken a walk. I could have at least gone downstairs to get the mail. As I thought about all these options, I found myself sitting down in front of my computer and then I found myself at the Neiman Marcus Web site, where they were having an online sale that would end in an hour, which meant I could discard the other options and focus on this. Because it was a big sale.

I found a Stella McCartney bag at 80 percent off and felt more powerful. I didn't love it, but I liked it a lot. And it was such a good deal. I added sunglasses to the cart. Where had my mother's collection of sunglasses gone? Did Caroline have it? Caroline had everything. Well, except for a loyal husband. But still, she had enough money to buy a whole country of sunglasses. I should get Mom's. I would ask her.

I had vaguely promised myself that I would spend only $1,000, just to see if I could stick to a budget, just for fun. When I went to check out, it was closer to $3,000. I didn't know if I felt more or less powerful when I hit Buy.

I ate some pretzels because I was supposed to eat more and then I went to take a shower because I felt dirty. The image of myself in that mirror—I couldn't believe it was me. My body had filled out nicely so far. I didn't look fat, I looked healthy. And my face, all done up in the makeup I would wear on my wedding day—it was flawless. I stood there for a long time. This is you, Catherine, on this day in this house in this life, and you are gorgeous. So why are you crying?

39

"I'm sorry I'm late, but I did bring flowers." He set them on the nightstand and kissed my forehead. I was in bed not reading the book about apartheid and not watching the late-night shows. I waited for him to notice that my eyes were puffy and ask me what was wrong, but he didn't. He was undoing his tie, unbuttoning his shirt, bending down to pet Herman.

"Geraniums," I said.

"They reminded me of you."

"How was your day? Did you have a client dinner?"

"No. In fact," he said from inside the closet, "I had dinner with Caroline."

I suddenly felt more awake. "My sister Caroline?"

"Yes, that one." He chuckled.

"Why?"

"Well," he said, appearing in boxers and a plain white shirt, "why not?"

"Okay, but why?"

"Are you upset?"

"I don't know. I . . . I don't know." I hadn't talked to another human being since Marty had left at noon, and it was hard to find words. "I mean, why didn't you invite me?"

"It was spur-of-the-moment, darling. Caroline happened to be downtown, and so we met for drinks and then ended up having dinner. I'm sorry, I didn't intend to be so late. You must have been worried."

"I wasn't worried. I assumed you were out with a client."

He sat on the bed, put his hand on my thigh. I wanted him to take it off so badly, but I didn't tell him that. "Next time we'll invite you," he said. "I'm sorry if you feel left out."

He still hadn't noticed how puffy my eyes were. "What did you talk about?"

"Bob, mostly."

"What else did you talk about?"

"Nothing of import, I would say. We remarked on how nice it was to get to know each other better. We are going to be family soon. I thought you would appreciate it that we made this effort to bond."

"Does she want to sleep with you?"

He took his hand off my thigh, put it over his heart. "Excuse me?"

"Just answer. And be honest. Caroline's in a weak and destructive place right now, so it's probably not even about you, but I still want to know. Does she want to sleep with you?"

"No," he said. "The answer is a firm, firm no."

It wasn't his words that convinced me. It was the look on his face. The idea of sleeping with my sister apparently repelled him. But that didn't mean it would in the future. Anything could happen. The future was always full of doubt.

"I don't want you to see her again unless I'm there."

"Whatever you want, Catherine." He furrowed his brow. Two wrinkles above his nose. Little indents, barely there.

"William."

"Yes?"

"Were you ever a smoker?"

"No," he said, disgusted. "Smoking is vile."

"It is vile," I said slowly.

After a long silence, he said, "How was your day?"

"Fucking hormonal." I knew he didn't like it when I cursed, and it felt so good when I did. In this small way, I was being true to myself.

"I'm sorry," he said. "Let me rub your feet."

I didn't want him touching me at first, but then I got lost in the feeling of feeling good. I'd had a long day. I deserved to have someone rub my feet at the end of a long day. He turned off the TV and put on classical music instead, something light and soothing.

"You know," he said, "I would never do anything to hurt you, Catherine."

"I know."

He moved from my feet to my legs, and up from there, and by the time his warm body was hovering over mine, I did want to kiss him. Was it to remind him that he belonged to me? Herman's bark rose above the music until he got tired and stopped. I may have cried while we made love, but not much, and afterwards, I let him hold me because I was cold.

•

In the morning he was gone. He'd left a note. No words. Just a drawing of a heart with a smiley face inside. I didn't know if that was cute or kind of lazy, but either way, I liked it. It was better than nothing.

I needed a Tums. I might have been abusing Tums because I felt so nauseous all the time. I grabbed my purse off the floor, pulled the bottle out of the side pocket, took two. Took one more. Got out of bed.

•

"Lucia?"

"Miss Catherine?"

I followed her voice to the kitchen, where she was unloading the dishwasher.

"You would like a coffee?"

"No, I need you to run some errands for me today, please. I need you to get fresh flowers from the Upper East Side, from where my mother used to go. Eighty-Third Street—do you remember?"

"Yes, okay, I remember, but why we no get flowers from Tommy?"

"I want them from Eighty-Third Street today."

Lucia looked at the flowers on the countertop, which had been bought the day before and looked perfect. "These no good?"

"I want new ones."

Lucia shrugged. "Okay."

"And pick up the dry cleaning, too."

"Yes, Miss Catherine, okay. I see you feeling better today, yes?"

"I don't know, Lucia. What does *better* mean?"

"Eh, okay? I don't understand."

"Never mind. Just go, please."

"I go now?"

"Yes, you go now. And take the subway."

"No taxi?"

"Subway."

She looked displeased, and I felt guilty, so I gave her $40. "And take yourself to lunch."

After she'd gone, I locked the deadbolt and returned to William's office. There had to be something. There had to be more. There had to be a reason he didn't want me in here.

The pictures again, the drawers again, the locked computer again. My tree outside the window again, losing more of its leaves. I expanded my search to the whole den. I looked behind the TV, behind the blankets in the cupboards, under the couch cushions, under the couch. Under the carpet. What did I expect to find there? Maybe a trapdoor he had built? I'd seen too many movies. I was going insane.

And what exactly was I looking for? Papers, an object, many objects? How big was it?

I had to sit down, I was going to throw up. I put his little trash can between my legs and waited. I needed more Tums.

And then I was opening the drawers again, looking again for secret drawers under the real drawers, for hidden compartments. A safe, maybe, a key to a safe, a gun. I didn't know.

I thought I heard my phone ringing upstairs. I waited, waited, waited. I couldn't decide whether it was actually ringing or not. I sat very still, made no noise. And then my eyes settled on the X-Acto knife. Why would William have an X-Acto knife? What would he possibly need this for? I remembered how he'd said he made cutouts as a kid but wasn't very good at it. Was he trying again now? I picked the knife up, pushed out the blade. There were little tiny bits of paper stuck to the serrated edge.

So I was looking for paper, cut-up paper. Nothing in the drawers; I already knew that. And then I looked at the books. Books were made of paper. I started opening them. I would flip through the pages of every book, and then I would call this mission off and go check my phone. William's books were alphabetized. I hadn't noticed that before. They were mostly coffee-table books, big sturdy things with big pictures. Of art and architecture and the castles of Scotland and the gardens of Europe.

Michelle Bellario's book. How had I not seen this in his library before? The cover was a subdued green that didn't stick out. Pictures of her sculptures. Yes, there were the pillows. Right, some of them had been installed in a park upstate. But there were so many books and Lucia would be home soon and I didn't have time to linger right now. I flipped quickly.

I almost missed it. I could have blinked a split second too early or late and missed it. But in the flipping, I saw a flash of green. A square had been carved through the pages of the second half of the book. With an X-Acto knife, probably. In the square, a pack of Kools.

"No."

Shock. I expected to cry, scream, something, but I stayed very still instead. William was a smoker. William was the guy. Mae was right. This stupid pack of cigarettes showed me everything I hadn't wanted to see. William was a liar. He was a person I didn't know.

They were menthols. Was this why he smelled like mint? And he was not only a smoker, but he smoked Kools? I would have expected something classier. Djarums, maybe. American Spirits maybe. Marlboros even. But Kools?

William was a person I didn't know at all.

I stared at the square. It was creepy, how well he had cut it. He hadn't done this just to be practical. He hadn't been in a rush. He had taken his sweet time. He had obviously used a ruler. He had felt proud making this little house for his secret.

40

At first I thought, A hammer. I need a hammer to remove the hooks in the wall. But I didn't know where the hammer was in my house. I walked to the tapestry. I touched it. All the work it had taken to make this, all those tiny pulls of string. I would get the ladder—I knew where that was, it was in the closet downstairs—and I would look for the hammer. But then something took over. I pulled. I pulled harder. I yanked violently. I broke into a sweat. Nothing mattered but taking this thing off my wall. The corners ripped. The fabric landed in a soundless heap. I'd like to say I forgot the image immediately, but I didn't. The hollow eyes of that woman. Even now I sometimes think of her.

.

I sat at the dining room table and waited for him. I'd put Michelle's book on the table. That would say everything. And then I would ask him why. Why had he come back? What did he want from me?

My phone beeped. William. "I'll be home in five minutes."

Good. He would explain why he had done this and then we would . . . what? Wait? Wait together for the baby to be born? Split the proceeds, never speak again? I had a hard time imagining he would leave quietly. And the next six months, waiting—it would be unbearable. There would be fighting. If I confronted him now, it would be worse. This was a bad idea.

I ran down to the office. I put the book back on the shelf. Just as I walked into the entryway, he opened the door.

"Hello, darling," he said. "Oh dear, did I scare you? You look like you've seen a ghost."

"No, no." I smoothed my hair.

"I thought we might order in tonight. What do you think?"

Herman came sprinting down the stairs. William picked him up off the ground. "Hello, little guy," he cooed, and kissed Herman's head. "And one for you, my darling." He leaned in to kiss me.

I turned a cheek.

"Is something wrong?"

"I think you have dog hair on your lip."

"Oh dear," he said, wiping his mouth with the back of his hand.

We walked up the stairs. "How do you feel about sushi?"

"I'm pregnant. Raw fish?"

"Oh, right, I'm sorry, I wasn't thinking."

"Let's just order a pizza," I said. "That'll be easy."

"The path of least resistance," he said as we reached the top of the staircase, "is always a good way to go."

•

It wasn't until we sat down to eat that he noticed. "Oh, the tapestry."

"I know," I said, looking straight at him. "It fell."

William scanned the wall. "Odd. The hooks are still in place."

"Very odd," I said.

We didn't like our pizza the same way. I liked cheese and he liked the works, so I'd ordered it just like that, half and half, split down the middle. It was passive-aggressive of me to ask for jalapeños on his side—I knew that—but I couldn't stop myself, or I didn't try hard enough. The words just came out and I let them. William hated jalapeños.

He bit into his pizza. He hadn't seen them. And then he was coughing, and spitting the pizza into a napkin, and sipping the wine I had poured him, which I might have spiked with cyanide if I had known where to buy cyanide. He was still coughing, his eyes red and watery. Herman was freaking out.

"Are you okay?"

"Yes. Ahh." He drank more wine, caught his breath. "Jalapeños."

"Oh no. I'm sorry—I just said 'the works.' I didn't realize it came with jalapeños."

"Usually it doesn't." He swallowed hard. "May I have a slice of cheese?"

I looked at the pizza like I really cared about it. "I was going to save my leftovers for tomorrow. I'm trying to be thrifty." I held his eyes. "That's what you want, isn't it?"

He sat back in his chair, studied me. "Are you angry with me, Catherine?"

"Fine," I said, "have some of my pizza." And then, because he was still staring, I said, "I know, it's only pizza. I can save in other ways. But like you've been saying, I don't get my monthly deposits anymore, so I should pay better attention to money. And I really agree with that. Darling. I think it's a great point."

"Yes, but now things are different. We don't need to be so frugal. When the baby is born, we'll be okay again."

"Will we?"

"It's a lot of money."

"It is, but we'll spend it, and what then?"

"I'm not sure. Maybe we'll have two children." He laughed. "Or three!"

"I'm almost forty-four years old, William. It's a miracle I got pregnant once."

He nodded in a serious way. "Well, one will have to be enough then."

"I worry nothing will ever be enough."

He took a slice of cheese. "Thank you for sharing with me."

"You're welcome."

"Catherine," he said, "this financial scare has put a good amount of fear into you, hasn't it?"

"I guess it has."

"Well, let's think logically now. Caroline mentioned that she received her payment two to three weeks after each baby was born. It takes that long to process the paperwork, apparently."

"She just happened to mention that in passing?"

"I suppose she did, yes. The point is, when we receive those funds, we can invest them properly so that they will last as long as possible. I'll make sure of that, trust me."

"Don't worry, I trust you." When I heard those words come out of my mouth, so cool and convincing, I knew that Marty was no longer right about me. I had become a good liar.

41

We awoke in separate bedrooms. After he'd fallen asleep in the guest room, I went back to the master. I couldn't sleep next to him. It was like the pizza. This was how things would be now. Together but separate. For the next six months, plus the few weeks it would take to process the paperwork, we would exist like this: side by side and never closer than that. I would avoid him as much as possible.

Before work, he came into the bedroom and said, "What are you doing here? Did you slip out during the night? I thought the Tempur-Pedic was out of the question."

"I changed my mind."

He knotted his tie. "Well, I'm happy to return to it."

"I want to sleep alone for a while, if that's okay with you. I can't sleep when I'm lying next to you. It's not you, it's me. It's the pregnancy. I just . . . Is that okay?"

A look of concern. He pressed his finger to his lips. "What am I to say?"

"That it's fine?"

"Sure, then, it's fine, darling." He took his watch off the dresser, and as he was putting it on he let out a loud sigh, which wasn't normal for him. He clasped the watch around his wrist, looked at the time. "I have to get to work, but tonight I'd like to have a talk with you. Something is not right here, and I need you to tell me what it is."

I blinked at him, said nothing. He was upset. I was surprised he was letting me see how upset he was.

"Answer me, Catherine."

I didn't answer him. We stared at each other. I thought he would accept my silence and leave. I waited. But he didn't leave. His cheeks turned red. He clenched his fists. And then he was standing over me, gripping my arm, saying, "Answer me."

"Let go of me."

He let go. "You, my darling, are making this difficult."

"You don't like difficult."

He was clenching his fists in quick pulses now, still standing over me. His red face, the fury in his eyes. I'd never seen him so angry. This was not the William I knew. This was some other man. He felt like a stranger, likc an intruder in my bedroom.

"Tonight," he said, and left.

·

"Ted."

"Catherine? How are you, dear?"

"I'm pregnant."

"Congratulations!"

"I need to talk to you about getting an advance on the will money."

"I see. I'm not sure that's possible, but—"

"It's an emergency."

"Are you all right?"

"Yes. No. Not really."

"If I remember correctly, you have to be married in order to collect—"

"I know. The wedding's in a few weeks. And I'm due in a few months. But we need the money now."

"Send me your fiancé's full name and Social Security number. I'll see what I can do."

•

Evelyn sat in the yellow chair. *The Price Is Right* was on. "Where's my mother?"

Evelyn flinched. "You damn near scared me to death, Catherine. She's right here. We are braiding Mrs. West's hair today, aren't we, Mrs. West?"

Half my mother's head was covered in tiny braids, each tied with a rubber band.

"With rubber bands? And why is she on the floor?"

"She's got a pillow, don't worry," Evelyn said. And then, to the TV, where a woman was spinning the lucky wheel, "Go, go, go!"

"Go," Mom said.

"Mom," I said, but she was watching the TV. Evelyn tied off a braid and started a new one.

"Mom!"

The wheel on the TV stopped turning. The audience sighed. "Oh no, she missed it. So close," Evelyn said.

"Mom," I said again.

Mom turned to look, and Evelyn quickly corrected her head so it was facing straight again.

"Evelyn, can you please stop that for a second? My mother isn't your doll."

She finished the braid anyway and tied it off. "Fine," she said, and sat back in the chair.

I went and stood in front of the TV and just said it. "Mom, I know you had an affair with William. How could you not have told me?" I held my hand up so she could see the ring. "Do you understand he's my fiancé?"

Mom touched one of her braids. Her eyes had gone dead.

But Evelyn had understood. I could see her wheels turning. And then she rubbed my mother's shoulders and said, "You slept with that William, Mrs. West? He's so young for you!" And then she was laughing, smiling. She thought this was hilarious. "You know, Catherine"—she laughed again; what was wrong with her?—"Mister William was here not two hours ago. You just missed each other!"

"What? What are you talking about?"

"He comes all the time, Catherine. William and Mrs. West like to play a little checkers together. Isn't that right, Mrs. West?"

"Right," Mom said.

"Sit down, Catherine," Evelyn said. "You look sickly."

A blur. A dry-heaving fit. My stomach pushing itself to a pinpoint, expanding into light, pushing again. The smallest, tightest point. That's where it hurt the most. I kept pushing toward it. I couldn't stop pushing toward the pain.

42

Caroline's housekeeper said, "She's taking a nap."

I found her in the bedroom, curled into a ball with a box of tissues by her head. She'd fallen asleep holding a tissue in her hand.

"Hey." I tapped her shoulder. "Caroline." And then I did the mean thing we used to do to each other as children. I squeezed her nostrils until she was fighting for air. She awoke, startled and out of breath and not aware of what had just happened.

"Catherine?"

"Did you know William's been going to see Mom?"

"No." She rubbed her eyes. "That's so sweet. Bob never does that."

"I need you not to talk to him right now. If he calls you, don't answer, okay?"

"Okay." She sat up. "But why?"

"It's . . . I'll tell you later. Just don't pick up the phone."

"Okay."

I stood up.

"Where are you going? Hang out with me."

Her bed did look comfortable. And I was exhausted. And the last place I wanted to be was home. But I didn't trust myself not to tell her everything if I stayed, and I wasn't ready to tell her yet. She'd be so upset, and she was already upset about Bob. I couldn't handle her crying all day.

"We can watch a movie."

"Fine, I'll stay, but I don't want to talk."

"Okay," she whispered, "I won't talk."

•

We stayed in bed all day. We ordered grilled cheese sand-wiches for lunch. Caroline's housekeeper brought them to us on a silver tray. At some point Caroline said, "Can I talk now?" I said, "Yes, but only about things that don't matter." She said, "I'm glad you're here, sis." She told me she'd gone paintballing to get her anger out, but it had been a bad idea. She showed me her bruises, and then the wart on her finger, which I told her to get iced off immediately. I asked her where Mom's sunglasses were. She said she didn't know. Whenever we were in bed like this, it felt like we were kids again, except for all the glaring ways in which we weren't. Like when Caroline said, "I know we're not talking about anything real today, but I might get a boyfriend. It seems only fair."

In the evening the kids came home with all their nannies. Did I want to stay for family dinner? No, I really didn't.

"Aunt Catherine has to go home," Caroline told the kids.

Only Spencer understood. The twins were too young. "Bye, Aunt Catherine," he said.

"Thanks for coming over." Caroline squeezed me. "Lunch tomorrow with Mom, right? I'll see you then."

•

He'd been texting me all day:

I'm sorry about this morning.
Shall we do dinner in or out tonight?

I think we'll both feel better after a chat.

Catherine, please write back.

I hadn't responded. I couldn't go home. The spot on my arm where he'd grabbed me was bruised. I didn't think he would hurt me more than this, but then, that's probably what every battered woman thought before the first time she got battered.

I wandered around the Upper West Side. I looked at shoes in store windows but didn't really see them. I went to a diner and ordered toast. I hadn't been alone like this since my junior year in France. I had felt very lost then. I had also been sure that when I got older, I wouldn't feel lost anymore. A naive thought.

I could go watch a movie, in a theater, alone. But that was crazy—I couldn't do that. I felt self-conscious sitting in the diner by myself. I knew the people who looked at me felt sorry for me. They wondered, Where is her husband? Where are her friends? There must be something wrong with her. The only thing worse than being lonely, I thought, is being lonely and exposed.

I checked into a hotel on Amsterdam. There was nothing sadder than the cheap landscape art of a hotel room. Nothing sadder than the crisp and sterile sheets of a hotel bed, with no one to remind you not to touch the cover because it probably hadn't been washed.

I poured the overpriced bottled water into the tumbler; I opened the small sad fridge. A mini vodka. I took that out, unscrewed the top. I would get drunk now. Fuck being pregnant. Maybe I still had Xanax in my purse. Give up, who cares, this isn't the life you want anyway. The balcony. I could jump off it. I opened the doors, touched the railing. It was cold outside. I took a small sip of vodka. This baby has no chance at a normal life anyway. A gust of wind. I set the vodka bottle on the railing. If the wind blows it away, I thought, I won't drink it. The wind did not blow it away. For a whole minute the bottle didn't move. "Fuck!" I threw the bottle over the edge. I didn't look to see where it landed.

43

"Bad news," Ted had written. "I was not aware that your fiancé was the son of Edward and Donna Stockton. As you will see below, this presents a large problem."

He'd highlighted the part he wanted me to read.

> *Following the death of Edward and Donna Stockton, no monies shall be distributed to the Stockton family in any way. If any beneficiary of this trust becomes involved with any member of the Stockton family, including any and all relations of Edward and/or Donna Stockton, said beneficiary's inheritance will be promptly annulled. Involvement includes any and all types of communication.*

Why would my father write this? Hadn't Edward been his good friend?

But.

And.

Unless.

No.

This could mean only one thing. My father had known about the affair. And if he'd been paying the Stocktons, then the Stocktons had obviously known. And they had blackmailed him. My father had paid for their silence. Until their deaths. Which was a very long time.

I read the words my father had written over and over. I imagined him in his old office, hunched over the desk, with the window cracked open because it always was, writing these words. How horrible that must have felt. How the name Stockton must have haunted him, and all of us, and how that family was still haunting ours now.

Now it was clear why William had come back. His parents had died; the bribe had died with them. He wanted more, and he'd returned to his old source to get it.

•

I opened the door, touched the railing, looked at the traffic down below. And then I called him. "We need to talk."

"Where were you last night? I was worried sick."

"Why don't you come to lunch today? Me, you, Mom, and Caroline. Da Castelli at noon."

"Oh, I would love to, but—"

"You need to come." A pause. I could hear him breathing. "I'll see you there."

•

Evelyn had taken the braids out of Mom's hair. "It looks like they crimped it," Caroline said. "And this makeup today?"

Bright blue eye shadow all the way up to her eyebrows, a Sharpie-thick line of liquid eyeliner both above and below her eyes. I would kill Evelyn. Or I wouldn't. Maybe my mother deserved this.

"Are you talking about me?" My mother's eyes. Muddy, bewildered.

"Yes," I said. "Your makeup looks like shit."

They were stunned. Caroline nervously grabbed a strand of hair and began twirling.

"What did you say to me?"

I was so angry. I hated my mother. This whole thing was her fault. "I said your makeup looks like shit, Mom."

My mother touched her cheeks with trembling hands. She looked hurt and insecure and so fragile. She seemed both like a child and heartbreakingly old at the same time.

"I'm sorry. I'm just angry."

Caroline touched my mother's arm and my mother didn't pull away. She looked up at me sadly. "Why?"

"I'm sorry I didn't tell you yesterday, Caroline. Maybe I should have told you."

I saw his suit in the mirror just as Caroline said his name. "William?"

"Caroline, hello," he said. "Catherine." He didn't try to kiss me. "Mrs. West." He nodded politely, sat down next to me. Quietly he said, "May we have a word alone please?"

"No," I said, too loud.

"Can I get you a drink, sir?"

"A dirty martini, thank you."

"Oh, that sounds delicious," Caroline said. "I'll have one, too." Apparently she was in a great mood now that William was here. "I didn't know you were coming to lunch! It's so nice of you to take time off during the day. Our dad never did that."

"Yes," William said. He did not look at my mother, who'd been gaping at him since he sat down.

"I know you," she said.

"Yes, Mrs. West, that's right."

"That's Catherine's fiancé," Caroline said. "Not Fernando. William."

"You and William have been playing checkers together, remember, Mom?"

"Oh?"

"Checkers?" Caroline said.

When I looked at William, he didn't seem uneasy or pissed off or even surprised. He just sat there twirling his hair with an eerie smile on his face.

"William's been going to see Mom because they have a history together."

"What?"

How to explain? There was nothing to do but just say it. "They had an affair."

"That's not true," Caroline said. "That doesn't even make sense. Catherine, what's going on with you today?"

William looked down. His eyes were closed. He was toying with his cuff link. My mother had no idea what was going on. She was buttering a piece of bread with a fork.

"William?" Caroline said.

"Please, I can explain," William said.

"Good. Please explain."

"Oh my God," Caroline said, and turned to our mother. "Mom?"

Our mother didn't answer because her mouth was full.

"Mom, did you have an affair?"

Mom inhaled sharply, too sharply, and then she was choking on her bread, coughing into her napkin.

"Drink water, Mom." I pushed the glass toward her. She drank, composed herself, patted her chest.

"Dear," she said.

"It was a long time ago," William said calmly.

"Oh my God. How old were you?" Caroline said.

"He was seventeen," I said.

"What?"

The waiter dropped off the martinis. Caroline took a big sip, took another.

"Are we ready to order?" the waiter asked.

"I will have the salmon pasta, light on the cream sauce, please," my mother said.

Caroline handed her menu over. "I'm not eating."

"Neither am I," I said.

"The martini is fine," William said.

"What is wrong with you?" Caroline glared at him. "She was married! And Mom, what is wrong with *you*? Oh my God! Seventeen! And what . . . why . . . Wait, and then you came back to marry her daughter? What the— Why? Why?" Caroline waited. William said nothing. Caroline said it louder. "Why?"

"Stop shouting right this instant," Mom said.

"Calm down, Caroline." William was stern. He was pointing a finger at Caroline. "Act like an adult, please."

Caroline looked stunned. "Excuse me?"

"William came back because the bribe ran out," I said. "How much did my dad pay you anyway?"

"Wait." Caroline's hands were up in the air, like she was angrily clutching an imaginary ball. "Dad knew?"

"He knew and he paid them off," I said.

"This is so disturbing." Caroline looked at my mother, who was staring into space, no longer part of this conversation. "Mom!"

"Yes?"

"How could you do this to us?" Caroline was basically yelling now. "How could you do this to us?" A guy eating spaghetti shot her a look. "How could you have an affair?"

I remember how my mother closed her eyes so slowly then. All that blue eye shadow. Weakly, she said, "I'm sorry."

And then Caroline, always so quick to forgive, let out an animal "Uuuaaahh" sound, surrendering, and wrapped our mother up in her arms. "It's okay, Mom."

"Catherine," William said, "I know it seems sick, I know that, I do. But when I saw you there at the gala, you were so . . . lovely."

His face was strained. I hated how much I wanted to believe him. A huge part of me wanted to say, It's okay, let's go home now, let's forget the past. I was so tired. "Please," he said, "please forgive me for not telling you. I meant to, but in the end I couldn't."

In the mirror my face looked upset, more upset than I wanted it to. "Why didn't you tell me you've been going to play checkers? I still don't understand that."

He sighed. "Elizabeth and I have an old bond. Even if she can't remember me most of the time. I wanted closure. I wanted her to get to know me now, as the man I am now. As your fiancé. I did it for us. If we spent enough time together, I thought she might let go of her negative feelings toward me."

"No," Caroline said, with sudden energy, as if she were about to spring up and grab his neck. "Catherine, this is bullshit—I'm not letting you fall for this. And you," she said to William, "you need to leave. You're not getting anything from us. You need to go pack up your dog and go back to the hole you crawled out of."

I loved Caroline in that moment—how fierce she was, how angry. I was angry, too, but I was too drained to show it.

William put his hand on the table next to mine. He was smart enough not to touch me. "Catherine, please."

"Leave!" Caroline yelled. Her face was red in patches.

The guy eating spaghetti threw his napkin on his plate, as if to say, I'm never coming to this restaurant again!

"Catherine?" William asked. His voice was soft and begging.

"Catherine!" Caroline smacked her palm on the table.

"The truth is, Caroline," William said, not raising his voice, "Catherine and I have an understanding. We both understand that we need the money from your father's trust. And in order to access that money, we need to be married."

Caroline looked like she'd just seen an explosion. "No. No, Catherine, no. You can't marry him. No. I'll give you money, I'll help you. Please don't do this."

"This is the problem, William." I pulled up Ted's e-mail on my phone, handed it to him. "Apparently no one gets any money if they're involved with your family."

"Dad wrote that in his will?" Caroline said.

"Apparently," I said.

"Is that a good thing?"

"It means that neither of us gets any money. It means you get nothing, William."

"Ha!" Caroline said. "Fuck-face."

William set the phone down and drank his entire martini. And then he was laughing. "You people." He slouched back in the chair like a bored teenager. He pressed his finger to his lips. "You disgusting, self-righteous, greedy fucking people." I couldn't believe he had cursed. I couldn't believe how he was sitting—I'd never seen William slouch like that. And at a restaurant? He looked like a thug. "You people ruined my family. Your father, the greediest person I've ever met in my life. What he paid us? Next to nothing! Only enough to scrape by. My parents settled for crumbs. But I—no, no, I will not settle for crumbs. And I will not leave this restaurant until I get what I want."

"What do you want?" Caroline said. She was still angry, but she looked a little scared now.

"First"—he looked at my hand—"I want that ring back."

"Fine." I tugged it off my finger and tossed it at him. It landed on the floor. He had to lean awkwardly to pick it up.

In a cool, menacing voice, he said, "Please don't make me any angrier, darling." He slipped the diamond onto his pinkie and slid it down until it touched the turquoise ring he never took off. "I leased this diamond," he said quietly.

My mother, who was working on her pasta now, stopped to say, "How tacky."

"Sshhh, Mom." Caroline's shoulder blades crept closer together. She seemed to be making herself as small as possible.

She made an *X* across her chest with her arms, as if that would protect her.

"I can't give you much money," I said.

"I know that. But Caroline can. I want $10 million. I think that's very fair."

"And then you'll leave us alone?" Caroline said.

"You might not want me to leave you alone, Caroline." His eyes flickered. "You might have questions for me."

Caroline tightened the *X* across her chest. "What does that mean?"

He looked at Caroline. He looked almost sad. "Things could have been different," he said. "I am not a bad man."

Caroline's face twisted. She pulled at a piece of her hair, rolled it between her fingers. She blinked hard and then opened her eyes as if that would make her understand. It didn't work. She still looked confused. "What are you talking about?"

William rubbed his lips together. He didn't respond. He touched the nape of his neck. He looked at my mother, who was drawing a line down the side of her water glass with her thumb. He looked at Caroline, who was tugging her hair now, her face still twisted in confusion. He didn't look at me.

"What *are* you talking about?" I said. My voice was only slightly trembling. "You will leave us alone. All of us. That includes the baby. I don't want you to have any contact with this child."

"That shouldn't be a problem." He sighed. "It wasn't a problem last time." William tapped the spoon on the table. "Elizabeth?"

My mother wiped her chin with the napkin. "Yes?"

"Who is Caroline's father?"

Her nostrils flared. She was doing something with the napkin in her hands—kneading it like dough. She tried to stand up and failed. She was panicking.

"Elizabeth!" William held up the spoon. "Tell them. Who is Caroline's father?"

Her eyes were darting around the room. She kept opening her mouth, about to speak—the words were right there, but all that was coming out was an *r* sound. I remember thinking, Please, God, please say Bruce and let it be true.

"Say it!"

The second he smacked the spoon on the table again, she did.

"William Stockton is the father."

Caroline and William looked at each other. They seemed to realize at the exact same second that they were both twirling their hair.

44

The end happened like a fire. It was amazing to me how everything we had built together could be burned down so quickly. Within the span of a day, a contract had been circulated and signed by the three of us, Caroline had wired the money, and William had moved out.

I stayed in the hotel for a few nights. When I went home, there were only traces of him: hooks in the walls where his art had hung, empty cardboard boxes the movers hadn't used, dust patterned around the feet of his desk.

But he had left one thing. Conspicuously, on my pillow, was the turquoise ring and a note: *For our child, on his or her tenth birthday.*

I didn't call anyone. I didn't cry. I didn't hesitate. I grabbed my coat and walked straight to the Hudson. It was freezing cold that day. My face had gone numb by the time I reached the end of the pier.

The water was so still, a barely moving reflection of the sky. The ring sent ripples through its clouds, and the note, pushed by the lapping tide, eventually joined the rest of the trash floating in the water.

•

We formed new routines, new ways to mark time. In the morning, after she sent the kids off with their nannies, Caroline would come over. Midafternoon, she'd go home again to make dinner for them, help with Spencer's homework. "This whole thing," she said. "I want to be a better mother."

Most of the time we propped ourselves up with pillows and stayed in bed. Life had become about the small comforts, maybe, the things you could count on: a pillow, a shower, a glass of water.

Every day we ordered too much takeout for lunch and promised ourselves that tomorrow we'd get less. We never got less. I think the extra food was another comfort. We were comforted by abundance, and always had been.

We watched the movies we had watched as children without really watching them. We knew the scenes by heart; we knew how these stories ended. Mostly it was background noise, something to look at during the pauses in our never-ending conversation about William.

•

"How are we ever going to trust anyone again?"
"I don't know," I said. "Do you think he's a sociopath?"
"I hope so. That makes him less human."

•

"Do you think I look like him?"
"A little bit, but you look more like us than him."

•

"I can't believe Mom let me watch them have sex," I said.
"There has to be more to that. I have a really hard time believing Mom would do that to you."
"I don't know what to believe anymore."

"If it makes you feel any better, Spencer walked in on Bob and me a few months ago."

"What did you tell him?"

"That we were playing a game."

•

"Do you think he stalked me? Like, do you think he ever followed me to school when I was a kid?"

"I hate to say this, but I don't think he cared enough to do that."

"At least I had Dad. I'm glad they stayed married. Can you imagine where I might have grown up if Mom had left Dad for William? And who I would have become? I could be a completely different person right now."

"But you're not."

•

"Maybe I'm an artist because my grandfather was an artist."

"Maybe."

•

"It makes sense now why Mom never liked me."

"She loves you, Caroline. I'm sure she just feels guilty when she looks at you."

•

"I decided I'm not getting a boyfriend. It's too complicated."

"Bob really does love you."

"I know. And at least he told me about his affair. At least he was honest."

•

"Do you think he'll ever come back?"
"No."
"I hope he dies."

•

"Do you love me less now?"
"No," I said. "I mean that."

45

Time passed. It passed in a way that felt both too quick and endlessly monotonous. Get up, brush teeth, drink water, pee, drink water, drink one cup of coffee, eat pregnant-safe foods, get dressed, get undressed. The weather got colder. I bought new sweaters. The leaves on my tree turned the colors of a baked and muted sunset.

I changed the configuration of the house to erase William. I put beanbag chairs where his desk had been. I had planned to hang my art in the empty spaces he had left, but then I didn't know if I liked my art anymore. The art I owned and the art I saw was either complete shit or so beautifully heartbreaking that I couldn't bear to look at it for too long. And I was having trouble telling the shit from the heartbreaking. How were you supposed to know what was good and what was bad? How were you supposed to know what you liked? How were you supposed to know what was you and what was someone else? Especially when you were scone-heavy and hormone-crazed and all you wanted to do was sleep?

And so I hung nothing. The blank white walls were soothing. They said, You don't have to be anyone right now.

Sometimes, especially in his closet, I thought I could smell that particular scent of his. It didn't make sense. I had already sprayed everything down with perfume. But I would spray again. And again and again and again, sometimes at three o'clock in the morning.

One day Lucia found a tie of his, rolled up in the couch. He must have taken it off after work and rolled it up and put it in his pocket, like he'd always done, and then it must have fallen out of his pocket. The tie was blue, striped. I didn't remember it. He had so many ties. When I went out later that day, I hung it on the side of a trash can.

·

Caroline was still coming over, but less. She'd moved on. She didn't want to ruminate anymore. Somehow she had completely forgiven our mother. As usual, but especially given the circumstances, I didn't understand how forgiveness came to her so easily. She kept asking me to come to lunch—"When are you coming to lunch? We miss you!"—but I just wasn't ready yet.

·

One day she showed up with cupcakes and said, "I have a surprise for you."

"Cupcakes?"

"No. Check your bank account."

"What did you do?"

"I decided it was only fair to give you $10 million, too."

"Oh my God, are you serious?"

"Yep. And I'm not even worried, because guess what?"

"What?"

"I'm pregnant again."

·

It was such a relief to be able to shop the way I wanted to again. I bought myself tons of shoes and hats and stretchy pants.

One emotional day I bought a $2,000 poncho I was pretty sure I would never wear.

Shopping for the baby opened me up to a whole new world of necessity. I bought parenting magazines and then I bought everything they recommended. I bought eco-friendly onesies and an entire zoo of stuffed animals. Handmade rattles from South Africa. A rocking chair from Roche Bobois, and a crib. At A Pea in a Pod, the salesgirl said, "You're basically getting the whole fall line—that's amazing," as if this were a real accomplishment.

With everything I did to prepare for the baby, I imagined how my mother must have prepared for me. All the care that went into this. I kept her journal by my bed and read it sometimes. I bought myself a journal, and I wrote my name in the front, and the date on the first page. And then, I don't know, something distracted me. A phone call. A pain in my side, in my foot. Or maybe it was more than that. Maybe I didn't know what to write about my life. Maybe I didn't know where to begin.

I bought a massage chair. Dan started coming twice a week. I needed the muscle work; I was stressed. He asked no questions about William. He was unconditionally sweet. He brought me little things from Brooklyn: a beaded bracelet to invite good energies (*energies* was plural, apparently) and yellow flowers he had picked from his garden.

He also taught me about holistic ways to feel better. Arnica gel for my sore hips, castor oil to keep my skin soft. One day we did a sage-burning ceremony at home to clear out the bad energies. We burned extra in the closet. We didn't mention William's name. We used words like *renewal* and *strength* instead. When the smoke from the sage set off the fire alarm, we ran to open the windows, me in a tizzy, screaming, and Dan quiet and useful, fanning the air with the newspaper.

Sometimes Dan came shopping with me. I tried to buy him a sweatshirt and he refused. He didn't need anything; he was just having fun going to all these stores he'd never been to. But I must not have believed him, because later in the week I said, "I can pay you for your time, you know. For hanging out with me."

He looked upset. I wanted to take it back.

When I told Susan about the sweatshirt, she said, "You two are spending a lot of time together."

"He's my new Marty now that I don't have Marty anymore."

"Yeah, but isn't he straight?"

46

October seventeenth came and went. It was a gloomy, shit-streaked day, the sky gray-brown and oily. The air was windless, stagnant, chilly on my legs as I walked down the block to meet Marty for an afternoon slice of pie, right across the street from the café where William had proposed to me. I couldn't quite go in there yet, but I was getting closer.

Marty and I sat at a table by the window. I kept looking over at the café. The outdoor tables were gone now. Inside, I saw the white flash of a waiter's starched shirt, the flickering of candles in the near-dark.

"What are you looking at?" Marty's leg jittered under the table; his eyes darted around. Sweat beaded his brow. He shoveled a piece of apple pie with cheddar cheese into his mouth industriously and chewed with the same productive energy, like eating was a job.

"William proposed to me at that café." I put my forkful of cherry pie on the plate. I was hot, uncomfortable. I slid my cashmere cardigan off my shoulders, too lazy to take it all the way off.

"Eh," Marty sneered. "I never met the guy, but he didn't deserve you, that's for damn sure."

"Thanks, Marty."

He ate the rest of his pie, pushed the plate away, drank his shot of espresso, added the empty cup to the plate. He did all of this in the most efficient way possible. "Having a kid, that's a miracle. Doesn't matter who the father is, it's a miracle." Marty adjusted the silk handkerchief in his breast pocket; it was purple today. "I have a kid—he's nineteen. Did I tell you that?"

"No."

"Yep. Thought I was straight once. I didn't want to have it back then—shit was cray-zee—but now I think it's the best thing that ever happened to me." Marty tapped the table a few times with the knife that was there. "He lives in New Jersey with his mom. He's a good kid. Plays baseball. We're cool now, but don't get me wrong, he was pissed about the gay dad thing for a long, long time. Long time."

"What changed?"

"Time," Marty said. "He got older. Older and wiser, thank God. He figured if you can't change it, you better accept it."

47

My mother gazed out the window, her chin propped on a ladylike fist, blue-green veins like skinny worms stretched across her hands. The wrinkles on her face were delicate, shallow; like me, she looked younger than she was. Her emerald silk blouse wasn't wrinkled at all. They did the laundry well here. If my mother knew that, she would have appreciated it. Draped over her shoulders was a green angora sweater, darker than the blouse. She had always loved to layer complementary colors like that.

"Here, Mom," I said, "I bought you a new lipstick." I had the small Lancôme box ready in my hand.

She took it from me carefully. "Thank you, Catherine."

"You look very pretty today."

The ends of my mother's mouth turned up, just barely.

"We took a long time doing that makeup today, didn't we, Mrs. West?" A woman appeared from the bedroom with a pile of towels in her hand. She was not Evelyn, though she looked a lot like Evelyn, except for her hair: it was very, very short. "She had me redo it about seven times," she bellowed. Her voice was deep, raspy, the voice of a chain smoker, though she didn't look like a chain smoker. Her skin was taut, unblemished. "Hi, I'm Denise."

"Hi Denise, I'm Catherine."

"Your mother talks about you girls a lot."

"Really?"

"Isn't that right, Mrs. West? You love your girls, don't you?"

Mom had uncapped the lipstick and was putting it on, but not very well.

"Oh, no, no," Denise said. "You let me do that, Mrs. West."

The door opened. "Knock knock," Caroline said.

"Well," Denise said, "I'll leave you to it. See you later, Mrs. West."

Mom gave a brief wave.

When Denise had closed the door, I said, "Where's Evelyn?"

"Oh my God, I meant to tell you. You're not going to believe this. They fired her."

"Why?"

"They found a duffel bag full of stuff from a bunch of different residents. She'd taken two of Mom's necklaces and a pair of earrings."

"Oh my God." I had to laugh. "Mom," I said, "I'm so sorry we didn't believe you."

"Believe what?"

"Nothing. Never mind."

Mom read, or pretended to read, the words on the Lancôme box. And then she was staring at me. "You're pregnant," she said.

"I know."

There was no reason to remind her who the father was. There was no reason to cause her more pain. There was no reason even to say, "I forgive you, Mom." The lipstick said that. My being there said that.

She gazed out the window. Maybe she looked lost. Maybe she looked more lost than before. But she also looked kind of peaceful.

"What are you thinking about, Mom?"

"We are here."

48

We went for a walk. The sky was bleach-white, dotted with dissipating gray clouds like ash tapped from a cigarette. I wore big sunglasses and carried a huge water bottle. I'd taken to carrying one of those everywhere I went. I mixed in pink-lemonade-flavored electrolytes so the water was pink. Dan wore sunglasses that hung on a blue cord around his neck. I remember that because I remember the mirrored lenses. I remember looking at him and seeing myself and thinking, God, you look so together and you're so not. I remember it was when we had turned onto Thirteenth Street that he said, "Do you ever miss him?"

"I don't know," I said, the words drawing out of me slowly. A mannequin had fallen over in front of a store. She was helpless.

We got to the crosswalk. I wasn't thirsty, but I took a sip of the pink water. Something to do. Something to avoid crying. Blame the hormones. We waited for the light to change. I tried to fit the bottle in the pocket of my coat. It wouldn't fit. I tried the other pocket, which made no sense.

Dan held out a hand. "Let me hold that for you," he said.

49

On Thanksgiving, Caroline and I went to St. Luke's, which was what we had done every year since college. My roommate at Sarah Lawrence had volunteered at a soup kitchen in Connecticut every Thanksgiving, and in an attempt to gain her respect (she was really cool), I had copied her. My mother thought it was a wonderful idea—great for my résumé.

We put on our plastic aprons, our nametags. Billy, the guy in charge that day, assigned me as a greeter and Caroline as a dishwasher. Caroline wore a long pretty dress and didn't seem bothered at all by how dirty it was about to get.

"Hello, hello, welcome, welcome, Happy Thanksgiving, Happy Thanksgiving," I said to the men and women who filtered in from the street, not overly excited, but like they had been here before, like this was part of the drill. On Thanksgiving you could count on food.

Some carried so much—plastic bags, backpacks, fanny packs, rolling suitcases—and others carried nothing at all. Maybe those who carried nothing were living in a shelter right now. Maybe those who carried a lot were also living in a shelter, and paranoid. They smiled when I greeted them, or didn't smile. Some said, "Happy Thanksgiving." One man—long face, pinpoint pupils, smelled like a porta potty—said, "Happy, happy!" and the man after him—button-down shirt; he could have been on his way to work—walked like a zombie, his head hung low.

Nothing at the soup kitchen that day had changed from the year before, or the year before that—they came, they ate, they complained that the mashed potatoes were too dry, and they left— but something about being there felt very different to me. I think it was this one woman. Her name was Jan. We got to talking in the line, which had started to move very slowly. She wore jeans and a sweater that I knew was a James Perse sweater. Maybe a good find at Goodwill, I thought. But then she told me she'd had a great job as a legal secretary until six months ago. They fired her for drinking on the job. She couldn't stop. She still hadn't stopped. She was trying. She didn't look like an alcoholic, or like a homeless person. She looked like anyone else with a nine-to-five. Maybe it was the pregnancy—I was so sensitive to everything. Blame the hormones. But I really had the feeling that I could have been Jan, I could have had Jan's life. Maybe I was only a few bad choices away from being Jan now.

•

The immaculate temple of the dining room at the Avalon seemed more immaculate than ever, and also more festive. Orange and yellow and brown leaves dripped from the ceiling, and a decorative arrangement of branches lined the wall. Mom wore pearls, a simple black dress, very light pink lipstick, and a confused expression. "Why are we here, why are we here?" she kept asking.

"It's Thanksgiving, Mom," Caroline repeated with incredible patience, each time as though she were saying it for the first time.

Mom's face would go lax—"I love the holidays"—and then, a moment later, "Why are we here?"

We gorged ourselves on Brussels sprouts and mashed potatoes

that weren't too dry. Mom and Caroline agreed that the turkey was cooked just right. I thought the same about my mushroom lasagna.

"Let's say what we're grateful for," Caroline said when the Indian man dressed in black placed our pumpkin pie slices in front of us. Each was topped with whipped cream in the shape of fanned turkey feathers.

"Pie," Mom said.

"You're grateful for pie?" Caroline said. "Okay, that's a good one, Mom. I'm grateful for . . ." She looked at us eagerly, sincerely, maybe about to cry. "Family, and that we're all here together."

The chandeliers cast a soft yellow-white light on the room; violin music played; the Indian man in black was refilling my water glass. The air was not too hot, not too cold. We were safe in here, protected from the foul smells of New York, its rat-infested subway tunnels, its litter and yelling, its choking heat, its bitter snow, its violence. Weren't we safe? The light and the violins and the sound of clinking ice cubes and the Indian man now scraping crumbs from the tablecloth with his special crumb scraper certainly made it seem this was so. Of course it wasn't so, but it was better than the alternative. It was much better than the alternative.

"I'm grateful for the two of you, that's the biggest thing." I looked at Mom and then at Caroline. "I love you both," I said. "And honestly?" I said, maybe more to myself than to them, "I am also grateful for money."

50

My tree turned black. Lumps of snow perched on its dark branches like skeletal fingers holding sugar. I thought it was kind of pretty.

I bought a tree for Christmas. I won't lie. It was a little sad, but it wasn't the worst thing that had ever happened either. I had planned to get a very small one, but the guy who sold it to me—Paulie with the gold tooth and the black bandanna around his head—talked me into a ten-footer. "You live right there? I'll have my guys bring it over, no problem. Consider it done."

I tipped each of the guys fifty bucks. Lucia and I strung white lights around the tree, Lucia on a ladder, me down below, feeding her cord. She tried to push tinsel on me, which was absolutely not an option. "It's good the dog is gone," Lucia said. "He will not eat the tree."

"Yes," I said, "it's very good the dog is gone."

I waited to feel sad. I waited to feel lonely. I knew it was irrational, but I waited for the feeling of missing him. But none of those feelings came. Lucia said, "It's good. You better now." And that was true. Maybe I wasn't the happiest woman on earth, but I was okay.

•

I wore a purple velvet dress by Carolina Herrera to Bob and Caroline's Christmas party. I ate a thousand gingerbread cookies and read Spencer a story on the couch. Tonia, his nanny, sat with us. She told me she was a student at LIU. I didn't know what that was. Long Island University. Oh. On Long Island? No, in Brooklyn. She was studying early childhood development. She said this with such certainty. "I am studying early childhood development." She looked straight at me, as if it were so obvious—what else would she be studying? I envied Tonia's youthful convictions for a second, and then I remembered that I'd been full of them at her age. No, it was good to be old. It was good to know that nothing was certain.

Caroline and Bob looked happy enough. Not that it mattered. How were you supposed to know who was happy or not? There was no way to know that.

My mother wore black velvet and pearls. She nibbled a cookie cautiously, like a baby tasting real food for the first time. From her perch on a chair, champagne elegantly in hand, she said, "That is a good marriage."

•

I went home and drank tea and stared at the blinking lights on my Christmas tree and the presents underneath, and then I decided to open them early.

Acquaintances had sent acquaintance gifts: chocolate, soap baskets, wine. From Ted, a Floridian ornament: a glass orb filled with sand. The little box from Susan contained a cute shrubby bonsai and a gift certificate for a spa treatment at the Mandarin Oriental. She had tastefully left the amount off the card. From Lucia, like every other year, a pair of pajamas from Target. This was a pants-and-top set with a pattern of flying pink pigs.

From Caroline, a little painting of the two of us, in pointillist dots. It was us now, just our heads, side by side. Caroline's rendition of herself was painfully honest: she had correctly included her fucked-up-tadpole eyebrow.

This was the first thing I hung on all those white walls. I didn't wait. I went downstairs and hung it in the entryway, so it would be the first thing people saw when they came to my house.

51

I still can't pinpoint the exact moment things changed between us. Dan made avocado sandwiches for lunch. We went for a walk around Washington Square Park, and to a tea shop in SoHo he liked. It was a windless, snowy day. Dan wore a rabbit-fur hat with flap ears, I wore a cashmere beanie. We drifted past Film Forum, decided to see a movie. When we came out of the theater, the ground was covered in white, everything was white. Cabs crawled along the streets, following the tracks of other cabs. New Yorkers walked tentatively, unsure of nature. The usual frenzy of the city was quieted to a deep lull.

He stayed with me that night, and then the next, and then he slowly started moving his things over from Brooklyn. He found Florence a great roommate; he interviewed the guy three times to make sure. He was worried about bringing Gandolf, his dog. He knew I thought pets belonged outside. When had I told him that? I said no, no, it's fine, and it actually was fine. Gandolf was an old chocolate Lab, the complete opposite of crazed Herman. I didn't love his dog hair on my couch, obviously, but it could be vacuumed.

Besides Gandolf, he didn't bring much. Florence's new roommate bought all his furniture. He brought his books and his clothes and the collection of baby avocado trees he had planted from seed.

"Did I ever tell you the apartment where I grew up was filled with plants?"

"No." He swiveled the cracked planter into the corner. "What do you mean by 'filled'?"

"I have a picture of it somewhere. I'll have to show you."

"Yes." Dan stepped back, considering the planter. "Is it okay there?"

"Yes," I said. "It's okay there."

•

Having Dan at home was wonderful. It was also an adjustment. Sometimes I would feel so exposed with him, like my chest had been unzipped and turned inside out and exploded into confetti in the air and there was nothing left of me but a scattering. When this happened, I would crawl deep inside myself and retreat to the shower and sit there for an incredibly long time, with the water pounding on my head, like I had done with William.

I was learning that a good relationship included work. It was hard. But we talked about it. That was the simplest and strangest change: actually talking it out.

We talked about money, which made me extremely uncomfortable. I couldn't seem to stop offering Dan money, or paying for everything. It was just second nature. Dan wanted to pay sometimes; he wanted me to let him do that. He also wanted to work. He enjoyed his work. He kept saying, "I'm not with you for your money, Catherine." I'd say, "I know, I know," but really, I didn't know, and honestly, I'm still not sure I know sometimes. I know Dan doesn't care about money like I do, and I know he cares deeply about me. But it's scary, putting yourself on the line for someone, really and fully, with no strings to attach them to you. How do I know he's not going to leave? We talk about that, too. There are no guarantees to change my fears. There is only trust.

We had many long conversations about moving—is this house cursed?—and for now we've decided to stay. Here in this house with its red door. We will not run away from the past. Maybe a house uptown later, maybe near the park. I'm still very resistant to the idea of living in Brooklyn—Manhattan girl, that's my thing, right?—though I will admit, Brooklyn Heights is very nice.

•

There are little rocks and pebbles all over the house now. A huge white rock from Long Beach on Dan's bedside table, a piece of flint from Arizona in a dish by his toothbrush. I opened a drawer the other day, looking for Neosporin, and found a bunch of tiny black stones inside.

"You collect rocks," I said to him.

"My mom has this thing about moving rocks around the world. I've been doing it forever."

"Why are you supposed to move rocks around the world?"

"I have no idea. I've never asked her."

After that I started looking for rocks. I'd never looked for a rock in Manhattan before. It never would have occurred to me. I didn't realize that finding a rock in the city—a real rock, not a piece of concrete, not construction rubble—is actually kind of rare.

•

I remember the day I looked at William and truly thought he was the answer. That with him, my life could be beautiful. I had thought that beauty was in the flashy, pretty things you acquired to prove that you were happy. But a flash is just a flash. It blinds you and then it disappears.

Now I think real beauty might be in all the small and obvious places I had overlooked. Oh, a rock in Manhattan. Oh, an empty street in Manhattan. Oh, my sister and me watching a movie. Oh, the sky. Our lives could be beautiful in the quietest ways, and already were.

52

I've avoided writing in you, journal, because I haven't been sure how I want to remember this time. If a story is constructed by the evidence it leaves behind, what do I want these little pages to say? Maybe I'm overthinking it. I'll just try to be honest. That seems like a good goal.

I am so pregnant. I am huge. I am a house. It's uncomfortable, but I kind of love it, too. I feel less selfish already.

I'm ready to have the baby. Also scared. What if he can't forgive me for choosing William as his father? He'll probably hate me for a little while when he's a teenager and then grow out of it. I hope that's true. And I guess it could be worse. It's not like William is an ax murderer. He was just greedy. And so was I, when I stayed with him after I knew who he was, just to get the money. I still can't believe I did that, and I wonder, if the circumstances had been different, if Dad hadn't written the no-Stocktons clause in the will, would I be with William now? I might be.

I can't imagine I would go the lengths that William went for money. Tracking me down, luring me in like that? It was so insane. But maybe if I'd had William's life, I would have made his choices.

According to my Google searches, the causes of sociopathology

*are more environmental than genetic, which means the baby will
probably be okay. Maybe William wasn't loved enough as a kid.
Maybe he was neglected. Maybe lots of things. I'm still not even
sure he was a sociopath. Google confirms they're hard to spot.*

*I feel conflicted. I hate his guts, I feel sorry for him, I hate his
guts, I feel sorry for him. Sometimes I actually still wonder if he
loved me. I really want this to be true because it means the baby
was created out of something good.*

*Caroline thinks the baby will be fine. If she turned out fine, the
baby will be fine. "William's not my real father anyway," she says.
"Dad was my real father, just like Dan will be your baby's real
father. William's just a sperm donor." She's been great at finding
the humor in the whole thing. She thinks it's hilarious that I slept
with her sperm donor, in a so-bad-it-has-to-be-funny way. In my
more forgiving moments, I think it's kind of funny, too. Caroline
and I are really close now, which I never thought would happen. I
think I was right. Disaster brings people together.*

*Dan. Without the William tornado, I might not have been open
to dating Dan. So I guess, okay, maybe I'm glad it happened. I
wouldn't change a thing, because it got me to where I am now. Isn't
that what people have to say when shitty things happen to them?
Oh, what a wonderful learning experience! Ha! I think it's a little
too easy, but I see what they mean.*

*I've started listening to violin music. I think I miss hearing the
boys play. Even though only Stan is playing now. Dan and I ran
into Max and Doreen at the farmers' market and Max was so
excited to tell us his mom had let him switch extracurriculars. He's
learning Chinese now, which Doreen thinks is better for college
anyway.*

*I apologized to Mae for being a bitch. She said she totally
understood—she would have been angry, too. I'm still not sure what
I think happened that night—did my mother really know I was
in the bathroom?—but maybe it doesn't matter. Mae is supposed*

to come over for tea sometime. I'll have to tell her to bring her rock crystals. Dan will probably be into that.

Mom's hanging in there. That's what we keep saying. But the truth is she's getting worse. Last time I saw her, she asked when we were getting on the boat. What boat? Was she thinking of the cruises we used to take? The worst thing about it is that there's nothing to do but hang in there with her. I'm trying to enjoy her as much as I can while she's still here.

I'll end this entry with an ode to my mother. Last night Henry and Susan came for dinner. Dan made a vegetarian feast—quinoa and sweet potatoes and kale—and we had carrot cake for dessert. Oh, and I may have bought two new pairs of shoes today.

C

53

Oliver West was born on April 13 at one o'clock in the morning exactly. It was a Friday. Dan assured me that Friday the thirteenth was just something Americans made up. In Japan the number four is unlucky. All that matters is what you believe matters.

I worried that when they put the baby in my arms, I would feel no connection to him. But it didn't happen that way. I loved him instantly, and so much. I had become a person who was capable of loving another person. For a long time I thought I was broken, but what does that actually mean? If you're broken, you can be put back together. I had never been broken. I had just been wandering in the dark, not aware that I was lost.

It's funny. My life only came together after it blew up. It exploded into all these pieces, and after I realized I hadn't died from the impact, I put the pieces back together in a slightly different way. I say slightly because I'm still the same person: I shop too much (I'm trying); I don't eat enough (I'm trying); meditating makes me want to punch someone in the face most of the time. I have, however, taken the subway a few times recently, though I still think it's gross down there and prefer cabs. The only hope we can have for ourselves, Dan says, is to change by one degree, or maybe two.

•

Oliver is almost six months old now. I've lost all the baby weight, thank God. If I'm going to be totally honest, yes, he looks like William. He looks a lot like William. He is devastatingly handsome. He is also a chatty baby. I wonder if William was a chatty baby. It's impossible not to think of William when I look at Oliver. I hope this gets easier with time.

I'd be lying if I said I wasn't worried about the future. I'm still not sure what we plan to tell Oliver about his father, or when. We can't tell him everything at once—that's too much for a child to hold. But eventually I do want him to know the whole story.

•

I had always pictured my perfect family like the little pink and blue peg people in the game of Life, moving through the world in set, safe, dry-cleaned moments. I had probably imagined a baby from a commercial, and a kid from a clothing ad, and a college grad with a very white smile, proudly throwing his tasseled hat up in the air.

It took me a long time to understand that what I had wanted was not a picture of something perfect. I already had that. What I had wanted was the feeling inside the pictures, the thing I had been trying to buy and drink and eat and not eat and fake my way to all my life. I wanted what everyone wanted. I wanted love.

Acknowledgments

I am so thankful to all the people who helped me get to the part where I get to thank them in a book.

This probably wouldn't be happening without my you-can-do-anything parents, and I'd like to thank Mark Huntley, in particular, for letting me take over the ohana many times, for many months at a time. I'm also very grateful to Rich Propper, whose relentless optimism gave me something to float on more than once.

Thank you to the MacDowell Colony and the Ragdale Foundation for the gift of quiet time and space.

Thank you to Ashley Nelson, Ann Hood, and the Eckerd College Writers' Conference.

Thank you to Sterling Watson and Dennis Lehane for being such generous mentors over the years. And to Stacey D'Erasmo: your support has meant the world to me.

This book actually wouldn't exist without the inspiration of my brilliant editor, Jenny Jackson, who made these pages much more beautiful, nor would it exist without the incredible enthusiasm of Allison Hunter, my wonderful agent.

Last, thank you to the people who've read all the versions, from the very beginning. Tasha Tracy, your so-honest feedback and your hilarious way of delivering it made writing this more fun. And Jen Silverman, your clarity and kindness inspire me all the time. Also: this is for us.